More praise for Maggie Shayne's *Eternity*...

"Maggie Shayne's gift for melding the mystical and the magical into her novels has made her one of the preeminent voices in paranormal romances today. *Eternity* is an awesome start to a series that promises to be richly textured and powerfully rewarding."

—*Romantic Times*

"Ms. Shayne's talent knows no bounds when it comes to romantic fantasy; her latest is a hauntingly exquisite tale . . . lush . . . heart-stopping suspense, spellbinding romance, and enchanting characters. *Eternity* is to be cherished like the precious gem it is."

—*Rendezvous*

"[*Eternity*] is one of the best of the decade as the magnificent Ms. Shayne demonstrates why she is ranked among the top writers of any genre."

—*Affaire de Coeur*

"A hauntingly beautiful story of love that endures through time itself."

—Kay Hooper

continued on next page . . .

Praise for a star on the rise . . .
The Novels of Maggie Shayne

"Maggie Shayne dazzles! She's on her way to the stars!"

—Suzanne Forster

"Maggie Shayne is a reader's joy. Fast-paced, witty, delightful, and shamelessly romantic, her stories will be treasured long after the book is done. A remarkable talent destined for stardom!"

—National bestselling author Teresa Medeiros

"Wonderfully creative . . . Ms. Shayne has the perfect touch with the vampire legend, unerringly focusing on the spellbinding romance and allure of this enduring myth. On top of that, she adds an ingenious plot twist which will knock your socks off. Brava, Ms. Shayne."

—*Romantic Times*

"Ms. Shayne definitely knows how to keep you guessing with the many suspects and different twists this plot takes. Her characters come to life in a way that makes you feel as if you know every one of them. A wonderful romantic suspense with edge-of-your-seat tension, steamy passion, and real emotions with which a reader can identify."

—*Rendezvous*

"Rising star Maggie Shayne proves that she has what it takes to shine with a work that combines elements of gothic melodrama and romantic suspense and turns the mixture into something rare and precious."

—*Affaire de Coeur*

"Just when you think there's nothing new under the sun, Maggie Shayne reinvents romance!"

—*The Literary Times*

"Maggie Shayne makes it very easy for her audience to willingly suspend belief and partake in a delightful fantasy adventure."

—*The Talisman*

"Ms. Shayne has delivered another knockout read. Once again she serves up another erotic vampire tale, filled with dark secrets and powerful longings, with surprising twists and turns."

—*The Belles and Beaux of Romance*

"Maggie Shayne has the ability and the know-how to create suspense, action, and intimacy that will keep you on the edge of your seat, whether it is vampires or covert agents. I love reading Maggie Shayne!"

—*GEnie Romance and Women's Fiction Exchange*

Jove titles by Maggie Shayne

INFINITY
ETERNITY

BEWITCHED
(an anthology with Susan Krinard, Lisa Higdon, and Amy Elizabeth Saunders)

INFINITY

Maggie Shayne

JOVE BOOKS, NEW YORK

INFINITY

A Jove Book / published by arrangement with
the author

PRINTING HISTORY
Jove edition / October 1999

For information address: The Berkley Publishing Group,
a division of Penguin Putnam Inc.,
375 Hudson Street, New York, New York 10014.

The Penguin Putnam Inc. World Wide Web site address is
www.penguinputnam.com

ISBN: 0-515-12610-1

A JOVE BOOK®
Jove Books are published by The Berkley Publishing Group,
a division of Penguin Putnam Inc.,
375 Hudson Street, New York, New York 10014.
JOVE and the "J" design
are trademarks belonging to Penguin Putnam Inc.

PRINTED IN THE UNITED STATES OF AMERICA

10 9 8 7 6 5 4 3

Arianna

Darkness
unfurled its shroud upon my soul,
long before Death could take his *toll*

I walked in place,
breathed air without taste
A blind man with eyes
A dead man alive
A corpse animated
A hunger unsated
A soul made of stone
A heart with no home

Sunlight
spilled Her gold and warmed my skin,
though I fought not to let Her in.

I emerged from the grave,
by the magick She gave
The dirt in my eyes,
swept away by Her sighs
A dead man, reborn
Night gave way to morn
My hunger She sates
My fear She abates
My soul, She does own
My heart has come home

Infinity
unfolds through space and time,
as soft I hold Her hand in mine

I've found Her again
and a love without end
As Her kiss I taste,
my tears are erased
My grief-crippled soul,
at Her touch is made whole
And the gift from above,
is the joy of Her love

—Nicodimus Lachlan

Prologue

I am lying in a shallow grave, immersed as if in the bowels of some great, black sea. I know not how long I have been captive in this void, nor do I care. But something has disturbed me, has stirred me to consciousness . . . of a sort. A sound. A steady beat, pulsing ever more strongly, forcing me back to the realm of coherent thought.

And thought alone.

The silk that once wrapped my body has rotted away. I have no coffin. Black, rocky soil is my tomb. But I am not dead. As dead as I can be, perhaps, and that is my greatest fear. I am . . . *immortal.*

I do not want this . . . to think. To know. To remember. But that drumbeat in my mind will not release me. And bit by bit, my mind clears, my past resurfaces.

My name . . . do I even know my own name?

I grasp in the darkness of my mind, fighting a momentary panic, and find it there . . . Nicodimus. That is my name . . . Nicodimus.

The beat that stirred me grows louder, as faint memories taunt me through the mists of my mind. There is no light, no return of feeling or sense. Only of awareness. Horrible, wrenching awareness. A living nightmare. The knowledge that I have been buried alive.

And the beat grows still louder.

Gods, it is my heart! It is near. I sense it drawing closer to me the way a lodestone can sense the north. I feel its beat growing stronger when logic tells me it should be weakening . . . slowing, fading, as its power is steadily drained by its greedy captor.

And yet, the proximity of the organ matters not. My heart is no longer my own, and without it, here is where I shall remain. I wonder, can the heart of an immortal ever cease its endless beating? And if it should, will the soul of its rightful owner find blessed release at last?

If not, then what remains for me? A living mind trapped in this undying body. A living soul held captive in a dead man's grave. How long can this go on? How long?

Forever.

The answer comes to me as if riding a whisper-soft breath. *Her* breath.

At the first thought of her, those teasing, distant memories break free at last, and rush through my mind all at once in a chaos of emotion too agonizingly shrill and sharp to bear. Images and fragments, painfully vivid, blindingly bright . . . that all begin with . . .

Arianna.

Arianna.

Arianna. . . .

Part One

1

1511, Stonehaven Village, in the Scottish Highlands

I rode my faithful Black, and he stepped high, as though he knew the man he bore to be of an utterly different breed than those others who surrounded us. Beside me rode an old friend . . . a mortal, chieftain of his clan, and laird as well. Joseph Lachlan welcomed my visit. He called me his cousin because I claimed to be. But though I supposed I might be some distant relative of his, the link was too old to trace now. I used the name and claimed the clan Lachlan only when it suited me.

Joseph didn't doubt me, nor did he ask why I might need to retreat here for a time. And that was just as well, for I couldn't have told him the answers had he questioned me. The truth was that resting from the constant battle was only one of the reasons I'd come.

Another was the skulking, dark-robed pair who'd been following me on and off over the previous seven centuries. Always silent, always faceless within the caves of their hoods. But I didn't need to look upon their faces to know. I'd avoided them sometimes. On other occasions, they had vanished without explanation. But more often than not, I'd fought them. Sometimes one at a time, frequently both together. Once I had nearly bested Kohl, but he fled before I could finish the job. And once—this last time—the two immortal brothers had done the same to me, and *I* had fled. To Stonehaven—my sanctuary.

I feared very little, almost nothing. But there was a cold dread in the pit of my stomach where my oldest and most bitter enemies were concerned. And it came, I believe, of knowing exactly why they had stalked me so doggedly, and for so long.

They blamed me for the deaths of their sister and their nephews . . . my wife and my sons. And they would never stop until they had taken my heart.

Or I theirs.

So I had come here to rest from the endless fighting. I put it from my thoughts in order to focus on the other reason I had returned to Stonehaven—the more important one. Her. The girl who had drawn me back here time and time again over the past seventeen years.

"You never age, Nicodimus," Joseph remarked. "You look to be the same fair lad I last saw five years past."

I sent a cocky grin his way. "And you've grown wrinkles about your eyes, Joseph. Soon I'll mistake you for my father." Joseph was perfectly bald, his pale head as shiny as his cheeks and his bulbous nose. He did have brows and lashes, but of a hue so pale it seemed as if he were entirely hairless. When he smiled, as he often did, it seemed even his bald head smiled along.

"No hope of that, lad. Your father was twice the man I'll ever be." Joseph lowered his chin. "I do miss him. But havin' you here on occasion is almost like havin' my dear cousin back with me again."

I had to avert my eyes. Joseph had never known my father. He had known only me. But when he'd seen me die at his side on a field of battle, I'd had no choice but to stay away for many years. And when I returned—as I had been compelled to do—I had simply claimed to be my own son. He had believed me.

"My father often spoke similarly of you, Joseph," I said

after a pause. I nudged Black's sides with my heels. The stallion trotted forward along the narrow, twisting paths of the village, chickens scattering in his wake. A fat man rolled a barrel of ale from a rickety wagon into the daub-and-waddle hovel that passed as the village tavern, while across the way a woman hurled wash water from a window hole where no glass had ever stood.

I'd seen London and Rome, Paris and Constantinople, great cities all around the world. Yet I marveled at how this tiny hamlet had grown. For when I had lived there it had borne no name. My home had been a thatched straw hut, cured hides stretched over the walls had served to keep out the cold. The meat I killed, my wife had cooked over a fire on the dirt floor.

Anya. Beautiful Anya. Meek, gentle, fragile. I could see her still, in my mind. Soft brown hair and eyes like the palest winter sky, her belly swelling with our third child as she watched over the other two. And I could see our boys. Jaymes, growing taller by the day and too skinny to stand up to a windstorm, though he ate more than his brother and I together. He had his mother's coloring, Jaymes did. And Will, a head shorter, but strong, already looking more man than boy. Hunting at my side, and outdoing me now and again. Begging to fight beside me as well.

The old pain trembled and howled and threatened to break free. I caught it with a will of forged steel, and forced it still and silent.

"The village hasna' changed since last you were here," Joseph said, pulling me out of my thoughts.

Ahead of me, the crofters' cottages leaned crookedly, their thatched roofs showing wear. I caught myself studying the villagers we passed, with their well-worn kilts and haggard faces, and realized I was seeking the golden child as I did on each visit. But I did not see her there. And it occurred to me then that I might not even recognize her at first glance, after so long.

I nearly smiled at the unlikelihood of that.

She stood out from the rest of the villagers the way a diamond stands out among bits of coal; her dark brown eyes gleaming against ivory skin. Her corn-yellow hair. Her upturned bit of a nose, and the gleam of life in her little girl eyes. And more. A spirit, a fire, undefinable, yet all but gleaming in its brilliance.

She had been a child, barely twelve years of age, when last I had seen her. She would be . . . seven and ten now. Quite possibly wed—though people here now married later than they used to. I'd made Anya my wife when I'd been but four and ten. But things changed a great deal in seven long centuries. And wedded or not, this girl, Arianna, was likely still unaware of what she truly was.

"Is that saddle maker still in the village, Joseph?" I asked abruptly. "Sinclair, wasn't it?"

"Aye. Is your saddle in need of repair?" Joseph eyed it, likely seeing that it was perfectly fine. Likely thinking that I never paid him a visit but that I needed repairs done to my saddle.

"Only a bit of loose stitching at the girth," I told him. "But I ought have it checked before I leave again."

Joseph nodded. "'Twas a cursed bad year for poor Sinclair. Cursed bad."

My head swung toward him. "Was it?"

"Aye." Joseph's lips thinned, and his bald head joined his brow in a frown. "Lost a daughter, he did."

At those words, my heart seemed to ice over. I had been watching the girl all her life, awaiting the time when I would explain her own nature to her. When she was old enough, and mature enough to understand and deal with the truth. Perhaps I had waited too long. I tried to speak, but couldn't.

Joseph never seemed to notice the force of my reactions. He was involved now in the telling of his tale. "Nearly lost the both of his girls, that sad day. Over a year ago, 'twas. They'd been up to no good, playin' in the loch when their father had forbidden it. My lads were about, heard the shoutin'. Kenyon pulled the one to safety, an' Lud went back for her sister. But 'twas no use . . . she drowned in the muddy waters of Loch Haven."

"Drowned?" I asked, nearly holding my breath.

"Aye. And young Arianna has ne'er been right since the day the loch claimed her sister."

I lowered my head and released my breath all at once. So Arianna was alive . . . Not that she could have died by drowning. She'd have revived . . . but to what?

Joseph nodded toward some distant point. "See for yourself, Nicodimus. She's there now, at the grave. 'Tis no place for a lass of ten and seven to be spendin' all her time. An' alone, no less! She's forever walkin' about alone." He ran a hand over his head, and slowly shook it.

I frowned, knowing exactly what Joseph implied. It was said that only a Witch walked about all alone. Only a Witch. And Arianna *was* one. But she couldn't know that. Not yet.

"Perhaps if I were to have a word with her," I suggested.

Joseph drew his mount to a halt, frowning at me. "Do you think it wise?"

"Why not? I've lost loved ones myself. I know a bit of what she's feeling." I knew, I realized, far too much of what she was feeling. It was a feeling she would have to get used to, for in time she would lose everyone and everything she knew. I sighed as I looked at her. Slight, so slight. Barely larger than she'd been at twelve. A golden wisp of a girl, the picture of innocence. She would have to learn to be hard. To close herself off. She would have to learn to stop caring, as I had done.

Looking worried, Joseph nodded all the same. "Take care, my friend. Dinna spend too long with her. She's promised to the cobbler's son, but even he's beginning to shy away. There's been some talk. . . ."

"What sort of talk?"

Joseph shrugged. "Ah, I pay it no mind, nor will I tolerate anyone persecutin' the poor lassie. We must make allowances, after all. Grief can twist a mind in all manner of—"

"*What sort of talk,* Joseph?"

Joseph cleared his throat. "Some claim she slips out alone in the dead of night. An' she's been seen speakin' to

The Crones more than once. What people will make of it . . . well, you can guess as well as I."

The Crones . . . the outcasts. The word "Witch" was never spoken aloud here. The people were too superstitious to dare it. Everyone in the village knew what the three old women were, yet The Crones were tolerated. Their shack outside the village at the edge of the forest was left alone. That happy state would likely continue, so long as only good fortune smiled down upon the flocks and the crops and the crofters here. As for the blue-blooded Christians of Stonehaven, most would no more exchange a public greeting with The Crones than eat from the trough of a pig. But they visited the old women every now and then, for a potion to cure the croup or a charm for good luck. In secrecy. In hypocrisy.

I turned again to stare at the girl. She knelt beside the grave of her sister off in the distance. Perhaps she knew more than I'd thought she possibly could. It would explain her visits to the village Witches. But who was there to tell her? I'd never met another High Witch, Dark nor Light, in this part of Scotland. Never. And our secrets were seldom shared with anyone else. I'd ascertained years ago that The Crones were mere mortals, and knew nothing of our existence.

"I'll speak with her," I said. "Before she lets the gossips ruin her."

Joseph nodded. "Perhaps 'twill do some good at that. Shall I wait at the tavern, then?"

"If the owner still brews that secret recipe of his."

"Heather Ale?" Joseph asked with a crook of his invisible brow that resulted in new wrinkles appearing in his forehead. "That he does, Nic. That he does." Joseph gave a wink, and wheeled his horse about, heading away.

I turned my attention toward the cemetery once more, and nudged Black's sides until he leapt into a spirited trot. Stopping him a short distance away from the girl, I tied him to a scraggly tree, then walked to where Arianna Sinclair knelt. For a moment, I only stood still and silent, looking at her.

Arianna had changed. In five short years she'd grown from a waif into a woman. And that aura of vitality that had always surrounded her seemed stronger than ever before. Her golden hair draped about her shoulders like a shawl of spun sunlight, moving in the breeze every now and again. And I'd been wrong when I'd concluded she had not grown, for she had. Her breasts swelled now, a woman's breasts, straining the fabric of her homespun dress. Her hips had also taken on a sweet roundness, while her waist remained small.

Kneeling, spine straight, chin high, she lifted a fist, and let some herb or other spill from it atop her sister's grave, as she muttered soft words under her breath.

A spell. For the love of the Gods, had the girl no sense? In full daylight?

"What is it you're doing?" I called. I expected her to stiffen with surprise and perhaps fear at being caught. The lesson would do her good.

She didn't start, didn't turn to face me. "Should anyone *else* ask, I'm plantin' wild heather upon my sister's burial site."

"And if *I* ask."

"I think, Nicodimus, you know better than to ask."

I blinked in surprise. Just how much *did* she know? And the familiarity of her tone with me . . . as if she knew me far better than she did. We'd spoken only a handful of words to one another in the past. Polite greetings at most, though my interest in her had always been more than that of a stranger. She was my kind. A rarity in itself. She was without a teacher, and . . . and something about her spoke to me on a level I had never understood.

The herbs gone, she pounded her fist thrice on the ground; a time-honored method for releasing the energy raised in spellwork. Then she lowered her head for but an instant. Finally, she rose, brushing her hands on her skirts and facing me. Her velvet brown eyes hadn't been so large before . . . nor so haunted. "It has been a long while since your last visit here," she said.

"Long enough so I must wonder how you could have recognized my voice."

"'Twas nay your voice, Nicodimus. Although 'tis true, you speak distinctly enough."

"Do I?"

"Aye," she said. "Almost like a Sassenach, rather than a true Scot. Careful, an' slow, without a hint of an accent, so a body could never guess where you truly come from."

"I come from right here," I told her.

She shrugged, and I wasn't sure whether she believed me or not. "Regardless of *how* you speak," she went on, "I knew you were there long afore you did."

Her words gave me pause. If that were true, her natural powers were incredibly advanced—particularly for one so young. "How?" I asked her.

She shrugged again. "I always know when you're near. Have since . . . why since I was a wee bairn toddlin' along and clingin' to my mam's skirts . . . an' you came ridin' into the village alongside Laird Lachlan. Do you recall?"

I did. It had been then I had first set eyes on her, and I'd known—even before I'd seen the crescent shaped birthmark on her chubby right flank—that she was one of us. "I remember it well."

Arms crossed over her middle, she sent me a steady look, and I studied her in return. Her small, upturned nose was the same as before. But her face had thinned. No babe's plumpness to her cheeks. Not now. It was a woman's face, touched by sorrow.

"I always wanted to ask you about it—that feelin' I get when you're near. But it seemed I should remember my place, and be neither impertinent nor disrespectful."

"But you've changed your mind about those things now?"

She glanced toward her sister's grave and her eyes grew darker, her voice softer. "They seem less important to me now than the dust in the highland wind, Nicodimus." Her eyes were round and filled with pain—and something else: rebellion. A dangerous wildness flashed from somewhere deep within her, and seemed to fit with the way her hair snapped whiplike with the wind, while her skirts flew about her ankles and bare, dirty feet.

"Propriety has its place, Arianna."

"Propriety," she whispered, looking directly at me again. "Society. Lairds and chieftains and crofters and slaves. What good is it, I ask you? What does any of it truly mean? Who cares whether a woman wears her hair unbound until she bears her first child, and bound up tight thereafter? Or if she walks about alone, or if she addresses a laird by his given name? What arrogant fool made up all these ridiculous rules that have us all hoppin' and scurryin' to obey?"

"You're angry," I said softly. "I understand that, Arianna . . ."

"Aye," she replied. "I am angry. 'Tis meaningless, all of it!"

Her voice had grown louder with every word, until I gripped her hands gently in my own and felt the jolt of awareness that occurs when one of our kind touches another. She looked at me quickly, shocked by that heat, wondering at it, I knew, but I said only, "Keep your voice low." And I inclined my head toward the village nearby, where already several sets of speculative eyes were turned our way. Hands shielding careworn faces from the morning sun. Squinting, searching gazes trying to see who dared raise her voice in the cemetery, of all places.

Arianna followed my gaze and saw her curious neighbors. She sent them a defiant glare with a toss of her head that reminded me of Black when he is agitated and smelling a battle; the way he shakes his mane almost in challenge. I moved to take my hands from hers, but she closed hers tight and clung with a strength that surprised me.

I looked down at our joined hands, and for the first time a ripple of alarm zigzagged up my spine to tap at my brain. For this was no child clinging to my hands. This was a woman, young and beautiful and full of fire. And her hands were slender and strong and warm.

"You *want* to make them gossip about you. Is that it?" I asked her.

"Let them gossip. I dinna care."

I took my hands away. "Do you care what pain you cause others, Arianna?" I asked, in a second attempt to put her firmly in her place, to let her know that what she might have been thinking just now when our hands were locked together, could never, never be. She was hurting, full of anger, confused and lonely for her sister. That was all it was. "You're promised to the cobbler's son," I reminded her.

She tilted her head to one side and shrugged. But it seemed her rant had ended, for her face no longer seemed like that of a warrioress about to do battle. "*I* never made any such promise to Angus MacClennan. Nor do I intend to abide by it. An' believe me, that clod has no tender feelin's where I'm concerned."

"No? Why, then, do you suppose he's asked for your hand, Arianna?"

She smiled slowly, eyes sparkling now with mischief. "You can guess as well as I. He wants a servant. Someone to cook an' clean an' mend for him. But mostly, he wants someone to lift her skirts when he demands it. Someone to relieve his manly needs with so he'll nay have to hide in his da's woodshed an' do it himself—"

"*Arianna!*"

"What?"

She was all wide-eyed innocence, but I saw the gleam beyond it. I only scowled at her.

"A tender young girl isna supposed to ken such things, I suppose!" Again that expressive toss of her golden locks. "Nay, we're to blindly agree to be some man's slave an' his whore in exchange for our room and board. Well, it willna be me, Nicodimus. Not ever."

I had to bite back a smile. So bold and outspoken, and so damned determined. "A wife should be none of those things, Arianna."

"Name one who isna *all* of those things," she challenged me, leaning slightly forward, hands on her hips, legs shoulder width apart in a cocky stance.

"Your mother," I said.

She lost a bit of her cockiness. "'Tis different with my mam."

"Why?"

"Because my da loves her, I suppose."

"And are you so certain your cobbler's son doesn't love you?"

She peered up at me from beneath her dark lashes. "Not so much as he loves his hand on certain nights in his da's woodshed."

I had to look away. To laugh aloud would only encourage her. And she needed no encouragement.

For a moment I thought about how seldom it was that I found myself inclined toward laughter. Genuine laughter. "I like you, Arianna," I said. "Just take care to bite your tongue from time to time. Not everyone appreciates a sharp wit and bold talk from a young woman the way I do."

She smiled up at me, all but glowing. And I thought I would enjoy spending a bit of time with Arianna while at Stonehaven this time, getting to know the astounding young woman she had become. And then I was shaken out of my thoughts, for she suddenly grabbed my hands and held them, and her thumbs caressed the hollows of my palms in slow circles. She stared up at me, her inquisitive eyes probing mine.

"You're different from other men, Nicodimus. I've sensed it always. You pay no more mind to the world and its silly conventions than I do. You . . . you're like me, somehow."

I averted my eyes. "I don't know what you mean."

"Dinna you? You're supposed to be Laird Lachlan's kin, yet you dinna live in his keep. You bathe just as often as you like, without a care that the church calls it vanity."

"And just how would you know how often I bathe?"

Her smile was slow, and it stirred something to life deep within me. "You smell good, Nicodimus. Clean. I like the way you smell." I looked away from the heat in her eyes. Her palm came to my cheek, turning my head until I faced her again, and then it remained there. "An' what's more, you dare to talk openly and all alone to the girl half the clan thinks is crazy—''

''And the other half thinks is dabbling in Witchcraft,'' I interjected, hoping to shock her into silence. She saw too much, this girl. And she was looking far too closely, tampering with parts of me that no one had dared come near in a very long time. Her touch . . . rattled me. Relief sighed through my chest when her hand fell away from my cheek at last.

''An' what if I am a Witch?'' she shot back, undaunted.

I stared at her in surprise. She was all fire and life and utter defiance, boldly blurting words that could easily get her killed. '''Tis no business of mine what you are, Arianna,'' I told her. ''And no business of theirs, either. Do as you will.''

She rolled her eyes. ''I intend to do just that!''

I gripped her shoulders to make her listen. ''But keep it to yourself, for the love of heaven! If you can't conform, then *pretend* to conform. And never, ever again must you say something so foolish aloud! For your own sake, girl, take the advice of one older and wiser. One who would like to see you live to grow into womanhood.''

''I'm a woman already,'' she told me, chin high, hair sailing in the breeze. ''A woman like no other woman you've ever known.'' She swayed slightly closer to me, gaze locked on my lips.

I dropped my hands from her shoulders and staggered backward as her bold, enticing eyes flashed fire at me. I'd come to her to try to help her. Instead, I felt as if I were under attack. Her forces battered my innermost tower, and I had a feeling they could bring it to rubble with minimal effort.

''An' since you've mentioned it,'' she went on, ''just *how much* older and wiser are you, Nicodimus?'' She smoothed the front of her dress as she spoke, her fingers brushing very near to her breasts, but her eyes never left my face.

I saw her meaning in those eyes. Saw it clear, for she didn't seem the least bit inclined to hide it from me. It unsettled me, shook me to my bones. I'd never thought of her in that way . . . not until this very moment—or perhaps a few moments ago, when I'd seen her again, a woman grown.

"Too old for what you have in mind," I said, hoping I sounded mildly amused and sardonic. "Go find your cobbler's son now, and torment him in my stead."

But even as I turned to leave her, my mind spun its arguments. She would be eighteen in a fortnight. Oh, yes, I knew the date of her birth. I knew more about her than she knew about herself. I was over seven centuries old . . . and yet at the time of my first death, I'd been twenty and eight. Physically . . . I still was. And never more aware of it.

"You're meant for me, Nicodimus," she called as I walked away. "You must ken that as well as I."

I froze where I stood. She came toward me, but didn't stop when she reached my side. Instead she kept walking, brushing past me, and dropping a kiss upon my cheek as she did. The touch of her lips sent heat through me all the way to my toes. "You'll be mine one day," she whispered. "An' then, Nicodimus, I will know all the secrets you hide behind your sapphire eyes."

A shiver raced up my spine as I watched Arianna walk away, golden hair dancing in the wind. She walked proudly right up to where a crowd of crofters stood pretending not to watch her antics. Her chin jutting high, she nodded hello to each of them, her entire stance oozing defiance—as if she were silently daring anyone to chide her for going about alone. Or for kissing a guest of their laird so boldly.

Or for muttering incantations over her dead sister—and in the daylight at that.

Daring them.

No one took the challenge.

She was right when she said she was a woman like no other. For there had never been another who touched my soul the way she did.

"Just what do you think you're about, Arianna?" her mother whispered harshly.

Arianna turned back toward the darkened cottage from which she'd just emerged, and hugged her dark cloak tighter 'round her shoulders. Her mother opened the splintery wooden door wider, and peered out at her. "I thought you were sleepin', Mam."

"How is a mother to sleep when her child roams about in the night like a wraith?"

Lowering her head, Arianna whispered, "I was only goin' for a walk. I couldna sleep."

Mara Sinclair shook her head, glanced up and down the path as if to be sure none of the neighbors were watching, and then stepped outside. She wore a nightshift that reached to her ankles and covered her arms to the wrists, over which she had thrown an old shawl for both warmth and propriety's sake. Out of long habit, Mara began twisting her long, gold and gray hair into a knot even as she sent her daughter a disapproving stare.

The sight of it made Arianna's temper rise. "Why do you do that?" she asked. When her mother tilted her head in confusion, she continued, "Your hair. Leave it, Mam.

Just this once, dare to ignore the rules of this foolish society and leave it."

With firm motions, her mother finished the job of binding up her hair and met Arianna's stare. "You so disapprove of me. Of all I am, all I stand for. I vow, Arianna, I dinna ken what's happened to you."

"You ken exactly what's happened to me, Mam. I've lost my sister," Arianna said.

Mara pressed one hand flat to her chest, and held the other up as if to ward off her daughter's words. "Dinna speak of Raven to me!" It was a shout. But then she bit her lip, tempered her voice. "I canna bear it, child."

Arianna shook her head. "Dinna call me 'child,' Mam, for I am a woman grown. An' I willna obey without question the way a child would do. The way . . . you do."

Her mother lifted her head slowly, staring at Arianna with hurt in her eyes. "Nay. You never did, lass."

"You scold me for my silence. You say I'm broodin' an' that I willna talk to you. Yet when I try to express my grief for my dead sister, you silence me. What am I to do?"

"Talk to me of something else," her mother whispered, gaze lowering, lids shuttering her eyes at once. "*Anything* else."

"I *think* of nothing else," Arianna said.

"Oh, but you do, lass," her mother said, speaking slowly and meeting her daughter's eyes once more. "You think of wherever it is you go on these midnight walks o' yours. An' of late, you think of Laird Lachlan's comely cousin. I've seen you spyin' on him now and again."

Arianna searched her mother's face. Barely a line in her skin and yet she looked old all the same. It was more than the gray in her once pure golden hair. It was something deeper than any wrinkle could ever be.

"Aye," Mara went on. "I've seen the way you look at Nicodimus, lass." Reaching out as if to stroke Arianna's hair, she paused and lowered her hand. Arianna told herself she'd have ducked away from her touch all the same. And yet she felt the pain of longing for her mother's caress, having been denied it. Not since Raven's death had her mother touched her in love. Instead they only hurt each other, over and over.

"Dinna wish for what you canna have, child," Mara warned. "He's far too old, an' above you as well. The kin of a chieftain, while you're but a saddle maker's daughter."

"You know nothing about Nicodimus Lachlan," Arianna said, feeling as if her mother were attacking her. "He cares no more for the silly ways of society than I, an' I *can* have any man I wish! You'll see!"

Mara frowned. "Child, you'll find only disappointment should you go dreamin' of such things. 'Tis young Angus you'll wed, an' none other."

"I've told you before," Arianna replied slowly. "I willna marry that whelp!"

"Hush!" Again her mother glanced around, seeking watchers in the night. More concerned, Arianna thought, with what her fellow clansmen and kin might think than with her daughter's feelings.

"You think I'm nay good enough for the likes of Nicodimus Lachlan, dinna you? You think I'm nay pretty nor smart enough. But I *am* equal to him. Equal to any man, be he peasant or king!"

When there was no immediate reply, Arianna met her mother's gaze again, saw her eyes soften, dampen. "I certainly believe you equal to any man, daughter. 'Tis the man you might have a wee bit o' trouble convincin' of it."

Arianna sighed hard, and shook her head in disgust.

"Child, we used to be so close, you an' I. Do you recall? I'd sit an' comb your hair, an' sing to you 'ere I tucked you in to sleep. . . ."

Arianna closed her eyes in response to a rush of pain. She missed those times. "An' Raven would sing along," she said, caught up in the memory for just a moment, in spite of herself. "She had such a beautiful voice. And when she—"

"Nay, you mustn't!"

Arianna lowered her head slowly. "You blame me," she whispered.

"Whatever are you—"

"Speak the words, Mam. 'Tis high time we spoke the truth, you an' I. You blame me for my sister's death. I was the elder. I should have protected her. She drowned because of me. I—"

"Nay, child!" Her mother reached for her, and perhaps wouldn't have stopped halfway this time. But Arianna ducked away before she could find out. "'Tis untrue, Arianna," her mother rushed on. "Your da an' I have ne'er once blamed you for what happened."

Holding back her tears, Arianna lifted her head. "Of course you do," she whispered. "An' I canna dispute it, for I blame myself as well." Sniffling, Arianna turned to walk away.

"Come back here! Arianna, where do you think you're goin', lass?" her mother demanded in a voice gone harsh.

"I'm goin' where I want," she cried. "An' doin' what I want, an' I'll marry who I want, as well. I'll nay be good nor obedient ever again, Mam, for I've seen the truth of where goodness and obedience find their reward! At the bottom o' some murky loch is where!"

"Arianna . . ."

"Raven was the good one," Arianna whispered, shaking her head and backing slowly away into the night. "She was the good one. It should've been me who drowned, Mam. It should have been me!" Arianna turned and raced away into the night.

She refused to cry. Instead she worked her rage out by running as fast as she could over the rutted paths of the village and beyond them, toward the woods. When her lungs burned and her muscles screamed, she slowed to a trot and then to a walk. Her heart thrummed and her breath rushed in and out of her heated body like the wind in the trees around her. And then she rested, waited . . . and listened. The nighttime woodland sounds would soothe her. They never failed to help her regain control when her tight grip on it faltered.

Soft, pine-scented air caressed her face, stroked her hair, filled her lungs. Padded feet stepped over the ground off to the left. Three steps, then a pause. Then an airy sound . . .

sniffing. A wolf. Yes, a wolf. Nodding in affirmation, she moved a little farther, stopping again at a familiar scent that tickled her nose. Standing still, she inhaled softly, closing her eyes. She smelled the heather growing thick on the moors, and rich earth and night air. She didn't smell the wolf, though the old women had told her such a thing was possible. The wolf could smell her, they'd said. So why shouldn't she be able to detect his scent in the night air?

She put all else from her mind as she made her way to The Crones' cottage just inside the edge of the woods. She chased away her sorrow, her guilt, her rage, and replaced them by focusing on her senses, on honing them as The Crones had taught her, on feeling as if she were one with everything around her. On trying to detect the scent of a wolf in the night.

"You're late," a rich, female voice announced, and Arianna looked up to see Celia, her skin smooth and unlined, her silver hair loose and flowing over her shoulders as if she were a young girl. Her smile was warm, and despite her scolding tone she enfolded Arianna's hands in her own. It was the sort of touch Arianna had been craving from her mother. What would she have done this past year without the companionship of these three women?

A small fire danced in the clearing beside the crooked little shack The Crones shared. The light of the fire was bathing their faces, gleaming in their eyes, throwing shadows upon their worn woolen shawls. Their home was a humble one, built of rough-hewn plank boards and filled with knotholes. It had weathered to near black over the years, and had moss growing on one side and vines creeping up the other as if embracing the wood. Its thatched roof sagged in the middle, as if it were tired to the point of exhaustion. The wild tangle of growth in the back looked to be a weed patch, but was in fact a garden of herbs and plants with healing properties. But no matter how untended this place looked, there was magick here. Arianna had known it from the first time she'd come to these three women and pled with them to teach her their ways.

"My mam tried to stop me," she explained.

"An' you came anyway?" Celia asked with an arched brow.

"I'm a woman grown. I'm a Witch. I do as I will."

Celia tilted her head. She exchanged an indulgent glance with her two companions. They each smiled and shook their heads helplessly. "Do what thou wilt is but a part of the Rede, child. Tell me the rest," Celia said.

"I dinna—"

"Tell me the rest."

Sighing, Arianna muttered, "'An' it harm none, do what thou wilt.' "

"Exactly," Celia said. "Do you think you harmed your mother tonight, child?"

"Nay! I dinna so much as touch her."

Celia's eyes narrowed. Arianna knew full well what she meant. She also knew that she likely *had* hurt her mother tonight—and that she would have to make it right.

Celia nodded, seeming to read Arianna's face. "Come," she said, and led Arianna closer to the fire. Arianna nodded her greetings to Leandra, the eldest of the three, a woman whose face was so lined it resembled the surface of the trembling sea. Her snow-white hair was piled atop her head, and when she spoke it was with the voice of gravel. Then Arianna turned to Mary, plump and always smiling, with steel-gray streaks in her thick ebony mane.

"Merry meet," Arianna said.

"An' to you, lass," Mary returned. "You ought be lookin' forward to this night's ritual."

Arianna smiled broadly. For a year and a day The Crones had been teaching her, letting her observe, answering her questions. But tonight, for the first time, she would be welcomed into the sacred circle as a Witch. And after her initiation, she would be allowed to participate in a magickal rite. She could barely contain her excitement.

So far, The Crones' "magick" had consisted mostly of concocting herbal remedies for various ailments, and they *had* managed to raise a cooling wind one hot summer's night. Arianna had been mildly disappointed. She'd been expecting explosions of smoke and light, thunderbolts, and evildoers changing into toads.

She'd been hoping. . . .

Well, what she *really* wanted to learn from the old women would take far more magick than what they'd shown her so far. But Arianna had learned one thing. Even in their minor workings, there was real power. Magick was real. Knowing that made Arianna certain she would one day learn what she needed to know.

Perhaps even from The Crones. For it may be that they were simply saving the stronger sorts of magick for later on.

"Tonight, you become one with us, Arianna. Our own sister in the Craft of the Wise." Leandra smiled, and more wrinkles appeared in her face before the smile died. "And then, we conjure rain," she said with a nervous glance at the sky. "For unless we get some soon, the crops could well begin to wilt."

"Aye," Arianna said, "and those fool villagers would no doubt blame you for it."

The three Crones exchanged glances, but didn't speak their fears aloud. Still, Arianna sensed their worry.

"Come, let us cast the circle," Leandra said.

I followed Arianna that night. I had been watching her often at night, hoping I could keep her out of harm's way, certain from what Joseph had said that she was too reckless to heed my warnings. I was right.

She went to The Crones on the night of the full moon just as I had suspected she would. Dammit, didn't she realize what a risk she was taking by sneaking out to that croft alone? What could happen to her if she were found out?

I followed, of course, and hid myself in the trees just beyond reach of the dancing firelight's glow.

Then I forgot why I had come. My mind became too involved in the beauty of what I witnessed.

The beauty of Arianna.

By the time I reached the edge of the clearing, the four

of them had cast their circle, and were well into their ritual. Arianna had removed her dark cloak, and beneath it wore a garment of flowing white, which reminded me sharply of the ritual robes of my first teachers—an order of Druid priests. In Arianna's golden hair was a ringlet of flowers, and as I looked on in silence, I realized this was some sort of initiation rite. Arianna knelt in the center of the circle, near the fire, and one by one each of the old women presented her with a gift.

Apparently, Arianna had studied long enough to be recognized as one of them now. It was almost laughable. Gods, if those Crones only knew.

In silence, one of the old women gave her a book. I recognized it as a *grimoire*, in which spells and rituals and ancient knowledge would have been painstakingly copied. The second old woman presented her with a pendant that I couldn't see in detail. The third gifted her with a dagger.

This made me peer more closely, for it seemed to be a very special dagger. One much like the one I carried—like the one *we all* carried at our sides.

But The Crones didn't know of our existence, or of their student's true nature. Did they?

There was no time to ponder this mystery, for the initiation rite concluded, and the four of them moved on to whatever magickal working they had planned for this night. I crept nearer, so I might hear them.

"Dinna be disappointed if the spell doesna work right away, child," the one who looked to be the eldest said softly. "It oft' takes several tries before the rains come. We simply repeat our rite until they do."

Arianna nodded and took the small pouch the old woman handed her, looping its drawstring 'round her wrist.

"In honor of your initiation, Arianna, we've decided to let you perform tonight's incantation."

I saw Arianna's huge eyes widen in surprise. "Oh, but I—"

"You know what to do, lass," the plump one said with a smile, patting Arianna's arm. "We've taught you well."

"Aye," said the third, the one who seemed to personify

grace, and whose face defied her years. "An' besides, 'tis in the grimoire."

Drawing a deep breath, Arianna opened the book. She clutched the dagger in her right hand. The pendant hung 'round her neck. The three Crones moved to the center of the circle, surrounded the balefire, and slowly began to move in a deosil direction. Arianna stood close to the fireside, so they were circling her, as well. Laying the dagger upon the open book, she opened the small pouch the old one had given her, and withdrew herbs, which she pitched into the dancing flames. Her face was a study in concentration as she worked.

Something about her touched me just then. I couldn't have said exactly what. But it had to do with the golden fire glow on her cheeks, and the light in her eyes. Or perhaps with the curve of her lips, or the slender grace of her neck.

Lowering her gaze to the book, she began to read the words written there in a voice that came soft and uncertain.

Ancient Forces of the Sky . . .
Winds and Clouds and Rain on high . . .
Rainbow Goddess, hear my cry . . .

I saw Arianna's shoulder's grow straighter, saw her chest expand as she inhaled, and I knew she was feeling it; the surge of power. In our kind, it was magnified, and in a rite like this, she would *have to* feel it. She may not know it for what it was, but its essence would fill her; the very essence of the Divinity she'd called upon.

She lifted her head, chin pointing skyward, and her voice came louder now, and firm.

Mother Earth is parched and dry,
Without thy dewy kiss, we die,
I call forth rainclouds. Draw thee nigh!

I glanced skyward, saw the barest hint of shadow crossing the face of the full moon. Quickly I fixed my gaze on Arianna again. Partly concerned for her, and for the reactions of her teachers, but mostly . . . I felt pride.

Her body seemed to elongate and tense as she let the book fall to the ground, and lifted her arms over her head, dagger pointing at the sky. Her voice came as strong as thunder then, deeper than before, echoing unnaturally in the night.

I call forth the rain!
I call forth the rain!
I call forth the rain!
And as I will it, so mote it be!

A clap of thunder punctuated her command. The wind came then. A harsh downward sweep of it sent her white robe snapping behind her and her golden hair sailing. The Crones stopped circling, went still, and looked at one another with wide eyes. Then they were staring at Arianna as if they had never seen her before, and looking skyward as if in fear.

Arianna noticed none of it. She remained as she was, arms stretched to the sky, eyes closed, body buffeted by the wind as she silently commanded the rain to fall. She seemed completely lost in the power she wielded.

Dark clouds surged as if from all directions, collecting in one grim mass overhead, blotting out the face of the moon. Thunder rumbled. Lightning cut a jagged swath across the sky. Then the sky opened, and the rains poured down.

Arianna's eyes blinked open. Her face still tipped back, she parted her lips as if to taste the raindrops that pummeled her. Slowly she lowered her arms and her head smiling as she sought approval in the faces of her teachers. But instead she found only shock in their eyes.

"I . . . I did it," she said. I could barely hear her words over the pounding rain.

Shaking her head slowly, the plump one backed away, and quickly walked the perimeter, chanting a closing rite as she did.

"Celia? Leandra? Did I . . . did I do something wrong?"

It was the elder who spoke. "Go home, child. This rite is ended. We'll speak of this on the morrow." She turned and walked back toward the cottage as Arianna stared helplessly after her.

The third gripped Arianna's shoulders. "I hope to heaven you know how to stop it, Arianna. Suppose it goes on until we're all swallowed up by floodwaters?"

Arianna looked wounded, then angry. "If I've the power in me to call forth the rain, then I can certainly halt it. An' I dinna ken why you all act as if you've suddenly discovered a demon in your midst! I only—"

"Celia!" the old one called from the cottage.

With a sigh, Celia turned and walked away, leaving Arianna alone in the deluge she'd summoned forth.

Arianna turned and strode back toward the village, filled with too many emotions to count. Gods! The power that had surged through her! Such a feeling had only come to her once before; as she'd knelt on the shore of that darkwater loch, moved beyond reason to shout her commands to the sky.

She'd made it rain. *She had made it rain!*

And yet The Crones had seemed stunned, and almost fearful of her afterward. She'd expected them to beam with pride. It was all very odd, and she had no idea what to think. She only knew she felt powerful. She could wield magick and command the elements to do her bidding. Her hair and her dress were even now soaked through with proof of it!

When Arianna turned to walk along the muddy path to her home, Nicodimus stepped out of the shadows in front of her, arms crossed over his broad chest, rust-and-gold hair plastered to his head. "This has to stop, Arianna."

She didn't jump, didn't cry out in surprise at his sudden appearance. She'd sensed him there in the instant before she'd seen him. So she simply stopped walking and stood facing him as the rain continued to beat down upon them both.

"Whatever do you mean?" she asked, feigning innocense.

"You know what I mean. The penalties for Witchcraft are not to be taken lightly. And if you continue on this reckless course, you'll surely be found out."

She tilted her head to one side, studying him. "An' how is it you know about me and my so-called reckless course?"

His eyes, when they probed hers, were piercing and sharp. "I've been watching you."

"Aye, so you have. I wondered if you'd admit it."

He lifted one brow slightly higher than the other. "You knew, then?"

"I have felt your eyes on me more than once since last we spoke." She shrugged. "'Tis all right, Nicodimus. I've watched you, as well."

That seemed to take him by surprise, for he looked up sharply. "Have you?" She nodded. "But why?"

"Why? What a silly question. For the same reason you've watched me, of course. We're connected, you and I. Linked together in some way . . . some way I've yet to understand. But you obviously feel it, too. Just as I do." She stared up at him, and when he said nothing, planted her hands on her hips and narrowed her eyes. "You're not goin' to deny it, now, are you?"

"I . . ." He seemed to think deeply before he spoke, his eyes studying her, as if seeing more than anyone else ever had. Or ever could. Pushing his wet hair away from his forehead, he pursed his lips, set his jaw. "I did not come here to speak of such things, Arianna, but to warn you."

"Warn me?" She shrugged. "I fear nothing, Nicodimus, so there's no reason to warn me of anything at all."

"I think there is."

Sighing, she rolled her eyes. "Speak your warning, if you must. I canna promise I'll heed it."

"You'll heed it," he said, and she thought she detected a hint of a threat in his voice. As if he intended to make certain she did. But he didn't say so. "You mustn't visit The Crones anymore," he told her. "There's no more they can teach you. And already they begin to wonder about you, Arianna. To fear you."

"Fear me? What rubbish, Nicodimus! Why would they—?"

"Because, foolish girl, you're a far more powerful Witch than any of them. More powerful than any Witch they've ever known. They have realized that even if you haven't yet."

His hands closed on her shoulders as he went on. The delicious tingling of his touch rocked her, and she closed her eyes in response, but he barely seemed to notice.

"They brew herbal potions to cure the croup while you cast spells to bring the dead back from their graves! Can you not see the difference?"

She blinked in shock as the import of his words sank in, but she did not pull free of his grip. Somehow he already knew her ultimate goal—something she hadn't dared confess to anyone.

He took his hands away, looking at his palms and shaking his head. He'd felt it, too. That sizzling jolt. That heat that had no place amid this cold, pounding rain.

She swallowed hard and voiced the suspicion she'd always harbored about him. "What do you know of spells, Nicodimus? Dinna tell me you're a Witch yourself."

"What I am or am not is between me and my Creator, Arianna. You'd do well to take a lesson from that."

She shrugged as if she didn't care, but took his refusal to answer as an admission. "Why should I heed your advice if you dinna even trust me enough to tell me your secrets?" she asked.

"I trust no one with my secrets. I have lived too long and seen too much to make that mistake." He studied her eyes for a moment, and his expression seemed to soften. "But I'll tell you a little of what I know, if you will promise to stay away from The Crones from now on."

She lowered her head. "I will promise this much. I shall be more careful, and will think about your warnings."

He dipped his head to search her eyes, seemed to resign himself to the fact that she would promise no more, and nodded. "All right. Then I'll tell you this much. Your sister will come back one day, Arianna. We *all* come back," he said softly. "The Crones must have taught you that much, at least."

She nodded. "Some would call those words blasphemy, Nicodimus."

"And some would call them truth," he countered. "But you cast a spell when your sister died, didn't you, Arianna? A spell to make her coming back . . . different."

"How do you know?"

He lifted a golden brow, tilted his head.

She sighed. "Kenyon an' Lud Lachlan told you how I shouted it to the heavens, did they? I made them swear ne'er to say a word."

He kept his gaze riveted to her eyes, only the raindrops, a misty curtain, between them. "What sort of spell was it, Arianna?"

Closing her eyes, she told him what she'd told no one, not even The Crones. "My sister sank into the cold embrace of that dark water," she said, lowering her head slowly as the pain of that day renewed itself in her soul. "I lay upon the shore, fighting to breathe, choking water from my lungs, searching for her. And Laird Lachlan's sons, Kenyon and Lud, they both went back for her. Frantic, shouting. But I knew she was already gone. I felt it somehow. Like a large, heavy stone where my heart should have been."

Nicodimus sighed, and when she looked up at him, he squeezed her shoulders. "I know the feeling well, child. Go on."

"I felt anger, rage, an' . . . something else. Like some other voice tellin' me what to do, only . . . nay aloud. I heard with my heart, with my soul, nay my ears. I knelt up, an' lifted my fists to the heavens, an' I demanded that my sister be returned to me. Aye, Raven will live again, but when she returns, she'll look the same, and bear the same name, and I'll know her again, for she will come back afore my lifetime is ended. Those are the words I shouted, the commands I sent forth, an' I tell you, Nicodimus, when

I did so I felt as powerful as the Goddess Herself."

Nicodimus expelled his breath. "That is because it was Her power you wielded, Arianna." He turned slightly away from her. "Within your lifetime," he muttered. "Sweet child, if only you knew how long that might be."

"Nicodimus?"

He faced her again, and she searched his eyes, not understanding what he'd meant. But he shook his head at her as if to tell her to forget about it. "Do you have any doubt your spell will be effective?" he asked.

Her chin came up. "None whatsoever."

"And who taught you such a conjure, Arianna?"

Slowly, she shook her head. "No one. As I said, it came from . . . within me. 'Twas as if the very Queen of Heaven put the words to my lips . . . or something."

"Or something indeed." His brows drew together. "You've no need of those village Witches any longer. There is no more they can teach you."

"But there is so much more I need to learn." She sighed heavily, pacing away from him, wringing her wet hands. "I want Raven back *now*, Nicodimus. I canna bear the loneliness without her."

When he didn't answer, she turned to face him again, only to glimpse a bleak expression in his eyes before he managed to shutter them. But deep in his eyes, she could still see a shadow of pain. Rivulets of rainwater ran down his corded neck, dripped from his chin. She wanted to wipe the drops away with her hands. With her lips.

Finally, he whispered, "I know how much it hurts. But there's nothing you can do to make her come back to you any sooner. Believe me, I've searched the world over for such a spell. It doesn't exist."

"Nay, it must," she whispered, clasping the plaid at his chest in her fists, staring up at him, pleading with her eyes.

"It doesn't. I would not lie to you about this, nor would I speak the words unless I knew them to be true. There is no way to raise the dead from their graves, Arianna. It *cannot happen.*"

"Nay . . ." Her knees buckled. She collapsed at his feet,

kneeling weakly in the mud. It was as if she'd been hit in the belly by a giant fist, the very breath forced out of her. She couldn't draw any air for a moment. For she knew, instinctively, that he spoke the truth. He wouldn't lie to her, not about this. So there was no way to hasten Raven's return. It was almost as if she'd lost her sister all over again at that moment. For she'd existed on a hope that had suddenly disappeared.

Gently, Nicodimus bent over her. He closed his big hands 'round her waist, lifted her to her feet again. "I regret taking your dream away. But 'tis best you know . . ."

She leaned against his chest and would have fallen once again had his arms not come 'round her to hold her upright. Sobs burst from her all at once, her tears mingled with the rain that soaked his clothes. He lowered his head and she felt his lips grazing the top of hers, heard his comforting whispers. "You cast your spell, Arianna, and I believe you cast it true. It will work. She'll come back to you one day, you have to believe it. Cling to it, child. At least it is something."

Sniffling, Arianna lifted her head, searching his face with her damp eyes. "Aye. 'Tis more than you had, is that what you're sayin'?"

He nodded. "Yes. It is more than I had."

"Who did you lose, Nicodimus?"

Licking his lips, he set her gently away from him, cleared his throat, schooled his features. Hardened them. "If you must practice your rites, Arianna, do it alone and in some secret place where you won't be found out. It is safer that way. That is what I came here to tell you, nothing more." He turned to go.

Arianna caught his arm and he stopped, his back to her. "*You ken all of it, dinna you*?" she whispered. "You ken the ways of magick, and far more than those village Witches understand. You have the secrets I've been seekin' all my life."

"I know nothing beyond what I've told you."

Slowly she moved around until she was in front of him again. She smeared the tears from her cheeks with one hand, and gripping his forearm with the other she probed his eyes. "I've been driven to learn the ways of the mystics, Nicodimus. Driven by some force deep inside me that I dinna even ken. An' drawn to you like a moth to the candle's flame from the first time I set eyes on you. And now I ken why. You can teach me, Nicodimus. You can tell me the things I need to learn."

"You're mistaken."

"Am I?"

He nodded.

"An' what of this, then?" Abruptly, she released his arm, and stepping back, bunched her skirts in both hands and lifted them high, baring her right leg and her thigh, and finally her hip, where the mark of a crescent moon stood in dark contrast to her pale skin. Clouds parted as if on command, and moonlight spilled down onto the birthmark as if in a caress. Nicodimus's gaze fixed to it in much the same way.

She saw him tremble, saw the sweat bead upon his upper lip. His hands reached out, and she closed her eyes in anticipation of his touch there on her bare hip. She held her breath, and felt the heat of his hands as they hovered a hairbreadth from her skin . . .

But he only took her skirts from her hands to lower them. If his fingers brushed her thigh as they passed, it was purely unintentional, though that touch left a burning trail of forbidden pleasure in its wake.

"Do not," was all he said.

Breathless, shivering, she stared into his eyes as if daring him to deny the truth. "You bear the mark, same as I do, Nicodimus."

He caught his breath. "How can you know that?"

She lowered her eyes. "I told you. I've watched you just as you've watched me. I've peered from my da's croft as you rode through the village upon that magnificent black stallion, an' I've spied on you from the tall reeds near the loch, long before the sun has risen in the sky. You go there to bathe in the coolness of the wee hours."

"You have no right—"

"Aye," she whispered. "I do. That mark you bear upon your hip gives me the right. An' if that were not enough, Nicodimus, there is the stirring I feel deep in the pit of my belly when you step, naked and wet, out of that water into the glow of the early sun, lookin' as wild an' magnificent as Cernunnos Himself. We're bound to one another somehow. When you touch me, I feel a force pass between us that is more than ordinary desire. An' you know 'tis true, Nicodimus. For you feel it, too."

"Arianna—"

"What does the crescent birthmark mean?"

He closed his eyes only briefly. So strong and steadfast, while she trembled at his very touch. "You're a young girl. The time when you'll need to burden yourself with all of this is far away yet. Far away. When it comes, when you need to know . . . I'll tell you. I promise you that." He stroked her hair with his big hand. "For now, that will have to be enough for you." He lowered his head, shaking it slowly. "An' as for this other—"

"Us wantin' each other, you mean?"

His jaw clenched. "You're too young, and I am too old for either of us to entertain such a ludicrous notion, Arianna."

But he didn't deny it was true. It wasn't an admission, nor even much of a concession. But it was something. He wanted her, too. She knew that as he turned and she watched him stride away. But it wasn't enough. She wanted a good deal more than a promise and a pat on the head from Nicodimus Lachlan.

A good deal more.

"You'll be mine, one day, Nicodimus. Heart an' soul you'll be mine. You canna see it, but deep down in your soul, you already are."

Nicodimus stiffened, but kept on walking.

3

Arianna was a girl in need of rescue. Yet at the same time, she was a woman . . . a woman in need of a man. And I knew that made her dangerous to me. I had a weakness in me for a woman in trouble. And with her that weakness seemed trebled. I had long ago vowed never to care again, and I feared that rescuing Arianna would mean breaking that vow. Already I felt the slow burn of desire for her in my blood. And more. A softness. A weakness. A vulnerability.

Just as there had been before . . . for Anya.

It had been a furious battle, between my own clansmen and those who dwelled in the lowlands. I no longer remember precisely when nor why it began, but in the year 764, I rode into battle beside my father, bow at my side and a quiver of arrows on my back. I fought bravely that day. I killed as many men as any of the other warriors, though I had but four and ten years, and this was my first battle. They congratulated me, my clansmen. Slapped my shoulders and sang my praises as we rode through the defeated village. Wounded men raced out of our path while women cowered.

As I looked around me, I saw her for the first time. A bit of a girl with wild hair as red as the sun before a storm. She tugged a wounded man by the arm, dragging his body from the path, though it was obviously more than she could manage alone. Her eyes met mine, and she stopped what she was doing, staring at me in silence.

Another man, younger than the wounded one, strode up to her and slapped her sharply across the face. "I told you to get him inside, Anya. Do it. *Now.*"

"Yes, Marten." She lowered her head in submission and began tugging at the man again. I drew my horse to a halt before her.

"Leave him," I said.

She looked up at me, wide-eyed. Her eyes were the palest blue I had ever seen. The blue of water, or ice. A thin, weak blue. And they showed me her soul.

"Leave him," I told her again, my voice more gentle this time, for she was small and timid and afraid.

She slanted a glance at the one who'd slapped her, as if seeking his permission.

"Anya," I said, calling her by name. "He's too heavy for you. Let this brute who slaps small women carry him instead."

She let go of the unconscious one's arm, and he thumped downward to the dirt.

"You," I said, addressing the young man now. "Are you her husband?"

"Her brother," he said, all but spitting the words at me. "An' she'll do as I tell her or suffer the consequences."

The men around me muttered, but didn't interfere. "No," I said softly. "You'll both do as *I* tell you. Marten, is it? If you want that wounded man carried inside, do it yourself." He didn't move. I pulled an arrow from my quiver. I'd fired them all in the midst of the battle, and I'd had to run about plucking arrows from dead men in order to rearm myself. The tip was bloodied. I strung the arrow, but before I lifted my bow, Marten had slung the old man—his father, I guessed—over his shoulder and was lugging him away. Anya turned to follow.

"Wait," I said, and she stopped, her back to me. "Does he strike you often?"

Her body seemed to stiffen. "Only when I do not work fast enough, or do my work well enough to suit him."

"And how often is that?" I asked softly.

I saw her shoulders slump. "Every day."

My stomach churned with the urge to kill the bastard. "Is he the only one who treats you this way," I asked. "Or does your father join in as well?"

She turned to face me. "My father is far harsher than Marten, and my other brother, Kohl, is just as bad." Her eyes flashed with the first life I'd seen in them. "And now that you and your clan have defeated ours in battle, it is bound to be even worse. Our women will bear the brunt of their anger. While you ride away with the spoils."

"Spoils?" I lifted my palms and looked at the men around me. "Have we taken any spoils?"

They all answered in the negative. It had never been our custom to loot a defeated enemy's village. I looked back at Anya once more. "But perhaps we should. I am the victor this day, after all. I ought to take a token of this battle back with me."

Her eyes widened slightly. She took a step backward as I held out my hand to her.

"Come with me, Anya," I said. "Come with me and no man will ever raise a hand to you again."

She simply stood there, her brows crooked together as if she couldn't understand. She took a hesitant step forward, then went still as a man yelled her name.

I turned to see what had to be the second brother rushing toward us, and I quickly leapt to the ground, snatched up a sword, and grabbed Anya's hand.

"Let go of her!" Kohl shrieked, and then he cried, "Marten! Marten, they're taking Anya!"

By the time Marten came running, likely after having dropped his father headfirst, I was lifting the girl onto my horse. I swung up behind her. She neither helped me nor resisted. And I remember wishing she'd give some indication whether she wished to come with me or not. I'd likely have taken her either way. It was my right to do so. But mostly I hated the thought of those men treating her so cruelly.

Marten and Kohl rushed me, and I could have easily killed one or the other of them with a single swipe of my sword, but I chose not to. Not in front of their sister. Instead, I simply kicked my stallion's sides, and we lunged forward. Tipping my head back, I bellowed a victory cry, and carried my prize away. And Anya whispered, "Goodbye, my brothers." Her voice was neither jubilant nor sad.

I'd made a pair of lifelong enemies that day. Their vengeance had cost me dearly, and would again, I knew. And yet here I was, once again, tempted by a woman in need of rescue.

Yet, I could not quite envision Arianna ever taking the abuse Anya had. I imagined the man who would lift a hand to her would suffer a thousand deaths before she'd satisfied her need for vengeance. She needed rescuing only from herself. And that, she needed badly. For if she continued on the course she'd set, only disaster awaited her.

I went into the village often. Daily, in fact. And each time, I made it a point to see her, to watch her movements. But from a distance, for my own peace of mind. Being close to her was far too disturbing to me.

Most often I found her at the grave of her sister—not mourning, but focusing very intently with a look of stubborn determination on her pretty, elfin face.

One morning I found her near the loch, sitting on the grassy bank alone—always alone. She stared out at the blue-green waters that had taken her sister, a haunted expression in her eyes. I'd vowed to watch over her, to keep her from ruining herself, if I could, but to do so without interacting with her any more than necessary. If she knew how often I observed her, she would read more into my actions than was truly there. And that would feed her romantic notions about the two of us. Besides, sparring with her was exhausting . . . and yet exciting to me.

So I'd decided to stay away. But the picture she made

there that morning was one so heartbreaking that I started forward. No one deserved to be as lonely as Arianna looked at that moment.

As soon as I took a step forward, I saw a young man approaching her, and decided to wait . . . and to watch.

He had to be the cobbler's son of whom Joseph had spoken; the lad to whom she was betrothed. His proprietary hand on her arm gave me to know as much. The way she shook it off only made me smile as I crept closer amid the rushes to watch this little scene play out amid a backdrop of sparkling water and rocky hillsides. The keep loomed tall and gray beyond them, looking almost like an extension of the cliffs beyond it. Its backdrop was the sky, the fluffy clouds drifting lazily past the sun.

"You've mourned your sister long enough," the lad was saying. Angus MacClennan was his name, I recalled. "It looks bad for you, Arianna, sitting out here all alone. 'Tis long enough, I tell you."

Arianna tilted her head to one side, studying him curiously. "How can one know how long is long enough? If I still miss her, if I still weep for her when I'm alone at night . . . then I still mourn her, Angus. And I *do* miss her. And I *do* weep for her. And I sometimes think that I loved her so much . . . a lifetime of mourning her wouldna be 'long enough.' "

Lowering his head, properly shamed, he whispered, "I didna mean you should stop missing her, Arianna. Only that 'tis high time you be happy again."

"An' how would you suggest I do that?"

He shifted his stance. Arianna remained where she was, sitting carelessly on the bank, knees wrapped within the folds of her arms, glancing at the boy occasionally only to return to her contemplation of the waves. It looked as if he was a bit of a nuisance to her, like a fly, and would get no more attention than one.

"You've long been promised to me," he said, seeming to choose his words with great care and forethought. "I want us to go forth with our lives, Arianna."

"Speak plainly, for heaven's sake."

He cleared his throat, thrust out his chin. "I want us to marry."

"Why?"

Very frank, very blunt, and spoken so quickly poor Angus nearly fell over backward. He blinked his surprise. "What sort of question is that?"

"A good one, I think. Why do you want to marry me?"

"Arianna, you're nigh on ten and eight! And I nearly twenty!"

"So we should marry because we are of a certain age, then." She frowned, shaking her head, still staring at the water. "Hardly seems reason enough to me."

Pushing both hands through his carrot-colored hair, Angus spun in a circle. Then he stopped and stared down at her. "Ahh, I see. So 'tis declarations of love you be wantin', is that it?"

She said nothing, but I saw her close her eyes as if in dread of what was to come.

Sure enough, young Angus rounded on her, dropping to one knee. "I love you, fair Arianna. I want you to be my wife. To bear my children. To—"

"So, you love me, do you?" she interrupted.

He licked his lips. "Aye. Do you nay believe it?"

She shrugged. "Why should I believe it? 'Tis the first time you've spoken of love, Angus, and only now because you think 'tis what I wish to hear. So tell me, what is it you love about me?"

"I-I dinna ken—"

"Well, do you love the way I go about alone when 'tis deemed improper?"

"Nay, not that, but—"

"Then 'tis the way I speak my mind, be my thoughts impertinent or not?"

"Nay, of course not, lass. But I—"

"Nay? Then it must be the way I mourn my beloved sister. . . . Oh, nay, for you've already told me you dislike that about me."

"You talk in circles!" he shouted. "I-I love your hair, lass, and your eyes, and the figure you fetch in your dresses.'' He gave a nod, looking quite satisfied with himself.

''My hair will turn gray and fall out in time. My eyes will dull and lose their glow amid the wrinkles that will pucker my face, and as for the figure I fetch, 'twill go to this childbearing you've spoken of soon enough. What will remain of your so-called love, then, Angus?''

He looked as if he'd been hit between the eyes for a moment. Then he frowned at her. ''It willna matter,'' he said, his voice growing sharper now. '''Tis time, Arianna, canna you see that?''

''Why?'' she insisted. ''Tell me why. Tell me now or go away. Why, Angus?''

''My mother is ailing, woman!'' he blurted all at once. ''How much longer do you expect her to run that household and care for me and my da and my younger brothers? 'Tis *your* place, an' the time has come for you to take it.''

She rose, and the look in her eyes as she glared at him made me shiver, even from the distance between us. I actually feared for the lad for just a moment. I rose from my hiding place in the rushes without a thought.

'''Tis *nay* my place.'' She poked him in the chest with a forefinger. '''Tis neither *my* mother, nor *my* household, nor *my* brothers need carin' for,'' she said, poking him three more times. ''I willna marry you, Angus. Not now and not ever, so you might as well stop with your askin'.''

''You . . . you . . .'' His face reddened. ''You canna do that! You're my betrothed! You canna—''

''Katie McDaniel would swoon on the spot should you ask for her hand. Go find you a woman who wants you, Angus. 'Twill never be me. I'd sooner go to prison, for that's what life as a wife here would be like. Prison. Servitude. But there is more than that out there awaitin' me, an' I'll find it someday. I vow I will, or die in the search.''

He stared at her, dumbfounded. ''Who's been puttin' such wild notions into yer head, woman?'' Then he looked at the ground when she didn't answer. ''Can it be true, what they're sayin'? Can it be true, after all?''

"Can what be true?" She looked exasperated with the entire discussion.

Angus lifted his head, and with a sigh of apparent surrender, reached out to her. "No matter. No matter at all, not now. Will you give me your hand, then? A gesture of friendship in parting?"

I went stiff, a little chill of warning creeping into my nape. Even as I started forward, she offered her delicate hand. Angus took it and gripped her hand hard. Too hard. I saw the alarm in her eyes, saw her try to pull free, and I raced toward them. But Angus had a blade in his free hand now, and with a ruthless swipe of it, he cut her. Blood sprayed from her wrist and she screamed. The sound cut right to my heart. Angus jumped backward, wide-eyed, terrified, first at the way she bled, and then as he caught sight of me bearing down on him.

"I dinna mean . . . They say a Witch doesna bleed when ye cut 'em! They say a Witch doesna bleed—"

My fist crushed the better part of his face, and when he landed hard on his back, he was blessedly silent. I turned and gathered Arianna close as her knees began to give. I closed my hand firmly around her wrist, slowing the blood flow with pressure. I didn't want her to die, only to revive into a new life; an endless life of fighting just to stay alive. Not yet. Not when she was so young, so innocent. She'd never survive.

"There, lie back, lass. I have you."

"I'll kill him," she whispered through grated teeth. "That simpering, superstitious lout!" She lifted her head to eye the wound. "I'll bleed to death."

"You know I won't allow that to happen. Lie back, Arianna."

She did, reclining half across my lap, her side pressed to my chest. I tore a strip of cloth from her skirt and wrapped her wrist up tight. She winced in reaction and bit her lip. "I'm sorry it hurts you, lass."

"Fear not, Nicodimus. I'm committin' every bit of this pain to memory, so that I can visit it back upon him."

"Hush." I tied a knot in the makeshift bandage. "You'll need stitching. Can you stand?"

She nodded, and then clung to my neck as I got to my feet. She tried to stand without aid and wobbled a bit. I eased her into the crook of my arm. "Come down to the water's edge, and I'll wash some of the blood away."

"My head is spinning," she whispered, but she walked beside me, lowering her head as she sank down into the grass beside the water. This time, she remained sitting up on her own, as I tore at my clothing and used the scraps to bathe her with loch water. Gently, I wiped the blood from her slender forearm. She sat still and silent, contemplating the loch as before. I rinsed the scrap of cloth, squeezed it out, and moved to her face, wiping as carefully as I could. Then I paused, my heart tripping, as I saw a teardrop slip down her cheek.

"Don't cry, Arianna," I said, and I washed it gently away.

She whispered, "'Tis ironic, dinna you think? Now both the Sinclair sisters' blood nourishes this water."

"Then this water must be very special indeed," I said softly.

She met and held my gaze. Her eyes were so brown and deep . . . and filled with far more pain and wisdom than a girl of nearly eighteen should know. She touched a palm to my cheek. "You likely saved my life just now, Nicodimus."

I shook my head, and concentrated on cleaning her face, trying to keep my touch cool and impersonal. "'Twould take more than a cut such as that one to do you in."

She opened her mouth as if she would argue the point, but as she did, she spotted her beau on the ground. Her eyes widened, and I followed her gaze to where he lay. His nose broken, lip bleeding. I supposed I hit him a mite harder than I should.

"Mercy," Arianna said with a gasp. "Have you done him to death?"

"I think not. He moaned a moment ago. And don't pity him, Arianna. He didn't get half the beating he deserves."

I scooped her up into my arms, cleaner now. At least not covered in enough blood to send her mother into a dead faint should she catch sight of her. "I never could abide a man who'd harm a lady."

Looking back at the lad, she told him softly, "Think how surprised you'll be, foolish Angus MacClennan, when you learn once and for all that Witches *do* bleed."

I knew exactly what she was thinking, though it didn't take any magick to do so. Her thoughts were writ clear across her face. "If you think you can go about wielding magick for such petty causes as vengeance, lass, then you've had poor teachers."

She blinked up at me. "Are you admittin' you know of such things personally, Nicodimus?"

I scowled at her. "I'm only saying young Angus has done you a favor. He'll consider this proof of your innocence." I nodded toward her bandaged wrist. "Though I'd like to throttle him for it, all the same."

Her smile was sweet and slow. "You care for me far more than you know," she whispered.

I ignored that remark, finding it far too close to the truth. "When word gets out that Angus cut you and you nearly bled to death, then the speculation about you might well die." I glanced down at her. "At least until you do something to revive it all over again."

"Superstitious fools, all of them. They'll never let it die. They'll say the blood was an illusion, a trick, that I conjured the blood to appear and flow just to fool him." She tilted her head. "At last Da canna expect me to marry the whelp now."

"Ahhh, you owe him for two favors, then."

She glared at me, and then sighed. "Where are you takin' me, Nicodimus?"

"To the keep."

"The keep," she whispered, and her eyes turned to stare off at the fortresslike structure. Her slender arms clung more tightly to my neck, and her head rested upon my shoulder as I strode with her along the craggy path up the hill to the massive stone structure at its top.

"Surely you've been in the keep before, Arianna," I said teasingly. "You've nothing to fear there."

"Aye, I've been inside before. An' I dinna fear it, Nicodimus. You've misread me entirely. I was born to live in a castle keep, and one far finer than this. . . ." She smiled up at me. "Just as I was born to be with you, Nicodimus."

4

Arianna rocked against Nicodimus's broad chest when he scooped her up into his arms and strode toward the keep. His arms were clamped securely around her, like some sort of protective armor. His scent surrounded her, warm and musky and male. And this close to him, she could see the tiny bits of stubble that made his cheeks appear shadowed. Beautiful, he was. She'd never known a man so beautiful. And she knew she'd never felt so safe. She didn't like the idea that she needed a man to make her feel this way. She'd never *needed* a man for anything, and she'd vowed she never would. But wanting a man, well, she supposed that was a far different matter. *Not* wanting this one, with his angular face and his wizard's eyes, *that* would be impossible.

Behind them, she heard Angus groaning. Raising her head to look back over Nicodimus's shoulder, Arianna saw that Angus's face was a mottled mess as he stirred himself to sit up. Nicodimus didn't so much as glance backward at the boy. And she knew, even more surely now than she'd known before, that he felt something very powerful for her. It was there in the hard set of his jaw, in the furrow between his brows. In the way he cradled her against his hard chest so carefully even while his broad strides ate up the distance to the keep. And in the way he paused ever so briefly, and closed his eyes tight when the wind blew her hair into his face.

Arianna felt a rush of uncertainty when he carried her through the outer gates and into the courtyard. Sounds of clanging metal rang in her ears. Men practiced with their swords, fighting one another in mock battle. Off to the left, there were men who shot arrows at straw stuffed targets fashioned in the shapes of men. Everywhere she looked, curious eyes in sweaty, wary faces seemed to greet her. To a man, they stopped what they were doing when they saw Nicodimus carrying her past. She could almost hear their thoughts as they stared at her. *What sort of trouble has the fool girl got into this time?*

Laird Lachlan would not be pleased with her. True enough, Angus's attack had not been her fault, but the laird would not likely see it that way. She was the one whose behavior had stirred suspicious minds to wild speculation. She was the one who'd caused the tongues to wag.

She couldn't help but stiffen in nervous anticipation as Nicodimus carried her nearer to the huge, banded doors.

Nicodimus looked down at her as he strode closer. "What is it, Arianna?"

She shrugged, averting her eyes. "I'm hardly dressed proper to be visitin' the keep. Look at me. Barefoot."

"You've been barefoot every time I've seen you." His gaze was indulgent and slightly amused.

"My dress is but poor tartan, an' stained with blood an' loch water at that, Nicodimus. Perhaps I ought simply return to my mam an' let her tend the wound."

When he didn't immediately respond, she peered up at him, only to see his deliciously full lips curving at the corners. "Was it not you I just heard telling your beau that there was more awaiting you in this world than a dirt-floor croft and a life of servitude? Or was that some other barefoot hellion?" He shook his head.

"So you were spyin' on us the whole time, were you?"

"I'd say 'tis a good thing I was." She pressed her lips

shut tight, but he ignored her lack of response. "Joseph will have to know what happened sooner or later, Arianna. I cannot believe a girl of your spirit is afraid of her own chieftain."

"I'm nay afraid of any man!"

Nicodimus lifted one brow. "Good. You've no need to be. And don't worry yourself about your state of dress, Arianna. You shame the sun, and I think you know it. What you might be wearing has little to do with it. And I doubt it would have any bearing on Joseph's mood at any rate."

A thrill of warm liquid pleasure spilled into her belly. "Are you sayin' you think I'm beautiful, then, Nicodimus Lachlan?"

Nicodimus's eyes darkened from a gleaming topaz-blue to the shade of sapphires at midnight. "You're beautiful. But there is more than mere beauty shining from those brown eyes."

"What more?" Her words came out on a breathless whisper.

He seemed to force his lingering gaze away from her face, and with a ragged sigh and a sharp shake of his head, resumed walking. "It is dangerous ground I'm treading. Best we speak of something else."

"Tell me," she whispered. "Tell me what *you* see when you look into my eyes, Nicodimus."

He looked down at her once more, and it almost seemed as if he could see right to her soul. He held her gaze with his, exerting some unseen force, even when she would have looked away. His eyes probed for a long moment, and what she saw in them . . . It was so intense, so powerful that it nearly frightened her.

An instant later the large, arching door opened, and he never answered her question. Laird Joseph Lachlan appeared in the doorway, a strikingly beautiful woman at his side. Arianna had seen the dark, exotic woman in Stonehaven before. She seemed to come and go as irregularly as Nicodimus himself did. But she seldom set foot in the village, and seemed to hold herself aloof from the clan in the keep. No one seemed to know from whence she came. That she was a foreigner was obvious. That she was well liked and welcomed by the clan chieftain, equally so. And if Laird Lachlan trusted her, then that was enough for his clan. Few asked questions.

But from the first moment Arianna had seen her, she'd burned with curiosity over the woman's background. The mysterious woman exchanged a lingering, searching glance with Nicodimus that made Arianna want to leap from his arms and claw out her eyes. 'Twas obvious they knew one another. And well.

Her eyes were ebon, slanted, and lined in black. Jewels dangled from her ears and a single ruby pierced her nose. So many bracelets adorned her wrists that they made music when she moved, and around her neck she wore at least as many pendants on chains. She was willow slender, and very tall—taller than most men, in fact. Her hair hung to her waist, blue-black and shining, and perfectly straight. And her skin was a flawless shade of bronze.

She met Arianna's gaze, and her expression did not change. She was stone-faced, no smile of welcome, no frown of concern. Nothing. Just a gaze that made Arianna feel measured and weighed and judged all at once.

"Come, bring her inside," Laird Lachlan said, stepping aside, holding the door. "I saw you comin' and summoned Nidaba. What's happened to her?"

Arianna stiffened in his arms as Nicodimus swept through the doors and into the great hall. Endless distance loomed above her, to the concave ceiling. She shivered at a chill so deep it seemed to reach out and touch her bones.

"Her devoted husband-to-be cut her," Nicodimus said. "To see whether she would bleed, he claimed."

The sound of conversation abruptly ceased as people in the great hall all turned toward Arianna. A lad with his arms loaded down with wood for the fire, the men who stood 'round the plank table deep in some discussion, the women performing various chores—everyone stared at Arianna so intently she thought their looks were burned into her skin. Nidaba muttered a word Arianna didn't recognize, but from the sound of it, it might have been a curse. She had no inkling whether it was directed at her or at Angus. The woman looked briefly into Arianna's eyes and then away.

"I will tend the girl," she said, her voice as deep and rich as a vat of spring honey, with an accent too exotic to identify. "Bring her to my chamber."

There was no trace of the highlands in Nidaba. Her dark skin was sun-kissed, her nails long and curving, with tiny stones somehow affixed to them. And her dress was as scandalous as any other Arianna had seen her wearing. Black and tight and anchored only at one shoulder, leaving the other, and both arms, completely bare.

She was frightening, and Arianna did not fear much. She bristled, and told herself she could hold her own against the strange woman, should the need arise.

The chieftain turned and waved a hand to those in the chamber. "Go about your business. The lass is nay in need of your gawkin' at her." His voice lower, as they scurried away, he said, "Angus MacClennan is a foolish lad, if ever there was one." He ran one hand over his bald head and sighed, walking beside Nicodimus as Nidaba led the way through an arching doorway and into one of the many dark stone corridors. Nicodimus carried Arianna past what seemed like endless doors, and his steps echoed like ghosts all around them. While Arianna had often been in the great hall and the kitchens, she had never before been in the private wing or invited into the chambers of those who lived here. And yet, she couldn't stop looking ahead, at Nidaba. The woman's black dress seemed to be made of some magickal fabric that shimmered when she moved and clung to her like skin.

"He could have killed her!" the laird muttered angrily. "How many daughters does he think her poor family can stand to lose?"

"You can see the damage gossip can do, Joseph. The tongue-waggers who started this ought to be horse-whipped," Nicodimus said quickly.

"Aye, indeed. Gossip can be a deadly thing, Nic. A deadly thing."

Arianna cringed a bit, knowing Nicodimus likely believed her own behavior had brought this upon her as much as the gossip of the villagers had done. He had warned her, hadn't he?

Nidaba opened a door, and they stepped into a large chamber. It was far different from the dark, rather barren parts of the keep Arianna was familiar with. The room seemed to be of some other world, filled with the most incredible collection of exotic items Arianna had ever seen. Glittering stones of purple and blue and pink, some colorless, some multihued, lined shelves on the walls. And there were daggers—countless different shapes and sizes, all from different lands, Arianna thought, perhaps even . . . different times. They hung on the stone walls, some crossing one another, some forming triangles, some fanning out like the tail feathers of some beautiful, deadly bird.

Nidaba waved a beringed hand toward her fur-covered bed, and Nicodimus lowered Arianna onto it. Then he stepped aside to let Nidaba move closer to her. The woman's black eyes met hers, and the ruby in her nose seemed to glow. Arianna shivered. And then the woman touched Arianna's forearm, clasping it to begin removing the makeshift bandage.

A jolt surged from her hand into Arianna's arm the instant the strange woman touched her. Just the way it had at Nicodimus's touch. Arianna's eyes widened. Nidaba paused, met her gaze, and seemed to will her to keep silent. Aloud, she said, "I have no need of you two men. You may go, take refreshment. I will bring her along to you when we've finished."

Arianna sought Nicodimus's eyes, her own pleading. She didn't know this woman. Nidaba frightened her, when she'd long prided herself on fearing nothing; not man, nor beast nor death itself.

"I'll stay," Nicodimus said, very softly. "She's been through a shock, and you're a stranger to her, Nidaba."

Nidaba's dark, probing gaze never left Arianna. "I am a stranger to most of the clan Lachlan. But few look at me with such wide eyes as these." Her hand clasped Arianna's chin as she studied her face, and Arianna fought to hide her inexplicable fear of the woman. "You are right to be afraid, young one, of those you do not know. However, I mean you no harm . . . just now." As she unwrapped the wound, she whispered, "I am not one of the Dark Ones."

Arianna only frowned, puzzled.

And when Nidaba saw that she hadn't understood, the woman sent Nicodimus a questioning look, to which he responded with a quick subtle shake of his head. There was another long gaze between them, but it broke off when Nicodimus came to the other side of the bed to watch over her as the dark woman worked. The laird himself, not some servant, fetched water and a cloth, and brought fine whiskey for her to sip, while Nidaba cleansed and then stitched the wound, and Arianna clutched Nicodimus's forearm in pain.

Twice, Arianna saw Nidaba move one hand over the cut in a circular motion; saw her lips moving as she whispered some words too soft to hear. Almost as if . . . as if she were casting a spell.

But nay. She couldn't be. Could she?

When the laird left the three of them alone in the room, Arianna cleared her throat, gathered her courage, and blurted the question on her mind. "Are you a Witch, Nidaba?"

Nidaba's hands stilled. Then she lifted one forefinger, and taking the needle, pricked it. A ruby-red droplet welled from the tiny puncture, and Nidaba met Arianna's eyes. "I bleed. Therefore, I cannot be, can I?"

Silent for a moment, looking from Nidaba to Nicodimus and back again, Arianna realized it was meant to be a joke. Though the strange woman never smiled.

"I am serious," Arianna insisted. "Is it only when I touch the hand of another Witch that I feel that . . . that surge of . . . of whatever it is that I felt when I touched you just now, Nidaba? Or when I touch Nicodimus?"

Nidaba met Nicodimus's eyes, her eyebrows raised.

"But it canna be that," Arianna continued, shaking her head. "I feel nothing when I touch Celia's hand, nor Leandra's nor Mary's."

Nidaba tilted her head. "And who are they?"

"The Crones," Nicodimus explained.

"Ahhh," she said. "The mortal village Witches."

Arianna frowned at them both while Nidaba bent to her work once again. " 'Mortal'? What do you mean, Nidaba?" But Nidaba didn't answer. "Nicodimus, what did she mean?"

Nicodimus cleared his throat. "Nidaba is not quite fluent in our language, Arianna. It is not her native tongue."

"Do you think I dinna ken as much?" Arianna said with a toss of her head. "The entire clan kens she's a foreigner." Arianna looked at her. "Where do you come from, Nidaba?"

"I believe you know it as Sumeria," Nidaba answered without looking up. Her hair hung over her face like a black satin curtain.

Arianna blinked. She was uncertain, but she thought Sumeria to be the name of some long ago desert land; a place that no longer existed. She must be mistaken. She certainly didn't want to show the two of them her ignorance by asking.

"And, how do you two know each other?" she went on, burningly curious about the nature of their relationship.

"Why do you ask?" Nicodimus asked her.

She shrugged. "You seem . . . well acquainted."

"We are."

Nidaba's head was still bent over Arianna's wrist, but not so much that Arianna missed the slight smile at Nicodimus's answer. "Nicodimus and I have been . . . acquainted . . . for a very long time. Longer than you could even begin to guess."

"Then . . . you are close. Close . . . as friends are close?" Arianna pressed.

The needle jabbed her, and while up to now she hadn't felt a hint of unnecessary pain under the woman's ministrations, this time it hurt. "The curious rabbit who pries into the scorpion's lair," Nidaba said softly, "gets stung."

"You did that apurpose!" Arianna all but shouted.

Nidaba said nothing more as she wrapped Arianna's arm

in a clean, soft cloth. When that was done, she straightened, and began putting her things away. "Finish the whiskey," she told Arianna. "The pain will ease soon."

The door opened and the laird peered inside. "How is she?"

"She will be fine," Nidaba replied. "But it could have been far more serious, had Nicodimus not been nearby."

"Aye, I thought as much. Rest awhile there, lass," the laird bade Arianna. "You'll take dinner here in the keep. An' I'll have no argument about that. Fear not, I'll send word to your mother with the same two men I'm sendin' to bring young Angus back here. A night in the dungeon might give the lad somethin' to think about 'ere next he harms a lassie. We dinna tolerate such behavior in the clan."

"No," Nicodimus said, almost under his breath. "No, we never have." And he exchanged yet another secretive glance with Nidaba.

Arianna forced herself to exercise the manners her mam had taught her. "I'm very grateful to you, Laird, and to you, Nidaba." It galled her to thank a woman she sensed might be closer to Nicodimus than she was. But she had no choice. The strange woman *had* helped her.

"Then you'll repay us by saying nothing of Nidaba's healing skills to those vicious gossips in the village," the laird responded. And as Arianna frowned at him, he explained, "If they persecute you for your strange ways, child, think what they'd make of her, did they learn she was a gifted practitioner of the healing arts. Nidaba is an old and valued friend, an' I'll nay subject her to such gossip."

Those words, and the truth behind them, made Arianna's chin raise. Women who practiced healing with any degree of success would soon raise the same suspicions in the superstitious members of the clan that Arianna herself had raised among them. "Aye," she said softly. "If 'tis my silence you want, you have my word on it, Laird. But were I you, Mistress Nidaba, I would march among the crofters proudly, and challenge anyone to say an unkind word and survive my wrath. Those ignorant fools need a lesson. 'Tis high time they had one, in fact, an' I—"

"And you're just the one to deliver it," Nicodimus finished for her. "Have you not learned a thing from all of this, Arianna?"

Nidaba looked from Nicodimus to Arianna, a worried glint in her strange eyes. "I approve of your spirit, child. And, if it is your own destruction you seek, you are going about it very well."

"My own . . . ?" Arianna shook her head. "That's not it at all."

"If that is true, then perhaps you will listen to someone a great deal older than you, Arianna. Sometimes it is better to wait in silence—to choose one's battles with wisdom rather than to rush headlong into each and every fight because of foolish pride."

Arianna blinked at the soft, poetic cadence of Nidaba's voice. She spoke slowly, deliberately, her tones deep and musical and hypnotic.

"I come here," she went on, "to rest from strife and conflict, Arianna. Lachlan Keep is a haven to me, as it is to Nicodimus. I have no wish to stir up trouble here, among Joseph's clan. There will be enough awaiting me when I leave these walls."

Arianna frowned, tilting her head to one side. "If your life is so filled with trouble, perhaps you ought to stay here for good."

"My troubles would find me soon enough," she said, and there was a sadness in her eyes that made Arianna think perhaps she'd jumped to the wrong conclusions when she'd judged the woman to be her rival and her enemy.

"What sorts of troubles do you—"

"No, child. You know nothing of these things. Not yet."

"Rest until dinner, lass," the laird said again. "Come, Nidaba. I could use some of that wisdom of yours myself as I ponder what to do with the lass. I've spoken to some of the clansmen, and the talk Angus has already spread will no doubt make matters far worse. Decisions will need be made regarding the lassie's safety."

Nidaba nodded as Arianna frowned, and the two left the room, the laird's head gleaming as much as Nidaba's nose ring did in the flickering lamplight. Turning her puzzled gaze on Nicodimus, Arianna asked, "What did the laird mean by that?"

Nicodimus sighed deeply, and sat down upon the edge of the bed. "Arianna . . ." He drew a breath and let it out slowly. "It is fairly obvious now that you cannot simply return to the village. Not when the talk about you has reached such a crucial point that people are out to cut your pretty flesh just to see whether you bleed. It is too dangerous."

"But I *did* bleed. Surely that should prove something to them."

"You said yourself that it meant nothing, and I fear you were right. If Angus is spreading more wild tales already . . . You're in danger here, Arianna."

She narrowed her eyes. "*Danger,*" she spat. "If my own clan is ignorant enough to come for me, let them. Next time I'll be ready."

"No, child, you're not nearly ready for such as that."

"Why will everyone nay stop callin' me 'child'? I am nay a child!"

His lips crooked as if he battled a grin.

Sitting up in the bed, Arianna frowned at him. "Nor am I ready to allow the laird to decide my fate! Nicodimus, I'll nay stand for it!" She swung her legs to the floor, went to stand, but Nicodimus gripped her arms in his, his touch tender, but firm enough to still her.

"All the laird has done up to now is show you his kindness, care for your wounds and invite you to dine here, Arianna. I'd suggest you try gratitude instead of rebellion, just this once. Wait to see what your chieftain has to say before you decide to flay him alive for it."

She blinked, released all her breath at once, and lowered her head. "You're right. I . . . I'm sorry. I'll try to behave better. Some things . . . just dinna sit well with me, Nicodimus."

"I know. And persecution of those whose ways are different is one of those things. Being told what to do is another. I'm aware of it. You wear your principles wrapped about you the way a knight wears his master's colors. What you don't understand is that Joseph shares those same concerns with you. It is why I come here when I need a rest from the . . . from the battles I fight. Why Nidaba has taken refuge here as well. Because he's not like the others out there."

She hung her head, a bit ashamed. "I suppose you think I'm actin' like a child."

"No. Like a warrior in search of a war. But you've no battle to fight here, not with me, nor with Nidaba, nor with Joseph. I promise you that."

She nodded slowly. "I suppose . . . you're right." Although she thought she might disagree about Nidaba.

"Of course I'm right."

"So what do you think he'll decide should be done with me?"

"I imagine you'd best wait and see."

"If I dinna like it, I will refuse. I . . . I will leave the clan if I must. I willna be forced into anything, Nicodimus. Not even by my own laird."

"Wild horses couldn't force you into anything, Arianna."

She looked at him, and he smiled. "You may take it as a compliment, if you wish."

She smiled back at him, just a little. She liked the way he made her feel. But she hated his secrets. Still, she supposed it would take him some time to come to trust her, to see her as a friend, the way he did Nidaba. But it would happen. She would see to that.

There was a sound outside the door, and then Nidaba stepped back inside. "I've come to tell you we eat in an hour, and to ask you, Arianna, if you would like to borrow a clean dress to wear."

Glancing down at her attire, Arianna sighed in relief. "I . . . would like that very much. Though your gowns will likely drag 'round the rushes on me. I thank you, Nidaba."

Nidaba nodded, her face expressionless, then sent Nicodimus a look that told him his welcome here was over. As soon as they were alone, she opened an ornately carved chest and pulled out gown upon richly hued gown, none conventional or even fashionable. They were all simply cut, many daringly so, with no sleeves to cover the arms, and only one strap to attach atop one shoulder. Nidaba chose just such a gown, in a shimmering amber-colored material. "This one is shorter. I made it so, for ease in riding."

"It's . . . very beautiful."

Nidaba handed it to her, folded her arms across her chest and watched with an unblinking gaze as Arianna undressed, and donned the gown. Arianna felt like a wanton when she put it on, but Nidaba only nodded her approval and reached for a silver comb.

"Sit," she commanded.

Arianna sat upon a stool, staring into a polished silver mirror that must be worth a fortune. And to her surprise, Nidaba began to run the comb through her hair. Arianna stared at her reflection, and that of the dark woman behind her, and she sighed. "My mam used to comb my hair this way."

"Why has she stopped?"

Arianna shrugged. "Nothing is the same since my sister died."

"And why should it be the same?" Nidaba asked. "There is grief now, where there once was joy. You miss her. Your mother misses her. Why do you not comfort one another?"

Arianna lowered her head, not saying what she felt. That it was her fault, and she felt too guilty to look her mother in the eye, much less try to comfort her, or allow herself to be comforted.

"No one knows the hour of their death, Arianna. You could not have known your sister would drown that day. You nearly drowned yourself."

"You know about Raven?" Arianna asked, meeting Nidaba's eyes in the mirror.

She nodded. "Nicodimus . . . has spoken of it."

Arianna swallowed hard. "Do . . . do you love him, Nidaba?"

Nidaba held her gaze in the mirror. "I have loved him for all of his life," she said. "And protected him, as well. I sense you are dangerous to him, young one."

Blinking, Arianna shook her head. "I would *never* hurt Nicodimus!"

Nidaba's gaze met and held Arianna's, and they narrowed very slightly. "Then you have nothing to fear from me. But if you do hurt him . . . I warn you, child, my wrath will know no bounds."

A cold chill rushed down Arianna's spine at those words.

Nidaba ran a slender hand over Arianna's hair, then gently pulled the strands back from her face and secured the tresses with a jewelled comb. She nodded. "There now. I believe you are ready for the meal."

Arianna stepped into the great hall feeling as if she were caught in a dream. Or perhaps a nightmare. The gown she wore felt foreign and strange, made of what Nidaba called "silk," spun by special worms in the Orient. Fit for a goddess, it was, dyed an amber hue that reminded Arianna of Nicodimus's golden hair. The gown hung from one shoulder, where it was caught with a brooch of glittering gemstones, leaving the other shoulder and both arms sinfully bare. One wrist bore the white bandages, but other than that, her arms were fully exposed, and it felt scandalous, but good. While the gown did drag through the rushes on the floor a bit, it was not nearly as long as she had feared it would be. She looked beautiful. And she knew it.

The moment she stepped into the hall, a hush gradually fell across the room as conversation ceased. Soon all eyes were turned to where she stood near the doorway. She seemed to have captured the attention of all those who had gathered in the hall for the evening meal. Even the laird himself stopped his talk to stare at Arianna. Was she so different then? Nidaba had arranged her hair in a most becoming fashion, with soft tendrils curling all around her face. And her eyes had been touched with some mystical powder to enhance their shade.

The laird stood near the hearth speaking with his two sons, Kenyon, who was just her age, and Lud, two years her senior. But it was not their eyes she sought, as she scanned the huge room. There . . . Nicodimus sat in an oversized wooden chair with a heavy brass goblet in his hand, but he'd paused with the drink halfway to his mouth and sat motionless, staring at her.

She licked her lips and boldly returned his stare, secretly wondering what to do next. Then the laird cleared his throat and Nicodimus blinked and quickly got to his feet. "Arianna. You look . . ."

"You look fit to take a man's breath away," Lud cut in, rushing to her side to offer an arm. He was a big lad of twenty years, with a belly that already bulged from too much ale. His face was ruddy, his hair, thick and uncombed.

"Nay, she looks better than that," Kenyon exclaimed. "She looks like an angel." And he came to her other side, also offering an arm. Kenyon was Lud's opposite, small and slight, fair of coloring, and always well groomed.

She glanced back at Nidaba, who only watched, her face expressionless. Not knowing what else to do, Arianna let the lads escort her to the laird's table, which sat on a raised dais at one end of the hall, where pitchers of mead surrounded platters piled high with steaming food. It looked to Arianna as though the laird's cook had been expecting a great many more mouths to feed tonight. There were several other tables on the floor nearby, just as laden with fare.

"Lovely as a sunrise," Laird Lachlan boomed, and headed for the high table. Nicodimus's approach was slower, his gaze enigmatic, as it slid from Lud to Kenyon, and back to Arianna again. Lingering on her. Nidaba watched him with her black almond eyes and expressionless face.

Nidaba and Arianna sat down, and then the men took their places. The others in the room quickly followed suit. Right away, beefy arms began reaching for the joints of meat and pastries. But Arianna's appetite fled at the thought of what Laird Lachlan might decree for her. Would he send her away? Would she have the spine in her to defy him if he tried?

Nicodimus glanced her way. "Are you not hungry, Arianna? Is it your arm? Is it paining you?"

She shook her head, and took a piece of mutton from the trencher set before her. "I'm nervous, I suppose. Laird, will you tell me what you've decided?"

"Food first, lass," he muttered around a mouthful of pork. "Talk later."

"I'm afraid I'll never be able to eat until I know what it is you're about to . . . *suggest* I do."

The feeding stopped momentarily. Lud glanced at Kenyon, and then the two grinned. "Never known our father to be one for makin' *suggestions*," Lud said.

"Aye," replied his brother. "Mostly he just gives orders."

"Enough," Nidaba said sharply . . . or, sharply, for her. But the lads fell silent. And Nidaba addressed their father. "Surely you can see the girl is frightened of what will befall her next, Joseph," she said softly.

"Nay, not frightened!" Arianna argued. "I dinna fear anything!" Her voice carried to the other tables. They all looked at her for a moment, perhaps surprised at such a declaration from such a small female. She focused her eyes on her food, waiting until they all went back to eating and the conversation grew loud again. Then, more softly, she went on.

"I canna wait endlessly for my fate to be sealed, Laird. I must know what you intend to do with me."

Drawing a deep breath, Joseph wiped the back of one hand across his mouth, then leaned back in his chair. "Very well, then," he said slowly. "The answer is obvious. Lass, what you need is protection. And a bit of taming, I might add. A man's name is like armor to a woman—his guidance, most needed. Especially in a lass as wild as you. You've got to get yourself a man. A husband."

Arianna felt her eyes widen, and she stiffened with tension. "You'll forgive me, Laird, but a husband is what the fool who cut me meant to be. I canna see that—"

"Now, lass, I said, you need a man. Angus MacClennan's a mere lad with half a brain an' less in the way of ambition. Bein' his wife would be no good for you. A woman with a nose for trouble such as you have needs a man stronger than she, not weaker."

It was too late now for discretion, for every man in the room was looking on in great interest. Blinking, looking around, desperate for any option to the laird's decision, she glanced wildly around the table. Her gaze met first Lud Lachlan's, then his brother's, and the expressions in their eyes as they stared at her made panic flutter in her chest.

"Who . . . who . . . ?" She sounded like an owl. But she couldn't seem to speak. Not the laird's sons. Please, not his sons. She'd never liked them in that manner. Lud was a slightly pompous bully who pushed his younger brother around with his weight and size, while Kenyon fought back with his keen intellect. Lud was too big and brutish, Kenyon too small and effeminate to stir in her the kind of reaction, the hot longing that Nicodimus did. And besides, throughout their childhood, neither of them had often let her forget that they considered themselves her betters. Although they'd changed their attitude toward her since she'd reached adulthood . . . since she'd grown breasts, at least.

They had even saved her life that day in the loch. But they had failed to save her sister . . . though they'd tried. They had failed, and she supposed she shouldn't hold that against them, but she couldn't help it. Each time she'd seen them since the day Raven had drown, had only served as a painful reminder of that horrible day.

She turned toward Nicodimus, but he was sitting very still, watching Joseph, waiting for his next words. He looked as if he were holding his breath. Joseph returned his gaze before turning his attention back to Arianna.

"You need the protection of a husband, lass. And I need to see to the well-being of the clan. I can't have this sort of talk dividing us," Joseph said slowly. "An' while I'm unsure it's wise to do so, my sons have insisted I consider choosing one of them as your husband."

"Aye," said Lud. "You'd be safe wed to the firstborn and heir of the laird." His eyes, friendly before, looked hungry now. And having seen the way Lud devoured the meat on the table, she nearly feared he'd do the same to her.

"Laird . . . surely there must be some other way to ensure my safety than—"

"Or the second born, who is far closer to the right age for her!" Kenyon shouted.

"Oh, but I—"

"Or the chieftain himself," said Nidaba, very softly. And when Arianna sent her a surprised look, she thought Nidaba looked smugly satisfied. So she thought Arianna would be out of Nicodimus's reach for good now, did she? "Joseph's wife has been dead this past decade. It is time he remarry," Nidaba went on, ignoring the desperate look in Arianna's eyes. "So, Joseph, which will it be?"

Arianna shoved herself away from the table, springing to her feet. As she did, so did two of the laird's men, one with a shank of meat still in his hand. "Nay!" Arianna cried. "I dinna mean to be rude, Laird, an' I am grateful to you—and fond of your sons, but I could never—"

The laird held up a hand to silence her. With a commanding look, he ordered his men to take their seats again. "Alas, Arianna, there's no other way. I'll leave the choice up to you. One of my sons, one of my men . . . But one way or another, lass, there's goin' to be a wedding. An' soon."

She shook her head rapidly, her eyes welling with hot tears. And she could feel the eyes of every man in the place focused on her, speculative and cold. Then she glanced down at Nicodimus, who remained just as still as a statue, and whose face had gone stony. He met her eyes, had to have seen the plea in them, the fear.

"I'll leave here," she said at last. "I'll leave the village an'—"

"An' what lass? Make your way through the highlands

alone?" the laird asked. "How would you eat? Or live? Nay, you'll marry. I promise whoever you choose, I shall see to it you're safe and protected, well cared for an' happy. An', lassie, you must know 'tis a great gift I offer you! My own sons, 'tis a match beyond your dreams."

"My dreams are far bigger than you could possibly know, Laird." Her voice grew quieter, until she had to swallow the lump in her throat in order to go on speaking. "An' I'm well aware of the gift you offer. I'm but a crazy wench with no prospects beyond marryin' a cobbler's son. Yet you offer your own sons. I dinna expect you to ken why I must refuse but—"

"Lass, you've no choice in the matter. I am laird of this clan. You will choose. Tonight. I'll speak to your father, an' I've no doubt he'll agree."

Blinking, turning her wide gaze from one of the men to the next, she felt as trapped as a hunted animal. And suddenly she felt as if she couldn't breathe. She drew in all the air she could, but it wasn't enough. Her chest constricted, and she pressed a palm flat to it, inhaling again and again. A pulse beat in her throat so hard it felt as if she were choking on her own heart.

Nicodimus got to his feet and went to her, searching her face worriedly. "Easy, Arianna," he whispered. "Breathe in slowly. Slower than that." He gathered her up, and took her back to her chair, then lowered her gently into it. "There's no need for all this upset. Joseph is only looking after you."

"I . . . w-want to go home."

His blue eyes softened. "Arianna, if you return home you'll not be safe. Your father is no fighting man. And with the talk in the clan being what it is . . ."

"I canna . . . I willna marry . . . not unless . . ."

"Unless . . . ?"

She got her breathing under control, sat up straighter, and turned to face Joseph Lachlan, while Nicodimus remained standing beside her chair. "If I must choose, then I'll choose right now," she said, her voice no longer shaking, but firm and strong. She turned to Nicodimus. "I choose you. If I must marry, I choose you, Nicodimus."

His face went as hard as granite, and his eyes turned cold. "I," he stated in a voice that made her tremble, "was not one of your choices."

She lifted her chin, turned her head quickly away so he wouldn't see the sudden, hot tears that sprang to her eyes at his quick, firm rejection. There was a satisfied look in Nidaba's eyes. "Then I'll nay marry at all," Arianna declared.

She got to her feet, walked directly toward the doors.

"Lassie!" the laird cried, getting up as well. "You mustn't go back into the village, 'twould nay be safe."

"If you wish to stop me, Laird Lachlan, you shall have to kill me." She jerked a heavy door open, stepped out, pulled it closed behind her . . . and then she ran.

I could only stand there and watch when Arianna rose as proudly and regally as a princess, and left us all behind her without a backward glance.

There had been no mistaking the pain in those brown eyes. Deeply felt, but quickly hidden. I had hurt her. I hadn't meant to. My reaction had been gut deep, the instinctive lashing out at that which caused me pain. I had done wrong, I knew that now. She had felt trapped, and she had reached out to me for help. I should have seen her desperation, should have realized she was only reaching for me the way a drowning man would reach for a sliver of driftwood. I had callously slapped her small hand away. And why? Because of my own need to preserve my solitary existence. Because of my own weakness where Arianna was concerned. I was afraid, I suppose, of a girl as small and slight as a butterfly. Determined that I would feel no more for her than I did already, and causing her pain in my attempts to ensure that. I was afraid, yes, but not of her. I feared being hurt again. The agony of the last time was still with me.

• • •

Anya, fiery haired, soft-spoken Anya, lying on a bed of furs, too hoarse and exhausted to scream anymore, while the clan elderwomen worked around her, grim expressions on their weathered faces. I'd been with Anya fully half my life, by then. For fourteen years, we had been as one. And no matter how often her brothers, Marten and Kohl, mounted raids on our village seeking vengeance, trying to steal her back, she'd remained safely at my side.

Jaymes had only just seen his twelfth year, and he huddled outside our hut, his face tearstained, his entire body shaking. Will paced, trying hard to be a man. To help, to be strong for his mother, his brother, and me. I couldn't even offer my sons any comfort. I was afraid right to my soul as my wife struggled to give birth to our baby girl, but to no avail.

Anya grasped my hand as I leaned over her. She stared up at me with her eyes of pale blue, and very softly, she whispered, "I never thanked you for taking me away from them, Nicodimus. You saved me, you know."

"I'd save you going through this now, if I could." Tears choked me, burned my eyes and my throat. *Saved her?* How could she say it? I had brought this on her. It was *my* child she carried, struggled to deliver. I was nearly out of my mind with the frustration of being utterly unable to help her. There was nothing I could do. Nothing, and it ate at my soul.

"Hush," she said. "It is nearly over."

My head came up fast in alarm when she said those words.

"I have had a good life with you. I have grown to love you, husband. And if I had to do it all over, I would change nothing. I promise you that."

"Anya . . . you mustn't speak that way. . . ."

"I will speak as I must. Time is short. You know it as well as I."

"No . . ."

She lifted a trembling finger, touched it to my lips. So brave. She even managed a smile for me. "Take care of the boys, my love. Jaymes is so gentle of spirit. He is not meant to be a warrior like you. And Will. Will is a bit too much of one. He needs to learn to master his emotions, to temper his anger.''

''I know. I know, Anya. But you'll be here to see to that.''

She shook her head side to side, just once. ''Keep them away from my brothers, Nicodimus,'' she whispered. ''Marten and Kohl must never come near my sons. They are cruel, arrogant men without a hint of conscience or decency. They made my life hell . . . until you came and took me away.''

''They'll never come near our sons,'' I promised her.

She nodded and was silent for a long moment. Her pain, I knew, was constant now. There was no rest in between. No time to prepare for the next bout. She stiffened as if it were growing still worse. Clenching her teeth, her voice broken and hoarse, she whispered, ''I love you, Nicodimus. I love you.''

Then Anya closed her eyes. Her entire body relaxed for the first time since it had gone taut with the initial birthing pangs. I cried her name again and again, but to no avail. My sweet Anya was gone. I was moved aside by the elderwomen, who'd done all they could to help her, as they frantically tried to save the babe. But I knew in my bones it was too late for the little one as well.

Weak, nearly lifeless, I went outside to face my sons. I didn't need to tell them. They saw the emotion in my eyes, and they knew. Young Jaymes rushed into my arms and clung to me, sobbing so hard I feared he'd tear himself in two. Will turned away and walked into the forest alone. I stood still as stone and silently vowed never to love another the way I had loved sweet Anya.

''Nicodimus? Nic?''

Nidaba's voice penetrated my mind, her hand on my shoulder, shaking me. I blinked away the haunting memories that still had the power to tear at my soul, even after seven centuries, and faced the woman who had saved my life more than once.

"You cannot mean to go after Arianna," she said, her voice a harsh whisper. "She's trouble to you, to both of us, you know that." Already, Joseph was speaking with his men, his meal disrupted, along with his appetite, I imagined. He would send them after Arianna, though it would pain him to do so.

"How much trouble can she be, Nidaba? She's only a girl."

"She's an immortal High Witch, same as you and I," Nidaba all but hissed. "One without discipline or a hint of discretion. Reckless and bold—"

I came very close to smiling at that description. "I have to go after her all the same," I told Nidaba. "Joseph, leave your men to finish their meal. I'll fetch the girl back."

Joseph stopped speaking, studying me curiously and finally nodding. "Aye, the lassie would likely react better to you than to a dispatch of soldiers."

Nidaba sighed, shaking her head as if in disgust or exasperation with me. In silence I turned to do what I must to save another girl. Even though there was a part of me that didn't want to try . . . for fear I might fail. Again.

Nidaba didn't try to stop me, but I could feel her disapproval following me all the way across the rutted courtyard to the gates.

Arianna had a head start on me. I could not follow her, so I went to the place I thought she would most likely go: her father's cottage. The village was dark this night. Silent. No light emerged from the saddle maker's cottage, but I saw a shadow moving through its plank door. Arianna. I went still as she stepped out again with a small pack slung over her shoulder.

Gods, she intended to leave then.

Pausing outside the doorway, she turned back, and in the glow of the waning moon, I thought I saw a shimmer of tears on her face. "I dinna know where you are this eve," she whispered. "But where e're you be, I hope you ken my love. I'm sorry, Mam. I wish things could've been different."

There was no reply. I'd assumed those inside to be

asleep, oblivious to what was happening without. But from Arianna's choked words, I discerned no one to be within the cottage. She hadn't even been allowed the luxury of saying a proper goodbye to her family. I cursed myself for being so cruel to Arianna and took a single step toward her, but she was already running again, fleeing into the night, heading toward the cemetery.

I sighed and stood still for a moment. Of course, she'd want to say goodbye to her sister as well. She would never leave Stonehaven without doing that. At least I knew where to find her.

I walked slowly, needing to collect my thoughts before I faced Arianna. I didn't know exactly what I was going to say to her when I found her. The wise thing, the *sane* thing for her to do, would be to obey Joseph and take a husband. Not me. Certainly not me, but one of Joseph's boys. They were both decent young men, and it was obvious either of them would be glad to have her as wife. It would solve all Arianna's problems. She could stay here, close to her family. The talk about her might go on, but not to such a dangerous degree. And certainly no one would dare to act on it.

And yet, some part of me rebelled at the thought of talking her into any of that. I couldn't imagine myself trying to convince her to marry either of the Lachlan lads.

So what options remained for her? Leave here, alone? Perhaps Nidaba would . . .

My musings as well as my steps came to a halt as the sounds of distant shouts reached my ears. Frowning, I glanced in the direction from whence the noise seemed to come, and saw an eerie red-orange glow lighting the night. My throat went dry. "Good Gods, is that The Crones' cottage?" It had to be. It was.

I broke into a run, rounding a corner so that the cemetery came into view. Arianna was not there. "No," I whispered. "No, she mustn't. . . ." Cupping my hands to my mouth I called, "Arianna! Arianna, come back!"

There was no reply. She must have seen the flames and headed out there. But she might not have heard the shouts, as I did. My senses were honed, sharpened, beyond mortal limits. Hers were not. Nor would they be, until after she'd tasted death for the first time, and revived into something new. She wouldn't understand what she might be walking into.

I whispered a spell of protection, and then I ran.

A prickling sensation ran up the back of Arianna's neck as she stood over her sister's grave, whispering her goodbyes. She'd realized, almost as soon as she'd left Lachlan keep, that the laird had been right. She *wasn't* safe in Stonehaven. It wasn't the gossip and the speculation about her that worried her. It was her father, and Laird Lachlan, and Angus—all of them trying so hard to marry her off as fast as lightning. Well, she wouldn't have it. And if it took running away to ensure her freedom, then that was what she'd have to do.

She could have borne wedlock, she supposed, had it been with Nicodimus. He understood her. No one else ever had, nor, she suspected, ever would. But he'd made it all too clear how he felt about the notion of being burdened with her as his wife. So she had little choice remaining. She didn't know how she would make her way, or even where she would go. She only knew she would survive. She never had any doubt of that.

She had glanced up at the sky as she'd contemplated which direction to take, and had glimpsed the fiery glow in the distance. The Crones! Their cottage must be ablaze!

Fear for the three women clutched at her heart, and she dropped her sack to the ground and raced through the village—the oddly *silent* village. It occurred to her that it wasn't all that late. Darkness had fallen, but there ought still be people about or some signs of activity. It was strange. Her own family's cottage had been empty, and it looked as if all the others were, as well. But perhaps the villagers, too, had seen the flames, and had rushed off to help douse the fire.

Imagine that—the fearful and narrow-minded villagers rushing off to help the outcasts. Never! Nay, it must be something else that had drawn everyone away this night.

Arianna's bare feet fell hard on the packed mud path through the village. She clutched a woven shawl around her shoulders to protect against the night's chill as she ran steadily. She could run like the wind. She'd always been proud of the fact, though she'd been told often enough 'twas unladylike to race with the boys . . . and unwise to beat them. The long gown Nidaba had loaned her slowed her only until she gathered its skirts up to her knees and held them bunched there with one hand. The night breeze rushed over her face and whipped her hair behind her. Her lungs worked hard, her heart harder, but she pushed on. Perhaps the balefire had got away from The Crones, she thought. Perhaps it was only some brush burning and not the cottage. Perhaps they weren't even home, but out gathering herbs, or . . .

She rounded a bend, and came to an abrupt halt as The Crones' cottage came into view. It was ablaze, every inch of it, with hungry flames shooting to the heavens. She could feel the heat from where she stood. And . . . and people. Arianna's own clan, all of them standing around, just watching it burn, some carrying torches. What in the name of . . .

She moved forward slowly, a frown creasing her brows, her eyes scanning the crowd for some sign of the old women.

She found them, not amid the crowd, but dangling high above it. Her stomach lurched so forcefully she doubled over and fell to her knees, gagging.

Celia, Leandra, and Mary each hung suspended by ropes from the sturdy limb of the giant oak that had shaded their home by summer and protected it through the cold winter months. Their bodies were completely blackened, charred, smoldering still as they turned slowly in the light of the nearby fire.

Overcome by horror and nausea, Arianna could barely understand the people muttering. Something about a lamb being born with two heads, and how it was a sign. Something about Angus MacClennan, and Arianna's refusal to wed him. Arianna knelt, heaving violently, shaking so hard she could barely remain on her knees.

Someone heard her retching and turned. "'Tis Arianna Sinclair herself," a voice yelled. The voice was vaguely familiar, though she was certain she'd never heard it raised in such an ugly tone. "She's been seen with the Witches! Out alone, at all hours, day an' night. An' she dinna drown when her own sister did!"

"A Witch just like 'em, no doubt," shouted another. "Did you see what she did to young Angus's face?"

"Aye, and he said when he cut her she bled only loch water!"

Arianna weakly lifted her head. The crowd turned toward where she knelt, and slowly began to move forward. She knew she was in more danger than she had ever been, and her stomach clenched with icy fear.

"God in heaven, nay!"

It was her mother's voice. Arianna managed to lift her head a bit higher, saw her mother and her father battling their way through the crowd to reach her. Her mother leaned over her, smoothed a hand over her forehead, and threw her arms around Arianna while her father stood at her side.

"My daughter is innocent!" her father cried, dropping to one knee, gripping her shoulder.

"Arianna," her mother whispered. "We tried to stop this. We did, I swear it to you, but they wouldna listen."

"Innocents dinna walk about alone at night, Sinclair," a voice accused. "Perhaps Arianna should join the other Witches in hell!"

Arianna managed to lift her head again, and saw the crowd moving still closer, while her mother hugged her hard, sobbing in terror. "I'll nay let them harm you, my girl! They'll have to hang us all!"

Stunned by the shock of seeing her friends so brutally murdered, and by the fear, her surprise took a moment to register. But then it did. This was her mother, the woman always so concerned with being proper and what the clan thought of her. On her knees, hugging her accused daughter, and defending her aloud! Tears stung her eyes. To have her mother defend her so fiercely and to show her love so openly! If only it didn't seem as if this would be the last moments they would share together.

Arianna looked up to see her father picking up a large limb from the ground. Lifting it high, he turned to face the threatening villagers. As if he'd fight them for her. But they'd kill him . . .

"Da, nay, you mustn't—"

And then a large shadow fell between Arianna and her neighbors. A tall, strong man, silhouetted by firelight. But she knew him just as she had always known him. She would know him even if she were blind.

"Nicodimus," she whispered, closing her eyes. "Thank the Fates."

"You can all stop where you are," he commanded. "Arianna Sinclair is under my direct protection, and the protection of your laird, Joseph Lachlan, as well."

His voice was harsh, powerful, and so icy it sent a tremor of reaction through Arianna, even though she knew she had nothing to fear from him.

"Any man who lays a hand on her . . . or any woman who speaks an ill word against her, will answer to me. And believe me, it will not go easy with them."

There was an angry murmur that grew louder. Nicodimus turned to her, ignoring the crowd. Gripping her shoulders, he helped her to stand. As her mother stood looking confused and afraid, and her father looked on in worry, Nicodimus searched Arianna's face. He pushed her hair away from her eyes, and brushed the twigs away from her borrowed dress. "Did any one of these pigs touch you, Arianna? Hurt you?"

She opened her mouth, but only a sob escaped. "Th-they *killed* them. They killed them. They—" She turned and pointed, and his gaze followed hers to where her beloved teachers dangled from charred ropes. As she stared, one of the ropes seared through, and gave way, sending one blackened corpse smashing to the ground.

"Celia!" Arianna shrieked.

Nicodimus pulled her close, tucking her head against his chest so she could no longer see. "They'll answer for what was done here tonight," he said, and he said it loudly enough so the crofters could hear. "Joseph will see to that. He won't tolerate murder being done in Stonehaven."

"An' just how is it you're speaking for Laird Lachlan," someone demanded.

"Aye," challenged another. "An' how is it Arianna Sinclair is under *your* protection?"

Nicodimus turned to face the crowd. "She's under my protection," he said fiercely, "because she is my betrothed. And I will kill any man who dares harm her."

Arianna stiffened in shock, dizzy now from the onslaught of so many emotions, all bombarding her at once. She was dimly aware of her mother's gasp, her father's perplexed frown, the shocked exclamations of the crowd. But all her mind could grasp at the moment were two things. That three innocent women had been murdered tonight because they were different. Women she had loved with everything in her. Women who had risked—and ultimately *lost*—their lives for her sake. And that Nicodimus had claimed her as his betrothed only to prevent her from being the fourth to die here tonight.

Oh, but his arms were around her now—strong, warm, and fiercely protective. Right now she never wanted to leave the haven they provided. Her heart pounded as if it would burst, and new tears welled to replace the old. He wouldn't go back on his word. He'd said he would marry her, whatever the reasons. And he would. She would be his wife. This man brimming with secrets . . . who yet made her feel she knew him as well as she knew her own heart. His wife. She was uncertain she could survive the pain she felt tonight. But if she had any hope at all of facing everything that had happened this night, that hope lay right here in his arms.

Hoofbeats sounded, and she lifted her head from Nicodimus's sturdy chest to see Laird Lachlan, his sons, and some forty of his men, come thundering into the clearing. The crowd broke apart. Cowards who didn't wish to be identified quickly melted into the trees. As far as Arianna was concerned they were all guilty. Every one of them had been a part of this evil.

"Joseph will see to this," Nicodimus whispered. "Come, you need to be away from here. This is no place for you."

Shaking her head, she drew slightly away from him. Yet his embrace remained as she stared up into his dark eyes. "Nay. I canna leave them like that." And as she spoke her gaze strayed to where two of her friends hung charred and blackened. And one lay bent and broken on the ground.

Nicodimus's palm cupped her cheek, turned her head gently, so she could only see him. "They'll not be left, Arianna. I promise you that. But remember all they taught you. Those bodies are but empty shells now. The Crones have moved on, and are beyond the touch of pain. They would not want you lingering here." One hand moved to stroke a slow path down her outer arm. "Gods, lass, you're shaking all over."

"He's right."

Arianna turned at the sound of her father's voice. "Come home, lass. I vow I'll let no harm come to you there."

Her lips pulled tight and her tears spilled anew. "Oh, Da . . ." Sniffling, she nodded. But when she looked down, she saw that her father still clutched the limb he'd snatched up in her defense. His hand held to it so fiercely that his knuckles had gone white. "You truly would have fought them all," she whispered in wonder.

Her father's brows rose in surprise. "You're my own child, Arianna. I'd fight the devil himself did he try to do you harm." His gaze lowered, but then he reached out and closed a hand around hers. "I love you, lass. I dinna always understand you. But I love you."

He hadn't spoken those words to her since her sister had drowned, and hearing them now brought a surge of emotion that left her weak-kneed. "And I love you, Da."

"Come, then. An' you too." He nodded to Nicodimus. "We have much to discuss, you and I."

"Aye, sir. That we do," Nicodimus replied. And without

warning, he scooped Arianna up into his arms.

"I can walk," she said, her protest mild, for she truly wasn't sure she could make it under her own power. She still felt weak and ill. She was afraid she might vomit again before they ever made it back to the cottage.

"You tremble still," Nicodimus informed her. "Besides, let them all look on and know that I meant what I said. I want there to be no doubt among the clan of my intent."

She battled dizziness. "You . . . had little choice, but to say what you did, Nicodimus. I'll nay hold you to such a promise . . ."

He was striding now toward the village, a step behind her father and her mother. She thought his arms tightened just slightly around her. But he didn't look down. "I meant what I said." He said no more as he carried her among the crofts and back to her home.

The Crones, her heart moaned again and again. Gone. Executed like murderers when all they had ever done was try to live in harmony with nature by the old ways. The ways of their ancestors. Gods! It was so unfair! They'd taught her, initiated her into the ways of magick. Aye, they'd wondered at the strength of her power, but perhaps their true fear had not been of her, but for their own safety. Perhaps they'd sensed the disaster building. Perhaps they'd felt it coming. And though she hadn't wanted to believe it, the blame for all of this rested squarely on her own shoulders.

She'd been careless—rebellious. Almost dared the clan to discover her activities—to learn where she went at night, what she learned, and at whose tutelage. They'd suspected for some time. And if Arianna's thoughtless ways hadn't generated so much talk of Witchery in the clan then perhaps The Crones could have continued living here peacefully. Perhaps . . .

But not now. They were dead. Murdered.

"And their killers must die. . . ." Arianna whispered, blinking her eyes open, looking through floods of tears back toward the clearing they were leaving behind. "They must die!"

Twisting in Nicodimus's arms, she pushed against his chest so suddenly she broke his hold on her. She stumbled to her feet and snatched the dagger from her side—the dagger The Crones had given her, and had told her never to be without. She'd worn it hidden beneath her clothes. And now the time had come to stain its blade with the cursed blood of killers!

As soon as she had the dagger in her hand, Arianna ran. A feral cry rose from her, and baring her teeth, she lifted the blade high and charged forward, determined to slash to ribbons every man she came upon. "Murderers!" she screamed. "Murderers all, and if it's hell you believe in, then I'll gladly send you there!" She glimpsed movement in the trees, aimed her deadly attack that way . . .

. . . and was snatched up from behind. Nicodimus's strong arm clamped tight 'round her waist, while his free hand closed gently, but firmly, about her wrist. "Let go the blade," he said hoarsely into her ear.

"Nay! I'll kill them all!" She struggled.

He held her, and let her fight him until all her fight was gone. Finally, her hand went limp, the blade fell to the ground, and her body began to tremble anew. Violent, back-bowing spasms that racked her to her soul. She couldn't breathe, and felt as if her throat had closed off. "They killed them. They *burned* them, Nicodimus. They . . ."

"Shh-shh." He turned her weakened body into his arms, held her close. She heard her mother's concerned questions, heard Nicodimus mutter, "It's the shock, Mara. I've seen it before. Come. She needs a warm bed, a cool cloth, and her mother's comfort. She'll be all right."

He carried her cradled in his arms. But not safe. She didn't think she would ever feel safe again. Not now that the enormity of it had finally hit her. The Crones were Witches, and because of that, they'd been brutally tortured and murdered. More than likely, their killers would be pardoned, for killing a Witch was not only legal, but morally acceptable.

And she . . . she was a Witch, too.

For the first time, she realized that that fact alone was enough to put her life in constant peril. She'd been in grave danger for some time now, only she'd been too blind to see it. Her mother had tried to warn her, her father. Nicodimus . . .

What about Nicodimus? Was he one, too? A Witch like her? He'd neither admitted nor denied it when she had asked. But sweet Goddess, if he were, then he had put his own life in jeopardy just now. By associating himself even more closely with her, his plan might go completely awry. Rather than restoring her good name, he might simply sully his own!

An image came to her mind. A vision too horrible to bear. Nicodimus, his body blackened and charred, dangling from a tree like The Crones. She released a horrified cry, and buried her face against his chest once more.

6

She could hear their voices, deep and hushed. Nicodimus and her father seemed intent on their conversation. A candle's gentle glow painted her mother's face as Arianna lay huddled, trembling still, beneath a mound of covers. How long she had been there, she did not know. She only knew dawn must be close. She must have slept at some point, though she only remembered the startled way she kept coming awake, the horrors of the night glaring in her mind's eye. And Nicodimus, coming to her each time, soothing her.

Nicodimus had carried her here last night, and had laid her gently down. Before he'd turned away, his gaze had touched her face, searched it, and she'd glimpsed genuine worry in the deep blue depths of his eyes. Or . . . she thought she had. His fingertips had danced over her forehead, brushing a stray wisp of hair aside. "Rest now," he had whispered, and then he'd straightened away.

She could see him now, for their home was small, and only a half wall and a curtain separated this room, and her sleeping pallet, from the rest of the cottage. Still here. He'd stayed all the night through. But why? He sat in a crude wooden chair, dwarfing it and the table and the room itself, not so much by his size, which was substantial but not unusual. Nay, Nicodimus's force of presence was what made everything around him seem smaller by comparison. He need only walk into a room to have every eye turned upon him. Men looked upon him with respect and not a little fear. The women, with something far different in their eyes.

My Nicodimus, she thought suddenly, and a fierce surge of pride welled up in her throat. *Mine, though he knows it not.*

There was a fire burning in the hearth, and his hair gleamed with the flame's red-gold shimmer. He listened respectfully to all her father said in careful undertones. Nodding his head in reply, he himself spoke softly and glanced her way, catching her eyes and holding them for a long moment. There was something there, some tension she could not identify. Then her father spoke, drawing his gaze away again.

"Have they been talkin' the night through?" she whispered to her mother.

"Aye, lass. They've much to settle between them."

"Nay, they have nothing to settle. I can settle my own life, Mam."

Aging hands soothed Arianna's brow and placed a cool cloth upon it. "This sudden betrothal o' yours gave your da and me a shock," her mother whispered. "An' there remains much to be decided. Dinna worry your head about it, lass. You've had enough worry to last a lifetime."

Closing her eyes, Arianna lay back and sighed. She knew what they were discussing out there. Her. Her future, her life. When would they realize that she could make her own choices?

"There's something you must understand, Mam," she said slowly, and her mother looked down at her with a certain expectation in her eyes. As if she knew and dreaded what was coming next. But it didn't stop Arianna from going on. "Nicodimus only said what he did to keep them from killin' me," she whispered. And the memory of her dear friends, her teachers, hanging charred and lifeless from the mighty oak, whispered coldly through her mind. She shivered and closed her eyes, but forced herself to go on, refusing to be distracted. "He canna truly mean to wed me, Mam."

Her mother's hand patted hers. "Aye, perhaps he did speak in order to save your life. But he's a man of his word, is Nicodimus Lachlan, an' if he says he'll make you his bride, you can be certain, he means to do it. You've naught to worry about on that matter, lass."

Arianna sat up a little, but her mother's hands urged her back again. "'Tis unfair to expect him to marry me, Mam. He saved my life. I canna hold him to the lie he spoke to do it. I'm certain he thought he had no choice but to say what he did."

"Perhaps *you* canna hold him to his word, Arianna, but your father can. . . . Not that it's necess—"

"He wouldna!" She sat up in bed so fast the cool wet cloth fell from her forehead. "I'll nay have a husband who needs forcin' to the altar!"

Her voice had risen. The two men in the other room fell silent and turned to stare.

"You'll have the husband your da chooses for you, lassie," her father said.

"I'll have a husband who wants me as wife, or none at all." Flinging the covers aside, she got to her feet. Bare, they touched the dirt floor, and her toes instinctively curled against the dampness and chill.

Her mother's hands came to her shoulders, trying to pull her down again, but she stood strong. "Darlin', how do you know he doesna want you as wife?" she whispered. "You dinna ken, methinks."

"Nay, Mam. 'Tis you who dinna ken. I proposed marriage to him myself only yestereve. An' he made his feelin's quite clear." She stared at Nicodimus as she spoke.

His lips pulled at one side, as if he battled a smile. So he was amused by her objections, was he? Was that what her pain was to him? Amusing? Did he not know how deeply his rejection had cut her?

"Can a man not change his mind?" Nicodimus stood up

from the table, his tone soft, but firm, his eyes holding hers captive whether she wanted to be held or not. ''Arianna . . . I was taken off guard by your . . . offer. I admit, my reaction was cruel, and thoughtless. But I swear to you, I regretted my words the moment I spoke them.''

Her eyes narrowed as she watched him. He was lying to her, she was certain of that. ''I would speak with you alone, Nicodimus.''

He didn't agree or disagree. He looked to her father, and her admiration of him grew another notch. For he was her father's better in every way, and yet determinedly gave him his due. ''With your permission, sir?''

Her father nodded but once and came to take her mother's arm in one hand. He drew her to the door, and took the empty water pail from its wooden peg on the wall beside it. ''We'll walk to the well and back,'' he said. His way of letting them know he wouldn't be far, and would return soon. He sent Arianna a stern look, while her mother's parting glance was only worried. She'd have offered them both a smile of reassurance, if she felt capable of smiling at all. But her stomach was churning, and a large empty pit seemed to have opened up in the center of her chest. What *was* this feeling? She'd never been nervous around anyone in her life, no man, no laird, no warrior. Yet the moment she was alone with Nicodimus, her hands began to tremble and the odd sensations in her belly intensified.

At the sound of the door closing behind her parents, Arianna's forced mettle deserted her. She let her legs give as they seemed determined to do anyway, and she sat down on her pallet gracelessly. Nicodimus could see through her false calm as if peering through clear water. It was no use pretending, not with him.

''You dinna want to marry me and we both know it, Nicodimus. So let's waste no more time with this foolish pretense.''

He walked slowly into the room, stood so tall above her that she wished she'd remained standing. But if she rose now, she'd be far too close to him, so she remained as she was and tilted her head up at him.

"I don't intend to lie to you, Arianna. I'm going to tell you the simple truth. You are a spoiled, selfish wild thing and it is high time you gave some thought to the well-being of someone else besides Arianna Sinclair."

She sucked in a shocked breath, her chin coming up fast. "How dare you!"

"Like you, hellion, I dare anything. And I think you know it. Now go on, spew your defenses. Tell me how unselfish you are, and then tell me why you'll refuse me."

"I'll refuse you for one reason and one reason alone, Nicodimus! I'll nay have a man who needs be forced to wed me."

"I've never been *forced* to do anything."

His tone was soft, but impatient. He knelt in front of her, gripping her shoulders and turning her body until she stared right into his blazing eyes. "And this is no longer about what you want."

"And what do you ken of what I want?"

"Oh, I know. I can see it in those cat's eyes of yours, Arianna, just as plain as the sun on the Summer Solstice. What you want are declarations of undying love, and a man on his knees begging for your hand—"

"Nay, not any man. You, Nicodimus. Only you."

That seemed to quiet him for a moment. His face paled and his lips tightened, but he never dropped his gaze. He drew a deep breath that expanded his chest, and blew it out, very slowly, before he spoke again. "You'll never have that from me. I've no love to give, and I have never begged for anything in my life. But I'll wed you, Arianna. And because of our marriage, your father, the man who just proved himself willing to lay down his life for you, will be respected and his wealth will grow. And your mother, who nearly fainted in terror at that clearing last night, will be spared the grief of losing another daughter."

"She wouldna have lost me. I'd have run away, nay let the villagers kill me."

"If you had run away, you'd be just as lost to her. And

your family name would be ruined, your father destroyed and known only as the sire of a fugitive Witch. Is that what you want for them?"

She lowered her head. "It mayn't have happened just that way."

"That's the only way it could happen. And *will* happen if you continue with this stubborn game you play. At the keep, Arianna, when Joseph bade you choose, you obeyed. You chose me. And if you regret that choice now, well, I'm afraid there's naught to be done. Your recklessness brought you to this. And now you've naught left but to deal with it."

Lifting her head slowly, she stared into his eyes, searching them, seeing a spark there, but so deep, so distant, she didn't see how she could ever reach it. Her voice quiet now, barely above a whisper, she asked him, "And what of us, Nicodimus? What sort of husband will you be to me?"

He rose then, turning slightly away, on the pretense of watching for her father's return. "You'll have my protection. I'll provide for you. And you'll bear my name."

"But nay your children," she whispered.

His head swung around. "Never that."

She lowered her head quickly when she felt the sting of tears burn her eyes. Gods but she did not cry. She *never* cried. And she blinked the dampness away. "Then . . . ours will be a marriage . . . in name only?"

Nicodimus came toward her, stepping close to the pallet. She got to her feet and turned her back to him, surreptitiously dabbing her eyes with one hand, reaching for a wooden comb with the other. He said nothing as she began drawing it through her hair.

"Is it because you dinna want me, Nicodimus?" she asked, very softly. "Am I nay beautiful enough to stir the desire of a man such as you? Have you nay once thought of tasting my lips, of holding me close with nothing between us save the heat of our own bodies?"

She felt his gaze on her, burning into her back. And boldly she turned to face him. "Tell me."

"My reasons . . . are my own. And an unmarried girl of

your tender years—a maiden—shouldn't be asking such questions. You know nothing of these things . . . nothing of . . . wanting."

She lowered her head until her chin touched her chest. "If I know nothing of wanting, then what is this feeling burning inside me, Nicodimus? Why do I so crave your touch, if desire is something I'm too young to feel? Why do I yearn to be in your arms? I want you, Nicodimus. And though you may deny it until the day you die, I think you want me, too."

She saw it clearly, the reaction that lit his eyes for but a moment, quickly concealed, a fire instantly doused. "I will set the terms of our marriage, Arianna. And as my wife, you'll honor them."

She stepped forward, closer to him, but didn't touch him. "Do you think you can live with me as my husband and never touch me? Never know me?" She laid her hand lightly on the front of his shirt, and slid it slowly up his chest.

His hand closed over hers, stopping its progress and moving it away. "We will not be residing together for long."

He could have slapped her and shocked her less. "I . . . but I . . ."

"You will reside in the keep, of course. And I will, as well, until I am certain of your safety. The talk in the clan will die down soon enough."

Her lower lip trembled, and she caught it between her teeth. "And then?"

"And then I go my way. I have . . . obligations. I come here only to rest in between them, Arianna. You know that."

"I only thought . . ."

"That I would change my life for you? No, Arianna. My destiny is set. Yours . . . has become entwined with it. Irreversibly so, I'm afraid, but not endlessly. There is no need for me to remain here once your safety is assured."

"I . . . I'll go with you!"

His surprise showed in his eyes. "Your family . . ."

"As my husband, Nicodimus, you will be my family."

He reached out to stroke her hair, gently, softly. "I cannot take you where I go, Arianna. There is only danger for you there. More, even, than there is here in Stonehaven."

"But where is this horrible place you must go? Why do you return there if 'tis so dangerous?"

"Because I must," was all he said. He took his hand away, and a darkness seemed to settle over him. A finality. There would be no arguing him around to her way of thinking.

"Then . . . you'll go. You'll leave me. Bound to a man I can never have, free to know no other. Am I to die a maiden, then, Nicodimus?"

"There is," he said slowly, "a long, long time before that possibility will arise."

She shook her head. "You are meant for me. This I have known since the day I first set eyes on you. And you *do* want me, Nicodimus. And you *will* know me. I vow it on all that I am."

He looked hurt by her words. Just a brief flash of some old pain flitted across his face. And then she saw anger. His jaw went tight, and he opened his mouth. She had the most peculiar feeling he was about to reverse his offer. She only held his gaze, praying he would not.

He did not speak, seeming to change his mind. She nearly sighed with relief, all the while gathering her courage. She *wanted* to wed him. But she wanted him to want it, too. Either way, it would not matter. She would be bound to him, aye, but he would be bound to her as well, she reminded herself. No other woman would know him. She would kill any woman who tried. It was her he would grow to love—Arianna Lachlan, his wife.

Finally, looking as if he were drawing on his last reserves of patience, he whispered, "So what of it, Arianna? Will you wed me or not?"

"Aye, Nicodimus," she said, before she could lose her hard-won courage. "Aye, I'll be your wife. If you'll give me your word that you'll be true to me. That you'll have no other woman. Including Nidaba."

He frowned at her. "That is an easy enough promise to make."

"I mean to see that you keep it," she declared.

"And to accept my terms?" he asked her.

"Terms? That you will never love me? Never touch me?"

He had to look away to answer. "Yes."

She moved to watch his face. And as she did, she knew that he was lying as much to himself as to her. He loved her already. Somewhere deep inside him, he knew it. She was meant for him, hadn't she sensed that from the very first? If The Crones had taught her anything at all, it was to trust her senses, the ideas that popped into her head like stray thoughts, the kind most people ignored. The wisdom of those old women had come from sources so ancient, even they had no longer been able to identify them. Yet they had lived by what they knew to be true.

The door creaked open and her parents stepped hesitantly inside, looking from one of them to the other, questions in their eyes.

All too aware that she had not agreed to Nicodimus's terms, knowing he was aware of it, too, she spoke aloud. "There is to be a wedding, then," she said, lifting her chin, holding his gaze and refusing to look away. "I have agreed to marry Nicodimus."

Nicodimus stared steadily into her eyes, and gave a nearly imperceptible nod of what she took to be approval, though there was more than a bit of wariness or perhaps, suspicion, in his eyes as he did.

"Thank goodness you've come to your right mind!" Her father's face split in a smile, and he clasped Nicodimus's hand in one of his own and shook it hard, slapping his shoulder with the other. "Welcome to my family, Nicodimus Lachlan."

"And glad I am to call myself a son of yours, Edwyn Sinclair," Nicodimus replied, to which her father beamed.

Mara hugged Arianna, and as she did, leaned near, and whispered, "What changed your mind, daughter? I've never known you to give in until you get what you want."

"I'm gettin' exactly what I want, Mam," Arianna said softly, watching Nicodimus and her father as they talked and gestured and planned. "A man who loves me. He doesna ken it yet, of course, but he will. In time."

"Bless me, but I believe you, child. Heaven help Nicodimus Lachlan. He canna ken all he's in for."

The celebration in Arianna's home that dawn was subdued and dulled by the grief so recently brought upon this clan. Dulled, too, I thought, by my own ominous thoughts. Arianna was a willful girl. She had given me fair warning that she would not abide easily by my dictates. The sooner I could get the vows said, and be safely away from her, the better.

It may sound foolish now. Arianna was beautiful, young, and just awakening to her body's yearnings. But she was dangerous to me, too. I knew my own heart too well. She was a girl I could come to care far too much for, far too easily—if I let myself. But I was certain of my fortitude. My lessons had been too hard won for my will to crumble at a look of yearning from a pair of beautiful eyes.

My Gods, I should have known I could never resist her for long. Should have known it that very day, as she looked me squarely in the eye and admitted her own desires: her desire to make love to me, to be my wife in every sense of the word. But foolish pride was my downfall. I told myself that a man who had lived seven centuries could easily win a battle of wills fought against a girl of seven and ten.

I could not have been more wrong.

Mara Sinclair took a bowl and pitcher of water into the small sleeping area with Arianna, and drew the curtain tight. Edwyn and I continued our discussion of the wedding and other arrangements. For his daughter's honor, as wife of the cousin of the laird, I would have a new cottage built for Arianna's parents. It was only fitting that my bride's family live in a dwelling grander than the one they now inhabited. And I would gift the family with food, sheep, and grain. All these things we discussed, as well as the date, a week hence, for the vows to be spoken. I was for having it done sooner, but Edwyn argued that there would be need of time to stitch a proper gown, and that it would only arouse more talk in the clan to have the wedding in such an unseemly haste. So I agreed.

I had a deep respect for Edwyn Sinclair. Always, I had liked the man, but since bursting into that clearing and seeing him there, standing alone, facing a murderous mob, defending his daughter with his life and a rotting limb, my respect had trebled.

Even as we discussed all these things, though, my senses were sharply attuned to what went on in the next room. I heard clearly the sounds of fabric against soft skin as Arianna removed her clothes. The trickling of the water as she bathed, and her own gentle sighs taunting me now and again. I grew agitated and restless, but tamped those feelings down and warned my foolish mind against them.

When at last she reappeared, freshly scrubbed, hair gleaming, in simple but clean garments, I saw a slight sparkle in her eyes. As if she had been aware of my attention the whole time.

But it dulled slowly, as she became aware of what was happening outside. Noise filtered into the cottage, voices, and Arianna hastened to my side as I opened the door to look without. Joseph sat mounted near the burial ground, three hastily constructed coffins in a wagon, beside him. The Crones. And a crowd had gathered at the cemetery gates. Voices rose in agitation, and Joseph shouted above them all. "They were murdered and shall be buried proper!"

Then the village priest, who stood directly in front of the death wagon, nearly nose to nose with the horse that pulled it, held his Bible high above him. "Not with good Christians, Laird. 'Tis blasphemy and will surely bring the wrath of the Almighty down upon us all!"

Before I could stop her, my timid bride rushed past me, bare feet flying as she raced toward the burial ground. She gripped the halter of the funeral horse, even as I ran forward. Her parents followed on my heels.

"You and your high and mighty notion of good and evil!" Arianna shrieked at the priest. "Where are the gallows, I ask you! Where are the executioners to make your faithful Christians pay for the sin of murder! Where?"

I caught her arm, tugged her back a step, but she jerked it free. "Nay, these fine women willna rest here among the hypocrites, for they were far too good to lie among refuse! 'Tis bad enough my own dear sister rests in such company!"

"Arianna, hold your tongue!" Edwyn shouted.

"I willna hold my tongue, Da. I canna."

Again I gripped her arm, and this time she relaxed at my touch, rather than fighting it. Turning slightly, she faced Joseph upon his horse. "Laird, I beg of you, dinna insist these women be buried here. They were taken from this life against their will an' before their time, tortured an' murdered because their beliefs differ from those accepted by the rest of the clan. Let their rest be as they would have had it."

When she turned, I could see her face. The tearstains on her cheeks. I'd never seen her cry the way she did for those three old women. And my heart seemed to soften.

"Did I know how they would have had it, lass, I'd gladly grant your request." Joseph shook his head sadly. "Alas, I ken nothing of their ways."

Arianna's lips curved into the saddest smile I had ever seen. "'Tis well, then, that I do."

A gasp went up from the crowd. They murmured against Arianna until I put my arm around her shoulders and sent a meaningful look over them all, meeting each pair of eyes, one by one. "You'd do well to heed my bride's words. She bears wisdom far beyond her years."

She glanced up at me in surprise, and I knew why. She'd been expecting me to quiet her. To order her to stop this nonsense, and tug her back inside, off the streets. Not to stand at her side and support her this way. But how could I not? I admired her so much that day. Gods, but I'd never seen the sort of courage this girl displayed. Even now that it had been made clear to her what happened to people outspoken in their differences, she stood among her enemies, and spoke loud and bravely against them. Even then she bore the heart of a warrior.

"The Crones would wish for a great funeral pyre to be built at the site of their destroyed home," she went on. "They would ask that these coffins be set atop it, an' that those who cared for them carry torches to ignite the flames." Slowly, Arianna turned, and stared off in the direction of the clearing where thin spirals of smoke still danced slowly skyward. The wind lifted her golden hair and sent it snapping, and blew her skirt about her naked ankles. A faraway look came into her eyes. "They would wish us to remember them, the good they did for us in life. I tell you true, I never could have survived the loss of my beloved sister were it not for the tender guidance of Celia, Leandra, an' Mary. They comforted me when no one else could." And then she faced the crowd again. "You, Maddy Hargrove, might think upon the time you nearly died giving birth to young Billy, an' how they came to you to ease your pangs an' save your life as well as that of your babe. An' you, Nathan MacGregor," she said, pointing an accusing finger toward the man and looking like an avenging angel. "You might recall the time they brought liniment for the cut on your leg which had already begun to fester. You might thank them that you still have a leg on which to stand."

Her gaze turned skyward, then. "By dark of night, we shall ignite the pyre. So the flames can dance an' spread their light far, even unto the eyes of the very Gods themselves."

"Blasphemy," someone whispered.

Arianna's gaze pinned the one who'd spoken. "Aye, an' was it blasphemy when Leandra stopped you as you walked, an' bade you hurry home an' tend the fire in your hearth? You obeyed then, an' found coals scattered on the floor, beginnin' to burn already, an' your wee children asleep in their beds, unaware."

Mara came forward then, a hand coming to rest upon Arianna's shoulder. "My daughter's views are not always my own," she said, her voice, unused to speaking above a meek and obedient whisper, wavered slightly. "But in this, I believe she is right. Or . . . if she's wrong, then perhaps we should call for the execution of everyone who used The Crones' ways to aid themselves. For if what they did was sin, then we all are as guilty as they."

"Well said, Mara Sinclair," Joseph declared with a firm nod. "Well said. It shall be as my cousin wishes it then." And by addressing Arianna as such, he was reminding them all of her new status in the clan and village. She might be different, but she was above them now. "'Twill be done. This night." He turned to where his sons stood behind him. "Lads, choose several strong men and take them to the clearing. Supervise them as they build this pyre." He glanced at Arianna. "Are there any special instructions you would give them, lady?"

She blinked in surprise, but quickly moved beyond it, falling easily into her new role. And no wonder. Hadn't she always sensed she was different from the rest? "Aye," she said. "The wood for the fire should be of oak, ash, and thorn. An' none of the men are to speak an ill word of The Crones as they stack the wood. This pyre is to be built in their honor, to see them out of this lifetime. 'Twould nay do to have their names besmirched during its building."

Kenyon and Lud glanced at their father, and he nodded once, firmly. "So be it then. The bodies will remain in my care, under guard, until nightfall."

He swung his horse around as if to go, but Arianna called after him. "Laird?"

He turned in the saddle. "Aye, lass?"

"I . . . Thank you. You are indeed a fine man, and an honorable one. I am more sorry than I can say for my behavior at the keep yestereve."

"Say no more," Joseph said with a gentle smile. "'Tis forgotten." Then he frowned. "You should ken, lass, the men who led the others in this murderous spree last eve are restin' now in my dungeon, and will remain there until they face their punishment."

She nodded. "An' what will that punishment be?" she asked, her throat sounding dry, her voice raspy.

"Much as it pains me, lass, those old women were murdered. As soon as the gallows is built, they shall hang." There was a murmur among the others, but it silenced when Joseph looked to see who would dare question his authority.

A slow, soft sigh escaped Arianna, and she lowered her head. "'Tis as it should be."

"Thank you, Joseph," I said, and in spite of myself, I found I was holding my young bride's hand tight in my own.

Joseph nodded once, kicked his horse's sides, and headed away to the keep, while his sons hastened to obey his orders.

7

Only a handful came to see The Crones on their journey. Joseph, Kenyon, and Lud. Nidaba, Arianna and her parents, and Nicodimus. They all stood a few yards, from the pyre, heads lowered respectfully, each thinking their own thoughts, saying their own prayers or whatever it was they believed in saying at times of parting. All of them let Arianna have enough room to grieve in privacy.

She stood apart from everyone, closer to the flames. It seemed to Arianna that she could hear the old women's voices as she stood very close to the funeral pyre and watched the flames dance for the sky. Leandra whispering that true love came but once, and that a person would always know it when it happened. Celia saying that was poppycock, that a woman must choose the man she would love, and set about winning his love in return. And Mary whispering that only the Fates themselves knew the answers.

Arianna thought perhaps they'd each had a part of it right. One could recognize love in themselves, but never know for certain if it would be returned. Doubts crept into her heart as she stood beside the fire. For how could she be so sure Nicodimus would ever love her, when even life itself was such a fragile and uncertain thing? Here a moment, and then gone. Fleeting as a stray breeze, and just as difficult to cling to. Life, love, joy. All so tentative, so slippery. She'd learned nothing if not that. Too much had been ripped away from her desperate grasp to doubt it.

Nicodimus could be torn from her as well. And it could happen all too easily.

Heat razed the front of her while the night's chill breath fanned her back. Firelight danced on her face, and her cheeks burned a bit, but she didn't step away. She only stared up at the burning coffins and heard the sharp snaps and cracks of the fire's teeth as it devoured them. The hiss of the green wood, the deep throated growl of the flames. Cinders rose like new stars flying heavenward to take their places among the rest in the inky night sky.

"Aye," she whispered. "Go, my sisters. May your souls rest and reflect and find the serenity you sought here among strangers. May you share all you learned with the exalted, and the ancient, and the enlightened. And may you return still closer to the state of perfection toward which we all strive. Live, love, die, and live again, my sisters. Merry meet, and merry part. I will miss you, until merry we meet again."

Hot tears slid down her cheeks, and Arianna opened the cloth in which she kept the flower petals she'd brought with her. These she scattered amid the flames.

A soft brush of warmth at her side made Arianna look down from the fire's brilliant yellow and orange glow. Nidaba stood beside her, her dark skin alight, her lined eyes shining the flames' reflection. She wore a white tunic, and silver crescents dangled from her ears, while a larger one hung from a chain 'round her neck. The ruby stone she wore in her nose gleamed red in the firelight. In silence, her eyes on the spot where the fire kissed the sky, Nidaba began to mutter in her own tongue. And the words had a music and a beauty to them that was . . . holy.

Her hand closed around Arianna's, sending the now familiar jolt through her. Slowly Nidaba lifted both her hands high, one of them still clutching Arianna's. "Farewell, innocent ones. Follow the moonlight into Inanna's embrace," she intoned in her jewel-rich voice.

Nicodimus came to Arianna's other side, clutched her other hand, and lifted his in similar fashion. "Go in peace," he said softly. His voice sent a tremor up Arianna's nape as it always did. Nicodimus's voice was like a physical touch.

Slowly, six hands lowered. Nidaba faced Arianna, bending her head slightly.

"Thank you for that," Arianna whispered.

"The loss of one is a loss to all of us, young one. Mortals seem to have much difficulty grasping the truth of that."

"Mortals? This is the second time you've used that word."

Looking up, meeting Nicodimus's eyes over Arianna's head, Nidaba licked her lips. "It is a lesson best learned on the other side, I think. That is all I meant."

"I see." She didn't. Not really.

"I am sorry for your pain, Arianna. Truly."

Arianna lowered her head. "I thought . . . you probably hated me."

"I do not hate. Except when my mind slips." She shrugged. "But how long can one live, really, without feeling the icy touch of madness every now and again?"

Arianna frowned and searched her face. "Madness? Nidaba . . . ?"

"What's this talk of madness?" Nicodimus asked, and he looked worried. "You're the most sane woman I know, Nidaba."

Nidaba lowered her head, and laughed very softly. "Speak to me when you've existed as long as I have, love."

When Nidaba's eyes met Nicodimus's once more, Arianna wondered anew at the depth of the link she sensed between the two of them. She experienced an unwelcome and unbidden stab of jealousy.

Nicodimus's strong hands closed on Arianna's shoulders from behind her. "Your garments are beginning to singe, little cat. Come away from the fire."

Turning to face him, Arianna caught her breath anew at the sheer beauty of the man. The way the firelight played on the angles of his face . . . the way it gleamed in his eyes. She tilted her head to one side. "What did you call me?"

"Little cat. It is what you remind me of, Arianna. With your curious eyes and volatile nature. Claws that can lash out in the blink of an eye to do a man to death. Your independent nature. In many, many ways, you remind me of the creatures."

Eyes narrowing, she studied him. "Then 'twas not an insult?"

"No, Arianna. 'Twas a compliment."

Her smile was slow, genuine, if tinged by sadness. "Then I thank you."

"You are very welcome." His palm flat at the spot directly between her shoulder blades, he urged her away slightly. A fallen log seemed to have become the gathering place for the others in attendance. This was where Nicodimus led Arianna. Easing her down to sit upon it, then standing beside her like a servant attending his queen as she rested on the throne.

Joseph approached her first, took her hands in his, and kissed them gently. "'Tis sorry I am that this happened, lass. I should have seen it coming. Should have done more to prevent it."

"Nay, Laird, you—"

"Ah-ah. None o' that. You're my cousin now, same as Nic. You'll address me as Joseph, an' nay by my title. As shall your family."

Lowering her lids to hide her surprise, she simply nodded. "You mustn't blame yourself for this . . . Joseph. Even I dinna see this coming, an' more than anyone else, I should have done."

He held her hands firmly for a long moment. "I suppose we all wish we'd have known, but the truth is no one could have. I only wish 'twere under more joyful circumstances I could welcome you into my family, lass. But welcome you I do."

"Thank you, Joseph." Leaning up, she kissed his cheek.

And the laird's smile was broad for a moment.

Less so, his sons, as one by one, they too came to her, kissed her hand, and welcomed her to the fold. Both seemed sad to see her pain, but their pride was far more wounded, she suspected, that she had refused to have either of them for her husband. Their eyes were shadowed, their mouths drawn and petulant, though she could see them trying to school their expressions.

Nidaba only met her eyes, and turned to leave with Joseph and the lads. The whole time Nicodimus stood his post by her side. He'd watched the boys carefully, closely, and had gone just slightly stiffer when they had approached her. Now he relaxed that minute amount she shouldn't have noticed in the first place. But she had noticed. She noticed every detail about him, even a hitch in his breathing.

Her mother and father had moved closer to the fire. Mam to toss flowers of her own upon the flames, simply because it was what Arianna had told her to do when she'd asked how to show her respect. Da simply stood with his head bowed, hands folded low. A moment of prayer and farewell.

She was silent, watching them. Nicodimus seemed more intent, though, on watching her.

When they returned, her mother said, "Come, child. We must get you in out of the night air, afore you take a chill."

Arianna bowed her head. "You spoke up for me, this morning, Mam. Despite what the clan might have thought of you, and despite that your own beliefs more closely mirror theirs than my own."

Her mother's hand stroked a slow path over Arianna's cheek. "I havena been the best mother to you, lass, since . . . since Raven . . ." Her voice broke.

Arianna knew how difficult it was for her mother to speak her sister's name, and she rose in one fluid movement to wrap her mother in a fierce embrace. "Nay, Mam, you've been the best mother in the world. 'Twas I who closed myself away."

"I was too crippled by my own grief, child," Mara went on. "But I do love you, lass. I never stopped. An' I'd lay down my life for you to this day, without a moment's hesitation. I love you, Arianna. My firstborn daughter. You're my soul, dinna you know that, lass? My very soul!"

Tears choking her, Arianna clutched her mother tight, and nodded hard. "Aye. Aye, I know. An' I for you, Mam. Even when I seemed distant, that remained true. I love you."

They embraced for a long moment, the emotions so powerful, Arianna couldn't tell which body was trembling, her own or her mother's. Perhaps both. But when they stepped apart, she looked at her father and saw his eyes were unashamedly red and moist. He met her gaze and nodded once, and she understood. I, also, he was telling her. She went to hug him as well.

Then she straightened. "I canna leave just yet," she told them. "I need to stay, to hold vigil by the fire until the flames burn out. 'Tis a tradition older than any of us, an' I wish to carry it through to the end."

"But lass, 'tis dark! An' the night air—" her mother began, but her father touched Mara's shoulder, and she bit her lip.

"She's a grown woman now," he said. "She can decide for herself how best to show respect to her friends who've passed on, so long as 'tis safe." At this he glanced at Nicodimus, who'd been standing apart, silent, until now.

Arianna met his eyes, saw the fireglow dancing in them. "She'll be perfectly safe," he said. "I'll stay for as long as it takes."

Alone with her, in the darkness, beside a blazing funeral pyre. It was not the wisest decision on my part. But I was learning more about Arianna every moment, and I knew full well she'd have stayed with me or without me. I still had concerns for her safety. While the crofters may have softened slightly toward her, their tongues would still wag were she seen out alone at night. Especially here.

She stood watching in silence as her parents walked back along the path toward the village. Within a few moments, the night swallowed them up, and yet she remained there, back to the fire, eyes fixed on the distant darkness.

"Are you all right, Arianna?" I asked.

Blinking away her thoughts, she nodded, and met my eyes. "My mam and my da . . . They love me again."

I almost smiled. Would have, except I thought it might hurt her to realize how her innocence amused me. She pretended such fierceness, such toughness. When in truth she was as tender as a babe. "They never stopped," I told her.

"I was certain they had."

Tilting my head to one side, curious, I took her arm and led her back to her stately throne—the fallen limb—and sat beside her. "Why?"

Shrugging, she shook her head.

"Because of your sister's death?" I prodded. I found myself wanting to know. Then realized it wasn't just this matter I was curious about. I wanted to know everything about Arianna Sinclair. Her deepest feelings, her darkest secrets. Everything.

"'Twas my fault. She drowned trying to save me. But I've told you this."

"Yes, and I've told you it was no more than an accident. Your family could never have blamed you, Arianna. Likely they were beside themselves with relief that one of you had survived, when for all they knew, the loch could easily have taken you both."

She nodded slowly, deep in thought. "But . . ." Then biting her lip, she stopped herself.

"Go on," I said.

She shook her head. "Nay, Nicodimus. I dinna speak of this. 'Tis my own demon that haunts me, an' I'll nay share its curse with you."

As she said these words, she turned her gaze away from me, staring instead at the fire. And I felt a shield go up, as if she were protecting herself from me, from the pain of the past, from intrusion.

Cupping her chin, I turned her to face me again. A more beautiful creature I had never seen. Arianna in firelight was something to behold.

"There is no demon you cannot share with me, Arianna,'' I told her. ''I'll not judge you, nor laugh at anything you say. Perhaps . . . perhaps I can help you to exorcize the beast that haunts your eyes.''

The eyes of which I spoke narrowed. ''And why would you want to do that?''

Her questions, as usual, cut to the bone. ''I . . . It is what a husband does.''

''Nay, Nicodimus. 'Tis what a lover does. Not a husband who is but a name. But a tender, caring man, out of concern for the woman he loves.''

I licked my lips, tried to swallow as my throat went dry. ''Arianna, you've mistaken my intent completely.''

''Have I?''

The wind played in her golden hair as she searched me with her wise eyes. It was more and more difficult to believe the girl had yet to see twenty years of life. ''You have,'' I said. ''I cannot be your husband in the way you would have me be, little cat. But I'll be more than a name to you. I'll be your friend.''

She frowned a little, a tiny pucker appearing between her delicate brows as she considered this. ''My friend?''

I nodded.

''Because you care about me?'' she asked, looking again into the flames, but peering at me from the corner of her eye as she awaited my answer.

''I always have,'' I admitted.

Her lips curved into a smile. '''Tis a start.''

The words startled me, as did the smile. ''It is the whole of it, Arianna. Do not read more into my friendship than what is there.''

She nodded hard, as if in firm agreement, but I knew better. I knew her too well, in fact.

''Will you tell me then? Your feelings about your sister?''

She nodded again. ''Aye, I'll tell you. When you love me, Nicodimus. When you love me.''

She rose slowly, and pulled her shawl from around her shoulders, to spread it upon the ground. Sitting down upon it she tucked her legs under her, and used her arms upon the log as her pillow. "I will rest now," she whispered.

I only nodded, and watched her for a time. She hadn't slept much the night before. Her grief had been too raw to allow it. I was glad to see her eyes this heavy, her head this relaxed. When her breathing became deep and steady, I knew she truly slept, and knew how badly she needed it. So when she shivered, I sat down close beside her. I did not wish for the cold to interrupt her rest.

I had not expected her to curl against me, drawn instinctively to the warmth of my body. I had not expected her head to rest upon my lap, nor her arms to curl tight about my waist. And when they did, I had no idea what to do about it.

I sat there a moment, looking down at the vision twined around me, debating inwardly. Finally realizing that this woman was to be my wife. I do not think it had hit me fully until that moment, when she rested against me, a warm weight of softness and beauty. I was to be not only her protector, but her husband. It would take every ounce of will I possessed not to make her my wife in every sense of the word. Every ounce of will.

Yet I was the strong one. I was older, wiser, and far more powerful. She needed my help, not my desire. I could handle my own body and its incessant demands. To prove this to myself, I relaxed there on the ground, and put my arms around her, held her gently against me. Kept her warm.

And died a thousand deaths before I finally fell asleep.

When Arianna stirred awake, she felt his arms pull her closer to him. As Nicodimus came slowly awake, his body went hard and tight, and his eyes when they opened, blazed with something she had never seen in them before.

For just an instant, its intensity frightened her, and she pulled away with a soft gasp.

Nicodimus closed his eyes, and when he opened them that look was gone. He said nothing. She wasn't certain of what to say either. Suddenly arousing this man's passion took on a frightening new prospect. She hadn't realized what a powerful force she might be bringing to life. Could she deal with his passion? Could she ever satisfy a man such as he?

He wanted to know her innermost feelings about her sister. But she could not yet confide in him her certainty that the Gods had made a mistake that black day. That they must have meant to take her, Arianna, the eldest. The troublemaker. The rebel. Never could they have intended to take the most gentle, tender soul ever to draw breath. She knew inside that it should have been her to surrender to the murky depths of the loch. Not Raven. And that perhaps, had she not fought so hard to survive, the greedy loch would not have taken her precious sister in her stead.

That was the secret she kept, and it was hers alone.

But even now Nicodimus's dark gaze searched her face, probing and seeing far too much. And there was more there. There was a heat blazing behind his gaze. One so intense it was frightening. And yet exciting to her.

"The—the fire has burned out."

"Yes," he said, watching her through narrowed eyes as she rose to brush the dust and twigs from her skirts. Nervous hands fluttered about her hair, smoothing it. She darted quick glances all around. Busying herself by picking up and shaking her shawl, and then arranging it with exaggerated care around her shoulders.

"Arianna," Nicodimus said, very softly.

She went still and looked down at him. He sat, still resting with his back to the log.

"You needn't ever be afraid of me."

She tried a smile, but it was forced. "I'm nay afraid of anything, Nicodimus. Why on earth would I be afraid of you?"

"You know why. I promise, you're safe with me . . . and safe *from* me. All right?"

Looking at the ground, she whispered, "An' that's supposed to make everything all right, is it? But what if I dinna want to be safe from you, Nicodimus?"

When he didn't answer, she brought her head up, met his eyes. "I dinna, you know. Not at all."

"Nonetheless, you shall be." He got to his feet, and it

was his turn to busy himself. He checked the smoldering ash which was all that remained of the fire, making sure no spark had spread. It occurred to her that Nicodimus might be as nervous as she had been. As shocked and shaken by the flare of awareness between them, as well.

But no. Nicodimus would not be shocked nor shaken by anything.

"Walk with me," she asked softly, deciding to go easier on him, just in case. Perhaps he only needed time to adjust to the idea that he loved her and desired her and would until the end of time. "Tell me of our wedding day. What will it be like?"

He finished what he'd been doing and came to stand beside her, looking relieved. "It will be everything you wish for, Arianna. You need only tell me what you want. The chapel will be decked in wreaths and buds, and the—"

"Chapel? But Nicodimus, I canna marry you in a chapel."

"But—"

"I'm not a Christian. I'm a Witch, and proud to be one."

He took her hand. "You mustn't speak it aloud that way, Arianna. It is unwise, you know that now."

"There is no one to hear me but you, an' I trust you with my life. Nay, I wish to speak our vows beneath the blazing fiery sun, our bare feet caressing Mother Earth's soft greenery and the air kissin' our faces, and the sea as our altar."

Nicodimus lowered his head. "The marriage needs to be recognized by the clan, and by the Church, Arianna. Such a one as that would not be."

"Then . . . canna we have both? One for the benefit of the Church and the clan, and another just for the two of us?"

He stared down at her. "We only need the one. The legal one, Arianna. For that's all there will be, that and friendship. No binding of two souls together as one, as you no doubt have in mind."

Closing her eyes to the disappointment, she sighed deeply. "Then 'twill nay feel like a marriage at all."

"Nor is it meant to. Only to look like one."

Her hand fluttered to her chest, very briefly. She fisted it and lowered it to her side again, an act of will. "Perhaps we should speak of something else."

"Perhaps," he said.

Nodding, she lifted her chin, staring straight ahead as they moved, side by side, along the path. "Tell me about Nidaba."

Nicodimus seemed surprised by the question, for it took him a moment to answer. "What do you wish to know?"

"How long have you known her?" She looked at him.

"I . . . it seems like forever. Surely for most of my life."

A vague answer. She wondered why. "Where did you meet?"

Searching her face, he tilted his head. "You're a curious little cat, aren't you?"

"Do I not have a right to be curious about the other woman in my husband's life?"

He shrugged, perhaps conceding the point. "'Tis a tale you may well enjoy, little one. The first time I met Nidaba . . . no. I will tell you about the second time. It was—"

"Why?"

He broke off, glancing down at her. "Like you, Arianna, I have some things in my past that are . . . too painful to talk about. Do you understand?"

She searched his eyes, saw the old wounds there, and nodded. "Aye. I ken it all too well. Go on, then, an' tell me the tale."

"I was traveling alone through the arid lands far to the east, when I was set upon by a group of desert bandits. Twenty of them, mounted on camels, surrounded me, swords drawn, demanding my horse, my gold, and my food and water. It was a three day journey to help, and that on horseback. On foot I'd have had no chance."

Arianna had stopped walking and stood staring at him, her eyes wide as she listened. "What did you do?"

"Drew my sword and prepared to fight. Actually, they began coming at me, long curving blades of their swords flashing with such skill I could barely follow them with my eyes, much less dodge the blows. And then there was this . . . this sound."

"Sound?"

"Yes. A cry, high-pitched and keening, rather like the shriek of an eagle before it swoops down upon its prey. The attackers whirled, and I turned to look as well. Pounding down upon us was a figure swathed in white robes to the point where only the eyes were visible. Each hand wielded a deadly blade, and they swung like windmills overhead as the white stallion thundered with guidance from neither hand nor rein. The bandits scattered. She didn't even have to kill any of them. They vanished like a distant mirage, and she sheathed her swords by crossing them in front of her and driving the left into the right sheath, and the right into the left. She was amazing to behold."

"She?" Arianna whispered. "Nidaba?"

"Yes. I didn't know it right away, of course. I blurted my thanks, but she only nodded and motioned for me to follow her. Only when we were safely inside her desert home, a veritable fortress, really, did she remove the headdress and reveal herself to me."

Arianna blinked. "She's . . . she's a very beautiful woman, I think."

"I have always thought so, too."

"Did you . . . did you and she . . . ?"

He touched Arianna's hair. "Nidaba and I are friends, Arianna. Only friends."

Her heart soared . . . but then began to sink a bit. Because she thought that if Nicodimus had been able to resist the allure of an exotic beauty such as Nidaba, she was in for more of a challenge than she realized. That Nidaba hadn't wanted him never occurred to her. No woman could fail to desire Nicodimus. Not ever. He was perfect in every way.

"You're very deep in thought about something," he observed. She started, unaware he'd been scrutinizing her face for several moments.

"Aye, I suppose I am." She shrugged. "It's occurred to me how very little I know about you, Nicodimus. You know every detail of my life, no doubt. But of your past, of your history, I know nothing."

His eyes became shuttered, and when her gaze searched them, he looked away. "You will," he said. "In time, I'll tell you all about myself."

"Would you care to begin now?"

He sent her a quick glance, then looked away. "Here, your mother is already awaiting us. Worried for your well-being, no doubt." He waved toward the distant figure, and Arianna saw her mother standing outside the cottage, waving back.

"She knows I'm perfectly safe with you," Arianna said with a sigh. "As your secrets seem to be, as well."

"You needn't be worrying about my secrets, little cat. 'Tis our wedding you ought be thinking of, planning for."

"Oh, I am," she said softly. "Believe me, Nicodimus, I am planning all the while."

His smile was warm, genuine, but there was a hint of something unreadable in his eyes. "Good."

Oh, but he wouldn't think it so good when she finished. Or perhaps he would, but not right away. She would fashion the most beautiful gown any woman had ever worn. She'd bathe herself in flower petals and smell like heaven to him. Her hair would gleam like gold. When Nicodimus bent to her lips, as he must—aye, he *must*—she would kiss him as he'd never been kissed before.

How she would manage that, she wasn't certain. She had never *been* kissed by a man before. But perhaps . . . someone could tell her how to best go about it.

If only The Crones . . .

Lowering her head, she sighed her regrets. Her teachers were gone. She would have to fumble through this as best she could. But come her wedding night, she intended to lie with her husband. In his bed, in his arms, whether he liked it or not. And she would, or her name was not Arianna Sinclair.

I watched Arianna change during the next few days, and the change at once relieved and troubled me. The pain that had for so long shadowed her eyes began to fade. The ghosts that haunted her, seemed to have been chased into a dark corner—for the moment, at least. She no longer spent hours each day sitting alone in the cemetery, and even the agony of The Crones' final fate seemed to be easing.

I actually heard her laugh one day, as she and her mother walked arm in arm along the heather-covered moor beyond the keep. Such a rare sound, and so beautiful, that it startled me into stillness. I found myself edging nearer, straining to hear it again, curious as to what had caused it.

"They have repaired the rift between them, have they not?"

I turned abruptly, unaware of Nidaba's silent approach. She moved like a cat and stood beside me now, observing the mother and daughter as I did.

"I believe," I replied, "that they are even closer than before the death of Arianna's sister."

"Good. The girl will not cling quite so tightly to you then."

I frowned, drawing my gaze away from Arianna to focus

on Nidaba. Her gaze held no contempt as she watched Arianna and her mother talking and laughing below. No dislike. It was only narrow and watchful.

"Why do you dislike her so much?" I asked.

Nidaba looked at me sharply. "Does it seem to you that I dislike her? I do not. The girl has spirit."

"Then . . . ?"

"It is the two of you together I do not like, Nic. You're not going to be good for her. Nor she for you. You'll destroy each other before you finish this ruse."

I shook my head at her. "I only want to protect her—"

"By keeping the truth from her? The truth of what you are, Nicodimus? Of what *she* is?" Nidaba's eyes again narrowed, falling on my young bride once more. "She ought to know, to have time to prepare."

"There is a long time before she will need to prepare for such as that," I told her.

"Only the Gods could know for sure. And you are not a God, my friend."

Her words troubled me. For I had seldom known Nidaba to be wrong about anything.

"Look at her," she went on. "You know full well that her laughter is not entirely due to her newfound closeness with her family, Nic. That kind of joy comes from only one place in a woman's heart. The girl is in love with you, and dreaming of things you have told her will never be. You cannot both come out of this unscathed."

My lips tightened. "I do not wish to hurt her."

Perhaps, I thought, I should tell Arianna again how it was to be with us. But two things kept me from doing that. First, the knowledge that Arianna Sinclair would believe exactly what she wanted to believe no matter what I might say to the contrary. And second, the simple fact that she was so incredibly beautiful when she was happy. Her smile, the sparkle in her eyes, the spring in her step, the confident tilt of her head. I loved seeing her this way. I did not want to be the one to put the shadows back into my lady's eyes.

She and Mara came 'round the bend in the steep path and saw us standing near the outermost wall. Arianna's smile died slowly as she met my eyes, searching them.

"Nicodimus, whatever is wrong? You look troubled."

I was troubled. For just an instant the thought had occurred to me that perhaps I *could* learn to love the girl. Could be her husband in the way she dreamed I would be.

And yet, I could not. I was a hunted man. More Dark Ones sought my heart than that of any other immortal, so far as I knew. Nidaba was older and more powerful, yes, but she'd lived so discreetly that few knew of her existence. My heart was the prize many Dark Witches sought. Two in particular, who had made it the mission of their endless lives to put an end to mine. Arianna would be in constant danger at my side.

Beyond that, I knew I was incapable of loving her. My heart was far too wounded to produce the tender emotion in any real quantity. Ironic, I thought, that a heart so damaged could be so prized by so many.

Frowning slightly, Arianna came closer, her small hands touching my cheeks. "My love, you are pale. Are you taking ill?"

My stomach clenched tight as the endearment fell from her lips. I glanced sideways, but Nidaba only stood in silence. "Arianna, you mustn't call me that," I said at last.

"And just why not? 'Tis what you are, and our weddin' day is on the morrow. Aye, sure and you might as well get used to it."

I closed my eyes. Such a stubborn girl. A smile tugged at my lips. "Aye, sure and I might as well," I said softly, imitating her beautiful speech.

"Is it teasin' me you like then?" she asked, stepping back a bit, hands going to her hips, eyes flashing with mischief.

There was, I realized, very little about Arianna that I *dis*liked. "I wasn't teasing, little cat. How goes the sewing, hmm?" I fell into step beside her, with her mother on the other side of her, and Nidaba walking along at my other side. We moved beside the blackberry briars that lined this side of the keep's outer wall. They blossomed just now, and their scents were heady and sweet.

Arianna shot Nidaba a sidelong glance, and smiled. "Nidaba has gifted me with the most wondrous material, and the gown is perfect, as you will soon enough see."

Any gown would be perfect if she were wearing it, I thought. We circled the keep, moving past the cobbled well, toward the gates. I paused, as a tiny shiver of warning skittered over my nape. What . . . ?

"I'll wear flowers in my hair," Arianna was saying. "And there will be such revelry afterward! Joseph has been more than generous, an' he has the cooks hard at work already. . . ."

As she went on, I glanced up, caught Nidaba's eye. She nodded just once, almost imperceptibly.

She felt it, too, then. The truly ancient among us could sense when another was nearby. And I sensed it now. Lifting my head, I scanned the horizon. But saw no one. Nothing.

"There will be barrels an' barrels of heather ale," Arianna was saying, "An' roast boar, venison, beef, an' mutton. Pastries to savor. Wine will flow, and fruits spill over. 'Twill be so . . . so . . ." She was looking more and more curiously from me, to Nidaba, and back again. "What *is* wrong with you two? You look as if you've seen a ghost!"

Snapping out of my state, I gripped Arianna's elbow in my hand. "Come, let's get you inside," I said, leading her and her mother through the gates, and across the courtyard toward the keep. I looked about as we moved among the men there, checking each face, but seeing only clansmen.

"But I dinna understand," Arianna protested. "What is it?"

"Do you not feel the rain coming, Arianna?" Nidaba asked, her tone unconvincing. "The air grows damp."

"You'd not wish to take a chill on the day before your wedding, now would you, little cat?" I asked her.

"You both be addled! 'Tis lovely outside!"

"Now, daughter, dinna argue with your bridegroom," her mother chided, but she, too, looked unconvinced.

I simply kept moving until Arianna and her mother were safely inside the keep. It was happening; the one thing I feared above all else. One of the Dark Ones had finally found me here—traced me to my only haven. Gods forgive me if I had brought disaster upon this peaceful village. Upon my friends. Upon my woman.

My woman.

Gods, why had I allowed myself to think of her that way?

When we entered the keep, Arianna turned to face me, her eyes no longer filled with mischief or joy, but that deep wisdom she was too young to possess. "A word, Nicodimus, in private."

Eager to be away, I nodded all the same, and sent a glance to Nidaba. She quickly excused herself, and Mara muttered something and vanished toward the kitchens.

"All right then," Arianna said softly. She came close to me, gripped my hand in both of hers. "I ken something is wrong. An' I can plainly see you're hidin' it. Now, tell me what it is."

Not for anything would I have spoiled the day to come for her with worries such as those plaguing me now. Gently, I stroked her hair with my free hand, as if I could soothe her the way I could soothe Black when he grew agitated or afraid. "Nothing is wrong," I told her. "Truly."

Tilting her head to one side, she searched my face with her velvety eyes. "Why are you lyin' to me, Nicodimus?"

Drawing a deep breath, sighing, I lowered my head. "All right. It's . . . sometimes, Arianna, I get . . . feelings. This, I know you understand."

Her eyes widening with interest, she nodded. "Aye, I do. The Crones taught me to trust those feelings, never to doubt them."

"And good advice it was," I told her. "Out on the path just now, I had the feeling that . . . that we were being watched."

Arianna frowned, nodding sagely. "Aye, I've had the same feelin' once or twice today, myself." She looked up into my eyes, worry clouding hers. "Who do you suppose it could be?"

She was too young to have such a sense of other immortals, I thought. But then again, she always knew when I was near, didn't she? Amazing.

"I do not know," I said, and it was only partially a lie. True, I didn't know *who*, but I damned well knew *what* sort of creature was watching us. "But I intend to find out."

Her eyes were narrow upon me. "You think this person . . . could be a danger to us?"

She saw too much. Read me far too well for me to lie to her easily. "I don't know. Perhaps. I cannot tell you because I'm not even fully certain myself. I am going to ask you trust me in this matter."

Nodding, she lifted her head again. "I do trust you, Nicodimus."

"Then please, Arianna, stay here tonight. Your family as well."

Blinking in surprise, she nodded. "Aye, Nicodimus. All you had to do was tell me the truth. If you fear there is danger, then I believe you. I will never doubt your word . . . so long as you speak the truth."

I very nearly smiled at that. Would have, had I not been nearly sick with worry. "Will you always know, Arianna, when I am not speaking the truth?"

"Only when you are as obvious as you were this time," she said. She smiled at me, and I knew I was forgiven.

"I shall go and fetch my father," she said softly, closing one hand around mine and squeezing. "We'll pack up our things for the wedding tomorrow, and—"

"No, Arianna. Let me go for him. It will be for the best." I started to tug free of her grip.

She held me fast. "You truly do sense danger, dinna you, love?" She searched my face. "Is there danger to you waiting outside these walls as well then?"

I looked her squarely in the eyes. "No, Arianna. I will be perfectly safe." Gently I tugged my hand free, and headed for the door, even as her eyes narrowed on me. And I think she knew, once again, that I had not been honest with her.

• • •

Gnawing at her lip and pacing the great hall did nothing to alleviate Arianna's worry, which seemed to intensify the moment the doors closed on Nicodimus's strong back. She recalled again the wisdom of The Crones. *Never mistrust your feelings, lassie. They be the core of your womanhood. The voice of your heart.*

Nicodimus was in danger.

Arianna stood a bit straighter, feeling a jolt of protectiveness surge through her so powerfully she felt as if she grew inches taller. Her chin thrust outward, she headed for the doors, pausing only once on the way, just long enough to glance behind her. But Nidaba was nowhere in sight, nor was her mother, nor any of the others, save a handful of servants spreading fresh rushes over the floor. She was more grateful than anyone would ever know for the privacy.

She ran a hand over her hip, and felt the reassuring lump there, where her dagger was strapped. Then she drew her shawl closer, and slipped away. Nicodimus was her man. She would be damned if she would stand by and let any harm come to him.

She crept, following on foot, ducking behind trees and bushes and any cover to be had, for she knew too well that Nicodimus would be furious if he saw her.

He did exactly as he had said he would. Rode to her home, fetched her father, and settling both Edwyn and the satchel he'd rapidly packed atop Black, Nicodimus led the stallion back to the keep gates. All this she witnessed from a spot high on the hilltop between the keep itself and the village proper, just at the edge of the woods, hidden amidst the trees.

But her husband-to-be did not go into the keep with his future father-in-law. Instead, he saw Edwyn through the gates, then remounted his noble Black and turned. He came toward Arianna, riding slowly, eyes narrow and scanning the horizon, peering into every clump of shrubbery in search of the watcher.

Arianna cringed backward farther, unable to believe she could hide from so piercing a gaze. But even as he rode slowly nearer, she forgot to fear discovery. For another shape rose up behind him. Another man, mounted upon a horse as pale as death.

Her eyes widening, she stepped out of her hiding place, and shouted a warning. But instead of heeding her, Nicodimus continued toward her, obviously surprised and displeased to see her there, and unaware of the danger coming upon him from behind. The white horse began to run, its rider a fearsome brute of a man, all swathed in a black cloak that covered his colors, did he wear them. His face was hidden behind a beaked black helm that completely covered his head. The reddish-brown tail of some unfortunate animal flew from the spiked top of the helm, like a banner. He thundered on, swinging a spiked mace in deadly circles. Arianna lunged forward, drawing her blade, even knowing she could never reach the man before he reached Nicodimus.

The mace flew directly at Nicodimus's head. But nothing happened. Eyes widening in shock, biting her knuckles to silence the cry that leapt to her lips, Arianna shook her head in confusion. Nicodimus had dropped low, over the side of his mount, just as the weapon came at him. Gods, he must have known all along.

Leaning low, he continued riding toward her, and when he swooped down upon her, he snatched her right off her feet, and settled her safely in front of him. One arm held her tightly to his chest, and he whirled his mount around, even as the other man thundered closer. Nicodimus continued to cradle her protectively with one arm as with his other hand he jerked a leather covered shield from the saddle, holding it before her.

The black-helmed stranger drew his pale horse to a stop, but the animal danced and pawed impatiently. Black tossed his head, shook his mane, and blew his angry retort.

"Who are you?" Nicodimus demanded. "What do you want of me?"

"You know what I want," was the answer, spoken so softly and yet so chillingly it sent shivers up Arianna's spine.

"I've no quarrel with you."

"The Dark and the Light live in constant conflict, Nicodimus. It is the way of things, with our kind."

Arianna turned to stare up at Nicodimus's face, but she saw no fear there.

"Then you know my name. You have me at a disadvantage."

There was a nod. Then the mask's beakish point seemed to aim her way. "Is this the latest leman, then? Or is she to be a replacement for the wife you stole away from her family and murdered?"

Arianna's breath caught in her throat. "W-wife?"

"Do not dare to speak of my wife," Nicodimus said, and he sounded even more dangerous than the other. "Or I'll kill you here and now."

"If you think you can."

"Oh, I know I can." He reached to his hip, hand closing on a weapon there, a dagger or blade. "And do not be so certain that the helm you wear hides your face from me. When your words tell me who you must be." He started to lift his weapon, but then he went still, looking down into Arianna's eyes, and she knew her tears showed. "I'll not do this. Not here. Not now. This woman and her clan are no part of our conflict."

"Perhaps you're right. About the village," he said. "As to the woman . . . Well, once I've cut out your heart, Nicodimus, she'll be mine to do with as I please. To the victor go the spoils, or so I was once told."

Nicodimus narrowed his eyes. "Show me your face, coward, that I might know which of my two oldest enemies I am going to have to kill."

"Not just yet I think. We'll meet again, Nicodimus. We'll meet again." He nodded toward Arianna. "As will you and I, pretty one."

She cringed closer to Nicodimus's chest, even as the man whirled his mount and thundered away. Pale hooves sent tufts of sod in their wake and left deep scars in the ground. Then Arianna turned into Nicodimus's arms as the full brunt of shock and fear finally hit her.

He clutched her shoulders, shook her gently as he stared into her eyes. "Why must you disobey? You could have been killed, Arianna! For the love of—"

"I'm sorry," she said, voice firm, even if her eyes were damp. "I should never have come out here armed only with my dagger. My Goddess, what help could I have been to you with only that for a weapon? I ought to have found swords, a mace like the masked man carried, a lance. . . ."

Nicodimus stared at her, opened his mouth, then clamped it shut again and shook his head. "I believe, Arianna, you're missing the meaning."

But she wasn't. "What did he mean, Nicodimus? About a wife you stole, an' murdered? What was he talkin' about?"

He dropped his gaze and looked away. "Come, let's get you back to the castle where you'll be safe."

"I'll go nowhere until you tell me. I know you have secrets you will not share, Nicodimus. But surely even a man as secretive as you would see a previous marriage as something he should discuss with his bride."

He held on tight to her waist, and nudged the horse into a trot. "It was a long time ago, Arianna."

"And you stole her from her family?"

"I rescued her from a den of brutes who beat her and treated her as their slave."

"He said you murdered her."

He looked down at her sharply. "No doubt he sees it that way." Then his throat moved convulsively as he wrenched his eyes away. "Sometimes, I do as well. It is true enough. Anya died trying to give birth to my daughter. So I suppose it could be said she died at my hand, yes."

"Nicodimus, nay!" Arianna pressed her hands to his face, forcing him to look into her eyes. "Nay, my love, you must never say such a thing. Never." Frowning at the pain that he tried so hard to keep hidden behind his eyes, Arianna forced away her own. "My Goddess, you loved her, dinna you?"

The skin drawn taut over his cheekbones, he gave a curt nod. "Yes. I loved her."

"And that is why, then. That is why you canna love me. Your heart belongs to another. Gone she may be, but alive within your soul." Lowering her head, she relaxed against him, eyes falling closed. "I understand now. I'm sorry for you, Nicodimus. So sorry. For I know your pain all too well."

"Arianna . . ."

She lifted a hand, pressed a forefinger to his lips. "Say nothing, love. There is nothing to say. You canna deny what you felt for her, no more than I would ask you to. I understand, now. I do, I vow it."

One large hand stroked down along her outer arm. "I know you do, little cat. I know you do." He touched her face, then drew his hand away quickly. "Tears, Arianna? I never saw you cry in your life until these last few days."

"'Tis only the shock, Nicodimus. The fellow frightened me well and clear to my bones. Next time he'll nay catch me so unprepared. Let him threaten you again, and he'll find himself skewered on my blade."

She dared peer up at him. Saw his lips curve a little. "You must promise never to disobey me this way again, Arianna. That man is a trained warrior."

"Aye. You know who he is."

He nodded. "One of Anya's two brothers, Marten or Kohl. I cannot be sure which of them. But either is as deadly as the other, and each is a danger to you, Arianna."

"I can learn to fight."

"He would kill you without a second thought." He looked deeply into her eyes. "He would kill you, Arianna. And I would not be able to live with that. So promise me you'll stay out of my battles. Let me fight them on my own. I'm very capable, you know."

She looked at him steadily. "That man will come back. He wants to kill you."

"I'm not going to let him do that, Arianna. But it's my battle. His and mine, and you are no part of it."

"He made me a part of it when he said what he did."

"Listen to me." He held her closer, harder, and a certain fierceness came into his eyes. "I will never let him touch you. I swear it to you, Arianna. You are safe with me."

Smiling slightly, she stroked a hand over his cheek. "Aye," she whispered. "You do care just a little."

Averting his eyes, he dropped a very chaste kiss upon her forehead. "More than is wise," he muttered, and kicked the horse into a gallop.

Her wedding day dawned clear and bright, like a new promise, and Arianna welcomed it. Her mother frowned at her when she refused to break her fast but didn't argue. For once, it seemed, she understood. Arianna seemed no more capable of eating than of coherent thought. She paced the spacious chamber assigned to her, until her mother went down to break her own fast and Nidaba came in her place.

"You sent for me?" Nidaba asked, closing the chamber door, turning to face Arianna.

"Aye." Arianna stopped pacing and gathered her courage. "I need to ask something of you, Nidaba. An' I fear you'll turn me down, for I know you disapprove of my wedding Nicodimus."

Nidaba averted her eyes. "It is not my place to approve or disapprove of your marriage, child."

Arianna lowered her head. "But you do, all the same. I hope you will change your mind one day, Nidaba, for I have come to admire you above any female I have known." Arianna looked up again to see the normally unreadable eyes wide with surprise, the lips slightly parted. "Does that surprise you? You're a strong woman, Nidaba. Independent. Getting along in this world somehow all on your own. And Nicodimus has told me of your skills in battle."

Nidaba schooled her features. "What is it you want of me, child?"

Arianna titled her head. "What do you know of this dark enemy Nicodimus encountered yesterday?"

Nidaba's eyes shifted away, toward the window. "Likely less than you do. Why?"

Arianna shrugged. "I dinna suppose it matters. Only that my husband could have been killed. An' if it had come to that, I'd have been of no help to him."

Meeting Arianna's eyes this time, Nidaba smiled. "You think Nicodimus needs your help, little one?"

"I only know that if he ever *should* need it, I want to be able to give it." Arianna squared her shoulders, lifted her chin. "I want you to teach me to fight, Nidaba. An' I dinna want you tellin' Nicodimus about it, for I know he would likely object."

Blinking several times and tilting her head to the side, Nidaba studied her for a long moment. And then, without an argument or a question, she simply said, "Yes."

Arianna gasped. "Yes?" She couldn't believe the woman had agreed so easily.

"Yes. It is a skill you'll need to master sooner or later anyway. So, yes. I'll teach you. In secret."

Smiling broadly, Arianna clasped Nidaba's hand. "Thank you, Nidaba."

Nidaba only nodded, and turned toward the door. She paused with her back to Arianna. "I . . . could stay, if you like. Assist you in preparing yourself for the wedding."

Arianna felt as if she might finally have gained a measure of acceptance from the strange, powerful woman. "I would like that very much. You could shadow my eyes again, aye?"

Turning, Nidaba nodded, and offered Arianna a tentative, and very slight smile, for the first time.

She came to me on the steps of the keep's small chapel, and I caught my breath. For the first time I saw the full extent of the danger represented by this one small woman. For the first time, I realized, I would never be able to withstand a full-scale assault on my senses such as the one she seemed determined to launch. Oh, I had thought I could. I had told myself so. But now I knew what a fool I had been to believe it, even for a moment.

Arianna wore silk as white as snow, which had been cleverly shaped to cup and lift her breasts, and hug tight 'round her small waist. Snugly covering—but not really covering—her arms were sleeves of delicate lace, which allowed incredibly seductive glimpses of creamy skin. Her hair had been rinsed in henna, so it gleamed like sunshine, and spilled about her shoulders, threaded through with tiny flowers—heather, forget-me-nots, and baby's breath. Her eyes—lined by the unmistakable hand of Nidaba—seemed somehow older, wiser, and a hundred times more sensual than before. And they shone with nervous excitement. Her lips were full and rosy and shining.

She came to me, and I could not take my eyes from her. Not to look toward the village priest as he spoke his words over us, nor even to spare him a glance when I repeated my vows. I could not stop staring at Arianna. The little cat who had somehow been transformed into a regal bride. Maiden bride. *My bride.*

Before my eyes she promised to love me, to obey me, to remain loyal only to me. In her small face was such solemn sincerity that I knew they were not just words. Not to her. She meant every vow she spoke. She would honor them. Her promises were real, and she would expect mine to be as well.

Honoring my vows to her . . . would not be difficult, I realized slowly. Keeping them would be no chore at all.

A tear slipped from her doe-brown eyes and glistened upon her satin cheek when I put my ring upon her finger. I leaned forward, brushed my lips across her face, and kissed the tear away. "It will be all right," I promised softly. Surprise and what looked very much like hope lit her eyes as she stared at me. Then at the priest's word, she let them fall closed and swayed very gently toward me. I caught her up in my arms, and pressed my lips to hers. It was to have been tender, our wedding kiss. It was to have been sweet, and reassuring.

It became something far different. Because her soft lips trembled ever so slightly when mine pressed against them. And her hands, featherlight and hesitant, fluttered and then pressed against my back. Then her body seemed to melt into mine. My hands had rested gently at her waist, until that soft sigh and tiny tremor that went through her. Shyly, she dared use her tongue to trace the shape of my lips. Then I forgot exactly why I had been determined to kiss her so gently. I forgot everything: who I was, who she was . . . and what we both were. My arms locked 'round her, and pulled her roughly to me. My mouth opened over hers, and my tongue pushed between her lips, stroking deep. I pressed her hips to mine, shamelessly rubbing against her as I drank my fill from her mouth. And even as I plundered her, I felt her response. Shock, yes, but arousal, too. She arched against me, arms twining 'round my neck, fingers digging their way into my hair. She tilted her head to grant my mouth greater access, and parted her lips willingly to my invasion. Her beasts squeezed so tightly to my chest that I could feel the pebbling of her nipples even through our clothes, and I imagined the feel of them between my fingertips . . . my lips.

The priest cleared his throat . . . loudly.

Slowly, I raised my head, parting my lips from those of my responsive little bride. But I didn't take my arms from 'round her. It took only a glance into her stunned and confused eyes to know that I could not. She would likely collapse if I let her go now. Her hands were trembling, her knees quivered. Her eyes were glazed and shining and wide. Her lips swollen and wet and hungry. She was breathing in quick, shallow little puffs. And she pressed one hand to her belly as if to calm the riot going on within. Desire was what she felt, I knew that. Though I was unsure she could correctly identify it. I knew no one else in the chapel would have any trouble. Particularly if they noticed the bulge beneath my kilt.

What had I done?

She held my gaze, and the stunned expression in her trusting brown eyes gradually gave way to a tentative smile. She slipped her small hand into my large one and we turned to receive our blessings from the clan crowding the chapel, filling all the pews and spilling out the door. Everyone in Stonehaven had come to see us joined.

Almost everyone.

The intruder was not here. For that I was grateful.

9

I could not frown upon the revelry Joseph had planned for the bridal feast. The doors to the keep had been thrown wide, and huge platters mounded with roasted meats, fish, and savory pastries were set upon all the tables lining the great hall. The entire clan was here to partake of the festivities. Jugs of heather ale, mead, and even precious wine were passed around freely, and mugs overflowed as all imbibed generously. Torches were lit in the courtyard as the celebration grew and spilled out beyond the confines of the hall. There was even a minstrel who moved hither and yon, strumming his lute and singing of love everlasting.

It was sad to hear of such things as those of which the mistrel sang, when I knew full well nothing was truly forever. I'd seen too much come and pass to believe otherwise.

But the wine and ale flowed like the twin rivers of Nidaba's homeland, and the food never seemed to run low. Feasting, dancing, singing, all of it ran together. Arianna was tugged away from me early on, pulled into the embrace of her family, and false-faced villagers (who, I reminded myself grimly, had been all too ready to see her hanged and burned only days ago) with well wishes.

I found myself torn. One side of me wanting to go, to

enjoy the festivities and let Arianna find her own way back to me. The other side, unable to do so. Unable to stop craning my neck to find her through the crowd. To make certain she was well, and safe, and not afraid nor tormented in any way.

Spotting her, I shook my head. Since when did Arianna Sinclair—Arianna *Lachlan*—allow anyone to torment her? It was a silly thought. And yet, she'd seemed so vulnerable today. So utterly open and vulnerable . . . to me. Only to me.

I gave up trying not to, and made my way through the crowd to her. I found her in deep conversation with the whelp who had cut her to see if she would bleed. My ire rose, my hand clenched into a fist, and my teeth, in all likelihood, bared.

"But that's when I realized what a fool I had been," the whelp was saying. "An' I'll never be able to apologize enough for hurtin' you. Never in all my days."

"Not if you live to be a hundred and ten," I put in, stepping close to Arianna, and in spite of myself, slipping a possessive arm around her shoulders.

"Oh nonsense, Nicodimus," Arianna said with a soft laugh. One that was off in some way, one that spoke of mischief. She was up to something. I looked down and saw that gleam in her eyes, and knew I should quiet her, and fast. I eyed the near-empty mug in her hand and wondered how many times it had been filled with wine. Her cheeks were pink, her eyes more sparkling than usual, and we had yet to sit down to the feast.

"I can forgive you, Angus. If you can forgive yourself. After all, you must feel a terrible fool for what you did. Far worse than the pain you inflicted on me, was the uselessness of the entire endeavor."

"*Arianna* . . ." I warned.

"Uselessness?" Angus echoed.

"Aye, that foolish old superstition that says a true Witch willna bleed if you cut her."

"S-superstition?"

"Aye, indeed. You saw for yourself the murder of The

Crones. You . . . were there, were you not?''

Angus lowered his head. ''Aye, I was there. An' ashamed I am to admit I did nothin' to prevent it. I know you were fond of them.''

''Yes, well, many of us were,'' I said, tugging at her arm.

''If you were there,'' Arianna rushed on. ''Then you must have seen their blood flow.''

His head coming up fast, Angus looked at her, wide-eyed. ''What's this now?''

''Aye, the ladies didna go to the noose without a struggle. They fought, and were cut, and when they were, Angus, they bled.'' She lifted her brows high. ''Just. Like. Me.''

''*Damnation,* Arianna . . .''

Angus interrupted me. ''Then . . . then they were nay Witches at all?'' he asked, eyes bulging.

''Oh, but they were. They were true Witches, through and through.'' Arianna tossed her hair behind her shoulder, and finally allowed me to pull her away, leaving Angus gaping and pale faced behind us.

I tugged her behind a tapestry, my hand firm on her arm, and made her face me. ''What the hell do you think you're playing at?''

Her smile didn't so much as waver. ''Putting the fear of the Goddess into him. Dinna fear, Nicodimus, I admitted to nothing.''

''No, just planted the seed in his fertile mind. He'll be convinced you're a Witch before nightfall.''

''And what's wrong with that? I *am* a Witch.''

''What's wrong with that? You saw what befell your mentors, Arianna, and yet you ask me what's wrong with that?''

She glanced down at my hand on her arm. ''You are hurting me.''

I eased my grip instantly, but didn't let go. ''I ought to be shaking you! Arianna, you're so reckless! So impulsive, so—''

''So perfectly safe,'' she interrupted. ''As your wife, I'm

safe. They wouldna dare harm me now, an' well you know it. So why do you care if I exact a bit of revenge for the wrongs done me an' mine? Hmm? What harm is there in letting young Angus spend the next several nights in a cold sweat, fearing my Witchly retribution? 'Twill do him no harm!"

I sighed, exasperated with her to no end. "'Twill do you harm, woman. Especially if he talks to others about the thoughts you've put into his head. This whole episode could turn itself back upon you, Arianna."

"Nay, it canna. For I have never felt safer than I do with you, my husband. An' I plan to spend the next several nights wrapped up tight in your arms." She snuggled close, twining her arms 'round my waist and resting her head on my chest. "Surely no harm can befall me there."

I stared down at her. My throat went utterly dry. Her eyes, heavy-lidded and gleaming from beneath thickly curling lashes, were filled with promise . . . and desire. Clearing my throat, I managed to force words through my lips, though they emerged rather hoarse. "You know that is not the way it will be. I have told you this."

"Aye, you have. But that was before our wedding kiss. An' I thought perhaps you'd changed your mind."

"I gave you no reason to think that," I said firmly, clasping her shoulders to move her slightly away from me.

"Nay? I rather thought near mating with me in front of the priest an' the entire clan was reason to think so, Nicodimus. Forgive me, though, if I misread you." Anger flashed in her eyes now.

I closed my eyes as painful memories reared up. I couldn't live it again. Didn't want to know her in that way, to come to cherish her any more than I already did, only to lose her. It would hurt too much. I would not love again, not ever. I had vowed it and I would keep that vow, for sanity's sake.

"I'm sorry. What you're thinking of can never be."

Her gaze fell, but not before I'd seen disappointment and pain cloud her expression. "Then let Angus rouse the suspicions of this clan. Let them come for me. If I canna be with you, I'd just as soon be dangling from a limb."

She whirled 'round as she said it, and stomped off toward the high table.

She was angry. Well, let her be angry then. It would be for the best.

I strode after her and joined my bride at the high table. As I sat down, she tore a leg from a roasted capon, and bit into it with a fierceness that was completely unladylike.

Arianna donned a nightshift so bold she could not believe she had the nerve to look at it, much less wear it. A wedding gift, presented to her by Nidaba during one of the more quiet moments of the celebration.

Sheer, made of a fabric she'd never seen before. Black, it hung to her ankles, but hid nothing. Every part of her was visible through the soft fabric. Arianna peered at a polished silver mirror, biting her lip. Even looking at herself dressed this way brought color to her cheeks. What would seeing Nicodimus looking at her do?

She snatched a blanket from the bed, and hastily tossed it around her shoulders. For now. Surely the courage to let it fall to the floor would come when she needed it. When Nicodimus . . . her husband . . . came through the chamber doors.

Her husband. Gods, to think of that man as her own. It was nearly too much for her mind to comprehend, and yet it was true. Or nearly true. She had yet to be his wife in the most important way. She had yet to lie in his arms, with less even than this scrap of cloth between them. She had yet to feel him inside her, filling her. Closing her eyes, she released a shuddering breath. It would be magick. True magick.

He would come to her. He would come to her soon.

Putting down the mirror, Arianna examined the room in which she and her husband were to spend their wedding night. Joseph had wisely assigned them to a chamber far from those used by the others. They would have complete privacy. Stone walls rose on all sides, with but a single window looking out and down to the outer walls, and the loch and woods beyond. She could not see the village from here. On one wall, a hearth stretched broadly, and a fire laid ready for the touch of a spark. Much like the fire inside her laid ready for the touch of her true love's hand.

His lips.

His body.

She closed her eyes against the roiling in the pit of her stomach . . . and lower. She was dizzy. Too much wine, surely.

When would he come? He should surely be here by now . . . if he intended to come to her at all tonight.

She whirled and stepped toward the door, even opened it a crack and peered out into the flickering, torchlit halls. But no sign of Nicodimus did she see.

He *would* come to her . . . wouldn't he? He'd said he would not. He'd said her dreams of being with him could never be. But she'd been certain he would at least come in long enough to wish her good night . . . on their wedding night. And when he did . . . and when she let the blanket fall away and he saw her in this scandalous shift, he would be unable to leave her to her lonely bed. He would take her, making her his woman in every way.

But no footsteps echoed in the halls. No sound at all came to her.

"Oh, Nicodimus, please," she whispered. "You wouldna leave me alone tonight. Not tonight, of all nights . . ." A tear burned in Arianna's eye as slowly she realized that was exactly what he intended to do.

The sound of hoofbeats accompanied a chill night breeze, through the window, and she hurried there. Hands braced on the stone sill, she leaned out, staring down into the darkness, to see the rider galloping away. Horse and rider both . . . unmistakable to her longing eyes. Nicodimus. Leaving his wife behind.

Her tears burned away under the blazing heat of her anger. Arianna let her blanket fall away, and snatched a dark, hooded cloak from her chest. Throwing it around her, she yanked the door open and strode out into the cool corridor.

He would *not* leave his bride behind on their wedding night. She would not allow him to.

I felt like a brute for the first time in my life, that night. Arianna . . . She was more than I could hope to resist, and I dared not face her. I knew too well what would happen between us if I went to her in the chamber where she waited. If I looked into those brown eyes and saw the raw yearning there as I had seen it earlier today when I had spoken my vows to her. If I touched her and felt the innocent trembling reaction of her body to mine. I knew she wanted . . . craved . . . what I could never give her. Not just coupling. I could provide that easily enough, and likely would have, had there been any way to keep her heart uninvolved. But it would not be possible with Arianna. It would mean more to her than the satisfaction of a physical hunger. It would mean I owned her, heart and soul. And that was a responsibility I did not want.

If I were to be utterly honest, I might admit that I feared for my heart and soul's well-being as well. Perhaps even more so than for hers. She intrigued me, enticed me, tempted me, in a way no woman ever had. No, not even my precious Anya. Arianna was so unlike my first love as to be a different breed altogether. Anya had been tame and timid. Arianna was wild and untamable. Anya had endured my touch, enjoyed it even, out of her desire to please me and her love for me. But Arianna was a bundle of passion awaiting release.

No. I could not go to her. I feared her, it was true. I felt as if she could easily destroy me, and lay to waste the solid stone wall I'd spent centuries building around my heart.

I knew now what I had done. I almost smiled when I realized that I had had a hand in destroying my own defenses by having put myself into this predicament. Her husband. By the Gods, I was the girl's husband now.

I rode Black hard, far away from the keep walls, into the forest beyond, and still farther, picking up the timeworn, but still familiar trail that led to my place. The sacred place of my people, and of those who came before them.

The Stone Circle.

When the towering pillars rose before me, I felt the first hint of peace beckoning me nearer. Tying Black's reins to a tree limb, I unlaced and removed my boots, out of reverence for the sacred site. My head bowed low, I stepped between the stones and entered the sanctuary.

Power pulsed here—from the stones, perhaps, or maybe from the ground itself. No one knew if the construction of the circle gave it the power, or if the power had been what had made the Ancient Ones choose this site. Perhaps neither was true, and it had been the constant use of this place for worship and ritual that had imbued it with magickal energies. I only knew the power here was real. A force I could feel thrumming like heady wine through my veins the moment my bared feet touched the soil within.

Moving to the center of the circle, I sat cross-legged and willed myself calm. Consciously, I slowed my breathing, deepened it, and one by one, relaxed every tense muscle in my body. I lowered my chin, closed my eyes, and opened my senses.

Gradually, the peace of the place worked into me. The sounds of the forest—for it was alive around me—made their way to me. The gentle breeze whispering amid the trees, and the stones themselves. The songs of nightbirds and crickets chirping. I could think clearly here. I would see the way I must proceed with Arianna. I had no wish to hurt her, and I knew I had that power. I had no wish to be hurt by her . . . and yet I suspected that power could belong to her all too easily. In silence, I sat. Until the silence was broken by a voice, deep and loud, calling my name from without.

"Nicodimus!"

My head came up fast, eyes wide, but sharp in the darkness. He stood outside the sacred place, a dagger already gleaming by the pale light of a crescent moon in his hand.

"The time has come."

Slowly, I got to my feet, my hand inching toward my own dagger, the one I never dared to be without. For this was my life. I never knew when a challenge would come.

He took a step forward. I held up a hand. "Not within the circle," I said, my voice low. "This is sacred ground."

He shrugged, his face invisible behind the beaked helm. "I've no care where I kill you, Nicodimus, so long as it gets done."

"Are you so certain you're ready to die, Marten?" I asked him, moving forward, coming out from amid the stones ten paces before him. "Or is it Kohl, behind the mask?"

"I am not certain at all that I wish to die," he said, his voice tinny and hollow. "But then I have no intent of dying, so what does it matter?"

He sprang then, and though I'd no wish to take a life here in this place, nor on the night of my wedding, I had no choice but to try my best to kill the man. For unless I did, he would surely kill me.

He plowed into me like a maddened bull before I could react. The pointed cone of his helm rammed my midsection and sent me stumbling backward, doubled over. Instinctively, I drew my knee sharply upward to pummel his face. An ill-planned move, since it only resulted in the beakish helm piercing my knee clean to the bone, by the feel of it.

I went down to the ground, and still he kept coming, roaring like an animal as he brought his blade down hard and fast. I rolled away, and his blade found dirt instead of flesh. Scrambling to my feet, even as he yanked his dagger free of the earth and began to straighten, I plunged my own blade deep into his back. My head clear now, I sought the spot where the bottom of his helm met the top of the breastplate he wore. My aim was true. The blade sank deep into the place between neck and back, and the force with which I drove it sent it clean through my enemy's spine.

He cried out but once, a cry that seemed cut off almost before it began. Then he went still. Motionless. Not a breath whispered from him. Not a sound. And yet he lived. Paralyzed and unable to breathe, but alive still. I sensed it.

I drew my blade from him and straightened, rolled him over with my foot, and crouching low, removed the helm. Blood poured from the thing, dampening the ground beneath him. And for a moment, it held my attention, and the familiar surge of regret swamped me. Spilling blood, taking lives, it had never set well with me. I did not like to be the instrument of death. Not even to one as evil as he.

But then my gaze went to his face. The bulging, unblinking eyes. The mouth, agape as he suffocated. And I stilled, as recognition flooded me. Kohl. One of Anya's two brutish brothers, as I had suspected. One less to torment me all my days.

Gripping his shoulders, I searched his immobile face, frozen in its dying grimace. "You were no immortal when I first knew you," I said to him. "And well I know how you gained your immortality, Kohl. By murder. What I wish to know is, how did you learn of this? Who taught you the way to steal unending life? Who?" But my voice trailed off, as I realized he could not answer me. And besides, what answer did I need?

It was obvious what had occurred, and it had been for a very long time now. Somehow Kohl and his brother had learned the secrets of the immortal High Witches. Somehow they had learned that to become one, they need only take the heart of another. And they had done so, long ago. A short time after Anya's death, as near as I could guess it. They had made themselves into a deadly pair of Dark High Witches, and likely I had been their reason for doing so. They had yearned to avenge their father's death, and then their sister's. On me. What did it matter who had taught them?

I lowered my head, closed my eyes, and thought of Anya. Lifting my head again, I saw the life slowly fading from Kohl's face. "I'll not take your heart until you die, Kohl," I said slowly. Knowing full well that had our positions been reversed, he'd delight in carving my own immortal heart from my chest while I still lived. "I'll do it before you have time to revive. You'll feel no pain. Make your peace, Kohl. You'll not be waking from death this time. Your life is over."

He blinked once and I sensed he would have spoken had he been able. To curse me? To thank me? How could I know? But taking his heart was the only way to ensure he stay dead. For immortals, be they Dark or Light, would revive from any death, so long as their hearts remained within them. And the hearts themselves would beat long into the future, even when removed. Imprisoned in small boxes, they were the stolen sources of the Dark Ones' power. My own immortality was earned in another way, for I was of the Light. My power came from the Source of all power, not from doing murder. I had no need of Kohl's heart nor the power it held. But I must take it all the same. And burn it, for that was the only way to release his soul.

The light in Kohl's eyes finally died. And still I waited, just to be sure. When his body began to grow cool, I removed his breastplate, and carved into his chest.

Arianna borrowed a horse from the stables Joseph kept within the keep walls. She headed out in the direction she had seen Nicodimus take, and then followed the deeply embedded tracks of his horse's pounding hooves. Once she had picked up the trail by the light of the moon, it was easy enough to guess where he was headed. To the Stone Circle. The Crones had shown her the place once. They had spoken of it with great reverence, but seemed afraid of the power they said the place held.

It was not difficult to find the place again. And when she neared it, she knew Nicodimus was nearby. She need only come within a short distance of him to feel his presence. And she felt him now. That tingling awareness that seemed to brush over her flesh. The dark sense of him filling her. Gods, how she loved him. Wanted him. Craved him the way some men craved their whiskey. Strong, he was, but so tender. His touch would be gentle and powerful all at once. He would teach her what this yearning in her belly meant. And how to quench it. He was the only man who could.

"Gods, how I love you, Nicodimus," she whispered. "Never has any man touched my soul as you have done." And now, oh, now, if only he would touch her body in the same way. Her fantasies of him had carried her this far, but they were no longer enough. She *needed* him . . . not in her mind, but in her arms, in her bed, inside her.

She closed her eyes, and the now familiar feeling of moisture gathered between her legs. It had been happening frequently of late, this new sensation, the dampness. The empty feeling, yearning to be filled. Maiden she may be, but learned as well. The Crones had spoken of such things, taught her what her mother would not. According to them, the pleasure to be had in mating was intense and wonderful and not at all sinful. A woman, they said, would experience as much pleasure as a man, and it was natural that it be so. Not shameful, not immoral, but good and right, and as our Creator intended. For did not the entire Universe come about by the mating of Goddess and God? Was not our Source truly the union of the two? As above, so below. All is but a reflection of itself.

She wanted to feel that magick with Nicodimus. She wanted to be one with him. It was meant to happen. She knew it was. He was the missing part of herself. She was his. He would realize it one day. He had to.

Shaking herself out of the deep contemplation into which she had fallen, she dismounted from the dun mare she'd taken, and moved forward, bare feet brushing the ferns and woodland grasses and mossy stones. And slowly, bit by bit, she emerged into the clearing.

Then she went still, and caught her breath. At first she saw only the Stone Circle, the sight of which filled her with as much awe and reverence now as it had the only other time she'd glimpsed it. It seemed to have been created by a race of giants, for she could think of no other creature capable of standing such massive structures upright, much less securing them deep enough within the earth to remain that way.

But then the scene taking place within the circle caught her attention, and her blood congealed at the horror of it.

Two men, within the sacred circle. One lying still atop a pile of brush, like a miniature funeral pyre about to be lit. He was obviously dead. His chest had been laid open, and his clothing was soaked in blood. The other man stood above him, his hands held high, and in those hands rested a bloody mass that nearly made Arianna retch to see it.

She whirled away, clinging to a tree with one hand, moving behind it as if to shield herself from the gruesome sight. Head bowed low, eyes closed tightly, she fought to catch her breath as her stomach churned. But something compelled her to look again. Something forced her to see . . . to know . . .

Slowly, she forced her eyes open, and lifted her head. Peering around the tree, she made herself look. Really look and see what was happening. And when she did, a soft sound rose in her throat entirely against her will.

The man standing was Nicodimus. And the thing in his hands . . . was a human heart.

A heart that was still quivering . . . beating. . . .

The sound she made was half gasp, half cry. And when she uttered it, she clasped a hand to her lips. But too late. Nicodimus's head turned sharply, his keen eyes scanning the woods, and landing unerringly upon her. His lips parted, as if he would speak, and he reached toward her with a hand stained scarlet.

Arianna backed away, shaking her head, unable to speak or even to cry. Good Gods, what was this? What sort of Witch was he? And what kind of evil drove him to . . .

She did not want to know. Suddenly she feared the man she had always loved. His secrets were far too many and too deep . . . and darker than she had ever imagined.

Even as he took a step toward her, Arianna whirled and raced away, frantically untying the reins before leaping onto the mare's back and wheeling her about. Kicking the mare's sides, she galloped into the forest.

She must run, she told herself. She must! For the hands that held a ghastly still-beating heart skyward in some sick offering to whatever Gods lived in Nicodimus's soul, must never touch her. Never!

10

Hastily, I built a pyre within the circle. Hastily, for I'd no wish to have Kohl revive before I did what must be done. His wounds would heal, and I would be bound to kill or be killed all over again. Already I felt my own torn flesh begin to tingle, mending itself as it always would—no matter the injury—unless my own heart were taken from me.

Slinging his lifeless body over my shoulder, I laid Kohl upon the pyre, and there I took his heart. Flint ready in my pocket, kindling laid, I held the heart high above my head, and whispered the words I had long used for such grim occasions as this.

"By the powers of the Ancient Ones, by the force of my Creator, and by my will, I commend this body to the fire, and this heart to the flame, and this soul to its Source. Go forth, Kohl, and ponder the lessons of this lifetime. And return, one day, to live again, enlightened by all you have learned. Go in peace, my brother. As I will it, and with harm to none, so mote it be."

For a long moment, I held the heart high, pushing my will into it, feeling it begin to slow, to release its life force bit by bit. But even before I could place it upon the pyre, a soft sound startled me out of my state of intense concentration. A sound so pained, so hurting, that it cut right to my soul. I snapped my head 'round in search of the source of that cry, knowing even before I saw her there, that Arianna had found me, had seen this wretched deed I did. And the knowledge brought with it a fierce surge of regret.

I spotted her there, clinging to a large oak, staring at me from beyond it. Her eyes were wide with surprise and shock and something I had hoped never to see in them. Fear. Fear of me. I tried to speak, not knowing what to say, even lifted a hand toward her, but she turned and fled as if she'd seen some monster instead of her husband.

And indeed, she likely believed she had.

With a heavy heart, I returned to my grim task. For to leave it unfinished would make me the exact monster my wife seemed to believe I was. It must be done. I would deal with Arianna later, though I had no idea how or what I could say. I should, perhaps, have told her what I was long before now. But I had not. Now I had no choice.

Calming my frantic heart, I placed Kohl's atop the pyre, near his feet. Then kneeling, I struck the flint until it produced a spark and ignited the kindling. There I waited until the flames danced high, and the body was too far consumed for there to be any hope of someone coming along and snatching it out in time. The heart, too, sizzled and oozed as the flames roasted it, burned it, then reduced it to smoldering ash.

Only when all was complete, did I dare leave and go off in search of my runaway bride, to try to explain what she had witnessed. And I must hurry, before her emotions made her do something foolish. For her to learn the truth was inevitable. For her to learn it like this, unforgivable.

Even now, I was uncertain just how much I should tell her. She was so young, and so incredibly vulnerable to me. To tell her what I was, how I must live, was going to be shocking enough to rock her right to her soul. But to tell her that she was the same . . . I was not sure I could bring myself to do that. Not yet. I resolved to wait, to see her reactions to the first of my frightening revelations before deciding if she were ready for the rest. The truth. The frightening, shocking truth, of what she was. An immortal High Witch, who would one day be forced to commit the same violence she'd just seen me do. Or have it performed upon her by one of the Dark Ones.

The knowledge could easily destroy my fragile little cat. And for the first time I realized that if it did, it might well destroy me, too.

I returned to the keep only to be told that Arianna had left with a small pouch of her belongings. Joseph's sons had already set out to search for her along the roads leading away from the village. But I didn't think she would leave Stonehaven. Not yet. I knew Arianna, or thought I did, better than anyone. So I went to the places where I knew she would go for solace. Her parents' home in the village, the cemetery where her beloved sister lay buried, the shores of the loch.

And finally, to the site of The Crones' cottage. That was where I found her. Alone, sitting on a small boulder with her knees drawn to her chest and her arms wrapped tight around them. Her face lowered, her dress absorbing her tears. Trembling and frightened, I found her. More kitten than cat just then. Vulnerable and afraid. I knew I would have to treat her gently, or see her bolt.

It twisted my heart into a knot to see her hurting, to know that her pain belonged to me.

The night wind whispered her name as I stepped slowly closer, and then I repeated its loving refrain.

"Arianna."

Her head came up fast, brown eyes wide, unblinking. Cheeks red with tear tracks, full lips trembling. "Leave me alone, Nicodimus." Her voice shook with emotion, with fear. Of me.

"I can't do that. I . . . I need to explain. What you saw, it wasn't . . ."

Her eyes narrowed on me, seeming to pierce right through my skin. "Wasn't what? Murder?"

Sighing deeply, I turned and sat beside her on the boulder. My elbows resting on my knees, bent forward at the waist, not looking at her, I said, "It was not murder. Kohl was trying his best to kill me, and I had no choice but to defend myself."

"By cuttin' out his heart?" Her voice broke on those words, and when I turned my head to look at her, I saw the grimace on her face, the horror of the memory in her eyes.

"It was . . . necessary."

"What sorts of Gods do you serve, Nicodimus, that would require such a gruesome sacrifice?"

I closed my eyes slowly. "I'll tell you, Arianna. If you'll listen, I'll tell you my secrets. Things you likely won't believe. But true, all of them, utterly true."

She said nothing, so I lifted my gaze to hers again, searched her face. And she said, "Goddess help me, for I am a hopeless fool. I want you to explain it all away, Nicodimus. I want to believe in you again. So I'm listenin'."

I nodded, drew a breath, nodded again. "All right. All right, then. But first . . . first, Arianna, know this. I would never hurt you. Never. Do you believe that?"

Again her eyes met mine, probed, searched. A little less fear, and more of her natural curiosity lighting them. "'Tis difficult to believe in the tenderness of a man I just saw holdin' a bloodied heart in his hands . . . a heart that . . ." She closed her eyes, gave her head a quick shake. "But that's impossible."

"Nothing is impossible," I said softly. "Nothing." It was going to be difficult to explain all of this to her. "What did you see, Arianna, that you believe impossible?"

She tilted her head to one side, remembering, and a little shiver worked through her. "It appeared that the heart was . . . was still beatin', Nicodimus. But 'twas only my shocked mind playin' tricks on me."

"You've no idea how I wish that were the case."

She blinked. "What are you sayin'?"

Drawing a breath, I said, "Let me begin at the beginning, Arianna. I only ask that you not run from me . . . at least, not until I've finished. The things I'm going to tell you will shock and upset you. But they are things you need to know and understand. Things I . . . likely should have told you a long time ago."

She thought a moment, then nodded once. "All right. I suppose 'tis little enough to ask. You've saved my life on more than one occasion. I owe you as much."

"You owe me nothing."

"I differ with you on that point. But let's nay argue. Just tell me these secrets of which you speak, an' make me understand why you butchered that man so brutally. For I trusted you, Nicodimus, an' what I saw frightened that trust away. I only want to understand, an' find it again."

"You want me to restore your faith in me," I said slowly, clarifying it in my own mind. Wondering if she'd be better off if I stopped here and now. But no. She had to know. We shared a fate, she and I.

"I was born into a tiny clan that once made its home here, at the site of this very village. And the year was seven hundred and fifty."

She smiled then. Smiled broadly, and punched me lightly on my arm. "Be serious, now, Nicodimus. An' stop jesting with me. 'Twould make you o'er seven hundred years old."

"Seven hundred and fifty, Arianna."

She stared at me. Her smile faltered and died.

I said no more, and gave her a moment to digest that bit of information. She clearly didn't believe me. It was evident in everything from the sudden worry clouding her magnificent brown eyes to the slight stiffening of her muscles. No doubt the question of my sanity was even now occurring to my lovely bride. And I disliked seeing it there.

"You mean," she began, slowly, cautiously, "you *feel* that old. But of course, you are not."

"Do you remember, Arianna, the way I looked when you first set eyes on me?"

She nodded at once. "Every detail," she whispered, then quickly turned her head away and I saw her cheeks color prettily, despite the darkness.

"And have I changed in all that time?" I asked her. "Aged at all?"

She frowned, pondering. "I . . . have often wondered how you hide your age so well."

"I hide my age so well because I do not age. My body hasn't aged since I was twenty and eight, Arianna, and it never will." I paused, turned to face her and took both of her hands in mine. Warm, they were. Soft as satin, with nimble, slender fingers that were quick and clever. I loved the way her hands looked—small and strong, yet willing to nestle into the grip of my larger ones. I liked closing mine around them, holding her. And I didn't give it any more thought than that. Though I recall very clearly the word that whispered insistently and in an unfamiliar tone, a possessive commanding tone, through my mind. The word was *Mine*.

"Arianna," I said. "I am . . . I am immortal."

Her head dipped slightly, eyes seeming to plumb mine even as they narrowed to mere slits. "Immortal?" she whispered. And now her hands turned, her beautiful fingers lacing with mine, and she squeezed. "Nicodimus . . . love, you know that canna be." Then one hand broke free, and her fingers gently probed and rubbed over my head, through my hair, searching every inch. "You may have been injured in the battle," she said quickly. "With that man . . . Kohl, you called him. Oh, Nicodimus, I know you didna do murder back there. I was only shocked to see such violence, an' afraid, an' still very upset with you for leaving me alone on the night of our wedding, an' so my emotions got away from me, I suppose, an' I—"

"Cease."

She did. Biting her lip, she stopped the stream of nervous words that had been spilling out of her without censure. I think she knew even then that there was some truth to what I said. How much, she could not know. But she needed to speak, and fast, to keep me from saying any more.

"I am not injured. I was, but 'tis healed now."

The worry in her brown eyes deepened. "No one heals so quickly," she said softly. "Where were you hurt, Nicodimus? Show me, and let me tend the wounds."

I nodded. "Yes. Yes, I must show you. 'Tis the only

way to get past your disbelief. There is much you need to know, my little cat, but we cannot proceed until we rid you of your skepticism.''

''Aye,'' she said slowly, humoring me. ''Aye, just show me. I am your wife, and tendin' your wounds is my duty. Let me help you, love.''

I nodded, and turned away from her, so my back blocked her view. Then, moving very quickly, I drew my dagger with its jeweled hilt, and pushing back my sleeve, I drew its blade across my forearm.

''Nicodimus, nay!'' Arianna leapt to her feet, seeing what I had done, but not in time to prevent it. Weeping aloud, she reached for the deep gash in my flesh, as if she would grip it tight and try to stop the bleeding. But I drew my arm out of her reach, held up a hand.

''Just wait, Arianna. Just wait.'' With one hand I smoothed her hair, my eyes on the gash, watching it. But when I heard her sobs I looked up, saw the distress, the twin rivulets of tears. She was shaking all over. And I was suddenly full of regret. I reached for her. ''Arianna . . .''

But her eyes were widening, and focused unblinkingly on the cut. And when I looked down again, I realized the blood flow was slowing visibly. Arianna took a stuttering breath as it stopped entirely, then stepped backward with a soft gasp as the skin 'round the edges of the wound began slowly, bit by bit, regenerating.

''Please,'' I asked her, when she took another halting step backward. ''Please, do not be afraid. It is what I am, Arianna. This is what I am.''

She searched my face, stared deeply into my eyes, her own growing less fearful by slight degrees. Her feet moved, but this time to bring her closer, and she reached out a tentative hand, to touch, drew away, and touched again. ''Oh . . . oh, my . . .'' she whispered, and sank to her knees at my feet, drawing my arm with her, clutching it in hers. She lifted the hem of her robe, and before I knew what she was about to do, wiped the blood away from my arm. Then she watched, trembling on her knees as the cut slowly healed. Her fingers trailed over the new skin, soft, erotic, sending a bolt of awareness straight to my soul, like lightning searing hot and shattering.

"Good Gods, 'tis true. . . ." She lifted her huge, innocent eyes to mine. "But how? How can this be?"

"For a very long while, I did not know. I still do not know all of it. The why of it, or how it all works. I only know that long ago, in my village, I believed myself to be an ordinary man. I hunted, I fought. I was a warrior, skilled and proud, and would have been chieftain of my clan one day. I had a wife and two strong sons."

At this point, Arianna's head snapped up. "Not just a wife then. But a family," she whispered. Slowly rising until standing, she faced me. "Tell me of them, Nicodimus. Tell me of your family. And of the woman who captured your love."

Nodding, I lowered my head. "Her name was . . . was Anya."

Arianna's small hand came to my face, cupping it, fingers tracing my cheeks. "You loved her," she whispered. "Nay, dinna look as if you regret it, husband. You've told me of your love for Anya before, an 'tis a relief to know you loved once. I'd begun to fear you were incapable of it."

I shook my head, considered telling her she had the right of it. That I was incapable of loving . . . now. But then decided I had hurt her enough, and my revelations would soon do so even more. Enough of causing her pain.

"How long were you together?" she asked, taking my hand now, leading me back to sit on the boulder as if she were the experienced sage, and I the innocent. She urged me downward, then curled her legs beneath her and sat on the ground at my feet, close to me. Her body leaning against my thighs.

"I was but four and ten when I found her. She was the daughter of an enemy chieftain. Our men took her father's life in battle, and I found her in her village, being beaten by her two brothers, Marten and Kohl. She'd been mistreated all her life. So I took her."

"As prisoner?" she asked. No judgment in her tone, just curiosity.

"The choice was hers. I took her, yes, but I may have left her behind, had she asked it of me." I shrugged. "Or perhaps not. At any rate, she did not object, so I took her. And back in my village, I made her my wife, and gave her my promise that no man would ever raise a hand to harm her again. 'Twas a promise I kept."

Arianna's hand touched my thigh, and she dipped her head, as if she were studying her fingers with great interest. "Was she . . . very beautiful?"

"She was comely. Small and frail. With the temperament of a mouse, Arianna. Wary and afraid, but eventually she came to trust me, and to love me. We had a good life together. She cared for my needs and I for hers. She gave me my sons, the most precious things in the world to me."

Arianna blinked and lifted her eyes to mine. "She sounds like my opposite. She couldna have been more unlike me."

"'Tis true enough," I told her.

And she quickly looked away, hiding her eyes from my scrutiny. "Tell me of the children."

"Jaymes was the younger. Timid and tall for his age. Sickly. But bright, beyond measure. He was constantly working figures, numbers and such. He could draw any likeness, and play the pipes like Pan Himself. Will was the elder. Strong, a warrior, a strapping lad with a temper to match. It was all I could do to keep that one in line. Had he lived much longer, he'd have been fully capable of besting his sire in a fair fight."

Darkening with understanding and sympathy, her eyes turned up toward mine again. "Oh, Nicodimus. You lost them."

I closed my eyes. "I lost them all. Anya died struggling to give birth to our third child, a wee girl who never lived to draw her first breath. After four and ten years with her, I didn't think I could live without her, but somehow I did. My lads needed me, then. I had no choice."

"You are very strong," Arianna whispered. "I've always known that about you." Her arms had somehow twisted 'round my waist, and her head rested on my thigh. "An' a fine father you must have been to those lads."

"I tried. By the Gods, Arianna, I tried. But Jaymes died when the Black Death swept through our village later that same year. And a year later, Will and I were cut down side by side, in battle with the same clan from whence I'd taken his mother."

"Oh, Nicodimus . . ." she whispered, head rising, hands stroking along my back. "Oh, my love, I am so very sorry. I know this grief that lives in you. I know it well."

"I know you do," I told her, studying her eyes seeing the tears pooling there. "You've felt it, too."

"So you and Will were wounded . . . in this battle?" she asked.

"No," I said. "No, Arianna, we were . . . we were killed."

She sat up straighter. "No, my love . . ."

"Yes. I'd a blade thrust straight through my heart, Arianna. There was no question. I died beside my son on the field of battle. But moments later, I lived again. Consciousness returned, and with it a blinding flash of pain and light. My body arched until I thought my spine would snap, and I dragged in a desperate gasp that failed to satisfy my starving lungs. I opened my eyes and stared, first at the blade which skewered me still, and then at my beloved son, lying lifeless at my side. And a rage filled me such as none I had ever known. I gripped the hilt of the sword, and pulled it from my chest. I howled in rage that Will should be dead, and I alive, with no one left, no one at all. Even before my grief abated, I felt a tingling sensation, saw the bleeding stop, and watched in awe as the mortal wound in my chest healed itself.

"Someone saw me then, and shouted that I'd been dead, my body already cooling, only moments before. I was confused and maddened with grief, and so I ran. I ran away."

Soft, cooling palms skimmed my face, and big brown eyes, brimming with tears, traced my features with healing tenderness. "Aye, Nicodimus. An' you've been runnin' ever since. From love. From carin' of any kind. Because it hurts to love and lose, you've decided nay to love at all."

I nodded, amazed, and not for the first time, by her insights. "You are very wise for one so young."

"'Tis nay my age which makes me know your heart, Nicodimus. 'Tis my own grief. I, too, wished never to suffer loss again. I believe 'tis why I drew away from those closest to me. Even my own dear mother." As she spoke, she lay her head down once again.

I looked down at her, blond hair spread over my legs as her head rested gently there. "Then perhaps you do understand."

"To have lost my sister nearly destroyed me," she went on, lifting her head now, and stroking my cheek with one hand. "I canna imagine the pain of losing a child . . . much less two of them, an' your newborn . . . an' your wife."

I closed my hand over hers on my face, and gently moved it away, for her touch was eliciting more emotion from within me than I had realized was hidden inside. "'Tis the way of things, for me . . . for my kind."

Her hand stilled in midair, eyes widening. "You mean you're nay the only one? There . . . there are others?"

I felt my lips pull into a smile at her innocence and wonder. "Hundreds," I told her. "And all of us cursed to outlive all of those we love."

Blinking rapidly, she finally averted her face. "I could never exist that way," she whispered, her voice choked with emotion. "Never!"

And my throat went dry, because I knew she must. But I couldn't tell her that. Not yet.

Eventually, she looked back at me. "I ken now why you canna love me, Nicodimus. I'll never ask it of you again."

I looked into her eyes, as dark and fathomless as the night itself, and I felt an odd tug in the center of my chest. It felt like . . . regret. But that made no sense, whatsoever.

But she gave me no time to examine the feeling.

"Where did you go?"

I only looked at her blankly, still pondering my own heart. "Where did I—"

"When you ran away," she clarified, staring up at me, wide-eyed and rapt with attention.

"Of course." I focused my mind back on my tale. "I wandered for a time, stopping at crofts and working for a meal and a place to lay my head before moving on again. Eventually, I decided to make my way back to my village, my people. I'd been searching for answers, but I'd found none. I'd been traveling aimlessly over the whole of Scotland for well over two years. And I was still no closer to understanding why I lived. But I had noticed things, changes in me. Though these things only served to puzzle me more."

"What sorts of changes?" she asked, nearly breathless now with anticipation.

"They were gradual," I explained. "There was a certain sharpening of my senses. My eyesight grew keener, and I began to see in darkness as well as I did in bright light. My hearing became . . . acute. My sense of smell became as honed as that of the wolf, and I seemed able to taste things more thoroughly, even things on the air. Physical feeling intensified, and with it, physical strength and stamina beyond that of any ordinary man. And then there was the healing . . . any wound I had would heal within a short while, just as I have shown you here this night. And while I suspected I could not easily die, I had no idea that I was immortal."

"How could you?" she asked. "Who would ever imagine such a thing?" She shook her head slowly, her gaze turning inward. "Even though you've shown me this miraculous healing power, I still canna quite grasp the fact that you canna die."

"I can die, Arianna. Just not easily, nor in the usual way."

She perused my features, her brown eyes narrow. "Go on, tell me what happened, how you found the answers you sought."

I rose from the stone to pace away from her. Apparently in thought, but truly because her embrace affected me far more than it should. Far more than I could bear.

"When I returned, it was to find my village destroyed. The crofts of my people burned, the crops lying exposed to the burning sun, withered and ruined, the livestock butchered, their carcasses stinking and bloated. And their owners, for the most part, alongside them in the same or worse condition."

"Oh, Nicodimus," she breathed. "Gods, I'd have collapsed in devastation."

I turned. She'd risen, but stayed near the rock, looking as if she'd like to run to me, to offer comfort, but perhaps, knowing better. "That is very close to what I did. Later, when I managed to move again, I erected a huge pyre, placing upon it the bodies of my clan—my friends and neighbors, my elderly father and my cousins." I lowered my head, shuddering at the memory. "I think I knew even then that the men responsible were Anya's brothers, Marten and Kohl. They'd vowed vengeance on me since the day I took their sister, and only the births of our sons had prevented them leading their clan against us sooner. Evil, they may have been, but even they had enough decency to refrain from embarking on a battle that might wound their own kin."

She nodded slowly. "But once your precious Will was gone, their restraint went with it."

I nodded, my lips tight, my stomach roiling with the memory. "After the fires burned low, I went to the ancient Stone Circle, where the holy men of my clan would go to commune with the spiritual realm, and find peace and wisdom. Common men such as I rarely ventured into the sacred space, but I still had no answers to the questions burning in my soul. And somehow, I thought I would find them nowhere else."

Eyes widening, Arianna tipped her head to one side. "The same Stone Circle where I saw you tonight?"

"Yes, little cat. I vowed I would remain there until the Gods themselves spoke to me, or I would die slowly within its embrace. And there I sat upon the ground, day and night, with neither food nor water. I sat there through rain and storm, through the chill of night and the heat of midday, until my mind became dulled with hunger, and my body parched with thirst. Until I became too weak to sit up, and so lay down instead, my knees curled to my chest, my body trembling. And still I waited, demanding the Gods either speak to me or take my life."

Arianna did come to me then. She stood very close, one hand sliding up my arm. "Obviously, they did not take your life."

"No. They gave me the answers I sought, in the form of a group of men whose roots went back in time, to unknown beginnings. The Druids. Holy men. As it happened, my vigil fell near their springtime rites, the one the Pagans call Beltane. And so they came from their secluded havens, to summon forth the spirits of the trees, and to dance in celebration of the spring."

"And they found you there?"

My hands had found their way to her waist, tiny in the span of my palms. I think I put them there to keep her at a safe distance, but it almost transformed into an embrace. It felt incredibly intimate, standing this way, holding her waist, her hands on my outer arms, her little face turned up to mine.

"One of the hooded, aged men carried me to the edge of the circle, and poured water down me, fed me, wrapped me in a blanket. Then left me there to witness their peculiar rites." I closed my eyes, remembering. "The fiddler played, and they danced and chanted. It was something of rare beauty and power."

I could see her face twist in confusion. No doubt she wondered why I would later sully such a sacred, mystical site with the blood of my enemy. But I would come to that.

"When they left again at dawn, they carried me with them. And at their temples, hidden deep within the forests, they patiently taught me what I was."

"What, Nicodimus? What are you?"

So much eagerness in her eyes. The fear was less now, than it had been before.

"I'm a Witch. An immortal High Witch, Arianna. Far different from village Witches such as The Crones were.

Most don't even know of the existence of the High Ones, the immortals."

She took my hand, and led me beside her along a path deeper into the woods. "How did you become this way?"

Her small hand was not cold, nor trembling, but strong, and firm. As if she could somehow comfort me. And amazingly, she was doing just that. "There are two ways," I told her. "It is said that when one dies while attempting to save the life of a Witch, that person will return to his next lifetime with the gift of immortality. He is born, and grows older as any mortal would do, until he experiences physical death for the first time. When that happens, he doesn't remain dead . . . but instead revives to life once more. And from that moment on, he will not age. His senses will sharpen, and his strength will grow. The older he becomes, the stronger he will be."

She nodded, listening intently. "You said there is one way you could experience true death, Nicodimus."

"Yes. Only should someone remove my heart from my chest, will my death be permanent. And even then, it isn't true death, for the body, though lifeless, will never rot away, and the heart, though bodiless, will beat on . . . perhaps forever."

She stopped walking, and with a soft gasp lifted her hand to her breast. "'Tis a nightmare!" Then she blinked . . . and slowly looked up at me. "Then . . . that man in the circle, whose heart you cut out . . ."

"Yes," I told her. "He was immortal. But not like me, Arianna. He was one of the Dark Ones, made immortal by far different means. For as I told you, there are two ways to obtain this endless life, and the second is far less pretty than the first."

She released my hand, and wandered toward the banks of a swift running stream, there to sit down on the soft moss, spreading her skirts beneath her. "Come," she said, patting a spot beside her. "Tell me."

I stood where I was, staring at her, so small and delicate to my eyes. "Perhaps I've shocked you enough for one night, Arianna."

"I'll nay rest until I know all of it," she promised. And again, patted the moss.

Sighing, I went to her, settled down beside her. "All right. Since I know your stubbornness to be legendary, I will go on. But if it becomes more than you can bear—"

"I am far stronger than you know, Nicodimus. Far stronger."

Looking into her eyes, I sighed and relented. "Where there is good there is also evil. You know this."

"Aye," she said. "There can be no light without darkness. 'Tis the way of things. Of nature itself."

I nodded my agreement. "Thus with Witches. There are evil ones among us, those without conscience, without love in their souls. When they find out the secrets of High Witches, they cannot resist seeking out immortality for themselves."

"And how can they gain it, Nicodimus?"

"By killing one of us. By taking the heart from our chest, and holding it captive in a small box. So long as they possess the heart, they possess the immortality, and the power of its rightful owner. In time, the heart will weaken, and the Dark Witch with it. So they are compelled to take another, and another. It is the only way they can live on."

"I see." She said it slowly, thoughtfully. Then, drawing a deep breath, met my gaze straight on. "You say you are one of the Light Ones, Nicodimus. And yet I just saw you take a living heart."

I stiffened. That she could, even for a moment, believe me to be one of the Dark Ones. . . . I nearly spoke without thinking, nearly told her of the birthmarks we all bear, the Light upon the right flank, the Dark upon the left, in order to prove to her my innocence. But I bit the words back in the barest instant before I would have spoken them. For if she knew of the birthmark's significance she would have to know that she was as I am. Immortal, just like me. And I was convinced my tender cat was not ready for that information. Not yet. Hadn't she already told me she'd rather die than to outlive all those she loved?

"I took his heart because it was the only way to ensure

he stay dead. And I did not keep it, Arianna. I burned it on a pyre, the heart as well as the body. For that was the one way to free Kohl's immortal soul."

She inhaled deeply, lowering her pretty chin, but then her head came up again, eyes wide. "Kohl? Nicodimus, this man was the one who attacked you before . . . he was . . ."

"My brother-in-law," I said, nodding slowly. "I have no idea how he learned the secret, but he and his brother did so. They both managed to take living hearts and capture immortality for themselves. And it makes sense to me that they did so. If they had learned I was immortal, they would have gone to any lengths to become the same. Their only wish was to live long enough to kill me, the man who killed their father, humiliated them before their own clan, stole away their sister. They blamed me for Anya's death as well. And they always vowed they would have vengeance on me one day."

"What of the other one, Nicodimus?"

I shook my head. "If they had been together they would no doubt have attacked me as one. Unfair, but they have never been men of ethics or honor. And Marten is a far more accomplished Witch than Kohl. He's even mastered the art of setting fires with but his will over the centuries. I'd have had much more trouble defeating Marten. No, Arianna, if Kohl attacked me alone, then his brother must be far away."

Her hand came up to stroke my face. "I'm sorry for you, Nicodimus. It must be truly horrible to know you have been hated so much for so long." Then she shook her head slowly. "And to live being hunted by the Dark Ones. For that is how you must live, is it not?"

"Yes. It is. Coming here, to this place, has always been my escape from that life. But one of them found me, even here."

"Aye," she said. "But that one is no more."

"I never meant to bring the darkness to this place. . . . To you . . ."

Her smile was gentle, and small. "I dinna doubt that, Nicodimus."

"But where one can find me, others may well follow."

She sat a little straighter. "They will have me to contend with, do they wish to harm my husband," she declared.

And that made me smile. But then she hugged me quite fiercely, her arms tight around my waist, her head pressing to my chest. "Dinna laugh at me, Nicodimus. I mean what I say."

My arms went 'round her, seemingly of their own volition. Such a strong, stubborn woman. She touched something deep within me. The scent of her hair seemed to tangle itself 'round my senses, and tug me gently closer.

"Take me to the Stone Circle, next full moon," she said softly. "The Crones were afraid to perform magickal rites there. But I wish to feel the power you spoke of, to know it for myself."

It was not in my power to deny her. I thought then, that anything she asked of me, I would gladly do.

Anything . . . except love her. I must never do that.

Never . . .

11

Arianna understood. Now so much more than before. Perhaps Nicodimus would love her . . . if only he could. But he could not. Oh, she did not believe for a moment that his heart had died with his family. No, his heart was strong in him, and filled with tender emotions. She had seen the pain in his eyes as he'd spoken of his lost family. One could not hurt if one were incapable of loving. Indeed, she had begun to think her husband had more love inside him than anyone she had ever known. But not for her. Nay, not for her. He could not risk loving her, nor would she ask it of him. For he knew—and now she did as well—the consequences loving her would bring. He would be forced to watch her grow old, while he remained young and strong. He would have to watch her die, leaving him behind. Immortal and utterly alone.

She thought on these things as she rode before him on his fiery black stallion, her back pressed to his chest, his hand at her waist. She thought on these things and more. And she realized that she had to give up her dreams of making him love her. For his sake. She loved him too much to ask him to suffer such unspeakable anguish because of her. She would not ask it of him again.

He glanced down at her, concern etched on his face. "The things I've told you tonight... they've shocked you."

She thought on that for a moment. "Shocked, aye. But enlightened, as well. I ken your heart more now than ever I have, Nicodimus. An' 'tis glad I am you finally shared your secrets with me."

His steady gaze made her wish for more than could ever be as he replied, "I always intended to tell you all of this. I only... thought to wait until I judged you ready to hear it. I thought..."

"You thought a girl so young and flighty too immature to deal with these truths. You thought I would run in fear of you, or give myself nightmares."

He frowned, a hint of guilt appearing on his face. "I only thought to protect your tender heart and mind from such dark truths as these."

At that, Arianna smiled. "My heart is far from tender, Nicodimus. I am strong. Far stronger than you know."

"And far more vulnerable than *you* know, little cat."

"Nay. 'Tis not so. In time, you'll see."

He returned her smile, but his was doubtful, tentative. And slowly a more serious expression replaced it. "I've trusted you with these secrets, Arianna. And secrets, they must remain. Understand that."

"Aye," she replied. "Nicodimus, I ken full well the need for secrecy in this. An' I would die of torture before revealin' a word of what you've told me this eve. I swear it to you on the name of my sister."

He blinked as if in surprise at the vehemence in her voice. But she meant what she said, and used the only words she could think of to convince him of that. He believed her, she thought. For he nodded firmly, and turned his attention back to the path ahead.

The keep rose dark and towering before them, and only as they drew near did she think of something she had not asked. "What of Nidaba? Is she... is she a High Witch as well?"

He glanced her way. "Nidaba's secrets are not mine to

share. But if you ask her, Arianna, I believe she will be as honest with you as I have been. She does not show it, but I sense that deep down she is fond of you, for some reason."

She lifted a hand to her breast as if wounded. "Am I so onerous that this surprises you?"

He met her eyes, a reluctant smile tugging at his lips. "Naught you might do could surprise me," he said. "And you know full well you're the farthest thing from onerous. It is simply that Nidaba tends to . . . shy away from intimacies, bonds of any kind where caring is involved."

"Aye," she said, smiling back at him now. "Except with you." He conceded the point with a nod, and Arianna told herself she'd no right to feel jealous.

Side by side they rode through the gates, and dismounted. Nicodimus took the reins, and led his horse into the stables. And he didn't object when Arianna walked with him into the dark, hay-scented outbuilding. He removed the saddle, the bridle, reached for a rag and began rubbing his stallion briskly.

She felt a bit guilty for not having taken proper care of the mare she'd borrowed earlier. And while Nicodimus worked on Black, she went to where the dun mare stood, and brushed her coat. When Nicodimus gave Black some grain, she gave some to the mare as well, and thought she saw approval in her husband's eyes.

Arianna tilted her head when he faced her once more. "I suppose your aversion to closeness must not extend to animals. For I believe you think more highly of your horse than your wife."

She was teasing. But Nicodimus didn't jest with her in return. Instead he took both her hands in his, and stared into her eyes. "You must never think that, Arianna. I do care for you. More than is probably wise."

Her hands warmed where he held them, and her heart seemed to quicken its beat. But she closed her eyes and reminded herself she must be strong. Must not give in to the yearning of her body . . . nor to that of her heart. "You needn't spew lies to comfort me, Nicodimus. I've told you,

I am the strongest person I know. An' now that you've explained your past to me, I'll be content to be your wife in name only. I ken why 'tis necessary, an' I willna go back on my word.'' He parted his lips to say more, but she shook her head firmly. ''Nay, no more. Save your carin' for your horse, husband. I've no need of it. Truly. You saved my life by weddin' me, an' 'tis enough. More than enough.''

He frowned at her, studying her there in the darkness as if unable to comprehend her words.

''Dinna you ken, Nicodimus? I'm only agreein' to the terms you laid down afore our marriage. I'll nay try to make you love me, only to watch me age an' die while you remain alone. Is this nay the very thing you wanted of me?''

As they walked together out of the stable and began crossing the courtyard, which was, for once, void of any clansmen, his frown deepened and he nodded. ''Yes, I . . . I suppose it is.''

''Then you have it.'' She lowered her head, bit her lower lip. ''However, I would ask one concession of you.''

''One concession?'' He crooked a single dark brow. ''Now you have me curious. Go on, what is it?''

Lifting her chin, she cleared her throat and met his eyes. ''I believe the laird and Nidaba would exercise discretion, but as for Kenyon an' Lud, I have doubts. Besides, servants are known for gossip, an' there are servants aplenty in this household. An' the rest of the clan, coming an' going all the while.''

''Indeed,'' he said. ''There are. And they do gossip.''

She nodded firmly. ''Aye. Were it known my husband preferred sleepin' in the hall or the stables to sharin' my bed, I'd be shamed, Nicodimus. Ridiculed an' a cause for amusement to the entire clan.''

Nicodimus kept his gaze trained on the ground rather than on her, no doubt displeased with the direction her thoughts had taken. But she forced herself to go on.

''I would ask, Nicodimus, that you at least make a pretense of feelin' . . . affection for me . . . of our marriage bein' a real one, rather than a lie designed to protect me from my own rebellious ways. Allow me to salvage my pride, an' walk without shame among my clan." Still he said nothing. Her voice softer, she rushed on. "After all, 'twill only be for a short while. Only until you leave me again, as you said you would."

He brought his head up sharply, his eyes intense now.

"I'm sorry," she said. "I've angered you. If you find the idea so distasteful, Nicodimus, then please, put it from your mind. I'll deal with the ridicule. The Gods know I have before." She turned away, striding toward the keep, a short distance away.

Nicodimus's hand on her shoulder brought her to a stop. "No, Arianna. 'Tis I who am sorry. My anger was with myself for not thinking of this sooner. Already, I've given the clan reason to talk, by riding off alone on our wedding night the way I did. I'll not give them any more."

She didn't turn around, for if she did, he would see the tears that burned inexplicably in her eyes. "Thank you, husband."

"I will say I went riding to give you time to prepare for me," he said, softly. "And as for your own jaunt tonight, the tale will be . . ." He thought for a moment, and when he spoke again, his voice was different. Quieter than before, and slightly coarse. "The tale will be that my passion for my chaste young bride was such that it frightened her. That she ran away, and that I fetched her back home only to ravage her still more."

As he spoke, his hand on her shoulder moved in what might have been an unintended caress. Soft, his touch. Calloused, his palm on her tender skin, she felt it even through the robe that covered her. The words he spoke brought a foreign longing alive in the pit of her stomach, and made her feel breathless and warm.

"'Tis . . . a good tale," she whispered. "I . . . I am feelin' a mite ill, Nicodimus. My stomach is behavin' quite badly just now. Flutterin' an' . . . odd."

When he said nothing, she chanced a look over her shoulder at him. He offered a strained smile, and swept her hair away from her forehead with a featherlight touch. "You'll be fine," he told her gently. "The feeling . . . will pass."

He didn't sound certain of that. Nonetheless, he turned her 'round, and gripping her elbow, walked her to the doors. But when they strode through the great hall, they were greeted by worried questions from a half dozen people. Joseph, Nidaba, and Kenyon and Lud, all while a handful of Joseph's men looked on with speculative expressions.

Nicodimus met her eyes once, and she saw the silent message in them. His pretense would begin now. Ignoring them all, he scooped Arianna up into his arms, and strode with her to the far end of the room and the stone stairway there. And as he did he spoke, his tone intimate, but loud enough so they could hear. "I'll be gentler this time, my love. I promise." And before mounting the first step, he bent and pressed his mouth to hers.

Arianna's heart nearly beat a hole through her chest. And yet that great emptiness remained. Oh, if only this were real. If only it could someday be . . . real.

I only wanted to protect her. No, that wasn't entirely true. I wanted her. I knew that. My body craved hers the way any healthy man's body would crave that of a beautiful woman . . . especially knowing that woman wanted him, too. Before, I had been half convinced Arianna would seduce me into her arms . . . into her bed . . . before we'd been married a week. I had told myself I would resist her, but I had already known I could never withstand her charms for very long.

But tonight . . . tonight everything had changed. *She* had changed. Suddenly so willing to agree to my terms. Vowing to leave me alone, and to have me play the part of the passionate husband only in front of the others. And I had realized then that not having her, not taking her, was again a possibility. Attainable, perhaps with ease.

That knowledge made me want her more than ever, however foolish such a thing may seem. So that when I spoke the tale I would spread among the clan, I saw the images of it in my mind. Fetching my runaway bride home, and carrying her up to our chamber to savor every inch of her, to exercise all of my husbandly rights. I had grown aroused beyond endurance at the thought, and more so when I realized she had as well. Stomach ailment, indeed. My innocent bride did not even recognize raw desire for what it was.

When I scooped her up, held her against me, promised to be gentle, and then tasted her succulent mouth, my desire for her burned still hotter, and for just an instant on that darkened stairway, I allowed myself to savor the fantasy . . . then became lost in it.

Hands tangling in her hair, I pressed her mouth open wide, and licked inside with my tongue. My hands began to caress the parts of her I held, one in perfect reach of a firm, rounded breast, and the other stroking her outer thigh. I felt her nipple harden against my palm, and nearly groaned with the force of the need that rocked through me. And all the while my feet carried her faster to the top of the stairway, then down the corridors. I kicked the chamber door open when I reached it, and strode through to lay her down upon the waiting bed.

It was her hands on my chest that finally made me realize what I was doing to her. My little cat lay breathless, her face flushed, eyes wide and staring up at me. I straightened slowly, pushing a hand through my hair as I turned away. Averting my gaze in shame, I walked to the door, pushed it closed. "I . . . I apologize, Arianna."

On a breathless sigh, she whispered, "I . . . I'd no idea you could be so . . . convincing. For a moment I thought you meant to . . . to . . ."

I looked back at her, but she clamped her lips tight and said no more. How was I to do this? Spend the night at her side and not touch her? It would surely take a saint to accomplish such a feat. I was no saint.

She tried a smile, though it was confused and tremulous. "Surely every person in the place was convinced as well," she suggested. Then slowly, she got to her feet. "'Tis so very warm here, dinna you think? I vow, 'twas not so when I left earlier."

She pulled at the ties that held her robe in place, and tossed it aside without a care.

What I saw then . . .

I could only stare for a long moment. "Arianna," I whispered. I sank to my knees to keep myself from moving any nearer. But I was unable to take my eyes from her body, for it was utterly revealed to me, every part of it, by the sheer fabric she wore. "By the Gods, woman, what do you think I'm made of?"

Blinking, she glanced down at herself, and then went so red the blush was like fire. "Damnation!" she cried, and she spun around, and snatched the coverlet from the bed to hold over her.

But it was too late, for the image of her was burned into my mind. And I knew it would haunt me. Breasts, high and proud, with full, sweet curves, and nipples elongated and dusky rose in color. The pendant she wore resting in between. A belly, flat and tight, and the silken triangle of hair between her slender thighs. Her perfectly rounded buttocks, and the tempting darkness in between. When she'd turned away, she'd aroused me even more.

"Where," I whispered, my voice barely more than a tormented croak, "did you get that . . . that shift?"

Holding the coverlet tight to her, refusing to face me, she answered, and her voice trembled. "Nidaba. I . . . I thought 'twould make you want me as I do . . . did you. I . . . 'twas before I knew, Nicodimus. 'Twas before I agreed to . . . I dinna mean to . . . I simply forgot what I was wearin', you see." She lowered her head. "Sweet heaven, but I've never been more ashamed."

Somehow, though shaking with desire, I managed to get to my feet. Still, I kept my distance. "You've nothing to be ashamed of, Arianna."

"'Twas an underhanded trick I'd planned to play on you. Indeed, you must think I've no shame at all. I dinna intend—"

"I know. It is all right." But the knowledge was there . . .

what she'd been planning. To seduce me in her innocent way. By the Gods, had I come to this chamber tonight instead of racing away on my horse like a fool . . . I closed my eyes against the desire that raged in me like fire in my blood. And still it came. Against my will, I heard myself say the words I all but bit my tongue to prevent.

"Let go the coverlet, Arianna."

She stiffened, her back to me. "What?"

"Let go the coverlet."

"But . . . but Nicodimus, you said you dinna want . . ."

"I am your husband, am I not?" I whispered. And I knew better, Gods, I knew better than to go on with this. "You wanted me to see you in this gown, and I find . . . I want to see you."

"I . . . I dinna ken you."

"I saved your life. Twice now. Do this for me. Release it, Arianna. Show yourself to me."

Her head tipping up slightly, she unfolded the coverlet in front and opened her arms, paused for just a heartbeat, and let it fall to the floor. I heard her breath catch in her throat when I whispered, "Good. Now turn 'round."

Slowly, she turned. Her chin high, and her eyes alight with too many emotions to name. Pride was there. Desire, too, and perhaps anger at my tone of command. And yet she had obeyed. I knew her too well to think she would have if she had not wanted to.

She stood still as I perused her, more thoroughly this time, slowly, feasting with my eyes on every part of her until her face was red and her breaths shallow and quick. Quicker now, as I moved foward. I was driven by sheer, base desire. My honor, along with any sense of self-preservation, and perhaps any hint of sanity, had fled me now. I only felt need. Hunger. Heat.

"How is your stomach now?" I asked her, when I stood so close I could feel every breath as she exhaled.

"It feels as if a flock of sparrows were set loose inside," she whispered.

Lifting my hands, I ran the backs of my fingers over her breasts, over her nipples. She sucked in a breath. So I turned my hands, and used my fingers, caught the distended peaks between them, and squeezed lightly.

"Nicodimus!"

I increased the pressure until I could feel the thrum of the blood pulsing where I pinched her. Until her every breath was a whimper of longing. And then I eased it, pressed once again, eased, pinched hard, and released her.

She was breathing in short, quick little gasps. "I-I-I dinna understand . . ."

"Shh-shh. You will." I slid my hands down her body, over the whisper-soft nightshift, caressing her belly, her hips, her outer thighs, then slid around to the insides of her legs, and ran my palms slowly upward again. "Part your legs for me, Arianna."

With a gasp that was half sob, she did as I said. I trailed my fingertips upward, and then over the soft mound of hair between her legs. A light touch that made her tremble. Then I parted her folds, and dragged my fingertips over the moist center of her. She released a sigh that stuttered out of her, and a soft "Oooh . . ." I repeated the stroking, a little harder each time, and then I found the tiny nub, the key to her pleasure, and rubbed it hard beneath my fingertips.

Arianna shuddered, her juices wet my hand. I moved my fingers inside her, dipping and stroking, rolling and pinching that pulsing nub harder and harder between my fingers. And she threw her head back, and clutched my shoulders with her hands; and cried my name aloud. I closed my arm tight 'round her waist and held her to me when her knees would have buckled. Working her with my fingers while she shuddered in sweet release. I held her longer still, close in my arms while her body trembled, and relaxed, and her breathing eased.

"What did you do to me, husband?" she asked in a whisper.

"Lie down on the bed," I croaked, my hands on her shoulders, pushing her gently backward as I spoke, for I could not wait. I could not wait to have her. No longer.

She didn't move. Her feet planted, she lifted her head, narrowed her eyes on me. "Nay, I canna."

"You . . . ?"

"I'll nay lie down on the bed for you, Nicodimus. For though you tell me 'tis what you want, I ken you far better than before. An' you dinna want this."

Looking down at her fiery eyes, her moist, succulent lips, I shook my head. "I want it," I told her. "And so do you."

"Nay, you're mistaken there, husband. What you did to me . . . felt like heaven. But if you think mating without any love is what I want, you're sadly mistaken indeed." And firmly she closed her hands over mine, where they rested 'round her tiny waist, and took them away. She turned from me, snatching up the dark robe she'd discarded before, and pulling it around her like armor. Hiding herself from me.

"I cannot love you, Arianna," I told her, lowering my head. "I know you deserve more—"

"Aye, on that you are correct. I do deserve more. But the fact remains, Nicodimus, that though you vow you canna love me, I could quite easily love you. Even more madly than I already do. An' this," she said, waving a hand toward the bed. "This will only make me more likely to do just that. An' perhaps already has." She dropped her gaze as she spoke the last words on a hoarse whisper.

Pushing my hands through my hair, I turned and paced away. I couldn't look at her, look at the bed, without feeling aroused beyond what was sane. I was awash in shame for losing myself to passion and forgetting to protect my fragile little cat's tender heart. "You've the right of it."

"Aye, I do. Just as you wish to protect your heart from being broken again, Nicodimus, I must look out for my own. I'll nay surrender it to you knowin' already that you'll crush it beneath your boot heel. A fool I would be, did I do such a thing."

"And I would be a cruel bastard to ask it of you," I told her softly. "I . . . Arianna, I didn't mean to be . . ."

"You dinna mean to be cruel, Nicodimus, but 'tis cruel you were. First you told me you dinna want me, though it cut me to the quick to hear you say it. An' now, when at last you've convinced me 'tis true, an' best for us both to accept it, you change entirely. Just when I promise to be your wife in name only, just when I steel myself against feelin' anything for you, you go an' . . . an' . . .''

She turned quickly away, but not before I'd seen her squeeze her eyes tight to prevent the tears spilling over. I touched her shoulders, turned her back 'round to face me again. ''I lost myself. You . . . you are a most beautiful woman, Arianna. And if you thought I didn't desire you, if that was what my words made you believe, you were wrong. It was more that I didn't *want* to desire you. But . . . but one look at you . . . in that . . . that scrap, and I simply lost all reason . . . and control. I apologize.''

Her eyes widened, and color crept into her cheeks. She dashed at the drying tears, and smiled tremulously. ''Then . . . you're saying you couldna help yourself.''

''A moment of madness,'' I told her. ''I have few weaknesses, Arianna. Did you ask me what they were, I'd be hard-pressed to name them. But I'm finding I do have one. And that weakness is you. I'm sorry if my desire confused or frightened you, little cat.''

''Dinna be sorry for that, Nicodimus. That you find me . . . desirable . . . makes my heart swell. An' my head, as well, I fear.''

''You've every reason to be proud. You're a remarkable woman, in so many ways.''

''Aye.'' She lifted her head, met my gaze head on. ''That I am.''

Her ready agreement made me smile. I must have been insane. Any other man would have been worshipping at her feet by now, promising her the moon if she'd only love him forever. I, on the other hand, was wishing I could erect barriers to keep her away from my heart, for she seemed to sling arrows at it with every glance, every smile, every word. I knew I had good reason to put up defenses. She was young, far too young to know her own mind, her own heart. Far too young to commit to me in any real way, or be expected to honor that commitment . . . for eternity. Far too young and too beautiful and full of fire to be satisfied by a tired old man such as myself for very long. She'd destroy me if I let myself love her. I would lose her. There was no doubt in my mind of that. It frightened me, right to my bones. Never had I been afraid of any foe. Of any beast or any danger. Never had I doubted my ability to survive.

But I would never survive a war of hearts with Arianna Sinclair. Arianna . . . Lachlan. My bride.

She cleared her throat, and drew my gaze. Innocence personified, with spun gold hair, velvet brown eyes, and satin skin kissed by the sun. She did not look like my potential executioner. A man unafraid to face down a rampaging lion, I thought. Ironic that he trembles in fear of a mere kitten.

"Perhaps 'twould be best if we dinna share the same chamber after all," she whispered.

Her words startled me out of my thoughts. "No, little cat. You're constantly proving yourself the wiser of the two of us, and you were right about the gossips and the damage they could do. I'll stay here, and I promise, lady, I'll not ravish you while you slumber."

"I never thought you would," she said softly, but kept her eyes carefully averted.

She should have, I thought. Because it wasn't beyond the realm of possibility. Sighing deeply, I snatched a tapestry from the wall. Then, drawing my blade, I sliced two lengths of thong from my boot laces, and bound one to each corner. Soon, the tapestry hung suspended in the midst of the room, dividing the portion where she would lie in the bed from the place where I would rest, alone and miserable, upon the floor.

12

I treated Arianna like a princess after that, more careful than I had ever been with anyone, so eager was I to protect her tender heart. I regretted letting my passion grow almost beyond my control, and was determined to offer amends. I was only making matters more difficult for myself, of that I was keenly aware. And yet I could not seem to stop my feet from treading eagerly upon the path to my own destruction.

She . . . mesmerized me. I took such pleasure in her company. Her wit, her laughter, seemed to fill the keep with a spirit which had never lived there before. Or, perhaps, not in a long while. Since the death of Joseph's own wife. But there was more than just this. Before my eyes, Arianna grew from the frightened, wild and rebellious child still mourning her sister, to a young woman filled with life and confidence. Part of what influenced her was, I believe, the companionship Nidaba and I offered. Two who shared her beliefs and practiced her faith. No longer did she question the legitimacy or even the sanity of it.

And more than that, too. Arianna was now a lady, my wife, and everyone in the household treated her as such. There was some resistance at first, but as I had already learned, no one could remain indifferent to Arianna for long.

It wasn't just me, I knew, who was slowly being drawn into the enchantment she spun. Within a fortnight she'd endeared herself to every servant, and many in the clan had gone from whispering suspicions about her to singing her praises, while others had at least grudgingly accepted her. Even the laird's men soon looked upon Arianna with fondness and affection.

Mara was so proud of her daughter. This was another part of Arianna that seemed to be flourishing here—the loving daughter, devoted and attentive to her parents. She had dresses made for her mother, and personally oversaw the early stages of construction for the home Joseph and I were having built for her family. Each day, without fail, she rode into the village to visit her parents. Often she would bring them back with her to dine at the keep, and sometimes she would take me along with her to eat at the humble cottage with them. She even attended morning mass at the village church with them on occasion. I knew how she detested it, so it moved me even more that she should do this just to please them.

The love in that tiny family grew steadily, day by day. And I was somehow included in that love. Arianna's father and I spent a great deal of time together in the stables discussing Joseph's horses as Edwyn repaired saddles, and even hunting together now and again. The man seemed to look upon me as a son, and an old scarred place in my heart seemed to soften and become tender all over again.

But it was not the strengthening bond between Arianna and her family, nor between her family and me, that unnerved me. No, more than anything else, it was my own unwilling fascination with her. I grew more and more reluctant to be away from her, and found myself seeking out her company at every opportunity. When she visited her family, I went along more often than not. Even to mass at the village church. I knew she was spending time with Nidaba every day in secret lessons of combat. I often hid myself to watch. The way she moved, the way she learned so quickly, her grace, her strength . . . all of it entranced me. When I exercised Black, I took her along, and our rides became more for sheer enjoyment than for the good of our mounts. Seeing her beside me upon a galloping mare, her hair flying in the wind, sent such sensations through me that I barely knew how to contain them. Or to understand them. And while these feelings frightened me, even while the warnings whispered through my mind, my heart rejoiced in them.

I told myself it was only friendship I felt for my young bride, a fondness like that of a brother for a sister. And yet I knew, deep down, these were lies. For I wanted her. More with every breath I drew, I wanted her. And each night as I lay in my nest of cushions upon the floor my discomfort and frustration grew. My young, beautiful bride only an arm's length from me, asleep in the bed we were meant to share, seemed to beckon me even from within the realms of her dreams. And often, I would part the makeshift curtain between us, just to look on her as she slept. When she rolled toward me, a soft sigh escaping her slightly parted lips, her hair spread over her pillows, I ached inside. When moonbeams streamed through our window to bathe her in silvery light, I held my breath as I watched her sleeping.

The moon waxed toward full, and with each night, I grew more and more uneasy. For I had promised her we would observe the full moon together, at the Stone Circle, and I felt a certain anxiety growing stronger and stronger within me. What I feared, I did not know. But there was a sense I had always possessed that warned me when danger was near. And I felt it now, looming larger with each night.

Until finally, the moon was full, and I knew the time was at hand.

Arianna was . . . remarkable that Esbat night. She wore a white tunic gown of the style I'd seen worn in Greece on my travels there, no doubt given to her by Nidaba. Silver clasps held the gathered fabric at her shoulders, a silver belt hugged 'round her slender waist. Her long, graceful arms were bare, save the bracelets she wore. And her pendant was fastened, as always, about her slender neck. For the first time I examined the pendant more closely, and the detail of it, the Moon Goddess reclining in the curve of a cradle moon, made me catch my breath. For it was the sort only worn by High Witches . . . but she did not know she was one.

She looked up at me as I entered our chamber, eyes wide, smile uncertain. Then she rose slowly as my eyes remained riveted. Her hair caught up with a silver clasp, then spilling free 'round it. A black cloak I'd given her for tonight was draped over her arm.

"Am I dressed suitably?" she asked me, her voice soft, hesitant.

"You . . . chose very well, Arianna." I'd seen an artist's conception of the Moon Goddess Diana once, and it had looked very much the way Arianna looked now. Silver adorning her, dressed all in white. As for myself, I wore my finest kilt, beneath a dark hooded cloak, and this night, I had donned my own pendant, so similar to Arianna's.

My gaze returned once again to the pendant she wore, I wondered what she knew of its significance. "Arianna . . . that necklace. It is . . . very unusual."

She fingered the piece, her touch reverent, fingers dancing over the circle, and the star in its center, and the cradle moon and reclining goddess that adorned its outer curve. "'Twas one of three gifts The Crones gave to me when I'd studied with them for a year and a day," she said. "'Twas at our last ritual together. I will cherish it always."

I nodded, not telling her I was wearing one very much like it, tucked beneath my cloak. Nor did I tell her that most of the High Witches I had known did as well. I did not usually wear mine when I was here at Stonehaven. I had no wish to advertise what I was to those few who might, somehow, know what the pendant symbolized. It was becoming painfully obvious that more knowledge existed out there than I had ever suspected. The Crones . . . could they have known of our existence? They had given her a High Witch's dagger as well that night as I'd watched in silence.

But how? And if they suspected what Arianna truly was, why had they not told her?

Then again, I thought, why hadn't I?

Perhaps they, too, had believed her too young, and not yet ready to know the truth.

"Come," I said softly, banishing the other thoughts. "It nears midnight." Taking the dark cloak she held, I draped it about her shoulders. It was silken, large, and loose, and had a hood. I had one like it.

"What is the meaning of the cloak, Nicodimus?" she asked as we moved into the corridors and through them, and finally out into the night.

Reaching behind her, I tugged the hood up to cover her golden hair. "It is practical. We blend with the night and are less likely to be seen. The Druids wore white ones much like these during ritual, and I followed their custom. However, with the advent of Christianity and Witch-hunters, I thought it wise to change it to black, at least for the journey to and from the sacred site."

She glanced up at me as we moved side by side over the meadows and into the woods beyond. "Ah. But what of your own people?" she asked as we picked our way along the old path. "Did they wear cloaks for their rites?"

"No. My clan were of the barbaric sort. We spoke to our Gods in solitude, and wore nothing at all, save the colors with which we painted sacred symbols over our bodies."

She blinked as if surprised, then smiled to herself. "I can see why you thought the Druid method might be preferable tonight, then."

I glanced down at the hint of laughter in her voice. But as I did, an image crept into my mind. One of my beautiful Arianna, naked and proud, unashamed, raising her arms and turning her face up to drink in the moonlight. And the image grew. Until I saw myself kneeling before her, dipping my fingers into pots of color, and drawing the ancient sacred symbols upon her pale, soft skin.

I shivered, and she looked up quickly. But when I said nothing, she faced forward again.

Soon the stones of the circle towered before us, and without being told, Arianna stopped and bent to remove her slippers before stepping inside. I nodded my approval and removed my own boots. Then I entered, and tugging the pack from my shoulder, I emptied it, setting its contents upon a large flat stone table in the northernmost quadrant. Wine, and two cups, four candles, and a staff.

"What magick will we work this night, Nicodimus?" Arianna asked me, her voice childlike with excitement.

I smiled down at her in the moonlight. "What do you wish for?"

She lowered her head at once. And I knew I had spoken too quickly. I knew what she wished for. And she knew it was impossible. Yet she spoke it all the same.

"I wish for your love, Nicodimus, but I ken that can never be. I wish for your touch . . . but nay for the consequences of knowing it. For those would only be pain for us both. An' I'd nay use magick to gain either of those things, for were they not given freely, they'd be worse than useless to me."

I did not speak. I could not, for I knew not what to say.

She lifted her head again, eyes meeting mine. "So instead I'll wish for something far simpler an' more mundane. A cooling North wind, to ease the dreary autumn heat."

Relief that she could smile in spite of the pain I'd caused her—was still causing her—made me breathe again. "Then a cooling wind it shall be. A wise choice, for the heat is wearing on the clan, making their tempers short. You've called forth the winds before?"

"Aye," she said. "With The Crones to guide me. Thrice we did so, an' each time the gentle breezes came within a fortnight of our casting." She tilted her head. "An' you, Nicodimus?"

I nodded once. "Usually the winds come within a day of my conjuring." I bent to make the preparations, building a small fire in the center of the circle, and lighting it. Then I placed a candle in each of the four directions, just at the edges of the circle. Returning to the center, I sat for a time, gazing into the flames. Arianna did likewise, and I knew she was letting her mind go quiet, gathering the energies around her. It seemed we both felt ready to proceed at the same moment, for we looked up simultaneously. And in silence, I took a flaming limb from the fire. I walked to the North candle, focused on the energies of Earth, and lit the candle's wick. Arianna met me in the center, taking the limb from my hand. She moved to the East candle, closed her eyes for a moment, and lit it. I could almost feel the Air move as she summoned its elemental energies to join us here. I repeated this process in the South, for the element of Fire, and she in the West, for Water.

Meeting at the stone table again, we locked gazes, and I saw something in her eyes . . . the swirling reflections of moonlight and fire. A shiver worked up the back of my neck. I took a breath, poured the wine, handed Arianna her cup. She held it up, as if to capture the light of the moon in the glistening scarlet liquid, as she chanted.

I am one with the light from above.
An' one with the force from below.
One with the beasts of the wild
One with the green things that grow.
One with the moon, one with the sun
One with the Earth and the Sky
One with All since afore I was born,
An' will be long after I die.

Then closing her eyes, lowering the goblet, she drank its contents. I downed mine as well, and walked her back to the fire. Dipping a hand into the deep pocket of the hooded cloak I wore, I drew out a palmful of herbs, and tossed them into the flames. They hissed and heated, burned fragrantly.

Smiling, Arianna reached her small hand into my pocket, and repeated what I had done. Then I faced North, palms up in front of me, and chanted in a long forgotten tongue the words to call the North wind.

Her eyes as she watched me were huge and luminous. And before I knew what she intended, she faced me, and pressed her palms flat to mine. The tingling contact rocked through me, right to my core, and the warmth remained long after that initial shock faded.

I felt it then. A power like I'd never known surging from below and above at the same time. And the place where it gathered until it nearly burned, was the very place where Arianna's palms pressed flat to mine. For just a moment, I swore an amber glow emanated from our joined hands.

There was a deep humming sound, as the wind picked up force, blowing through the trees, whistling over twigs, and groaning past limbs. Then it grew to a roar. The mighty oaks 'round us seemed to bow beneath its force. Arianna's hair blew and danced and her white gown seemed alive. Leaves and twigs swirled 'round us like miniature cyclones, and the air cooled so rapidly my skin shivered. My gaze swung 'round, seeking shelter. But before I could think on that further, the air filled with snow. Snow! In the midst of a highland autumn!

It coated my garments and melted there, wetting me to the skin in a matter of seconds. Amazed, I faced Arianna.

But my little cat stood with her face turned up to the snow, and her arms outspread as it fell on her. Turning in a slow circle, she faced me again, a look of wonder in her eyes as her hair grew damp, and crystalline flakes sparkled on her cheeks like tears. Smiling, then laughing aloud, she flung her arms 'round my neck.

"Do you see what we've done!" she cried. "Nicodimus, this is powerful, this magick we work together!"

Her body close to mine, my arms tight 'round her waist, I nodded against her snow-damp hair. "I've never seen the like."

She drew back just a little. Enough so she could look up at me, her face only inches from mine. "The Crones said 'twould be so. They said the power of magick is strongest when there is balance . . . between feminine and masculine energies, such as those of a man an' a woman."

"Yes." I nodded my agreement. "I've been taught much the same . . . and yet it has never been quite this . . . startling."

"Ah, Nicodimus, do you nay ken, even now? 'Tis nay just any combination of man an' woman who could bring about such a force as this. But of you an' me, husband. Two who . . . belong to each other."

"Arianna . . . I—"

She held up a hand. "I know, dinna speak it. I know you canna love me," she whispered. "An' I've no wish to hurt you. But I know you want me as I do you, Nicodimus. An' I'm tired of protectin' myself from future hurt by refusin' to live life. I'm tired of fightin' against feelin's over which I've no control. 'Tis like fightin' against nature."

I stared down at her. She stepped back another pace, and drew the cloak from her shoulders, tossing it to the ground. "I know you canna love me, husband. But I can love you." Her hands went to the shoulders of the tunic, freeing the clasps there, and the dress fell down to her feet as if washed away by the snow. "Let me love you," she whispered. "Just this once . . ."

I stood staring at her. Perfect, her skin glistening with the snowflakes that drifted down on her. Breasts round and soft, nipples growing stiffer with each icy flake that touched them. She stepped over the discarded dress, closer to me.

And what was I to do? How could I . . . or any man, resist such an offering? Before I could even consider my answer, my hands were on her, palms skimming over the wet skin of her belly, cupping her breasts, caressing her. I drew her tight to me, and bent my head to capture her mouth. I tasted the snow on her lips, and the warmth beyond them when I pushed my tongue inside. I fed at her mouth as her yearning body pressed against mine, and I dreamed of drinking every melting droplet from her skin. I slid my lips to her cheek and down slowly over her neck. She tipped her head back and moaned softly as I nipped and suckled the tender skin there.

Lower. I licked the beaded moisture from her shoulder. And all the way down her arm to the inner bend of her elbow, and she cried out when my tongue darted over that sensitive flesh. I moved to her hand, sucking the moisture from each finger, and then kissed a hot path across her belly and began again at her other arm.

She was trembling, clinging to me in order to stay upright when I moved at last to one tender breast. I took my time, circling the peak slowly with my tongue before finally closing my lips on the crest. I drew on her there, and she shivered. I suckled harder, and her fingers curled in my hair. I bit lightly, and she pressed herself closer.

"Nicodimus," she whispered. "Oh, but you give me such pleasure. An' I . . . I dinna ken how . . ."

I bit again, and this time she tugged against my teeth, whimpering in rapture at the sweet touch of pain. My hand slipped between her legs, and I touched her inner lips, tracing them, feeling the moisture there for me. I drew a forefinger higher, circling the tiny nub that was the key to her pleasure, and then touching it, rubbing it, pinching it so that her knees began to buckle, all the while still feeding at her breast.

My other arm 'round her waist anchored her to me, else she'd have surely fallen to her knees.

"Nay," she whispered, and it was a plea. I pinched her harder, and her voice grew hoarse. "You must tell me what to do, Nicodimus. Tell me how to please you."

I closed my eyes in sweet anguish. "You please me, Arianna, with every breathless whisper, and every sigh and every touch." I slipped my fingers inside her, gently, carefully. "And to see you in the height of pleasure will please me even more."

"Make love to me, Nicodimus," she whispered.

I lifted her then, and carried her to the stone table. My cloak I flung down beneath her, then I lay her upon it. Quickly I took off my clothes until I stood naked in the falling snow. And gently I parted her legs and watched as the snowflakes kissed her secret places. Then I bent to kiss and lick every droplet away until she squirmed and cried out and opened wider to my questing tongue.

I moved upward until I lay atop her, and carefully, I entered her slick, tight passage. The wind swirled icy cold 'round us, and the wet snowflakes fell upon my back. I moved deeper into her, and still deeper. I felt her pain, brief and sweet as I tore through the barrier of her maidenhood, and I held her still beneath me, waiting, giving her time.

Timidly, hesitantly, she moved her hips against mine, taking me deeper. And again, drawing away and moving once more. Fire licked at my loins, and I took her then. Deep and hard and fast, I took her, and she lifted her hips to meet my every thrust. I kissed her fiercely, swallowing each breathless whisper, each sigh, each moan. And finally, her entire body tensed around me, squeezing and drawing on me, convulsing around me until I felt myself shatter inside her. I pumped my seed into her, and with it, it seemed, my very soul. And then I eased my body down beside hers, and held her, and wondered how I could ever let her go again.

Oh, Gods, she'd done it. She'd made her way into my heart. I knew, with everything in me, she would break it before she was done.

13

" 'Twas wonderful, Nicodimus. I . . . thank you."

He sat up slightly, blinking at her in surprise. But then his face changed even as Arianna lay in his arms, feeling more alive than she ever had. He frowned, tilting his head to one side. "What . . . what is that sound?"

Arianna listened, but heard nothing. "I canna hear—"

"Shh-shh." He held up a hand, sat a bit straighter. "Horses. Oh, Gods, battle!" He surged to his feet as Arianna's heart leapt into her throat.

"But Nicodimus, I hear nothing!" Even as she said it, she rushed to retrieve her garments.

"It is yet another part of being immortal, Arianna. The sharpening of the senses . . ." He struggled into his own clothing and drew his dagger, then came to stand over her, his eyes alert and scanning the trees around them as she finished dressing. As if he'd protect her should any threat appear.

And that gave her to know he truly believed there was trouble afoot. "Nicodimus . . . what is happening?"

He closed his hands around hers and stared intently into her eyes. "I want you to stay here. Right here, Arianna, wrapped in the cloak and concealed amongst the shadows of these stones. The clouds have covered the moon. If you are still, no one will see you, even should they look, and you will be safe—''

''Nay! I'll nay stay safe while you rush into danger!''

He shook his head firmly. ''I must go, little cat, and there's no time to argue with you. The village . . . I believe the village is under attack. Joseph and the boys . . . Nidaba—''

''Mam!'' she cried. Suddenly it seemed her stomach turned in on itself. For now the sounds were reaching her ears as well, and in the distance, an eerie glow began to reach into the dark sky, despite the falling snow. She screamed aloud, hands pressed to either side of her head as panic took hold of her heart.

''I'll see to your family, I vow it, Arianna. Please, please, remain here, safe.''

Trembling from head to toe, she nodded, knowing even as she did so that she lied to her husband. She lied blatantly. For no force on earth could have kept her from her family.

He studied her face for one lingering moment, then drew her dark cloak tight about her, and led her to a shadowy niche between two of the standing stones, where one had toppled slightly and leaned against another. ''In here. You'll be all but invisible, in here.''

She nodded, eyeing the cavelike space. Then Nicodimus gripped her shoulders and pulled her against him. He kissed her long and hard. ''Stay safe,'' he said, and his tone was one of command. ''I'll come back for you.''

''Aye, Nicodimus. Go, now. Go do what you must.''

With a quick nod, he turned to leave her. But she rushed after him, a sudden knot of cold fear hitting her fiercely in the chest. Flinging her arms around him, she fought to control her sobs. ''Oh, my love, please take care. Stay alive, for though I've fought against it I—''

''I know,'' he said softly, stroking her hair. ''I know. Go now, hide and await my return.''

She nodded hard, pressed her lips once to his warm neck, then fled to the spot where he had told her to hide. He watched until she had crawled into the darkness between the stones, and only then did he hurry away.

But the instant Nicodimus was out of her sight, Arianna crept out of her hiding place, and picked her way quickly and silently through the woods, taking the shortest route to the village. And as she went the sounds of battle grew louder. Shouts, screams, thundering hoofbeats. The snap and hiss of fire. The snow fell and fell, and as she finally drew nearer the village, she realized the shouts and cries were coming less and less frequently with each step she ran. Until, only the hoofbeats, and the crackling of flames remained.

What she found when she emerged from the trees made her heart turn to stone.

Cottages burning, flames licking at their thatched roofs, and hissing against the snow; fueled by something that burned despite the wetness from above, but burned more slowly because of it. And as she raced closer, she saw torches born by men on horseback who thundered through the village. Swords and clubs smote the few crofters who ran like frightened animals through the muddy pathways. And when the clouds skittered away from the face of the moon, she saw the bodies, battered and bloodied. *Everywhere.*

"Mam? Da?" she whispered. Her own family's cottage stood in the distance. Arianna paused to bend down and scoop up a discarded blade as she moved urgently toward it. Her dagger was at her hip, aye, but she wanted something bigger. The sword hung heavy in her hand, too long for her, its tip dragging through the mud when she stumbled. She expected to be struck down before she reached her parents, and quickened her pace at the thought. But the darkness and her cloak must have been her aids, for none of the rampaging beasts seemed to notice her. Most were far too busy, looting the homes, murdering the few who remained alive, and putting the torch to every building in sight.

She heard a cry from within her parents' house. Her mother's cry . . . a cry that was cut off before it ended. With a growl of absolute fury, she lifted the sword high, raced forward, and burst through the door.

Her mother lay upon the floor, limp, her head bloodied, while a soldier bent over her, tearing at her dress. Without hesitation, Arianna brought the blade flashing down with all her might, aiming for the man's neck.

He cried out only once as his blood shot from his veins, and then he crumbled at her feet, his head tipped at an impossible angle. Arianna stepped over him, giving him not a second look. She rushed to her mother, knelt over her, gripped her shoulders.

"Mam! Mam, 'tis all right. I'm here now an' . . . an' . . . Mam?" She shook her mother, but saw now what she'd failed to see before. Or refused to. The once bright eyes were already filmed over by the glaze of death. Staring sightlessly, their light forever extinguished. "Nay!" Arianna cried. "Nay, this canna be!"

Rising to her feet, she backed away, turning her gaze from the sight of her mother there on the floor, only to see her father lying still in a corner, a dagger in his belly, a pool of blood around him.

Arianna's head began to spin. She did not want to believe any of this, for it could not be real. She had barely survived losing her sister, but to lose her parents, too, and just when they'd begun to mend the rift between them? Nay, 'twas too much to bear.

She lifted her head to gaze into the dark, snow-damp night, and saw the herd of swine who had brought this destruction upon her people, her family, her clan. Looking down once again at the sword in her hand, she muttered, "I will kill them. Aye, I'll kill them all!"

In a fury she raced into the wet snow, bare feet slapping through the mud, as she attacked one man after another. Her rage drove her, gave her strength. She killed more than she could count. Until at last, when she lifted the blade high above her head about to bring it down on another of them, she felt her body pierced from behind, and went still, her mouth agape, eyes bulging. Looking down, she saw the point of a blade protruding from her belly, blood flowing to soak the white tunic dress she'd worn to please Nicodimus.

Nicodimus. Gods, where was he? Where on earth was he?

She dropped to her knees, and knew death would come soon to claim her. So be it, then. 'Twas preferable to going on, dealing with such a crippling loss. No one left to her but a husband who could never love her. A husband who would leave her in the end just as Raven, her sister had done. Just as her beloved teachers and her parents had each done in turn. She would lose him. She had lost them all.

Better than living, was dying just now. Better than living . . .

Arianna fell, facedown in the mud—never having glimpsed the face of the man who had killed her.

I never should have left her alone. It was a mistake that led to my destruction, and for it I take full blame. Things may well have ended differently had I kept my promise to protect her family. But those promises were words I never should have spoken, wrenched from me without forethought, and my judgment was poor. I wanted only to comfort her, to take away the pain I saw in her soft brown eyes. To take away the fear. To be her hero, I suppose. Foolish. Foolish to make promises I could not keep simply because I loved the girl.

Yes, it was true. I loved her. In spite of my best efforts not to. Arianna had conquered me. I hated the feeling, the vulnerability it created in me. And yet it was that feeling that drove me to protect her and all those she cared about. A feeling that made me willing to face battle—to face anything at all—for her.

So I spied the flames, heard the thundering beats of hooves, and knew the village and clan were under attack by a large number of soldiers, whose motives I could not imagine. But I simply knew that this was no ordinary raid. I raced to the keep for weapons, and to stir Joseph and his sons in case they remained asleep and unaware. Every man in the household would be needed to defend the village. Every last one.

I broke from the woods, and raced across the moor, up the hill to the front gates, my lungs burning, my body alive with immortal power.

It was only when I found the gates flung open that I slowed, and took more careful stock of things.

The huge wooden door leading into the great hall was not open, but lying flat—a battering ram made of half a tree trunk dropped upon it. And from the gaping, dark windows, thin spirals of smoke whispered forth.

"Nidaba," I whispered. "Joseph . . ."

Forcing myself to pause, to take care, I slipped inside, keeping to the shadows. The intruders were long gone, now. But everywhere I looked were signs of their carnage: broken bodies were strewn on the rushes, slaughtered like sheep. I found Joseph at the base of the stone stairs, still in his nightclothes. His neck broken. His sons had never even made it out of their chambers. Both of them lay dead within. And of Nidaba . . . of Nidaba there was no sign.

My heart clenched and my blood boiled. Damn these bastards, whoever they were! Attacking a peace-loving clan, murdering Joseph, a man who had shown nothing but kindness and understanding to all who'd known him. My friend. He had been my friend, and one of the few I still possessed.

But I had no time to mourn, nor even to bury him. Kicking open the bolted door of the weapons room, wondering why the invaders had not bothered to loot it to the bare walls, I snatched a sword and scabbard and belted them in place. Ignoring the rest, for I'd no need of maces nor shields nor crossbows, I strode quickly outside again, needing the air to cleanse the stench of spilled blood from my lungs.

Glancing toward the stables, I saw the tongues of flame beginning to lick up the sides. No doubt the straw and hay inside had been smoldering even before I had arrived. The doors stood closed up tight, as if the bastards had not even bothered to steal the horses, but simply wanted to destroy them. Destroy everything associated with this clan.

Gods, who could have cause to hate the clan so much?

I ran, yanking the stable doors open, and in only seconds, managed to send several horses galloping to safety with no more than a slap of my hand. The last few were panicked by the flames, and I had no time to lead them free one by one. Not when Mara and Edwyn were in their cottage at the mercy of the attackers. I gripped Black and leapt upon him without benefit of saddle or rein. He obeyed as easily as he always had, and leapt free of the burning building with barely a flick of his eye. He'd seen fire before, Black had. The stallion knew no fear.

Leaning low, I kicked him into motion, and we sailed through the night, pounding ever nearer the village, but my heart sank as I saw the yellow glow battling the snow-drenched darkness, and I whispered the names of my wife's parents as I raced closer. I drew my sword, rounded a bend in the road, and then tugged Black to a halt as I saw the destruction. The death all 'round me. The ruin. There was nothing left. Nothing.

And the soldiers were gone. They had rained terror and destruction down upon an unsuspecting, peaceful clan, and then left just as quickly as possible. Tears burned in my eyes as I moved closer to the saddle maker's cottage. Because there was no hint of life from within. No one moved or breathed. I heard no tears, no cries for help, though the thatched roof was already alight with flame. No moans of pain. I knew death, and this was it. I felt it in the very night, heightening my awareness with every wet snowy droplet that struck my skin. I was the only man alive here.

Black halted in front of Arianna's former home, and I dismounted slowly. My boots sticking in the blood-soaked mud, I stepped inside. And then I felt the pain rip through me as I saw them. Mara, her head caved in. Edwyn with a mortal blade wound to the gut. And in the corner . . . who was that?

A soldier, one of the attackers, his head nearly severed. Someone had fought back then. Tried to help. But too late, too late.

My eyes burned with unshed tears as I thought of telling

Arianna that her beloved parents had been brutally killed. I had been unable to tell her the truth about her own nature, to spare her the pain of knowing she would one day outlive all those she loved. But now that day had come all the same, and there was no way I could spare her this. No way.

And I'd promised her. I had *promised her* that I would protect them.

"I'm sorry, Arianna," I whispered. "Damnation, if I had only come here sooner. If I had only . . ." But I shook my head, for my words and my regrets could not change what had befallen her family tonight.

Edwyn . . . he had been as kind to me as if I were his own son. And Mara . . . I recalled her smiling face, the reborn joy in her eyes as she and her firstborn had found each other again.

Gone, now, both of them. Their precious lives snuffed out without a care, without a cause.

My every instinct told me to go after the vermin who had wreaked such tragedy on Stonehaven. They had headed north, and their trail—the hoofmarks of so many horses—would be easily followed. But I needed to return to the Stone Circle, to Arianna. Thank the Fates, I thought, that I had left her there. The soldiers had headed in the opposite direction. She was safe. They would pass nowhere near her.

Stepping outside, I reached for Black's mane to pull myself up, but as I did, I glanced down, and a gleam caught my eye. Not a blade, but something silver, stomped into the mud. Instinct caused my stomach to quake, and I dreaded what I would find. I bent, and picked it up.

A silver pendant with a cradle moon adorning one curve. Exactly like the one Arianna had been wearing. And it had been lying here, right outside this house of death—her parents' home.

"No," I whispered. "No, it cannot be hers. She wouldn't have come here, she couldn't have. . . ." Terrified, I scanned the bodies crumpled hither and yon, but I did not see the ethereal white tunic she had worn, nor the gleam of her spun gold hair. Not at all. Still, my gut was telling me what my mind already knew. It was hers. She had been here . . . and something terrible had befallen her.

I draped her pendant 'round my neck to join my own there. Then, leaping upon Black, I whirled him around, kicked his flanks hard with my heels, and headed at breakneck speed back toward the Stone Circle. But the emptiness in the pit of my stomach told me even before I reached the sacred place, that I would not find my bride there, either.

A jolt bent Arianna's body backward so suddenly and so acutely she felt as if her spine would snap and her lungs burst from the force of her gasp.

Then slowly, her body eased again, and she opened her eyes. But even as she did, memory came flooding back, and she squeezed them tight against the onslaught. The attack. The bodies. Her parents lying dead . . .

"Nay, it canna be," she muttered, and turned instinctively into the shoulder upon which her head rested. The arms around her tightened, and a deep voice whispered, "There, lass, it will be all right now, I promise you that."

And that voice, she realized, head coming up fast, eyes widening, was *not* Nicodimus's.

He held her to him, seated behind her on a horse; a large man, and strong from the feel of him. She found herself staring into pale blue eyes that reminded her of a wolf in winter, and ashen hair that gleamed nearly white in the moonlight. Not with age, but with the fairness of its hue. His face was soft, with a gently rounded chin and cheekbones, and a bulbous nose. No harsh angles, no cragginess like her Nicodimus. But softness. He seemed a gentle soul, this man who held her in his arms.

And yet she stiffened, pressing her hands to his shoulders to hold herself away.

"Aye, lass, 'tis natural you'd be confused now. But you've naught to fear from me, I promise you." He studied her face. "'Twas your first death, was it not?"

Her brows bunched together, she whispered, "First . . . death?" And then she recalled the sensation of being run through, the horror of looking down to see a blade thrusting out of her own belly, and of falling dead into the mud.

Dead.

"Nay," she whispered very softly. "Nay, 'tis nay possible. I . . . I *died.* I . . ." Lowering her chin she saw the bloodstains all over the front of her tunic, and even the slit in the cloth where the blade had torn through. Hooking her fingers in that tear, she ripped it wider, and then searched her skin, her belly, for some mark or cut or flaw. But only found the stains of drying blood. She pressed her fingers to the spot where it seemed she could still feel the phantom pain of the wound . . . but there was nothing there. No injury. Not so much as a nick nor a scratch.

Wide-eyed, she lifted her head once more.

"You canna mean to tell me you dinna know, lassie! You're immortal. A High Witch, just like me. Nicodimus must have told you. . . . Damnation, he dinna tell you at all, did he, child?"

She blinked rapidly, searching her mind, hearing the warnings it whispered. "Immortal? Nay . . . nay, it canna be. . . ."

"You're the living proof that it is, lass. It is. You're alive, and unmarred by the blade. I found you lifeless in the mud, but knew you for what you were, and vowed to take you away from all the carnage. And from the reach of Nicodimus."

Nay. She would never be beyond the reach of Nicodimus. He would find her. He would come for her. But this man . . . this man knew his name. "You . . . you know my husband?" she asked.

"Aye. He's been my arch enemy for centuries, lass. One of the Darkest of the Dark, he is—"

"Nay!" Arianna felt her anger rise to drown out her confusion and grief. "My Nicodimus is good and pure, and I'll kill any man who says otherwise!"

He studied her for a long moment, drinking in, it seemed, the anger flashing from her eyes. "I can see you believe it to be true. I vow, lady, at least now I understand why a woman like you would bind herself to a man such as he. You simply dinna ken the truth."

She narrowed her eyes on him. "I'll never believe a

word spoken against my husband," she all but hissed at him. "Who are you that I should take heed of a word you utter?" Then she tilted her head. "You're one of *them*, aren't you? One of those who attacked my village!"

He nodded slowly. "Aye, lass, though it pains me to have to tell you. I am their chieftain."

"Bastard!" Arianna clenched her hands into fists and pounded his chest. But he easily caught her wrists and held her still, though she struggled. His horse came to a halt.

"I dinna fault you, lass. Indeed, I canna. But if you'll only hear me out. I tried to get to the village in time to halt the bloodshed. I tried, I vow it on the name of my own father. But I was too late. And my men had already done that poor defenseless village to death."

Grief made her weak, and she stopped her fighting. "Aye, and they'd done my mam to death, as well, and my da along with her. An' I vow I'll see every one of them die before I rest."

His eyes, soft with sorrow, moved gently over her face, and releasing her wrists, he stroked her hair. "Gods, but I'm sorry. More sorry than you can know. The men . . . they were crazed. Their chieftain—my older brother, Kohl—was murdered . . . by your husband, lass. By our lifelong enemy, Nicodimus, that Dark Witch of old."

"'Twas nay murder! Nicodimus had to kill him in order to stay alive!"

He shook his head. "An' I suppose he gave you some reason why he had to take my brother's heart as well, did he not? But pretty one, only the Dark take the hearts of their victims. Only they and no others."

She shook her head, confused. Nicodimus had told her that . . . but then he'd said he'd had to take Kohl's heart to set his spirit free.

"The men adored Kohl," this fellow went on. "And they . . . took vengeance on the village. One lad knew what was about to occur, and raced off to find me. But I dinna arrive in time, and the men, without a leader . . . acted in anger and unleashed a mighty fury upon Stonehaven." Again, he shook his head slowly. "It pains me more than

I can say that your family perished in the attack, lass."

She studied his face. "You're naught but a liar," she whispered, but his words made her wonder. Not about Nicodimus—nay, never that, he was good and true, and she loved him—but about the rest. Perhaps this man *had* tried to stop what had happened.

Then more things clicked into place in her mind. "Your name is Marten. Nicodimus told me about you . . . the brother of Kohl, and of Nicodimus's wife of so long ago. Anya."

"Aye, I imagine he told you much. I only hope you'll nay believe the worst of me too easily. Nicodimus . . . he hates me. It has always been so."

"An' you hate him in return," she whispered. "Nonetheless, he dinna tell me that he was one of the Dark Ones, nor that you were one of the Light."

"Nay, lass. Nor did he tell you that you yourself were an immortal High Witch just as we are."

She blinked. "He . . . he knew?"

"Of course he knew."

Shaking her head slowly, she knew it couldn't be true. "Nay, he'd have told me if he knew. He . . . he trusted me with all the other secrets. Why would he keep this one from me? Nay, he'd have told me. He would!"

"Perhaps," Marten said slowly. "I suppose 'tis possible he dinna know of your nature. Tell me, did he ever see the mark of the crescent moon upon your flank, child? The one that marks all immortals as who and what they are?"

She felt the arrows of his words piercing her soul. The crescent birthmark. Nicodimus bore one. So did Nidaba, and so did she. He knew that. So if it was the mark of immortality . . .

"And has he ever touched you, lass?"

Frowning harder, she said, "I dinna ken your meanin'. What are you—?"

"Take your hands from my shoulders, pretty one. Just for a moment, an' you'll understand."

Still confused, she did, sitting away from him slightly, taking her hands from his shoulders.

"Now, put them back again."

With a nod, she lay her palms lightly upon his shoulders once more. Immediately, a jolt of something passed through her. The same sort of jolt she felt when she touched Nicodimus, or Nidaba.

"The initial contact you make with any other immortal will give you just such a sensation, child," Marten explained slowly, patiently. "So even if Nic had never seen your birthmark, he'd have felt what you were the first time he touched you. Do you ken?"

She nodded, very slowly. So it was true. Nicodimus had known what she was. He had to have known. And yet, she defended him. "If he did keep the truth from me, then he likely had reasons for doin' so."

"Aye. No doubt he and that she-wolf of his planned to take your young heart, once it grew powerful enough to sustain one or the other of them."

"Dinna be foolish!" she shouted. "Nicodimus is my husband, and Nidaba my friend!"

"Aye. And the two of them sharing a bed for nigh' on eight centuries now, lass. Can you not see what is before your face?"

She felt as if he'd punched her in the belly with a fist made of cold iron. Blinking with reaction, battling tears, she whispered, "Nicodimus . . . and Nidaba?"

"Lovers, child. Lovers all along, even right under the nose of my sweet-natured sister, who died more of heartache than childbirth all those years ago. For she knew."

She shook her head slowly. "Nicodimus . . . he loved Anya."

"Loved her? Nay, child, he took her. Destroyed her village and her family and took her as his captive. By force, he took her."

She lifted her gaze. "Just the way your men destroyed my village, Marten? An' just the way you've now taken me?"

"Aye, lady. I'm afraid so. I'm sorry your life is being turned 'round because of it, but justice is justice, and for Nicodimus, 'tis long overdue."

Dropping her chin, releasing a sigh, she whispered, "You're so wrong about him."

"An' if I'm wrong about him, then where is he? Hmm? He was nay among the dead, I can tell you as much. Neither he, nor the dark woman who owns his heart and soul. Nay, lady, he dinna come looking for you, nor so much as try to protect your family. He vanished, he and his Nidaba. Vanished, without givin' you a second thought. He lied to you, little one. He lied to you about what he truly is, and kept the truth of your own nature a secret from you. And then he abandoned you. He's not worthy of a woman so fine as you are. Oh, sweet lady, I dinna even know your name."

Blinking, eyes burning, she whispered, "My name is Arianna. Arianna Sinclair . . . Lachlan."

"Arianna," he said slowly. "Dinna cry, Arianna. He's nay worthy of a single tear from such as you."

But the tears fell all the same.

Her captor pulled her gently closer, his touch exquisitely gentle, his body warm and soft. "I'll make it all up to you, lady. I vow I will. You'll know nothing but joy whilst you reside in my keep. Nothing but joy."

14

I stood in the center of the Stone Circle, hands clenched, arms taut and quivering as I howled my rage. My cry echoed through the forest and the surrounding moors, bounding from the silent monoliths that surrounded me. And yet no one heard. There was no reply.

Arianna was gone. Gone.

"I'll find you," I promised hoarsely when the echoes of my fury finally died away. "I swear to you, Arianna, I'll find you, no matter where they've taken you. And when I do I'll kill the bastards. I vow, if they've harmed a hair on your head, I'll . . ." My voice dropped to an anguished whisper. "Gods, don't let them harm her."

I lowered my head, staring through pools of tears at the pendent I clutched in my hands. Tears. How long had it been since I'd shed them? A century, perhaps? Longer?

Dammit to hell, why was I still pretending? "I love you, lass," I finally admitted in a whisper, wishing for all the world that I could just hear her voice, that joyful lilt, one last time. "I love you. I should have told you. But I will, I vow it, I will. And I'll make it right again, make all of this up to you—somehow."

My hand fisted 'round the pendant, and then I brought

it to my lips, and kissed it to seal my vow. Silently, I fastened it 'round my own neck. Then I mounted Black, drew the horse about, and kicked his sides. Black lunged into a gallop, and I headed north, as I knew the attackers had done. Their trail was well laid and easily followed. I would catch the blackguards before this night was through.

"Stop looking for him, Arianna," her captor said, his voice soft, his eyes gentle. "Nicodimus will nay come for you. The sooner you accept that harsh truth, the better 'twill be."

She shook her head slowly. "He will. He'll come for me, you'll see." But would he? Maybe the more important question was, *could* he? Oh, but she was no fool. She knew well enough what was happening here. This Marten and she were alone, no one within sight nor earshot around them. Yet there had been dozens upon dozens of warhorses and soldiers in the village. So many men. Obviously, they had all ridden off in another direction, perhaps to plunder some other village, perhaps to battle some other clan. But wherever they had gone, it was obvious Marten's goal lay elsewhere. His horse's hooves, she noted, were wrapped in thick layers of cloth. And he guided the beast over the hardest terrain, where leaving a sign of their passing would be all but impossible. Marten pushed onward at a terrible pace. The miles seemed to fall away between Arianna and her home, along with all she had known there. All she had ever held dear, all she had loved. Perhaps Nicodimus would be unable to find her, even if he tried.

If he tried.

And what if he didn't? What if all the things Marten had told her . . .

But, nay. That could not be. She knew Nicodimus. Knew him . . . and loved him. She believed in him. Aye, he had kept things from her—vital things she should have been told. She was immortal.

By the Gods, she was immortal. And unsure now, what that meant to her. How it would change her life. She only knew that even the girl she had been only hours before was now lost to her. As lost as her mother and father. As lost as her dear sister. She no longer knew who Arianna Sinclair Lachlan might be, who she would become.

Gods, why had Nicodimus not told her?

She sighed, closing her eyes. If Nicodimus had kept so vital a truth from her, then he must have had some reason. He must have!

He would come for her. And when he did, she realized slowly, through the haze of grief and shock that clouded her mind . . . when he did, she could be with him . . . forever.

Aye, forever. He would not have to watch her grow old and die, as she had believed, for she was immortal, just as he was. And could be with him!

If . . . if he wanted her.

Doubts assailed Arianna then, new ones that had not occurred to her before. For Nicodimus had known these things all along, hadn't he? So maybe he did not want her after all.

I followed the horde of men for three nights before I finally caught up to them. I had not expected them to be moving so quickly. They had left no survivors behind, and had no reason to assume they were being pursued. Why, then? The question dogged me. Why such haste?

If they knew, somehow, that I was following, if they were ready and waiting when I finally arrived at their camp . . .

But, no, it didn't matter. Whether they expected my attack or not, my course would not change. I had to rescue Arianna. I had to find her. Hold her in my arms again, and know that she was all right.

It was full night, the fourth one of my journey, when at last I heard the sounds in the distance that told me they were near. Keeping to the thickest patches of forest, I moved Black slowly, quietly nearer, until I could see by the pale glow of distant fires that they had set up camp for the night. Good. Good.

Tying Black in a grove of pines, I crept closer, walking softly, using the skills I had learned as a warrior long ago, and wondering as I neared what I would find awaiting me in Arianna's eyes. I had promised to protect her family, but I had failed. And more than just that ate at my soul. For those butchers had killed every clansman they saw. No one was spared, no prisoners taken. The lifeless corpses of beautiful young women had littered the muddy village road alongside those of their families. So why, then, had they taken Arianna alive?

And what if they had not? What if she, too, had been cut down, only to revive again? What if they had only taken her captive when they'd realized that they *could not* kill her?

What if she knew now, what she was? What I, in my arrogance, had kept from her?

I paused to lean against a tree, swamped with a sudden weakness brought on by regret. "I should have told her," I murmured hoarsely. "By the Gods, I should have explained it all to her, whilst I still had the chance . . ."

But it was too late for regrets now, and when I lifted my head again, I could see the camp of my enemies. No less than fifty men in this troop, I judged. Four separate fires burned, and men surrounded each. Some eating, some drinking. Some still as stone, contemplating the flames. Some already lying down. And at the center of them all, a ragged tent had been erected, with men standing guard at each of its four corners.

"Arianna," I whispered, and my heart tugged as if trying to leap from my chest. She must be alive! That well-guarded tent had to be where they were keeping her. Every inch of my body seemed to stretch forward. My feet itched to run to her. And only by a supreme act of will did I manage to hold myself back. To draw a breath, and crouch down beside the large tree, and wait.

The hours crept by. Too slowly, too damned slowly. It seemed ages before the men in the camp truly slept. All except for those standing guard outside the tent. I could not hope to outfight fifty armed soldiers. Four, on the other hand, should pose no problem. But I would have to move quickly, carefully, and in utter silence. They must not be given the chance to sound the alarm.

I crept closer, then moved silently among the sleeping men, picking my way with great care. Still concealed in shadows, so the men guarding the tent could not see me. Not yet. But I could see them, for my vision in the night was excellent, honed by the kiss of immortality.

I took another step, then went still as I saw one of the men turn toward the tent flap, as if in response to some sound from inside. I strained to hear, and finally did, even from this distance. The voice was a whisper, barely more than a breath.

"Please. Only for a short while. I am so cold and afraid, and alone . . ."

No, I thought in silence. By the Gods, what did she think she was doing?

Even as I willed him not to, the man to whom she spoke gave a nod, and ducked inside. While the other three exchanged lewd grins, and muttered their speculation. Fury built in my blood, a hot, pulsing thing. The bastard was alone in that tent with my wife. My woman. My Arianna. He would not live to see another sunrise.

In a moment, he poked his head back out, and I could see that his chest was bare now. My jaw clenched, teeth grated, hands fisted.

"Why dinna the three of you go an' fetch a bite to eat?" the man asked softly of his companions. "A mite o' privacy is called for at the moment."

One of the men frowned. "We were told nay to leave our posts," he argued, keeping his voice low.

"Aye, so you were. But if you do this for me I'll return the favor . . . in just a while when your own turn comes 'round."

The other man's brows rose high. "The lady's willin' to take each of us?"

And the man inside the tent gave a shrug. "The lady's a prisoner. Who cares if she's willin'?" He grinned broadly, his meaning plain.

The other three exchanged glances. "I dinna think it

wise,'' said one. ''The chieftain, and Master Dearborne as well, warned us against that one. They say she's evil, same as the outlaw Nicodimus.''

Another man nodded. ''Aye, and the lad Nedmond himself witnessed the demon, cuttin' the heart from the very chest of Master Kohl.''

''Ah, she's but a woman. You can well imagine Laird Marten is takin' what pleasure he wishes from his own captive wench! An' I intend to do the same.''

Nicodimus stiffened. Marten . . . Gods, he should have known Marten would come to avenge his brother.

But there was no time to think, for the other men sighed, and nodded their agreement. ''Dinna be too long,'' said one who hadn't spoken before now. ''An' dinna untie the wench, either.''

The bare chested one grinned again. ''Nay, my friend, I willna. I prefer them bound, I do.'' Then he ducked back inside the tent, likely to ravage my wife.

I drew my dagger as the three men wandered away from the tent; heading toward me. I saw the fire they'd chosen, one with a barrel of ale standing nearby, and a pot half full of stew near enough the flames so it would still be warm.

I got closer, crouched down, and waited, though it nearly killed me to do so.

Two of them dipped out a cup of the stew, and sat down, while the third went straight for the ale, a short distance away. Even as he drew the foaming brew from the spigot, I crept up behind the other two. A silent slice, and the first one's throat was cut along with his windpipe. The second never knew a thing was wrong until his mate's legs began thrashing and the stew he'd held tipped to the ground. He glanced sideways, his eyes widened, and my hand covered his mouth even as my blade drove into the base of his neck, cleanly severing his spine. He did not move or breathe again.

His cup full of ale, froth spilling over his hand, the third man turned with a smile and started toward them, frowning when he glimpsed his comrades lying still on their backs. As he paused, squinting at them through the darkness, and then moving closer, I crept 'round until I could come up behind him. I knew the instant he saw the blood, the second he realized death had visited his camp this night. For his body went taut and his head turned as if to shout to the others. But the sound never emerged, for my arm clamped tight 'round his neck from behind, and my hands gripped his head and twisted hard. He went limp when his neck snapped. I lowered him to the ground, and he looked for all the world as if he were sleeping.

Then I turned toward that tent again, and the blood thundered in my temples as I moved quickly, quietly forward. If the bastard had touched Arianna, if his hands were upon my woman, his death would be slow.

Wrenching the tent flap open, I leapt inside, dagger drawn.

The woman before me was standing, naked except for the shift she was pulling on, over her head. The guard lay at her feet, his face frozen in a surprised grimace. He wore nothing except the dagger that protruded from his chest, and the blood that slicked his skin.

"Arianna," I whispered, reaching for her.

Her head and arms poked through, and she straightened the shift around her legs, turning to face me. Not Arianna. Not her at all.

"Nidaba? But . . . but I thought—"

"Exactly what the bastards intended you think, no doubt," she whispered. She gripped my hand. "Come, we must go before we're found out."

"But Arianna . . ." I began.

"She is not here, Nicodimus. Come. *Now.* I'll explain as we go." And she drew me from the tent.

In silence we made our way from the camp. Nidaba led me to where the soldiers' horses were picketed, helping herself to one as I quieted the others. I loosed the remaining mounts, and led them into the forest, before slapping their rumps and letting them run free. We raced quickly to where Black was tied, and were far away before we heard the shouts of alarm. Far enough away so I knew they would have no chance of catching us.

"Where is she?" I asked Nidaba.

She lowered her head. "Their leader took her, Nicodimus. His home is to the south, from what I was able to overhear. A keep called Kenwick. Do you know it?"

I did not. But it would not stop me. "Their leader," I said with distaste. "Marten. The bastard has hounded me for the last time. I do not know this Kenwick, but I will find it," I vowed. "And when I do, Marten will die."

"He knew you would follow the others," Nidaba said slowly. "So he sent them in the opposite direction, with me as their prize."

I glanced at her quickly, for once forgetting my own anguish. "Nidaba . . . did they harm you?"

She averted her gaze. "They were ordered not to touch me until I was safely in the dungeons of this . . . Kenwick Keep. I was to be delivered unharmed to a man called Dearborne, for what, I do not know."

"They were *ordered* not to touch you," I repeated, watching her face closely. "Was it an order they obeyed, Nidaba?"

For a moment, she was silent. Then she only whispered, "Most of them did." She met my gaze and said no more. And I knew she would not. "This is far from the matter at hand, Nicodimus. There is something you must know. Arianna . . ."

I closed my eyes as she paused, drawing a breath, sensing what was to come.

"She was run through," Nidaba told me. "She experienced death for the first time, my friend. And likely revived to realize the truth."

I closed my eyes against the pain that flooded my soul. "I feared as much. I should have told her."

"There is naught to be done about it now. She knows. And likely knows you did as well, and kept it from her. You should be aware of it before you face her again."

"Why did he take her, Nidaba? Why, when I'm the one he wants?"

"I do not know, I only know he took her and rode south.

If it were Arianna's heart he wanted, surely he'd have simply taken it and been done with her."

"A heart so young would be of little use to a Dark Witch as old as Marten," I protested.

She nodded. "I have thought of that. And realized, Nicodimus, even before I knew who he was, that perhaps it is your heart he is after. Now I am even more certain. Arianna is simply serving as his bait. If you go after her at Kenwick, you will be walking directly into Marten's trap. Just the way he wants you to do."

I looked up sharply. "I've thought of that, as well. But if he wanted me to follow him to Kenwick, then why the ruse to lead me away?"

Nidaba shrugged. "To give him time to prepare? To set this trap of his in such a way that there will be no chance for you to escape?"

I knew she was trying to warn me, to prepare me. To dissuade me from rushing headlong into disaster, perhaps even death. But it did not matter. Nothing would keep me from Arianna. Nothing.

"I have no choice in this. She is my wife, you know this, Nidaba. I must go after her."

"Even if it costs your life?" she asked, softly, for she already knew the answer. "Even . . . if it costs you your immortal heart?"

"I love her," I whispered, the confession draining me. Saying it aloud to Nidaba solidified the feelings in my heart. With the confirmation came the fear, more intense, more vividly real than before. Certain disaster awaited me, I knew it in my gut. Yet I was powerless to divert it. "Gods help me, Nidaba, but I love her."

Closing her eyes, she nodded. "I feared as much. I . . . can only hope she's worthy of that love," she whispered.

"I only hope," I said, my voice hoarse, "I didn't wait too long to realize it. For though she loved me once, Nidaba, she could very well hate me by now."

His keep would have held Lachlan Keep twice within its solid walls. Huge blocks of chiseled rock towered high above the tall sturdy outer wall. Kenwick was a dark, dreary place. Large, but made of dark stone, with few ornaments and only a small number of torches for light. The gate itself seemed to have been built of entire tree trunks. Surely not even an army of men could gain access to such a fortress.

But could Nicodimus? Would he even attempt such an impossible feat?

Upon her arrival she was given into the hands of serving girls, not one, but two of them. A few men lingered about the great hall. One who wore a dark robe with its cowl pulled over his head stood silent and watchful. He made her shiver, that hooded man.

"You are a lady, Arianna of Stonehaven, and as a lady you shall be treated," Marten said, as he waved the serving girls closer.

"I am a prisoner," she replied.

Marten lowered his head, and his eyes seemed saddened. "'Tis my hope that will one day change. That you will grow to be happy here, Arianna. And that you will wish to stay. But until that day comes, aye, lassie, you are my prisoner."

She shook her head firmly, tears burning in her eyes. "I will never wish to stay with you. My only wish is to be back with my husband again."

One of the serving girls, the younger one, by the looks, caught her breath. Marten glanced up at her, a sharp reproach appearing, then vanishing in his eyes. He cleared his throat. "These are your servants, Arianna. They will attend to your every need. Lydia and Kathleen." He indicated each of them with a wave of his hand. Lydia was younger, with dark hair and eyes, and she reminded Arianna of the sister she had lost. Her beloved Raven. The thought gave her heart a painful twist. The other one was of her own dear mother's age, she guessed.

Looking again at the hooded man, she asked, "And who is this?"

Marten said nothing, but the man moved closer, lowering his cowl to reveal a thin, aged face. "I am Nathanial Dearborne. I am Marten's . . . spiritual counselor."

Marten cleared his throat, and the old man moved away.

"Your lady is in need of a bath," Marten addressed the servants. "And garments suitable to her station. I leave her in your care."

Lydia came forward and curtsied before me. "Come, my lady. You look weary and worn. Let us tend you."

Arianna glanced up quickly, and saw her first chance for escape. Surely the two women could not hold her by force. Not against her will.

Marten looked into her eyes, and seemed to read them. Without looking away, he lifted a hand behind him, crooked a finger. At once a burly man came forward, standing at the ready, weapons at his sides.

"You will attend the lady as well, Gorden. And dinna allow her out of sight even for an instant, for she has yet to realize that this is her new home. Until she does, I fear she will bolt at the first opportunity. And does she escape, Gorden, I'll have your head. Do you ken?"

Gorden nodded, his eyes flicking over Arianna briefly. She shivered at his cold glance. As if she were a possession to be guarded, or an animal in need of tending.

"I regret this is necessary, Arianna," Marten told her softly, and he lifted her hand and brushed his lips across the back of it. She shuddered in revulsion. "Perhaps the day will come when it no longer is."

She knew her disappointment showed in her eyes. Her hopes for escape crushed, at least for now. But she would not stop trying, nor stop seeking an opportunity. If she were patient, and cunning, one would surely come.

"It willna matter how many guards you place upon me, Marten. Nicodimus will come for me. Nothin' will stop him."

Marten spared her a pitying glance and stroked her hair, but she shied away from his touch. "Poor Arianna, clingin' to false hope. But you'll see soon enough that your husband will nay come for you. Because he doesna care. But I do, lass. I do."

Turning away, she hurried off, unsure where she was going, only needing to be away from this man who spoke so horribly of her beloved Nicodimus. Lydia caught up, gripping her elbow gently and steering her in the right direction. "Come, my lady. This way." And then leaning close, she whispered very softly, for Arianna's ears alone. "Take heart. My dear mother used to say that true love always prevails. Dinna give up hope, no matter what Laird Marten says."

Arianna glanced sideways at the girl, and sensed she might have found an ally here, in this strange, impenetrable prison. And perhaps, in time, a friend. Having one might make the short time she would be forced to spend here a bit more bearable. But there would not be *much* time, either way. For Nicodimus would come. She clung to that hope.

But when a full week had passed, with no sign of her husband, hope began to fade.

Each day she was dressed in fine, costly gowns, her hair styled in ringlets, and glittering jewels and gold adorned her fingers, her wrists, and even her earlobes. Gifts, all of them, from her captor. They felt to her like chains more than jewels, but Marten insisted she wear them. She dined in the style of royalty, seated at the high table, Marten's table. Unlike Joseph Lachlan, this laird seemed to hold no fondness for eating among his clansmen, and his table stood far apart from theirs, all the way on the opposite side of the gray and somber great hall.

Marten's table was near a hearth, where a fire always burned. No one else dined at the high table except for Dearborne. The man seemed to be considered of great importance to Marten. She was not certain why. The others sat away from that warmth, and if the evening were cold, and the men uncomfortable, it seemed not to disturb Laird Marten at all.

The chambers she had been given were large, but just as gloomy and dark as the rest of the hideous place. And always, wherever she went, her guard, Gorden, stood to one side of her, watching. Always watching.

His dark eyes watched her as she dressed, or undressed, or bathed. Lingering where they would, for as long as he wished. It seemed he had his master's consent to ogle her.

Each evening, Marten came to her, and spoke for long hours of Nicodimus's past deeds, all of them evil. And of Nicodimus's longtime lover Nidaba, and the way he would touch her, and likely was spending every night in her arms. He would talk on and on, while she was forced to sit and listen to the details of the things her husband was likely doing with his lover, even now.

A dark cloud settled over Arianna as the days passed by, slowly, so slowly. Her hopes faded with each night that Nicodimus did not burst through the gates, sword in hand, to rescue her. She cried often. It seemed each time she did, Marten appeared there. As if someone were reporting her every whisper to the man. He would speak soft words, words of comfort, and make promises that he would one day end her terrible pain, mend her poor, broken heart.

At last . . . at long last, she realized the truth. Nicodimus was not coming for her, for if he were, he would have been here by now. But she could not stir a tender feeling for Marten, nor did she wish to do so. She could never love another as she did her Nicodimus, nor would she even want to. And she would not live her life as Marten's possession, no matter how richly she would be kept.

Without hope, her mind seemed to sharpen. And at last, she was able to think clearly once more. Without Nicodimus to depend upon, a bit of the rebellious girl she had been stirred back to life in her soul. Stirred from beyond the depths of grief and shock that had, for a time, silenced her. And Arianna came to understand that she had no one to depend upon but herself.

Silently, she vowed never to forget that lesson again, nay, not for as long as she lived.

Secretly, Arianna began to plan.

She need only pretend. She need only convince Marten that her feelings had changed, and that she was willing to stay with him, to be his woman. And once he believed the lie, his defenses would relax. Gorden's constant watchful eye would turn away from her. And that would be the time when she would make good her escape.

But she would need to be convincing. Marten was no fool, and would not believe easily. So she began slowly, offering him a slight smile when he spoke to her at mealtime. Forcing herself not to draw away when he took her hand, or touched her face. Even seeking him out once or twice in the castle, and claiming she had been lonely and wished his company. She asked him to tell her about her new nature as an immortal, and to explain to her the tingling jolt that rocked through her each time he touched her.

And finally, one day when they were alone in the great hall, Marten kissed her without warning. Arianna knew she would never have a better opportunity. She swallowed her revulsion, and linked her arms 'round his neck, letting her body go soft, and parting her lips in invitation. She felt his reaction. His body hardened, and his heart hammered in his chest as he held her tighter, plundering her mouth in a way that made her want to retch. But she held her ground, refusing to let him see the truth. She pressed herself against him, closed her eyes, and told herself it was necessary. Necessary. She would do anything to get free of him.

Anything.

When at last, he lifted his head away, she breathed heavily and deeply, and stared deep into his eyes. "I have missed being held in a man's arms," she whispered.

His eyes filled with fire, he slid a hand up the front of her to cup her breast. And when she gasped in surprise and disgust, he took it to be a gasp of sheer pleasure. "Give yourself to me, Arianna. And I promise, you'll nay miss a man's touch ever again. For I will touch you often, and thorough, and well."

She released all her breath. "Aye, Marten. Aye. Touch me. Touch me everywhere."

His smile was one of victory, one of possession and ownership and pride. But also, one of doubt. "I am nay so certain I believe you, lass."

Her confidence wavered, but she stiffened her resolve. "How shall I prove myself to you?"

He looked at her, his hot gaze roaming from head to toe. Then slowly, he reached out, and began unlacing the front of her gown. Panic made her heart race, but she only stood still, eyes closed. Whatever was necessary, she reminded herself. For her freedom.

His hands worked steadily, but slowly, so she had ample time to object. When the laces were loosed, he spread the bodice open still wider, and then clenching the fabric in his fists and giving a brutal tug, he tore the dress wider still. Her breasts spilled free, bared to his hungry stare.

He touched them, his hands cupping and squeezing them, his fingers closing on her nipples, and tugging at them. "I want you very badly, Arianna," he said, his voice thoughtful as his hands worked, pinching her, kneading her. "Do you want me, too?"

"Aye," she whispered.

"Then tell me. Make me believe you, Arianna. Convince me of this desire you claim."

With everything in her, she resisted, and yet forced herself to speak the lies to him. "I want you, Marten. More than I've ever wanted any man."

He smiled again, and bent his head and nursed at her breasts, first one and then the other. Arianna placed her hands at his head fast, instinctively, her intent to push him away. But she fought her heart and won. Instead she held him to her, tipped her head back, closed her eyes, and sighed loudly. Marten's hand caught her skirts and pulled them up high on her thigh, and higher, baring her down below, and plunging his hand between her legs. He worked her there with his hand, rubbed her hard and fast with roughened, cold fingers, as his mouth tugged and his teeth nipped at her breast. And she whispered, "Please, Marten . . . please . . ."

A sound, a broken gasp, gave her to know someone else had entered the great hall. Mortified, she looked up quickly. And then her soul seemed to shatter, for Nicodimus stood in the open doorway, sword in hand, eyes . . . so tortured she couldn't bear it. He only stood there, staring in anguish as Marten laved her breasts and drove his hand ever deeper.

"Nicodimus, nay!" she cried. "It isna—"

Marten bit down hard, and she uttered a sound that was

a cry of pain, but she knew it would not seem so to Nicodimus. To her husband. And even as she pulled against Marten's hands and his mouth, she saw another form—a dark, hooded form—enter behind Nicodimus. Nathanial Dearborne! She cried a warning, but too late. The Dark One moved fast, lifting a blade, and plunging it into Nicodimus's back.

He sank to his knees. With a sudden desperate push, Arianna finally jerked free of Marten's embrace, and ran to Nicodimus, falling down beside him. His eyes were already beginning to glaze over. . . .

"Nicodimus, 'twas an act, all you saw! I vow, 'twas only a trick!"

"And a fine trick it was, Arianna," Marten called, his voice tinged with glee. "Our plan to lure him here worked perfectly, wouldn't you say? You did it so perfectly. You shall be well rewarded."

Nicodimus shook his head very slightly, his fading eyes holding hers. "How . . . why, Arianna . . . ?" he whispered. And then the light in his eyes died out.

"Nicodimus, nay! Nay! I love you, I vow to the Gods, I do. No one else. Only you!"

But he didn't hear her. He was beyond her words now. Marten was laughing as he came forward. He said, "Your plan worked perfectly, old man. And I thank you. Now, at last, I shall have the most powerful heart in existence. And I will have vengeance on my dear brother-in-law as well."

He yanked Arianna by her hair up from where she knelt on the floor. "And for you, my little liar . . . Gods, you know you almost had me believing you." His fist smashed into her face, and she crumbled to the floor atop Nicodimus. Consciousness fled in a sudden rush of blackness. Gods, if only she would never have to wake again.

15

I could not believe my eyes when I saw her in the arms of another. Not after she'd sworn to me that she would never give herself to any man but me. Not after she had spoken of her love for me so many times. And when I glanced to the side and saw that the man who held her was none other than Marten, I drew my blade. *He must die!* My mind screamed the command. He had stolen the hearts of innocents and fed on their power for seven long centuries. He and his brother, both determined to kill me, to have their vengeance, had murdered Joseph Lachlan, his entire family and clan. There was nothing they would not do to destroy me.

And nothing they could have done to torment me more than what Marten was doing now. Ravishing Arianna—my wife—right in front of me. My mind exploded in a blinding rage, so white hot I ignored the senses I should have been heeding. And the attack came from behind.

As I lay dying, Marten congratulated my wife on her plan having worked perfectly. I looked up into her eyes, which were wide and afraid. Her entire body trembled as she held together the gaping front of her dress and shook her head slowly from side to side.

It did not fit. The way she looked, simply did not fit with what she had done. But there was no time to ponder that, indeed, no time for anything at all. My time was over. I died as the blood drained from my body, and knew as the light faded that this would be my final death. For the bastard would have my heart this time.

Marten would have my heart . . . or as much of it as Arianna had left for him. For truly, she had the bulk of it. I could feel it bleeding in her small, slender hands.

When Arianna regained consciousness, it was to see Marten lying dead upon the floor. And farther away, near the door, Dearborne, that frightening old man, was just straightening away from Nicodimus, a bloody, still-beating heart cradled in his palms.

She screamed her husband's name and raced forward. But the old man only backed away as she hurled herself down upon Nicodimus's bloody form. The gaping wound in his chest, the scarlet wetness staining his clothes, the utter lifelessness of his body, all of it too terrible to look upon. And there was his dagger, still clutched in his fisted hand.

"Do not be so upset, child. You're young. You'll find another," Nathanial Dearborne rasped.

Rage welled up in her. Rage and violence, and a burning lust for the killer's heart. "You tricked him," she whispered. "You and Marten. This entire scheme was created just so you could kill Nicodimus."

"How very astute of you, Arianna. Yes, indeed, I've been planning this for a very long time. I was there, you see, when the brothers learned of their sister's death, and heard the tales of their brother-in-law, whom they detested, having apparently risen from the dead on a field of battle. It was I who told them the way to gain immortality for themselves. I who showed them how they might live long enough to have their vengeance. Of course, Marten believed Nicodimus's heart would be his." He glanced at the dead man. "He had no idea I was only allowing him to do my work for me, nor that I would collect the prize for myself.

And his own heart will be my bonus in just a moment. I win,'' he said. ''I always win.''

Arianna's fingers inched forward, and she eased the blade from Nicodimus's dead hand. Then she turned her head slowly. Dearborne had placed her husband's heart in a small box, and this he dropped into a drawstring sac that hung at his waist. Then he pulled out his blade, already stained with Nicodimus's blood, and started toward the dead Marten.

''You're mistaken,'' Arianna whispered, straightening to her feet. ''You dinna always win. You willna win today.''

Dearborne stopped where he was, facing her, his silver-gray brows lifted high. Then he smiled. ''Child, you cannot mean to challenge me. You're barely a newborn.''

''You'll nay leave this castle alive, Nathanial Dearborne,'' she whispered. And then she charged him.

Nathanial's eyes narrowed, but he drew his dagger to defend himself. However, he had obviously not expected so furious an attack. Arianna was driven by rage, a fury more powerful than his need for a living heart had ever been. He fought, yes. To preserve his life. She fought for the loss of her love, and there was no power stronger. Her anger seemed to surge from her in waves that sent him staggering. She had no care for her own life, and was so numb that she did not feel the blows he returned. There was nothing, nothing but rage, all of it directed at the old man.

''He died thinkin' I betrayed him,'' she said, panting, slashing with her blade. Tearing through the old man's robes, and his flesh more than once. ''I'll ne'er have the chance to tell him the truth. An' all because of you!'' She slashed again, slicing his chest clear to the bone.

Gasping, staggering backward, the old man shook his head. For the first time, Arianna saw fear in his eyes. He continued backing away until he reached a heavy chair, then he spun, snatched it up, and threw it at her.

The piece was far heavier than a man of his age should have been able to so much as lift, much less use as a weapon. She hadn't been expecting it, but should have recalled what Nicodimus had told her about the increased strength and honed senses of immortals. The chair hit her hard, and drove her backward, smashing her into the wall. She shook herself, shoving it away and surging to her feet again, only to find Dearborne gone. He'd fled from her, leaving the door wide open on the carnage he'd left behind.

Gone. And Nicodimus's heart gone with him. So final. It was so final. Her husband was dead, and the enormity of that was more than she could bear.

A sob was wrenched from her breast as Arianna once again went to her husband. Her fault, she realized. Her fault, all of this. If only she had obeyed him, if only she had stayed safe in the Stone Circle as he'd bade her do. Oh, if only . . .

But he was gone now. He had explained enough to her so that she knew this. He would not revive. His heart had been taken from him and he was lost to her now. Just as Raven, her sister was lost to her. And just as her dear parents were, as well. Arianna was alone. More alone than she had ever been.

A low moan made her turn fast. Marten! His heart had not been taken, and he moved slightly now. Slowly, he opened his mouth as if to draw a breath—and she recalled that stunning, painful first gasp she herself had drawn, upon waking from the dead.

She lunged toward him, flipping the dagger in her hand so she held the blade end, and brought the jeweled hilt crashing down on his head.

He did not move again.

He would, though. Unless . . .

Biting her lower lip, she bent over Marten, and with her dead husband's blade, she sliced through the fabric he wore, baring his chest. She positioned the blade, point down, above his heart, closing both fists 'round the hilt. Grating her teeth, she closed her eyes tight, and drove the blade deep into his chest.

The body went rigid, and when her eyes flew open wide she saw the blood bubbling forth from around the embedded blade. She saw his eyes bulging, pain burning in them.

Shaking her head slowly, grimacing and trembling, she jerked the blade free of him, and rose, backing away. "I canna," she whispered. "Gods forgive me, but I canna cut a livin' heart from a man's chest!"

Marten slumped back into temporary death, as Arianna fought not to choke or faint. She couldn't do either of those things. She was immortal. A High Witch, alone in the world. She would need to be strong to survive. She would need to eliminate her weak stomach as well as her soft heart. She would make herself hard and powerful, and no foe would ever take her. No man would ever use her.

But first . . .

She looked at her husband once more. His face still and relaxed as if he were only sleeping. First she would see he had a proper burial. And it would be in the place he loved best.

The servants had fled. She would have to work on her own. She fetched a silken coverlet, tucked it beneath her arm and went outside to seek a horse and wagon.

She'd traveled only an hour, Nicodimus's lifeless body in the back of the wagon she drove. When she came to a stream, she stopped, and carefully, lovingly, she stripped away his torn, bloodied clothes. Then she bathed him, as much she thought, with her tears as with the cold water. As she did, her gaze fell upon the twin pendants he wore.

With trembling fingers, she lifted one of them, fingering it with sobs all but choking her. He must have found it. He'd had one like it, all along. It must be . . . it must be something worn by High Witches. And he'd donned hers . . . almost as if he'd cared for her after all . . .

Aye, and he must have, or he wouldn't have come for her. Died trying to save her from Marten. But she'd made him hate her in the end.

Swallowing her tears, she lifted one of the two pendants from his neck—the one that seemed older, more dulled with age, for it was his—and lowered its chain over her own head. She pressed a kiss to it, and then to her own pendant, which she left upon the body of her beloved.

"Remember me, Nicodimus, wherever you are. And perhaps . . . someday . . . forgive what I did here this day. For I love you. I love you still."

Tears rolling fresh down her face, she continued bathing her husband's violated body.

When he lay clean and glistening with droplets, she wrapped his body in the silken coverlet she'd taken. It was a deep blue. A fitting shade, she thought vaguely. A sad color.

When all was finished, she reached for the wagon to pull herself once again into the seat.

"Arianna!"

She turned fast, finally realizing she was not alone, and saw Nidaba thundering toward her on a horse.

"I've just come from Kenwick!" she shouted as the mount slid to a hasty stop and Nidaba leapt to the ground. "There was blood everywhere, and no more than a quivering servant to be found. Gods, what happened there?"

Arianna opened her mouth to speak, but found the words would not come. Nidaba gripped her shoulders, shook her. "We were coming for you, Nic and I. He kept ordering me to stay behind, but I refused. Then he slipped away last night while I slept. Damn him for being so protective! He knows full well that I—" She stopped there as her gaze fell upon the silk-wrapped body in the back of the wagon. She fell silent, searching Arianna's face. "Oh, Gods no. Tell me it is not him," she begged.

When Arianna still said nothing, Nidaba rushed to the wagon, and pulled the silk away from Nicodimus's face. "Oh, no," Nidaba whispered, her voice gone soft and coarse. "Oh, please, no . . ."

"I am sorry, Nidaba. 'Twas my fault, truly. Marten . . . and this other immortal, Dearborne, they set a trap for Nicodimus. An' it worked, just the way they both intended it would. I . . . I . . ."

"You cost him his life! Damn you, Arianna!"

Arianna lowered her head, unable to deny the charge. "If I could exchange my life for his, I would gladly do it," she whispered.

Nidaba stepped away from the wagon, and stood facing Arianna. "I ought to kill you myself," she whispered. Her entire body quivered with rage, her face was snow white and her dark eyes gleamed.

"If you wish," Arianna said softly. "I'll nay fight for my life. I ask only that you finish what I've begun. Bury him, Nidaba, at the Stone Circle he so loved. An' if you've a hint of mercy in you for me, you'll lay me to rest beside him there. For I loved him. I love him still."

"You loved him so much you let him die for you," she seethed. "The one servant I found blubbered that Nic had burst through the doors to find you in Marten's arms. Marten, the man who hated Nicodimus above all others! What were you doing with him if you loved your husband so, Arianna?"

Her shoulders slumped, Arianna whispered, "I was bargaining for my freedom. Like any common whore." Hands trembling, she took the blade she now carried at her side, and held it out to Nidaba. "Use Nicodimus's dagger," she said softly. "'Twill be fittin', dinna you think?"

Snatching the blade away, Nidaba growled fiercely, and finally lifted it high above her head, and drove it downward, toward Arianna's chest. Arianna stood motionless, awaiting the blow. But it never came. The blade sank instead, into the wooden side of the wagon just behind her. "Stay clear of me, Arianna Sinclair," she whispered. "Stay clear of me, for if I see you again, I *will* kill you!"

Spinning away from her, Nidaba took a step toward her horse, only to fall to her knees. For a long time she remained there, sobbing so hard she scarcely breathed except to mutter "Nicodimus" over and over again, brokenly. She shook all over, and her cries grew louder all the while. Until finally, they abated, and she went utterly silent. It was as if there were nothing left inside her.

"The man who killed my Nic," she said at last, "You said his name was Dearborne?"

"Aye, Nathanial Dearborne."

Nidaba nodded. "The same who wanted me brought here as his captive for some sick reason. Well he shall have me then. He shall have me and rue the day he harmed my beloved Nicodimus!"

She lunged to her feet, mounted her horse and rode away at a murderous gallop.

Arianna felt no relief that Nidaba had left her still alive. It would have been easier had the woman simply ended it. Her limbs heavy, like lead weights, she tugged Nicodimus's dagger from the wood. Then dragged herself into the seat to continue the journey.

She buried Nicodimus in the center of the ancient Stone Circle near the place that had once been her home. She covered his beloved, silk-wrapped body with earth. Then she sat upon his grave, drew his dagger, and grasping a handful of her long, golden hair, began sawing. Lock upon lock fell to the ground around her. And tears upon tears fell with them.

Eventually, she left that place. Left Scotland. Left all she'd known, and began her new life as an immortal High Witch. For the first time, she understood the pain Nicodimus had known so long ago, when he, too, had lost all those he'd loved, only to find that he must live on. No wonder he had been unable to love her. Unwilling to risk his heart that way. She understood now. She knew that she would never love again, either. But for far different reasons.

Oh, she feared the pain, the loss, just as Nicodimus had. She feared it. But it wouldn't matter if she feared it or not. She was incapable of loving another as she had loved her Nicodimus . . . as she still loved him.

One day, she vowed, she would find Nathanial Dearborne again, and make him pay for what he had done. And one day, perhaps, if her long ago spell had worked, she would find her beloved sister again, as well. That dim hope was the one thing that gave her the strength to keep going.

Until then, she had nothing to do, except prepare. She would learn. To fight, to kill . . . to survive.

Part Two

16

Arianna spent almost two hundred years alone. More utterly alone, she thought, than the last star to fade in the morning. And in that time, she nursed a hatred for Nathanial Dearborne and for Marten, that rivaled the sun for its blazing fury. She didn't see Nidaba in all that time, and didn't search for her. The woman hated her with good reason. Besides, seeing her would only be a painful reminder of Nicodimus and the brief, sweet time Arianna had spent with him. In his arms. Loving him, even though he couldn't return her feelings.

But that was history. She was no longer a seventeen-year-old girl in love. She was different now. She didn't look the same; she'd kept her hair short and liked it that way. Though perhaps if she looked very deeply, she would find somewhere inside, buried in the deepest part of her being, the notion that she left her hair short in memory of Nicodimus. In some kind of meaningless penance for the long ago mistakes that had cost him his heart.

She didn't *sound* the same. The lilt of the highlands had long since faded from her voice. She was hard, solitary, and she spent every moment she could honing her skills with a blade. She fought. She killed. She survived, with one thought foremost in her mind. Someday she would cross paths with Dearborne and Marten again. And when that day came, she would kill them for what they had done.

But almost two centuries after Nicodimus's brutal murder, something happened that softened Arianna's rocklike soul, and restored a sense of joy to her existence; in the summer of 1691, she found her sister. Raven at long last, lived again. Arianna's long ago spell *had* been true. Raven looked the same, bore the same name, and Arianna recognized her at once. And even though Raven didn't know who Arianna was at first, there had been an immediate connection, and a slow rebuilding of the bond they'd once shared. For over three centuries, they remained together almost continuously.

And then, a year ago, in 1998, another figure from the distant past had reappeared in Arianna's life. Nathanial Dearborne. He'd been determined to kill Raven, to take her heart for his own. He'd hated her for capturing the love of the man he'd thought of as his son. He blamed Raven for turning Duncan against him, and sought vengeance. But he hadn't counted on Arianna's presence, nor her intervention. Deaborne's attempt on Raven thwarted, he had run back to his rooms to gather his belongings and flee Arianna's wrath. . . . At last, her chance to avenge Nicodimus had come. . . .

Arianna walked into the room while Nathanial Dearborne gathered up the tiny wooden boxes, all of them filled with stolen, still beating hearts. The sources of his strength, his very life. For a moment she only stood in the doorway, watching him as he packed the hearts in a case, and began reaching for the volumes of journals that lined the shelves. It amazed her that her hatred for him could still be so strong, after four hundred eighty-seven years . . . for that was precisely how long it had been since she'd seen the bastard plunge his blade into Nicodimus's back.

Arianna drew a breath, and stilling her emotions, began to speak. "You took the man I loved," she all but growled. "And I'll kill you for it."

Dearborne froze, then turned slowly to face her. And Arianna knew he feared her. She'd nearly bested him when she'd been but a fledgling immortal, after all. He had to know she could kill him easily now. He'd always known. It was why he'd been so carefully avoiding her for so very long. She could see it in his eyes.

"Don't be so certain, Arianna," he said to her slowly. "I was unprepared for you before. But never again will I underestimate the power of hatred."

"It wasn't the power of hatred, Nathanial. It was the power of love." He took a step forward, but she moved to block the door fully. She stood there with her legs shoulder width apart, knuckles on her hips, chin high. "Hatred has no power. The power that nearly killed you then was the power of love. My love for one of the many you murdered. And it's that same power that will destroy you now."

He took a step backward, setting his packed case on the floor to free his hands. She watched his every move, ready to react. "Which one was he, this victim of mine? It's been so long . . . I can scarcely remember them all. Was he the barbaric Celtic warlord? The Mayan Shaman?" He shrugged. "Not that it matters. They all died on their knees, begging for mercy."

"I can hardly wait to see how you do," she said, and drew her dagger, held it lightly, tossed it from one hand to the other. "But to remind you, his name was Nicodimus, and he died with the blade of a coward in his back. And you remember him perfectly well. I know you do."

His Adam's apple moved as he swallowed his fear—or tried to. "Will you kill me unarmed, Arianna, or give me a chance to draw my blade?" His hand inched toward the leather pocket at his side.

She narrowed her eyes. "I'll kill you in a fair fight or not at all," she told him. "Go on."

He drew the weapon from its sheath. Not his dagger, but she didn't see in time. Dearborne pulled out a handgun, and even as Arianna gasped and tried to dart out of its line of fire, he leveled the barrel and pulled the trigger.

The bullet hit Arianna in the chest like a freight train,

driving her backward through the open doorway, and into the hall. The pain exploded even as the floor fell away, and she realized she was tumbling head over heels down the stairs. Her body crashed and pounded, twisted and turned, and when she came to a stop at last, her limbs were bent beneath her, broken, and she knew the healing wouldn't have time to take place, because Dearborne wouldn't let it.

It was over. She had failed . . . failed Nicodimus. Again.

She opened her eyes and saw the evil bastard standing over her. "It's a shame you prefer a fair fight," he said. He crouched low, tore open her blouse and she could do nothing to prevent it. "I prefer a sure win, myself." And then she felt the fiery tip of his blade slicing her flesh.

"Raven . . . will kill you for this . . ." The thought of her sister's grief was nearly as painful as the rest.

"Oh, I'm sure she will try." Dearborne tilted his head thoughtfully. "Do you ever wonder about the bodies of slain immortals, Arianna? They die, but don't really. They remain ever new, ever young. Do you suppose their minds are still alive, as well? Do you suppose they *know* they've been buried alive?"

She did wonder, had wondered endlessly, ever since Nicodimus had been taken from her. But she had no more time to wonder, because Dearborne chose that moment to drive his blade into her chest to the hilt. Arianna's mind exploded in a screaming blast of agony . . . and then she descended into blackness.

But it was a blackness that faded.

The next thing Arianna felt was the jolt that seemed so much like electrocution. Her back arched sharply as she sucked new breath into her lungs. And as she relaxed and blinked her eyes open, it was to see her beloved sister staring down into her eyes. Fear and shock raged inside, and Arianna clutched at her chest, which throbbed and tingled. "How . . . how did you . . . what . . . ?"

Raven stroked her hair. "It's over, Arianna. You're all right." She smiled through her tears. "You're really all right."

Raven hugged her close, but Arianna couldn't stop her

own violent trembling. "B-but . . . he took my heart."

"I know, I know, darling. But now I've taken his. And yours . . . yours beats still, back inside you where it belongs."

"But—"

She was interrupted then, by Duncan, her sister's lover, the man who'd once thought of Dearborne as a father. "It was Nathanial," he said. "He seemed to want to clear his conscience before he died. So he told me how to bring you back."

"But how could he know that?" Arianna asked, amazed. "I didn't even know that such a thing was possible, and . . ." She blinked then, as the magnitude of what this meant hit her fully. "He has other hearts here."

"Well, yes," Raven said. "Weak ones, nearly lifeless, some of them, but—"

"Don't you see?" Arianna sat up slightly, grasping her sister's shoulders. "My Goddess, Raven, don't you see what this means?"

Raven hadn't seen. Not fully. Not then. But Arianna had. She'd taken all those captive hearts, knowing that one of them, one precious heart, belonged to Nicodimus. And if there was a chance in creation that she could return it to him, restore him as she had been restored . . . she had to try.

She'd taken Dearborne's journals as well, pored over them. And what she found in them horrified her. The man had considered himself some kind of scientist. He'd taken other immortals captive, kept them and experimented on them to find their strengths, their weaknesses, all with the intent of becoming the strongest of them all. He had killed and revived his victims time and again, observing the effects, making notes. He had taken hearts, and returned them, just to see what the results would be. His notes made mention of one "subject" in particular. One he called only "the dark woman," whom he'd tormented longer than any other, before she had finally escaped him. Dearborne had written that this woman had been the oldest High Witch he'd ever known, and that even her strong mind had begun to flirt with madness, in time. He had intended to kill her once and for all when he'd finished with her, but she'd managed to break free before he'd done so. As she read those words, Arianna thought of Nidaba. The last time Arianna had seen the woman, she had been going after Dearborne.

Gods, could this victim have been Nidaba? That strong, proud immortal Arianna had admired—and envied—so greatly?

Arianna, Duncan and Raven, had burned Dearborne's body. But before incinerating his heart, she'd performed an incantation over it, willing all its stolen power to return to the captive hearts where it belonged.

Once that was done, Arianna left her sister behind to begin the longest journey of her life. Armed with the six captive hearts, all beating strongly now in their little boxes, and the reams of information recorded in the journals of a madman, she set out to locate the bodies of Dearborne's victims, and to try to restore them to life.

But the first one . . . the very first heart she returned to its rightful home . . . would be that of Nicodimus. The man she had loved and lost. The man who believed she had betrayed him. The man . . . who had been her husband.

17

Stonehaven, Scotland Autumnal Equinox, 1999

Arianna stood upon the hill overlooking Stonehaven. It was rebuilt, isolated—backward by modern standards, space-aged in comparison to the way she remembered it. The ship had seemed to take forever to cross the Atlantic, and though she'd been impatient, there had been no other way. She certainly couldn't have boarded an airliner with six human hearts beating in her carry-on bag.

In her hands she held the small wooden box that contained the heart of Nicodimus Lachlan. Its beat had been weak, barely there, until she'd cast the spell to return all Dearborne's stolen power to its rightful owners. Now it beat strong and steady. And now she would try what her one-time husband had told her no Witch could do.

She would try to raise the dead.

The wind blew, riffling her short hair, brushing her cheeks with the scent of heather and the sea. Midnight now. The Witching Hour children spoke of in whispers on All Hallows' Eves. She walked slowly into the woods, leaving her vehicle, a small Jeep, parked nearby. A heavy backpack hung from her shoulders, and the jugs of rainwater suspended from either side of it bounced against her hips, and made it even heavier. But she had grown strong in four centuries of immortality. The weight was no burden to a High Witch as old as she. Deeper and deeper into the woods she trekked, until she located the site where the sacred Stone Circle had once towered.

Those monoliths were tumbled down now. A few remained upright, leaning drunkenly inward. Some lay flat and broken, large chunks missing, ruined by time or overzealous tourists who stumbled upon the circle and thought to take some of its magic home with them. Sacred souvenirs. The place was overgrown by vines and brambles. Few even knew it existed.

Arianna paused at the very center of the circle, where she had buried Nicodimus. Closing her eyes, she remembered him as he had been, and in turn, herself as she had been. She was not the same anymore. There was, she mused, a large difference between a girl of seventeen and a woman who had existed for centuries. But one thing remained the same. Her guilt. She blamed herself for Nicodimus's death just as surely as *he* had blamed her for it while the life drained away from him. And what she did now, she did to right the wrong she had done him. And for no other reason.

"You likely won't even know me now, Nicodimus," she murmured. According to Dearborne's hideous journals, others had been revived. Some right away, some more slowly, but all to varying degrees of confusion. And they had been relatively recent kills of his. The madman had noted that the longer he allowed an immortal to remain in death, the more disoriented they were upon their resurrections. Arianna herself had been dead only moments when she'd been revivified.

But Nicodimus . . .

Nicodimus had been lying in this dark mockery of death for centuries.

Even without that, he might not recognize her. Her once long golden hair was cropped short now. Her voice no longer carried the lilt of Scotland, and every shred of innocence had been burned from her eyes.

She no longer vomited at the thought of taking a heart. Indeed, she'd taken many. Quickly, coldly, and without remorse. For it was the way of things. She had come to learn that very early on in her new life.

Above all else in Arianna's mind, was the knowledge that if Nicodimus *did* somehow know her, and remember her, he would likely hate her for what she had done. His last glimpse of her had been in the arms of his darkest enemy. The man who'd hunted him all his life, and from whom he had come to rescue her. And he had died because of it.

"It doesn't matter," she told herself again. She had been telling herself the same things over and over all night as she'd made her preparations. "It doesn't matter. I'm righting a wrong. It isn't as if I still love him. It's been centuries. And that love belonged to an innocent girl—a girl who died along with her family back in that tiny cottage on that darkest of days. A girl . . . who no longer exists."

With a sigh of resignation, refusing to acknowledge the slight trill of anticipation singing through her veins and making her hands tremble, she set the box with its precious contents down, and shrugged off the large backpack. She set the water jugs aside, quickly loosing the knots that held them. Then, unzipping the pack, she took out the foldable shovel, the flashlight, the four white candles, and the soft, down-filled sleeping bag.

The moon sailed high, and the night breeze made the trees 'round her seem to whisper. Trees sacred to long ago Druids. Oaks, tall and mighty, so old they'd seen entire races come and go. These very trees had been in attendance at Nicodimus's burial. It was fitting they look on now, at this, his restoration.

Her hands still shaking, Arianna began to dig.

She hadn't buried him deeply. Her preternatural strength had only begun to manifest then, and besides, she'd been emotionally and physically drained. So firmly entrenched in her misery, she'd barely been able to hold her head up, much less dig a proper grave. But she had made it deep enough so that Nicodimus would be safe. No animals would have reached his perfectly preserved body.

She pushed the blade in with a foot, scooped out mounds of soil and flung it behind her. Over and over she did this, never tiring in the least. As the hole deepened and widened, she dug more carefully, inserting the shovel with great care, feeling for his body lying helpless, lifeless beneath the black earth. Her heart pounded harder with every bit of dirt she removed—but not from the exertion.

Finally she glimpsed a rotted scrap of deep blue satin. Her breath caught in her throat, and she fell to her knees, picking it up carefully, shaking the dirt away and then running her fingers over the fabric. "Nicodimus," she whispered.

Using her hands, now, she clawed more soil away, and finally saw one large hand, icy cold and so . . . so very still. Coated in dirt, damp with it. A sob escaped her as she brushed the dirt away. She dug faster, frantically now, scraping the dirt away from his forearm, then upper arm, and shoulder . . . until at last, she uncovered his face.

Earth was caked upon his skin, but she whisked it away. Soil had crumbled into the creases around his closed eyes . . . Gods, how she wanted to see them open again! She continued working, refusing to give in to the foolish urge to just sit and stare at him. She could not be discovered here. How would she ever explain herself? No, she must work quickly, and put her emotions aside. Close them off. Refuse to feel. It was easier than it might have been once. She had been practicing this very thing for a long time, after all.

When his body was free of its earthen tomb, she paused briefly, brushing the soil from her hands and staring down at him. He lay motionless, in some kind of suspended state. Neither alive, nor fully dead. Bathed in moonlight at the bottom of an uncovered grave, caked in earth. Naked, except for the few scraps of satin that remained. And the pendant—her pendant.

Her breath caught in her throat at the sight of it lying

there, and it was as if the centuries, the very ages, melted away. The pain of losing him was as fresh and new in her heart as it had been on that day.

And yet, it had been so long. It had been so long since she'd looked at this man. Since she'd touched him.

Stop it!

Closing her eyes briefly, Arianna put a mental stronghold on her heart, and listened only to her mind. The practical voice telling her, step by step, what must be done. She had planned this all carefully. She knew what to do, how to proceed.

She went to the sleeping bag, unzipping it and laying it open, just to the left of the grave. Then she moved around to stand near Nicodimus's head, her feet in the grave on either side of it. Bending low, she gripped him underneath the arms, and tugged him out of the hole, onto the damp, mossy ground. The wound in his chest lay open, gaping, and filled with soil and stones, but no insects, thankfully. Evidently the insects had sensed this was no ordinary body to be feasted upon, and had stayed away. As she scooped the dirt and stones away, she wondered what Nicodimus felt, if anything, what he thought—if thoughts were still something of which he was capable. What he remembered . . . or would remember when he revived.

If he revived.

Over four hundred years. Gods, even Dearborne had never attempted to raise an immortal this long dead.

"It will work," she whispered, squaring her shoulders. "It *has* to work."

Arianna set the white candles around him, and lit them, one by one. Then she dug into the very bottom of the backpack for the large bowl and the clean cloths she'd brought along. Kneeling beside Nicodimus, she poured water from one of the jugs into the bowl, dipped a cloth, and held it, dripping, above his face. She squeezed gently, and the water trickled over him. Soil streamed away in dirty rivulets. Bending closer, she began to wash him.

Like history repeating itself, she thought, and the memories came vividly. Memories of the last time she'd washed his lifeless body this way . . . at a stream as she'd carried him back here to be buried.

Just like last time, tears mingled with the water. When the first one dropped from her face to his, it startled her. She stopped what she was doing, sat up straight, and touched her own cheek, only to find it damp. "You're a fool, Arianna. A hopeless fool," she told herself.

She bathed Nicodimus's face, and his neck. She washed his hands, gently working the soil away from each strong finger and from the creases in between. His arms and his chest, she cleansed. No movement came from him. No life. She spent a great deal of time on the wound in his chest, the place where his heart would rest once again, when she had finished. One entire jug of the fresh rainwater she had brought went to this purpose. She rinsed the gaping place again and again, and shone the flashlight upon the open wound, to be sure it was perfectly clean.

Then she moved lower, washing his strong thighs, and the place in between. His calves, and his feet. She rolled him over, and cleansed the ages of soil from his back and buttocks. And with the remaining water, she rinsed his hair, running her fingers through it to scrub the dirt away.

Finally, all was ready. All that remained was to replace his mighty heart. Arianna paused to brush a lock of gold and russet hair from his forehead. "Come back to me, Nicodimus. Fight your way back, if you must . . . but come back."

Closing her eyes, drawing a deep, steadying breath, she reached for the box with trembling hands. It was small, intricately etched with symbols and designs. Engraved upon the lid of each of Dearborne's tiny prisons was a single letter. She could only guess, only hope, that the N on this one stood for the initial of its rightful owner. Nicodimus.

Carefully, she lifted the lid, and gathered the heart in her hands. Lifting it high, tipping her face up to the moonlight, she held it, and it seemed to Arianna that its beat grew stronger as she spoke. "By the powers of the Ancient Ones, by every force of the Universe, I restore this heart. I revive this body. I resurrect this man. Nicodimus, I call you forth. Return to life. Live, Nicodimus. Live. *Live!*"

Slowly, she lowered the heart into his body, positioned it carefully, and took her hands away. "As I will it, so mote it be," she whispered.

She sat back on her heels and waited, watching. She stared until her eyes watered, willing his chest to heal, his body to accept and embrace its heart. But nothing happened.

Tears once again stood in her eyes, but she angrily blinked them away. "It might take time," she reminded herself. "That's all. Just time." Nodding hard in affirmation of that belief, she gently eased Nicodimus's body onto the waiting sleeping bag, and folding it over him, zipped it up. One by one she snuffed the candles, and packed them away. She attached the empty jugs to the sides of the backpack. She scraped the earth back into the empty grave, and the bits of rotted silk along with it. Then she folded the shovel and put that in the pack, as well. She packed the basin, the soiled cloths, the flashlight. All that remained was a length of rope. This she tied to the sleeping bag at either side of Nicodimus's head, then looped the rope around her waist, and set off.

The journey back to her Jeep seemed endless. His weight behind her seemed to increase with every step, and even with her tremendous immortal strength, she grew tired. Not physically so much as mentally. She wanted the journey over. She wanted him safe inside, out of sight. At last her vehicle came into view, just as the first blush of purplish predawn light painted the horizon.

Nicodimus was heavy, even for one with her power and strength. But not too heavy. She wrested his body into the car, closed the rear door, and leaned against it for a moment, sighing in relief. It was done. Or all but done.

But would it work? Would he awaken?

And if he did . . . what then?

With a sigh of resolution, she vowed to deal with that when the time came. Climbing behind the wheel, she started the engine, and drove over the rutted track and down into the village of Stonehaven; to the cottage that sat on the site of her onetime home. The place where she'd been born. Where she'd lived. Where she'd found her parents brutally murdered.

She had returned here several times over the centuries. Drawn back like a moth to the candle's flame. She had come back to the memories; the pain, the hurt, the loss. As if testing her resolve to feel none of it anymore. She had purchased the lot on one of those many visits, and had a modest home built there. She rarely visited it anymore—simply paid a local resident to see that the place was cared for, kept up. But somehow, she couldn't seem to let it go. It was as if that place were her one remaining connection to the mortal, headstrong girl she had been, and the happiness she had once known. It was as if selling it would be cutting herself off at the very root.

The house was a simple, two-story structure, with clapboard siding painted white, and black shutters at the windows. Closed now, those shutters. All of them. It wouldn't do to have anyone peering in just now. The house had two bedrooms and a bath upstairs, and one below, in the back. That would be Nicodimus's home . . . for now.

She peered again at the paling horizon as she shut off the engine. She'd best hurry and get him inside before the villagers began to wake. Quickly, she moved to the rear of the Jeep, opened it, and tugged him out. She paused only long enough to shut the doors, then dragged him quickly over the flagstone walk to the house. His body bumped up the three front steps to the door, and she opened it and pulled him through. With a surge of relief, she closed the front door, and turned the lock.

"Almost done," she whispered. "Perhaps it's good you're taking your time about waking, Nicodimus. I doubt you'd like being dragged around by a female."

She peered down at his pale face, but saw no change. Trying hard to keep disappointment from consuming her, she dragged his body across the living room floor, and through the door at the back, into the bedroom there.

She let him lay on the floor alongside the bed, while she

hurried back to close and lock the bedroom door, just in case. And finally, she tugged back the covers, opened the sleeping bag, and with no small effort, maneuvered his limp form into the bed. Only then did she look again at the wound in his chest, eager to make sure his mighty heart hadn't been jostled out of place. It hadn't. It remained precisely as she had placed it. Was there more color to the pale, steadily beating heart than before? Was the tissue around it pinker? Or was it only wishful thinking?

No way to tell. Patience, she must have patience.

Drawing the covers over him, tucking them gently around him, Arianna finally slumped into the chair beside his bed, where she would wait . . . for as long as it took. Much like a funereal vigil, she thought. Only . . . in reverse. In times of old the bereaved would sit up the night through with the recently deceased corpse, the idea being to remain until the soul had surely left the body.

Arianna's strange vigil . . . was the wait for Nicodimus's soul to return. If indeed, it had ever been gone.

The silence of the room seemed to expand as she sat there. Until she could hear the beating of her own heart, and his, and no other sound.

Arianna drew Nicodimus's hand into her own and held it. The hours passed slowly, endlessly, and after more of them than she cared to count, she lost her battle with exhaustion and closed her eyes as sleep crept in to pull her under.

I emerged from a state of *nothing*, to a state of *everything*. Every part of my body burned. Every bit of my skin sizzled. My head felt as if a spike had been driven through my skull, and my chest, as if it were about to burst. The gasp I dragged in was noisy and painful. And then, just as suddenly, I went limp. Weak. Terrifyingly weak.

I opened my eyes.

A woman rose to her feet from where she'd been sitting in a chair beside the odd bed in which I lay. A beautiful woman. Her hair was cut oddly short, but golden in hue, and her eyes were as wide as all the world, and brown as a doe's. She clutched my hand in hers. And I felt it. I . . . I *felt* it!

"Nicodimus," she whispered. And one trembling, very warm hand touched my face. I thought I glimpsed teardrops dampening her eyes, but she blinked those away quickly enough, and leaned closer. "Nicodimus," she said again. "Can you hear me?"

"Yes." My lips formed the word, but the only sound that emerged was a rasp of air. I closed my eyes in frustration. The name she called me by—*Nicodimus*—yes, it was familiar to me. But my mind seemed lost in a fog I could not explain, and that my own name would seem so strange startled me. Who was I?

A coolness touched my lips, whilst a soft, strong hand lifted my head. A drinking vessel, made of glass and filled with water. I sipped from it, then drank deeply, closing my eyes once more. The liquid felt good on my parched throat. So good.

When the water was gone, the woman lowered my head again to the softness that pillowed me, and set the vessel aside. "How do you feel?" she asked me.

I had to think on that for a moment, for so many feelings were coursing through my body that it was an effort to identify any one in particular. "Weak," I finally answered. "Heavy. My head . . ." I tried to lift a hand to press to my temple, where a dull throbbing sensation lived, but found my hand barely moved. It rose slightly only to fall again, limp and useless at my side. I believe my eyes widened in alarm.

"It's all right, Nicodimus." She took my hand again in hers, and lifted my arm, bending it at the elbow, then lowering it again, bending, then lowering. Over and over. Then she began moving my fingers one by one. Her touch as gentle as a caress. And slowly, more sensation returned to the arm, the hand, though the rush of it was tingling and intense to such an extreme that it made me grimace. She then moved to the other side, manipulating that arm, that hand. By the time she finished, I found I could indeed move. Slowly, weakly, but my limbs were at least functioning now.

She moved lower, to my legs, tugging the covers aside, and as I lifted my head with great effort to glance down at her as she worked them, I saw that I was naked.

"Lady," I whispered, in a voice so choked and raw it was unfamiliar to me. "You might at least leave me covered."

She met my gaze and smiled very slightly. "I've never known you to be shy before, Nicodimus." But she tugged the covers over me from the lower part of my waist to the upper part of my thighs.

She knew me, this woman. That smile had triggered a reaction in my mind, but it was a reaction so fleeting I could not identify it.

"Who are you?" I whispered. "What has happened to me that I am so weak?"

She'd been massaging my feet, wriggling my toes, drawing the feeling back into me as if by magick. But she paused at my question, looking up slowly this time, her smile gone. "You don't remember me then? Or anything that has happened to you?"

Staring into the huge velvety wells of her eyes, I searched my mind, but found nothing. I shook my head slowly.

"Try, Nicodimus. Try to remember."

I closed my eyes, strained to find the information in my brain, but to no avail. "I am sorry. I cannot."

She nodded slowly, returning to her station at my side. "Would you like to try sitting up?" she asked.

I nodded, and her warm hands slid underneath me. She eased me upward, into a sitting position, but dizziness spun my brain in circles, and this time I did press my hands to my head.

"It will pass," she whispered, still holding me. "Easy. Take it easy."

I clung to her voice as if to a lifeline. And knew I would have tilted right off the bed had her hands not been my support. But in a few moments, the rush of dizziness passed. I lowered my hands, lifted my head tentatively, and opened my eyes. Yes. It was gone now.

But her hands remained at my shoulders.

"I . . . It is better now. Gods, what ails me?"

She drew a breath, and I sought her face. Small, with an elfin, turned up nose, and wide full lips. Eyes wide set and almond shaped, cheekbones high and sculpted. And yet she did not answer me. And it occurred to me then that she was very oddly dressed.

"It would be better," she said softly, "if you could remember on your own."

I frowned at her. "Then you'll tell me nothing?"

"I'll help you to remember, Nicodimus."

"Then do so, woman! I did not even recall my own name until you spoke it to me!"

"Calm down." Her hands on my shoulders moved higher, to the tops of them, and began a smooth, rhythmic motion of pressing and easing and moving in circles. It sent the breath rushing out of me, made me to bend my head forward. Her touch . . . it felt good. Soothing.

"Look at your right flank," she told me, still rubbing. Her hands slid behind me now, her thumbs pressing against the base of my neck, then lower as she rubbed the unbearable aching from my back.

I looked where she told me and saw the birthmark I bore. The berry-colored mark of the crescent moon. Something sparked like a near-dead ember in my mind.

"We all bear a similar mark, Nicodimus. I bear one just like yours. Now, look at the pentacle you wear around your neck."

Lowering my chin, I did. A pendant, with a quarter moon on one curve of the circle that surrounded it, and a woman—a Goddess—reclining there.

I lifted my head, and eyed the strange woman's neck. She wore a pendant just like mine.

"What are you, Nicodimus?" she asked me very gently, those eyes probing mine.

"I . . . I am a Witch." The words rolled off my tongue without forethought. "I am an immortal High Witch."

She nodded. "Yes. As am I. You see? It's coming back to you." Her voice was so soft, so encouraging to me. "Now, tell me, if you're immortal, how can you die?"

I frowned, searching the murky, blackwater depths of my mind. "I . . . my heart. I can only die if a Dark One takes my . . ." Alarm flashed in my mind then, and I found myself instinctively reaching to my side, for what, I did not know. A weapon. Yes, a dagger.

"It's all right. I am not a Dark Witch, but a Light One. Do you know how to tell the difference?"

Eyeing her warily, I nodded. "The crescent appears on the right flank in the Light, the left in the Dark."

Nodding slowly, she reached down to the odd fastening of the breeches she wore. Blue, they were, and of sturdy make. Yet they hugged her body obscenely close. The fastener slid lower, an ingenious device with teeth of metal, and she pushed the breeches down, revealing a scrap of shiny, flimsy material underneath. A minuscule pantlet that covered her perfectly rounded backside, and concealed her woman's charms from me, though not by any great degree. Turning, she showed me the mark on her right flank. Then turning again, she revealed the left, as smooth and flawless as satin.

"You see?"

I blinked, but could not take my gaze from her body. "Yes. I see."

She pulled the breeches up again, fastening them. No modesty, I thought. Not in this female.

"Someone took your precious heart, Nicodimus," she told me slowly. "A Dark Witch. I found him. He's dead now. And in his home were countless journals filled with secrets of our kind, which he spent centuries compiling. From him, I learned that it is possible to restore the life to one who has been killed in this way. By retrieving the heart, restoring its power, and replacing it in the body of its owner."

As she spoke, she pressed her palm to my chest.

"I . . . I was dead?"

"As good as dead, yes," she whispered. "But now you are alive."

I was not certain I believed this far-fetched tale she told. And yet, were it true, I owed her a great debt. Far greater than I would ever be able to repay. "I . . . Thank you." I shook my head. "You are a stranger to me. I do not even know your name, and yet you did this for me?"

Her smile wavered. "I'm not a stranger to you, Nicodimus. We knew each other once. But you'll remember, in time. My name is Arianna."

"Arianna," I whispered. "Arianna." There was something about the name, but my mind refused to tell me what. I gave my head a shake, frustration eating at my gut. "Tell me, Arianna. Have you performed this feat before, on others? This raising of slain immortals from their graves?"

She held my gaze, shook her head. "You are the first. But that other one, he had done it many times."

"And were those he restored this confused, this weak and dizzy, when they awakened?"

She averted her gaze from mine as she spoke. "All awoke confused and weakened. Some to greater degrees than others. But it passed, Nicodimus, in each of them. And I'm confident it will in you as well."

"Yes, but when?"

Her hand, trembling slightly, stroked my hair. "I cannot say when. Be patient, Nicodimus." She offered me a smile that was meant to comfort and reassure. "Come, try to stand. See if you can walk at all."

I was hesitant, but I turned obediently when she pulled me to the side, and my legs dangled over the edge of the bed. Then she came to stand in front of me, wedging her thighs between mine to get closer to me. Her arms slid beneath mine, and around to my back. "Now slide toward me," she instructed.

I did so, wondering at her lack of shyness in pressing her body against that of a near-naked man. I felt a stirring of awareness in my loins, but my body did not respond in any physical way. No hardening took place. And what I felt was, I sensed, but a faint shadow of true desire. Not because she was less than desirable. She was very desirable.

My mind knew that. My body simply seemed slow in acknowledging or reacting to the information.

My feet touched the cool floor beside hers, and my body straightened slowly upright. She held my chest tight against her, waiting, as I tried to get my balance and test my legs to see if they would support my weight.

I was shocked at how much effort this cost me. How weak-kneed I felt. Yet I managed to stand. She moved to stand beside me, rather than in front of me, all without letting go, but the change in her position caused the cover she'd placed over my body to fall away.

She ignored that. And I decided if she were not offended, I would not worry over something so insignificant as modesty. It was, I knew, the least of my troubles just now.

She slipped an arm around my waist, holding me hard against her, and then she began to move, very slowly. "Just once around the room, for now," she said. "Then you can rest until your strength returns."

My feet did not move from the floor, but rather slid along it with each step she took. The floor covering was odd. Thicker than any tapestry or floor covering I'd ever seen, and soft, but not like any fur I'd known. It was no more than ten paces to the doorway at the end of the room, and yet by the time we reached it, I was drained and struggling to remain upright. To my shame, I was leaning upon the slight woman far more heavily than she should be able to bear.

But immortals grow stronger, their senses more acute, with each passing year.

The voice of my mind whispered this information to me. I realized it was true, and that the knowledge I had once possessed was still within me, awaiting recovery. It reassured me a great deal.

Arianna paused at the closed door, turned me carefully, and then waited, giving me time to rest before starting back to the bed.

It gave me a moment to examine the room. I saw the bed. A large affair finer than any I had ever seen. The wood seemed like oak, but it gleamed with a luster unknown to me. A shine so bright it reflected the light of the oil lamp on the table beside it. The table, too, shone like glass, though it again was wood. There was a window at one end, but its curtains were drawn tight, affording not one glimpse of the world without.

We walked back to the bed, and Arianna used one hand to pull the covers back out of the way. Soft quilts, but different from those I'd known. And crisp white linens underneath, spotlessly clean. She eased me onto the bed, and I lay back gratefully. But was shocked anew at the plushness of the plump pillows, and the way the mattress seemed to cradle me like a cloud. Surely these were not stuffed with straw. No, they definitely smelled different. Their scent was one that seemed new and clean, and yet foreign to me all the same. She must be, I mused, a very wealthy woman, to afford such luxury. And yet, this place did not appear to be a castle. The room was small, its ceilings low. Still, it was far finer than any cottage I had seen. Far finer.

Arianna tugged the covers over me. "I'll bring food," she said. "You need to eat and drink a great deal in these first hours. It will help get rid of the lingering weakness."

I nodded, wondering if I could stay awake long enough to sample her fare. Surely I ought to have had enough of sleep, if I'd been dead, even for the short while it must have taken for her to find the secret in my murderer's journals and restore my heart to my body.

"I am hungry," I said.

"Of course you are. Now, I'll only be a short while. Please, Nicodimus, promise me you won't try to get up while I'm away. Just lie here and rest, all right?"

I stared at her, fussing over me like a mother over a sickly child. I dared not admit to her that I was afraid of falling asleep. Afraid I would not awaken again.

"I give you my word, Arianna," I said.

She squeezed my hand and turned to go, but I found myself gripping her hand stubbornly. Tilting her head, she gazed down at me.

"Do not be long," I said softly, hating that she might realize how confused and afraid I was.

At first I glimpsed pity in her eyes. But then she chased it away with a smile. "You really are hungry, aren't you? I promise, I'll be so fast you'll barely have time to miss me."

I returned her smile. I liked the woman. Odd, she was—as were many of her words and phrases, her clothing, her hair, and many, many other things about her—but direct, too. And seemingly very concerned with my well-being.

She glanced down at my hand on hers, and bit her lower lip. "You'll be all right," she told me. "I promise." Then she tugged her hand gently from mine, and hurried from the room.

Arianna pulled the door closed behind her, leaned back against it, and quickly blinked her eyes dry.

He was alive! Nicodimus was alive! Gods, the magnitude of it stunned her to the soul. Every emotion she'd ever felt for him had flooded back into her being as soon as she'd looked into his deep blue eyes again. For a moment, she'd forgotten that so many years had passed.

And that he'd died hating her.

She knew she mustn't let herself forget those things again. Eventually, he would remember. And there could be no doubt in her mind that he would hate her all over again.

Or would he?

Worry gnawed at her as she hurried through the small house and into the kitchen, yanking a platter and glass from the cupboard, and utensils from the drawer. He was in far worse shape than any of those written about in Dearborne's journals had been. Oh, they too had been weak at first, but according to the notes, their memories had returned within moments, and their strength to a far greater degree as well. Nicodimus had lain in the grip of death for far longer than any of them had, though. Surely it was only a matter of time before he recovered fully.

She closed her eyes, and willed it to be so—even as she feared the opposite would prove true. Dammit, maybe she should have kept the journals rather than boxing them all up and shipping them back to Raven in the States, for safe-keeping.

But no. She'd read them so thoroughly, and so often, that she had practically memorized their contents. They'd be no help to her now.

Arianna filled the platter with food. She had guessed Nicodimus would awaken ravenous, and she'd planned for it. She piled slices of ham and roast beef on the platter, added soft rolls, potatoes, and vegetables, then slathered the lot of it in gravy. She popped the feast into the microwave, and pressed a button.

Watching the modern wonder heat the food in record time, she mentally reviewed the precautions she had taken. She hadn't wanted Nicodimus to be shocked upon awakening. He had no idea how much time had truly passed, and Arianna thought it best he not learn the truth until he'd had time to adjust to simply being alive again. So she'd covered the bedroom's light fixture with a pretty scarf, and draped another over the wall switch. She'd placed furniture in front of every outlet, to prevent him seeing them and growing curious. She'd closed the shutters and drawn the drapes on the room's single window. It was a rear room, not near the road that passed by in front of the house. And it was solid. With the door closed he shouldn't detect the traffic passing by—what little of it there was here.

Not at first, anyway. Gradually, though, his immortal senses would regain their former acuity. He would hear the passing cars then. She closed her eyes and drew a breath. The timer *ping*ed. She would just deal with that when the time came. One problem at a time was more than enough to handle.

She filled the glass with milk, took the platter from the microwave, and headed back into the bedroom.

Nicodimus blinked at her in surprise, his gaze going from the heaping, steaming platter to her eyes again. "Surely you did not have time to prepare such a meal as that?"

"I had it ready and waiting, Nicodimus. I knew you'd need sustenance." She moved closer as he slowly, painstakingly, sat up in the bed. The covers fell away from his chest, and her heart tripped over itself in response to the sight of him. Glorious, as he'd always been. A flare of desire sparked to life deep in her belly. Gods, how pathetic was she? That she could want him still, just as she always had. And yet, why had she thought that would be different now? Why had she been foolish enough to believe the years would have changed that?

She hadn't prepared herself for this. She wasn't even certain she could have.

She set the platter on his lap. He frowned at it for a moment, then gripped the stainless steel fork in his fisted hand and turned it slowly. "What sort of tool is this?"

She could have kicked herself. Her first mistake. Gods knew there would be more. "It's a fork," she said. "It's to eat with."

He eyed the fork, turning it this way and that. "I have seen one before . . . in . . . Greece, I believe. But they were not the custom in my country. I never saw the need." Shrugging, he speared a hunk of meat with the fork, and drew it whole, to his lips. He bit off a chunk, while gravy dripped from the rest back onto the plate.

Arianna settled into a chair beside the bed, grateful that he seemed more interested in the food than in the fork. He ate with gusto, cleaning the plate, and using the remains of a roll to swipe the last droplets of gravy away. Then he chugged the milk and set the glass aside, wiping his mouth with the back of his hand and sighing in content.

"My praise to your cook," he said, nodding at her.

"I don't have any cook," she replied automatically.

He seemed surprised by that. "Then you are truly a woman of many talents."

Not as many as he thought, she mused, but she couldn't very well tell him the food had been purchased already made, and needed only heating up. "Would you like some more?" she asked.

He pressed a hand to his belly. "No, I am sated. Thank you. It seems I am growing more deeply indebted to you all the while."

She shook her head quickly. "No, you mustn't think of it that way. You were . . . You are my friend, Nicodimus. I would do as much for any friend."

"Then you are an exceptionally generous soul," he told her, but as he spoke his eyes seemed heavy.

"Lie back now," she whispered, leaning over him to take the dishes away, pulling the covers over him once again. "Rest."

"But there is so much I still do not know." His protest was mild, and spoken even as he settled himself into the nest of pillows.

"You have time, now. I promise you. So much time. It's safe to go to sleep Nicodimus. You'll wake again feeling stronger and more like yourself than you do now."

"That would be more reassuring," he muttered, "if I knew who 'myself' might be."

She smiled as his eyes drifted closed. "Oh, I can tell you that much, at least. Who you are, Nicodimus, is the finest man I've ever known."

His eyes opened, and he stared deeply into hers. "I fear I shall never equal such high praise."

"You already do," she told him. "You're strong and brave, honorable and honest. Intelligent and loyal."

"You . . . sound as if you know me very well."

"I did . . . once." Closing her eyes, she shook the lingering sadness away. Sadness for what she'd lost so long ago, when she had lost him. "Go to sleep now. I'll stay with you. I'll be right here when you wake."

His breath escaped on a drawn out sigh, and his eyes fell closed once more.

18

Memories came to me slowly as I slept. Dreams came to me. Dreams of a woman . . . a beautiful, fragile woman called Anya—my wife—and of two sons, Jaymes and Will. The images fluttered in my mind like a breeze through the branches of a leafy tree. None solid, just brief glimpses. A small village, the hut where we lived, Will and Jaymes hunting at my side. The happiness we'd shared.

I sought for some memory of Arianna—something to tell me who she was, and what she had been to me. For I sensed that there had been something . . . more than friendship between us. But what came was a feeling of foreboding. A certainty that the woman was not to be trusted—the feeling of pain . . . deep, intense pain, that I sensed she had caused. It was vivid, this feeling. So real that I woke to the grim certainty that she was no friend of mine, but perhaps an enemy of the most dangerous sort. That all of this caring was but a ruse, a trick of some kind.

Yet, as I opened my eyes, it was to see her there, asleep in a softly stuffed chair. She did not look like a dangerous enemy. Nor had she acted like one, thus far.

I was confused. More now than I had been before. The images creeping into my mind were disjointed and made no sense. All but one . . . a single piece of knowledge that lay there, bright as the glaring sun at midday, and just as undeniable.

Arianna stirred and opened her eyes, her gaze meeting mine, and the words tumbled from my lips without forethought. "I remember you now," I said. "You're the woman who killed me."

Her brown eyes widened as she rose from the chair. But behind the shock in her expression, I saw the guilt. Obvious guilt. It was true then.

"Nicodimus, no. I know it seemed that way to you at the time, but—"

"Where is my wife?" I demanded of her. "Where are my sons? Tell me where they are."

Closing her eyes slowly, standing motionless, she shook her head. "You . . . you remember them then."

"I love them," I whispered. "It should be my Anya, my heart, tending me now, not my betrayer."

She lowered her head as if in great pain. "She would be here if she could. But it's not possible just now, Nicodimus. I'm afraid you're stuck with me."

"The hell I am," I muttered. I flung back the covers, swung my legs to the side, and made as if to stand, but my knees buckled quickly, and I collapsed in an ungainly heap upon the floor.

She was beside me in an instant, gripping my arms, but I shoved her hands away. As she stood back, looking down on me helplessly, I gripped the edge of the bed and managed to drag myself back into it. Weak as a kitten! And completely at her mercy. It infuriated me.

"You mustn't try to get up," she told me, standing by the bed, hands clutched in front of her. Her knuckles were white, her arms trembling.

"I'll not lie here at your mercy, woman," I replied harshly. "I'll not become dependent for my very life upon my enemy."

Her expression grew hard and cold. "Right now, Nicodimus, you have no choice in the matter. You're too weak to leave here. And until your strength returns, here is where you'll stay."

I clenched my jaw until my teeth ached. Frustration burned in my belly. This weakness... I was a warrior, damn it. A fierce fighter, a skilled hunter. I was not this weakling who required a mere woman to tend to my every need.

"Don't look so devastated, Nicodimus. You're healing fast. Your body will be well again, soon, and I hope your mind along with it. The answers you demand will come. And when they do, and your strength has returned, you'll be free to leave here."

"I've no wish to wait that long," I muttered.

"No doubt tolerating my presence will be a great burden to you until then, but as I said, you have no choice." She dropped her gaze, turning away. "I'll get you some breakfast."

"Where is Anya!" I demanded in desperation as she started for the door.

She froze, her back to me. "I cannot tell you that. When you're ready to remember, you will."

She left, giving me no time to issue the threats hovering on my lips. I wanted to leap from my sickbed and close my hands around her tender throat, to choke the answers from her if need be. She knew the answers to the questions burning in my mind. I could see plainly that she did. I wanted to make her tell me of my wife and my sons. But I was unable. Weaker than a woman, when I had once been the strongest man in my clan. I could have howled in frustration.

The tale she'd told, of having brought me back to life by replacing the heart in my chest... it was untrue. It was no more than a well-spun web of lies. She was responsible for my downfall, she'd all but admitted as much. Why would my enemy wish to help me now?

No, she had reasons for what she did now. Reasons for keeping me here, keeping me from my family, and from knowing the truth. Some plot, some scheme I couldn't begin to fathom. Else why would I feel this certainty of her past treachery burning so strongly in my gut?

I would find the truth behind the lies she told. I would!

Arianna sank down at the kitchen table, burying her head in her hands. Her back ached from the night spent in a chair, and her heart ached from Nicodimus's rejection of her. His mistrust. When she ought to have been prepared for it. She had told herself that she was, that she would be able to handle it when his memories of her began to return.

"He has every right to hate me," she muttered. "I knew that before he ever awoke."

And yet she'd hoped . . . foolishly, perhaps, that it would be different now. Stupid. She was stupid and her heart was behaving like the heart of the young girl he'd known. It would only get worse when he remembered all of it. The true extent of her betrayal, as he had perceived it. He would hate her even more when he remembered seeing her in the arms of his worst enemy. And Marten's words as Nicodimus lay dying. She ought to prepare herself for that. Until this very moment, she'd thought she knew what to expect and how to cope with it. But now . . . Gods, she hadn't expected it to hurt this much!

At least she knew now the true reason he'd never been able to love her. It went beyond his past pain. The truth was, he'd never stopped loving his wife. His Anya. He loved her still. Remembered her, even when he'd forgotten everything else.

It was going to devastate him all over again when he remembered Anya's death, and his sons' as well. And he would refuse to let her offer any comfort at all.

A knock came at the front door, and Arianna lifted her head slowly. Brushing the tears from her eyes, giving a quick glance toward the back of the house to be sure Nicodimus hadn't dragged himself into sight, she rose and went to answer it.

Her beautiful sister stood there, brows instantly furrowing as she searched Arianna's face. And then Raven was hugging her close. "What's happened? You look terrible, Arianna, what's happened?"

Arianna hugged her sister in return, looking over Raven's shoulder to Duncan, who stood just behind her. Sighing, she stepped back. "Come in. How on earth did you find me?"

"Not easily," Duncan said, ushering Raven through the door. "We've been trying to catch up to you since you left Sanctuary, but you've been difficult to catch up to, Arianna."

"I might not have been, if I'd known you were looking," she said, raising a brow in question.

"We finally gave up and went back home," Raven explained. "Then the package arrived, containing Dearborne's journals . . . with this address on the return label."

Arianna sighed resignedly. She should have known her sister would follow her here. "The journals, yes. Did you . . . did you read them?"

Raven closed her eyes and nodded, no doubt recalling the horrific tales those journals held. Then she faced Arianna again. "Did you find him?" Raven asked. "Did you find this man you were so determined to resurrect?"

Arianna nodded tiredly, and led them into the kitchen, and to the table. Raven and Duncan sat down, and she put a pot of coffee on to brew, and a kettle for tea, which Duncan still preferred. "I found him."

"And?" Raven leaned forward in her chair.

"He's weak, confused. His memory is sketchy. But on one thing, he's very clear. Nicodimus hates me, blames me for his death, just as he did then. But . . . I'd expected as much."

"Oh, Arianna." Raven got up quickly and came to take the kettle from her hands. "Sit, darling. Rest. Let me do this."

She ushered Arianna into a chair and took over.

"Why don't you just tell him the truth?" Duncan asked softly.

Arianna lifted her head and looked at him. "You don't even know what the truth is, Duncan. How can you be so sure it would do any good?"

He offered her a gentle smile. "I know you well enough to know you didn't betray him the way he seems to think you did. You couldn't. Not a man you love."

"Loved," she corrected quickly.

Duncan sent Raven a swift glance, a silent message. "Okay. If you say so."

Arianna leaned back in her chair, shoulders slumping. "He doesn't even remember that his first wife and his sons are dead, Duncan. He keeps asking for them, and I just can't . . ."

As her voice trailed off, Duncan covered her hand with one of his. "Don't you think you ought to tell him, Arianna? Wouldn't it be for the best? I know it might seem a cruel thing to do, but it seems to me it's more cruel to let him go on not knowing."

Arianna shook her head. "His memories are coming back slowly. He'll realize soon enough." She shrugged. "Besides, I doubt he'd believe a word I said at this point."

"But Arianna, you saved his life!" Raven protested, turning from the small range and coming back to the table.

"I don't think he believes that, either. He'd be out of here if he had the strength to leave."

"Well then, thank goodness he doesn't! Arianna, he remembers the world as it was centuries ago. He has no clue how to get by in it today."

Arianna nodded slowly. "I had planned to help him, to teach him . . . but . . ."

"No matter. What do you say I pay the fellow a visit, hmm?" Duncan asked. "Perhaps he'd feel a bit better talking to another man."

"You're welcome to try," Arianna whispered.

With a nod, Duncan got to his feet, but Arianna gripped his hand. "Be very careful what you say, Duncan. Nicodimus has no idea how much time has passed, and I'd prefer he not know just yet. He has so much to deal with already."

"I won't give anything away, I promise, though I disagree with you on the wisdom of that." He squeezed her hand.

"Tell him I'll bring his breakfast soon."

Duncan nodded and left the room, following the directions Arianna gave for finding her houseguest. Arianna rose to begin preparing a meal for the lot of them, and Raven got up as well. "Don't cook. Let's walk to that lovely little bakery in town and get bread and pastries for breakfast, instead."

Arianna smiled at her sister. The sunshine on her face would feel good today. But then she sent a worried frown toward the back of the house.

"It'll only take us a few minutes," Raven insisted. "I'm sure Duncan can hold his own against a man who can barely stand upright for that long." She looked deeply into Arianna's eyes, her onyx ones filled with reassurances. "You're not on your own anymore, big sister. Duncan and I are here to help, and we'll stay for as long as you need us."

Blinking away the unexpected rise of tears, Arianna finally nodded. "All right. Let me just put on some fresh clothes."

When the door opened, I looked up, expecting to see the wounded eyes of my captor again—and they *had been* wounded. As if my suspicion of her caused her inexplicable pain. If she truly were my enemy, then why would she react that way to my accusations? It made no sense. And yet the certainty that I had indeed hurt her remained.

But it was not Arianna who entered my prison. Instead, it was a man I did not know. Tall he was, dark of hair, with a well-muscled frame that bespoke strength. As I had possessed once. His clothing was as strange as Arianna's was to me. I stiffened, instantly suspicious of him.

"Easy, big guy. I'm a friend."

I did not relax, though his eyes were indeed friendly as he perused me. "If you are a friend, you will take me out of this place," I suggested.

He smiled. "As soon as you're strong enough, I'll do just that—if you still want to go. You have my word on it."

I narrowed my eyes on him. "Who are you? If I know you, I have no memory of it."

He came closer, extending a hand. "Duncan Wallace," he said. I took the hand he offered. His grip was cool and firm, and the jolt that passed between us gave me to know he was an immortal, like me. "And this is the first time we've met."

"Then you are a friend of Arianna's?" I asked him.

He hesitated. "She has been a friend to me, yes."

"Trust her at your peril, Duncan Wallace," I told him grimly.

He sighed deeply, drew up a chair and took it with ease. "I do trust her," he said. "But she seems to think you don't."

"I do not. And with good reason."

"Wronged you once, did she?"

I nodded. "No doubt you disbelieve it."

"No," he said. "I believe it. Arianna is impulsive and wild and often reckless. But her heart is good. And if she did wrong you, Nicodimus, then I believe she regrets it with everything in her. And she's trying very hard to make it up to you now."

Those words gave me pause. I lifted my brows, searching his face for a sign he was lying to me, but saw only openness and honesty in his eyes. "Has she told you the details of how she betrayed me?"

Duncan shook his head. "No. Do you remember them?"

"No," I said. "Only small bits of certainty that she did, and that it cost me dearly."

Duncan drew a deep breath and sighed. "Perhaps it would be best to reserve final judgment until you remember what truly happened. Maybe . . . maybe there's some explanation for what she did."

"It is so infuriating to not remember!" I closed my eyes tightly.

"I know. I've been in a very similar situation myself, you know. And not so long ago."

This caught my attention and I eyed him again. "Truly?" I asked.

He nodded hard. "That's why I thought I might be of some help to you now. I know how maddening it is to have bits of memory that tease at the edges of your mind, only to vanish again before you can grasp them. I know how difficult it is to put those bits together in some way that makes sense. But it will come together, in time. I promise you."

I believed him. And for the first time since I had "awakened," I felt some semblance of hope come to life in my chest. I was unwilling to believe fully in a man who was a friend of my enemy, and yet I felt instinctively that he could be trusted. That he wished to aid me in this, just as he said he did.

"How long?" I asked him.

His lips thinned. "I wish I could tell you. In my case, it was only a matter of a couple of weeks. It might very well be less with you."

"Or it might be a good deal more," I said softly.

"It's only time, my friend. You're immortal. Time is something you have in abundance."

I nodded. "Patience, however, is not," I said.

He grinned at me. "We must be related then. Distant cousins, perhaps?"

A reluctant smile tugged at my lips. I could easily come to like this strange man. "What land are we in, Duncan, that the natives dress so strangely?" I nodded at his clothes. The sturdy blue that covered his legs, much like those Arianna had worn. And the garment on top that buttoned up the front and tucked into them.

He seemed taken aback by my question, and relief filled his eyes when the door opened again and Arianna entered, carrying heaping platters of fragrant baked goods. Another woman, taller, and very dark of hair and eyes, entered behind her, carrying a tray laden with drinking vessels and containers of brew that steamed.

"Breakfast has arrived," the dark one announced cheerfully. The two women lowered the feast to a nearby table, as I eyed the newcomer. A woman of rare beauty, she was. And her coloring reminded me of someone else. Another woman, very dark and tall. Slender as a reed, I thought, as a brief, flickering image of her crept into my mind. She'd loved me very dearly . . . and I her, but . . .

The image vanished as quickly as it had come, and I blinked away my frustration.

"Who are you?" I asked the woman.

Arianna parted her lips, but before she could utter a word, the woman said, "My name is Raven," she said. "I'm Arianna's sister."

My brows lowered, and my mind whirled. "But . . . but Arianna's sister is dead . . ."

Three pairs of eyes widened, and Raven clapped a hand to her mouth. But already, more memories were returning.

Marten had watched Arianna and her female companion as they walked the short distance to the bakery, and again as they returned to the small house, their arms loaded down with food. He'd always hoped to come across the beautiful Arianna again, someday. The few times he'd had word that she'd been seen in any given place, however, he'd arrived only to find her gone. Or, if he did glimpse her, she would be in the company of this other woman. He supposed he could have found her, if he'd put his mind to it. And yet he hadn't. He didn't like to think too deeply about why that was. But he knew, and the knowledge was a bitter pill indeed. She'd been very convincing that day so long ago. And in the time he'd held her captive . . . he'd come to care for her in a way that was completely foreign to him. When she had come to him, when she had returned his ardent kisses . . . there had been a few brief moments when he'd allowed himself to believe she cared for him as well.

The truth of her motives had cut him deeply. Her rejection . . . it had shamed him. So much that he still felt pain when he recalled it.

Part of him feared that when he saw her again, he would see pure hatred in her eyes as he had seen that day. It was an experience he had no desire to relive. So while he had fantasized about seeing her again, he'd done nothing to make it come about.

Now, however, events had taken a strange turn. Perhaps he would take this chance to have her, at last. He'd always wanted her. She, he reminded himself, had rejected him, tricked him, used him. Now that she was here, and he was so close to her, he found he had an urge to extract his revenge. Perhaps he would at that, when he finished with his other business.

Every year on the anniversary of Nicodimus's death, Marten visited his burial site to dance on his grave and gloat over his victory. It had been easy enough to find the burial site of his oldest enemy. For a beautiful young woman driving a wagon alone, with a satin-wrapped body bouncing in the back had been a remarkable sight in those days. So the few people who'd seen Arianna pass by had remembered her.

It ate at him that he'd never had the chance to take Nicodimus's heart himself, to drain it of its very life. Dearborne had stolen that from him.

He'd heard old Dearborne had finally met his match. He was nearly as glad to see that old immortal dead as he had been Nicodimus. He'd hidden from that old man for centuries, in fear Dearborne would find him and kill him for no more reason than the sport of it.

At any rate, this year, Marten's annual visit to the grave of Nicodimus had been different. This time he'd found the grave empty, barren, though refilled with freshly turned earth. And thoughts began to pound at his brain.

Dearborne, the treacherous cur who'd used him and would have likely killed him had the opportunity not been wrested from his grip, had hinted that the second death was not necessarily the final one for immortals. That there was a way even *it* could be reversed. And if anyone would know, it would have been that old man. For he'd captured and toyed with countless immortals in the time Marten had known him. He'd made use of Marten's own dungeons for his gruesome experiments on Light High Witches, before killing them in the end. He reminded Marten of a cruel cat, the way it will torture and tease a mouse until there is so little life left in the creature that the sport is gone. Then the cat will devour it.

Yes, Dearborne had hinted, but he'd refused to tell Marten what he knew. And he'd kept his precious journals under lock and key. But now . . . now the thought Dearborne had planted in Marten's mind returned. Was resurrection from the second death possible? Could an immortal whose heart had been taken, be revived? The possiblity tormented him, especially when he saw that open grave, and learned that Arianna was right here in this town. Had Arianna somehow learned of Dearborne's secrets, and used them to revive his blood enemy? Was that bastard Nicodimus once again alive and breathing?

If he was, Marten vowed, he would not be for long. And there was only one way to find out. Watch Arianna. If Nicodimus were alive somewhere, he would come to her, sooner or later. The beautiful Arianna would serve as bait for Marten's trap.

Just as she had done before.

Arianna could have choked her sister for the slip. But it was an honest mistake. Raven had known Nicodimus as a child, in another lifetime, one that had ended centuries ago. Naturally she would have no memory of that. And Arianna had only given her sister the sketchiest of details about her own brief time with Nicodimus. No, this was her own fault, not her sister's.

"I'm so sorry," Raven whispered, backing away, eyes wide.

"No. Don't be." Arianna moved closer to the bed where Nicodimus sat, as still as stone. "You know, Nicodimus is going to need clothes. Why don't you two go into the village and see what you can find? My purse is in the kitchen."

Raven nodded, understanding. Duncan gave Arianna's shoulder a squeeze before they both turned and left. Alone with Nicodimus, Arianna wondered how much to tell him, how much he already might know.

"I . . . assumed I had only been in the grave a short

while," Nicodimus said softly, slowly. His gaze seemed turned inward as he searched his mind. "But if she is your dead sister . . . grown now . . ." He lifted his gaze. "Did you revive her in the same way? I . . . I thought you said I was the first?"

Arianna sighed, pushing a hand through her hair. "No. No, Nicodimus. My sister drowned when she was but a child. That memory will likely return to you soon. She wasn't immortal then. She didn't die because some Dark One had taken her heart as you did. She died . . . trying to save my life."

Nicodimus closed his eyes, nodding slowly. "And so returned to her next lifetime as an immortal."

Arianna nodded. "Yes. And I had to wait until she was reborn into that new lifetime to find her again."

His brows rose, but other than that, there was no reaction. "Your sister is grown," he murmured. "Born again, and a woman grown." It was as if he were clarifying this in his own mind. "Immortal, this time."

She nodded. "Yes. She's one of us now."

"And her age?"

He wanted to know how much time had passed. He wanted her to tell him. Gods, it would be so hard for him. She didn't answer him. She couldn't.

"I remember my Anya," he said slowly. "Young and fair. Hair like fire. My sons, just lads . . . but they must be grown now. And Anya . . . older . . . 'Tis more than my mind can grasp. She . . . she was pregnant with our third child when last I recall seeing her. A girl." Then his brows bunched in concentration. "But how could I know the child was a girl unless . . ."

"Nicodimus, don't push yourself," Arianna pled, but it was too late. His head came up suddenly, eyes wide and anguished as the memory hit him. She saw it come, saw the utter pain that made his face into a mask of torment.

"Oh, Gods, she died! Anya died and our babe with her!" He pressed his hands to either side of his head as his eyes moved rapidly from side to side, seeing nothing but the memory, she knew. His breaths came fast and short. "She died, she died in childbirth. Oh, Anya, sweet Anya . . ." Tears brimmed in his eyes, and he lowered his head, covering his face with his hands.

Unable to bear seeing him in so much agony, Arianna went to the bed, sank onto its edge, and put her arms around him. She hugged him close, stroked his hair. "I'm sorry, Nicodimus. I'm so sorry, more than I can tell you. I wish . . . I wish I could take this pain away."

He straightened slowly, staring hard into her eyes. "What of the boys, Arianna? What of my sons?"

She blinked, and shook her head. "I . . . in time you'll remember. . . ."

His hands clutched her shoulders hard, more strength in his grip than she had realized he possessed, and his eyes stabbed into hers like daggers. "Tell me!"

Closing her eyes, Arianna took a deep breath. "There was a plague . . . it claimed the youngest. And your firstborn died at your side during a battle."

He released her all at once, tipped his head back, his hands like claws clutching at his face. His cry was one of such intense despair she felt tears streaming down her own cheeks. And she could only sit there, crying, watching him fight the pain, for a long time.

When at last his body stopped trembling, and his breaths came more evenly, he faced her again, eyes red-rimmed and dull with grief. "Why did you do this to me?" he asked her. "Why did you bring me back to this grief? This heartache?"

"I . . . I thought—"

"My family is gone. I belong with them, but instead I live on, alone and too weak to do more than lie in this cursed bed! Damn you for this!"

"You were not with them, Nicodimus!" Arianna got to her feet, determined to make him understand. "And you'd lived for a long time without them when my foolishness got you killed. But even then, you were not with them. You were lying in a shallow grave in some state of limbo. Not dead, but not alive. Trapped there, in some in-between place . . . forever. I . . . I only wanted to free you from that."

"There was another way!" he shouted, glaring at her in undisguised fury. "You could have freed me by burning my heart and my body. You could have returned me to my family!"

She lowered her head. "Yes, I could have. But I didn't. I foolishly believed you would prefer life to death, Nicodimus."

He shook his head slowly, his back bent, shoulders slumped. "At least . . . there was no pain there," he whispered.

"No, there wasn't. No pain. No joy. No pleasure. No life at all."

He sighed, a deep, wounded sound. "Why did you bring me back?"

She closed her eyes. "Because I owed you. I wronged you, and it was the only way I could see to make it right."

Grating his teeth, stiffening his spine as if making ready to receive a blow, he asked, "What is the year in which I now live, Arianna? Just how much time did I lie mostly dead in the grave?"

She felt her eyes widen. "I . . ."

"Tell me. And speak the truth. I must know sooner or later, you realize that. Simply tell me, for the love of the Gods!"

Nodding, she bit her lower lip.

"Tell me," he went on when she didn't speak right away. "I am not a fool, Arianna. I see that the window is blocked from without. I see what care you and the others take when speaking to me. It is obvious now that time has passed. The way you speak, the clothes you wear. . . . It is all very different. Has it been a decade?" He stared hard at her. "A century?"

He waited for her to give him the answer. Waited, and silently demanded she tell him what he needed to know. "It has been," she whispered at last, "nearly five centuries."

"Five?"

Lifting her gaze to meet his, she nodded slowly. "The year is nineteen hundred ninety-nine," she told him. "We are at the dawn of the third millennium."

He sat there, still and silent, searching inside himself for understanding.

"You'll be all right, I promise you, Nicodimus. I'll help you to adjust, and to learn, and you'll be fine. You're a strong man, an intelligent man, and—"

"A man who cannot walk across a room without help from a woman. A man held captive by his own betrayer."

"I am not your captor, Nicodimus," she whispered. "And I didn't betray you. Not the way you think—"

He shook his head slowly. "Take a dagger to my chest, woman. End it here. Undo what you've done. I've no wish to linger in this place."

She swallowed hard. "Now you're feeling sorry for yourself. I won't let you do that. It's not like you."

"And what do you know of me?"

She leaned close to him, touched his cheek with her palm and turned his face so she could stare into his eyes. "I know you well enough to know that this pain will ease. Never end altogether, but ease. I know your strength, Nicodimus. It's unlike that of any other man I have ever known. And I know, too, that even now, somewhere beneath this crippling grief, you're curious to see what the world is like, how it has changed after all this time."

He pulled from her touch, averting his eyes. "You know nothing."

She shrugged. "Maybe not. But I do know you won't get strong again unless you eat. And the food is here, waiting, untouched. I don't imagine your appetite is very good just now, after all these shocks. But force yourself, Nicodimus. If for no other reason than to hasten the time when you'll be able to walk out of my house, and never have to see me again."

He sent her a narrow-eyed glare. "That is all the reason I need," he muttered, and reached out to snatch a pastry from the tray. "Leave me in peace," he said. "Give me that much, at least."

She nodded, heaved a sigh, and headed out of the bedroom, closing the door behind her.

And as she stood there with her back to the living room, she knew she was no longer alone in the house. Someone else was here . . . and not Raven or Duncan. There hadn't been time for them to return from their errands in town.

She turned, a shiver of foreboding working up her spine. A woman stood facing her. A woman she hadn't seen in a very long time. Dark and exotic as ever, but no longer beautiful. Nidaba's hair hung in tangles, dirty, its sheen faded. Her eyes were sunken and hollow. Dark circles surrounded them, and she wore a dress that seemed to be rotting with age before Arianna's eyes. Even her jewelry—and she wore as much as she always had, right to the ruby stud in her nose—was dulled by the touch of time.

"You," Nidaba whispered. "I told you once I would kill you if I saw you again."

"Nidaba. Gods, where have you been? What's happened to—"

"*Where is he?* What have you done with Nicodimus's body?" She shot forward on unsteady legs, her hands clutching Arianna's shoulders. "I went to visit his grave and he's gone! I should have known it was you! I should have known! Tell me, wench, where is he?"

Arianna pulled free, only to stagger to one side, banging into a small stand. A vase tumbled to the floor and shattered with a loud crash. And still Nidaba came at her.

"My Gods, Nidaba, what's happened to you?" The darkness of insanity seemed to glow from within Nidaba's once flawless eyes. "Calm down. Nicodimus is fine. He's fine, Nidaba."

"Fine? He's dead, and it's all because of you! You!" She made a growling sound in her throat, teeth drawing back from her lips in an ugly snarl, and she came at Arianna with her hands bent clawlike.

Arianna reacted instinctively. Years of fighting for survival had given her reflexes too strong to override. She reached to her side for the dagger that hung there, concealed by her blouse, but then her hand froze. She couldn't harm Nidaba. Not the woman who had been some kind of heroic figure to her once. Something horrible had happened to put Nidaba in this maddened state.

Suddenly the haunting words written in Dearborne's journal came floating back to her mind. "No," she whispered. "Gods, it *was* you, wasn't it?"

Nidaba brought her clawed hand flashing down as if to strip the skin from Arianna's face. Arianna lifted her hands to cover her eyes in self-defense.

But Nidaba stopped suddenly, one hand still gripping Arianna's shoulder, and she stared wide-eyed at something beyond Arianna. Slowly, Arianna realized Nicodimus stood behind her. She felt his presence, as she always had.

"Nicodimus?" Nidaba whispered. "How . . . ?"

"Release her, Nidaba."

Arianna turned, sighing in relief when Nidaba's hand fell away. Nicodimus stood near the open bedroom door. He wore a blanket tied around his middle, and one hand was braced on the door frame to hold him upright.

Arianna took a step toward him, but Nidaba shot past her, and Nicodimus enfolded the trembling woman in his arms and held her close. "There," he whispered. "It will be all right, Nidaba. It will be all right now."

Arianna stood watching them, and remembered all the poisonous things Marten had told her . . . that the two were lovers, that they had been for centuries, and that there was no room for anyone else in Nicodimus's heart. She hadn't believed it then . . . not completely. But now . . . now she wondered.

Nidaba sobbed in Nicodimus's arms, sobbed as if she would never stop. And gently, Nicodimus stroked her tangled hair and murmured words of comfort to her. His eyes met Arianna's over Nidaba's head. Some unspoken questions in them. *What has happened to her? Are you responsible for this, as well?*

Arianna only shook her head slowly. She didn't know. She didn't know what hell had befallen Nidaba. Not for certain. But she had suspicions. Dark, nightmarish suspicions that made her sick to her stomach.

Had Nidaba been one of Dearborne's captives? The dark woman he spoke of, who had escaped him after months, perhaps years, of torment?

The front door opened, and Duncan and Raven stepped inside with packages and bags in their arms. Arianna met their puzzled glances, and held a finger to her lips for silence, as Nicodimus slowly drew Nidaba back through the door and into his bedroom.

19

Nidaba. The memory of her came rushing back to me all at once. I knew her. She had been closer to me than anyone in my life. My friend. My one and only friend at many times during my long, lonely life. My *best* friend, always.

She clung to me, crying softly for a time as I eased her into the bed I'd been occupying myself. And then she clung to me still as I sat down beside her. She didn't speak a coherent sentence in all the time I held her. Only sobbed, and kept repeating my name. Other words, phrases, made no sense to me. And I knew her mind was more than simply troubled. I feared for Nidaba, my heart ached with it.

She calmed, gradually, begged me not to leave her alone, and finally, she cried herself to sleep in my arms.

She had been the strongest woman I had ever known. To see her reduced to this quivering, childlike state of hysteria frightened me right to the core.

Arianna entered the room. I could have snapped at her for intruding, but I knew it had been some time since I'd drawn Nidaba in here. She had been patient, I supposed. Considering this was her home, and this strange woman had attacked her on sight. No doubt she'd have Nidaba thrown into the streets now. Or try to. I would not let that happen without a fight.

Arianna didn't speak, just stood quietly near the door, apparently ready to leave the room, should I order it. I looked up at her. Her gaze seemed very vulnerable, and slightly wounded as it lingered on Nidaba's sleeping form, her head all but in my lap, her arms locked 'round my waist.

"She was the one who found me with the Druids, where I'd gone to nurse my grief. It was she who convinced me to live again, when I only wished to die. I had lost my wife, my sons, my unborn daughter, and then my entire clan had been destroyed. I had revived to a life I did not understand," I said, very softly, for I did not wish to wake Nidaba. Still, she shuddered now and again with residual sobs.

"She was the one to take me from that temple, when my studies with the holy men had ended. She was the one who taught me the many things they could not."

Arianna walked farther into the room, and her eyes seemed to well with sadness, not the anger I had expected, as she gazed at Nidaba. "What things didn't they teach you?" she asked softly.

"To fight, to kill. To stay alive," I told her. "I laughed at first. I, a warrior, being taught to fight by a mere woman. I remember the narrow-eyed look she gave me when I said those words. The haughty indignation. But indulgent." Reaching down, I stroked Nidaba's hair, and gently moved her arms from around me, easing her into a more comfortable position upon the pillows. "She has always been indulgent with me. And so we fought our mock battles and I realized that fighting the most skilled mortal warrior was not even close to battling an immortal. But I learned fast."

"I imagine you did," Arianna said.

"We have parted many times, gone our separate ways, but always, we find each other again. I love her," I stated emphatically, as I slid from the bed, keeping my blanket anchored like a kilt around my hips. "I love her the way I imagine you must love your sister."

Arianna stared at me, then eyed the sleeping woman

again. "She does not cling to you in a way that seems exactly sisterly to me, Nicodimus."

I blinked as her meaning came clear to me. "What you are thinking is incorrect, Arianna. Though why this concerns you I cannot know. My memories are broken, but of this, I am certain. Nidaba and I have never been lovers." I tilted my head, studying the color in Arianna's cheeks, and the glint of jealousy in her eyes. Unmistakable. "But I wonder now, what of you and I?"

Her gaze flew from Nidaba's sleeping form to my face, eyes going wider. "What do you mean?"

"What were you to me, Arianna?"

She shook her head vehemently. "Far less than Nidaba was," she whispered. "Or Anya or your sons. That much should be obvious."

"Why?" I asked, moving still closer to her. "Because I remembered them before you? Tell me, Arianna, did I know you before them, or after?"

She looked up slowly. "After. A long while after."

I shrugged. "Then it could very well be that my mind is pulling the past to me in order of chronology, rather than of import. Could it not?"

She bit her lip, looked away. "I think not. And besides, it's unimportant. What is important is Nidaba." She looked again at the sleeping woman. "Poor thing. She was so strong when last I saw her. So fierce. To see her like this . . ." She lowered her head, shaking it slowly.

I nodded, seeing the sincere worry in her eyes. Could this woman truly be evil if she cared deeply for Nidaba? Even after Nidaba had attacked her, in her own home?

"When was it . . . that you saw her last," I asked, as eager for answers as Arianna seemed to be.

She hesitated and looked up at me. "It was right after . . . after you had been killed by a Dark One named Nathanial Dearborne. I tried to kill him, but he fled, taking your . . ."—her eyes focused on my chest—"your heart with him."

I felt my own eyes widen with surprise. "You fought him?"

"I was out of my mind with rage." She shook her head. I wondered that a girl as small and delicate as she would try to avenge my death on an immortal strong enough to have defeated me in battle, but I said no more.

"I took your body back to the ancient Stone Circle to bury you. It was a place you loved very much," she said. "On the way, I stopped near a stream to bathe you and wrap you in a satin coverlet. That was when Nidaba came along. And I . . . I had to tell her you'd been taken from us."

I nodded slowly. "She would have been devastated by the news."

"She was. She screamed to the heavens, blamed me, told me she'd kill me if we crossed paths again, very nearly decided to do it right then and there."

"You didn't fight her?" I asked suddenly, certain I had known no immortal who could outfight Nidaba.

"No."

She did not elaborate, leaving me to wonder what, exactly, had transpired between the two.

"When she left," Arianna went on, "she demanded the name of the man who had killed you. I was certain she would go after him herself. And if she found him, Nicodimus, she didn't kill him. I know that, because I saw him again only recently. Duncan was the one who finally ended his cursed existence."

I nodded thoughtfully.

"You must find out if Nidaba spent any time with this Dearborne," Arianna said softly. "When she wakes, if you feel she is ready, ask her, Nicodimus. But ask her very gently. And if she reacts strongly, then let the matter rest. Don't press her."

I narrowed my gaze on her. "Why? What do you know of this man?"

She focused on Nidaba again. "He kept journals. He was obsessed with becoming the strongest immortal alive, and to do that, he felt he must learn of our every weakness. It was through his studies and notes that I learned how to replace a heart, to bring a victim back, as I did with you."

I nodded. "But there is more."

"Yes, there is more. He . . . kept captives at times. Immortals he would weaken through many methods. Pain, torture, starvation. He would kill them by mortal means, and make detailed notes on how long it took them to revive, and whether multiple deaths and resurrections seemed to weaken their hearts. Sometimes, he took hearts, only to wait a time and replace them." She closed her eyes and shuddered. "He used them to experiment on, Nicodimus. The notes of these experiments read like the transcriptions of nightmares. And I fear . . . I fear Nidaba might have been in his hands, for a time."

I felt my blood boil in my veins. "Where are these notes?"

"They're at my sister's home. I can have them sent here, if you wish. You're free to read them, Nicodimus, but I can tell you already you will not find what you're looking for. Dearborne didn't name the captives he kept. Nidaba's name was never mentioned. There is no way we can know for certain . . . unless she tells us."

I closed my eyes in pain. Gods, the thought of Nidaba going through such torment! "If the man lived still, I would kill him myself."

"He deserves a thousand deaths for what he did, Nicodimus, but he had only one. I burned his heart to release his spirit. Had I known then, what crimes he'd committed, I might not have had the generosity to do so."

I paced toward the bed, vaguely surprised that my legs seemed to be functioning more readily than they had until now. "What will become of Nidaba now?" I asked softly.

"What do you mean?" Arianna asked. "She'll stay here, with us, of course. We can care for her. Perhaps in time . . . her mind will heal."

I turned toward Arianna, searching her face for the villainess I had believed her to be. But found no sign of it in her deep brown eyes. "She attacked you," I said. "She threatened to kill you. Might have done so, had I not come out in time."

"She loves you," Arianna returned, her voice gentle. "And she needs our help."

I nodded slowly, watching her face. "You . . . did not fight back, when she attacked you."

"*You* love *her*, as well, Nicodimus. I couldn't take away another person you love. I could never do that."

She confused me, this woman, who admitted betraying me, admitted costing me my life, and yet seemed to be nothing but goodness to her core. And beauty. Pure beauty such as I could scarcely bear to look upon.

"She should sleep for a while," she said quietly. "You're getting stronger. Perhaps you'd like to bathe, and put on something besides that blanket while she rests."

I glanced down at myself and nodded. "If she wakes . . ."

"I can lock the door in case she bolts. And station Duncan outside in case she needs anything. But truly, I think she'll sleep for a long time. Look at her. She's exhausted."

I nodded my agreement. "I think . . . perhaps the door should be left ajar. If she's been held captive in the past . . ."

Arianna nodded. "You're right. We'll leave it unlocked and open a bit."

"Good. Then . . . I shall bathe."

She smiled gently, and took my hand. And at her touch, the familiar jolt rocked through me, but something else accompanied it. Another jolt. A physical awareness so very powerful it left my knees weaker than they had been before. Her skin . . . her scent . . . her touch . . . all were familiar, and tickling to life some distant memories from deep beneath the surface of my mind. A flash, and no more. A sudden recollection of my own feeling of intense arousal, of longing. Her mouth beneath mine as I tasted and probed its recesses. Her breath near my ear, promising things, whispering secrets my mind still struggled to keep from me. *You will love me one day, Nicodimus. You will love me just as I love you. You'll see.*

• • •

She watched his expressions as she led him through the house to the stairs. She wanted him to use the upstairs bathroom. There was a bath below, of course, but they'd be less likely to disturb Nidaba with the noise if they used this one.

His gaze danced around each room they passed through, fixing on light fixtures, the refrigerator, the switches and plugs in the walls, the stereo system, and other things he couldn't possibly identify. The television set was, thankfully turned off just then.

"What's up?" Raven asked as they started up the stairs.

Nicodimus leaned heavily on the bannister, so Arianna paused to let him rest a moment. "Nicodimus is ready to be out of bed. So we're going to try a bath and a shave."

"Here, you'll need these." Duncan quickly snatched up a pair of shopping bags. "Meanwhile, what about our . . . other guest?"

Arianna felt a rush of pain. "Nidaba is a friend . . . or was once. When I last saw her, she was going after Dearborne. And from the state of her now . . ."

"Oh no," Raven whispered. "Gods, no, tell me you're not thinking . . . what we read in those journals . . ."

Arianna nodded at her sister. "It's possible. I can't be sure, but my senses are telling me it's true. I thought of Nidaba when I first read Dearborne's account of the prisoner he called 'the dark woman.' " Sighing, Arianna pushed the gruesome memory from her mind. "She's resting now. But the bedroom door is unlocked. Just keep an eye on her, will you?"

Raven nodded.

Nicodimus turned to Duncan. "Nidaba is dangerous in this state," he warned. "Take care."

"I'll be careful. Don't worry," Duncan said. "Go on, enjoy your pampering. We'll yell if we need you."

Nodding, Nicodimus began moving up the stairs again, slowly. At the top, Arianna led him into the small bathroom and eased him onto a chair at the vanity.

"It is," he murmured, "as if I've entered an entirely new world. I see everything, yet recognize . . . almost nothing."

"It must be very upsetting to you. It will get easier, I promise."

He nodded, but looked doubtful.

"I guess we'd better start at the beginning. We use a power called electricity for just about everything now. It's the same kind of energy that creates lightning. Mankind has learned to generate the power, and it is connected by wires to most homes. With this power, we no longer have to use candles or oil lamps for light." She moved the light switch on the wall, and the lights came on in the dim bathroom. "See?"

Nicodimus stared up at the lights overhead, and the rounded bulbs lining the top of the mirror. "No," he said. "I do not see at all."

"I'll show you the wires later, and try to explain in more detail how it works. The same electricity powers the pumps, so we can have water pumped in as we want it. It also heats the water, if we like." She leaned over the tub, closed the plunger, and turned on the water, adjusting the temperature and letting the tub fill.

Nicodimus watched it with awe. "It is amazing. Truly amazing."

He turned to the sink, seeing the spigots there similar to the ones in the tub, and reached up to turn a knob. Then he jumped backward when water shot out.

"It's all right," Arianna soothed. "Go ahead, play around with it a bit. Get a feel for how to work it."

"I have seen such things before. The bathhouses in Rome. But the water there was heated by the earth. . . . Hot springs fed the baths." Nodding, he turned the knob further, increasing the flow, then cranked it in the opposite direction to turn it off again. He tried the other knob, getting hot water this time, and nodded in understanding as he shut it off. Then he pointed toward the toilet. "And what is this?"

"Um . . . that's a toilet. You um . . ." She opened the lid. "You sit on it, to uh . . . answer nature's call."

He tilted his head, then his brows rose as he understood. *"In the house?"*

Smiling, she nodded. "Look." She flushed the thing, and he watched the water swirl and vanish, only to refill again.

"Where does it go?" he asked her.

"A tank buried underground outside." She pointed to the roll of paper. "You use this to . . . uh . . . clean up afterward. It goes down, too."

He shook his head in wonder. Arianna liked not seeing open hostility and suspicion in his eyes for a change. She went on, showing him the razors and shaving cream, the hair dryer, the soap and shampoo. The toothbrushes and how to use them. When finally the tub was filled, she turned to the door.

"You are leaving me?" he asked. He didn't sound worried, just surprised.

"I . . . thought you'd want some privacy."

He studied her face. "You have bathed me before, Arianna. Twice now, I believe. Surely you are not embarrassed by this now?"

As he spoke, he dropped his blanket, and stepped into the steaming water. He lowered his glorious body slowly into the tub, and leaned back with a sigh. Arianna tried, but she couldn't take her eyes off him.

"You uh . . . you were dead then, Nicodimus. Both times."

"And those were the only times you ever saw me in a state of . . . undress?" There was speculation in his eyes as he studied her face.

"No," she admitted.

"Then we—"

"We aren't going to talk about that, Nicodimus."

"Why not, Arianna?"

She looked down at his body beneath the rippling water. "For many reasons. The main one being that you'll remember everything on your own, and I think it's better for you if you do."

"And the other reasons?"

She swallowed hard. "It was a painful time for me, Nicodimus."

"Because you wanted me, and I did not return the feeling?"

She met his gaze suddenly. "Because I loved you, and you did not return the feeling. Wanting me was never a question." She turned again, gripped the doorknob.

"I think, Arianna, it still is not a question," he said softly to her back.

Arianna felt her eyes widen. Swallowing hard, she stepped out of the room and into the hall, and closed the door firmly behind her.

So that was why she had resurrected me from the very bowels of death. She had loved me. *Had* loved me. *Once.* A very, very long time ago. How she felt about me now, I did not know. How *could* I know? Certainly all she had done for me thus far, from bringing me back to life, to taking me into her home and caring for me, seemed to indicate that she still cared for me. But caring and loving were quite different matters.

I was getting stronger at a rapid pace now. By the hour, it seemed, I felt the life force moving more powerfully through my body. And she had told me that once I was able to do so, I would be free to leave here.

To leave her.

Never to have to look upon her face again, as she had so eloquently put it.

But I had a new interest in staying. I did not want to leave until I had unlocked all the secrets of Arianna. Of our past together, of what she had been to me, how and why she had betrayed me and cost me my life, and what . . . if anything . . . she felt toward me now.

And Nidaba. What horrors had befallen my beloved companion, Nidaba?

I bathed thoroughly, washed my hair in the water, using the sweet smelling stuff she had called "shampoo." I likely used more than was needed, for the suds the stuff created nearly suffocated me, and I had to turn the water flow on once again and thrust my head beneath it to rinse it all away. Huge white mounds of froth floated upon the water in which I soaked, rendering it useless for rinsing. But quite fragrant for all that.

Finished, I dried myself with the thick, soft "towels" she had left for me, and performed the shaving ritual with some difficulty. The little razor seemed too small for my large hand, and I longed for the honed edge of my dagger instead.

Briefly I wondered what had become of my dagger. Stolen, no doubt, by the bastard who'd killed me. I would have to acquire another, for as my memory came clearer, battles of the past emerged in rapid succession in my mind. And I knew that for an immortal to go about unarmed was foolish beyond words.

Next, my chin bleeding from several small wounds, I approached the clothing Arianna had left for me. One by one, I examined the items in the neatly folded stack beside the water basin. A shirt of soft fabric, with little round discs sewn at the sleeves and along the edges up the front, much like the one Duncan wore. It was fairly obvious how to don that, so I did. There were no laces for closure, and after studying the garment more closely I realized that there were tiny openings in the cloth that the little discs could be pushed through to hold the edges of the garment together. Next was a small white scrap of cloth with three openings. Two of which seemed to be for the legs, and one which was hidden by a flap. It must be . . .

I nearly laughed aloud as I realized its intended use, and tossed the small garment to the floor. The day had not dawned when I would need to maneuver my rod through a minuscule portal when I required use of it! Ludicrous!

The final item was of the sort Arianna wore. "Jeans," she had called them. Sturdy and well made, with a metal fastener at the front, and a little round metal disc atop it. I stepped into these easily and tugged them up to my waist, drawing them closed and feeling how tightly they hugged me. I was unused to clothing of such close fit, but I assumed this was the mode of the day, and I must adjust. I toyed with the odd fastener, but found no way to make it work. Finally my fingers stumbled over the tiny handle at its base, and I deduced that I needed to pull this upward. I did so.

Tiny metal teeth bit into the flesh of my manhood and I howled! Hopping in agony, I tried to grasp the minuscule handle again, to tug it downward this time, but I could not seem to find it.

The door burst open, and Arianna stood staring wide-eyed at me. Then she lowered her gaze, and her hands flew to her lips—to hide her amusement, I was certain.

"Get this thing off me, woman, before it cuts clean through my—"

"All right, all right, just stand still." She dropped to her knees at once, and the moment I stilled, her nimble fingers gripped the evil little implement of torture and gave a tug.

Sharp pain screamed through me, but the device let go its teeth. My hands went instantly to cup my groin, my face contorted in residual pain.

Arianna looked up at me. "How bad is it?"

"It damned well feels as if I've been cleaved half through," I muttered, sucking air through my teeth and stomping one foot twice as if that could somehow ease my pain.

She looked at the floor, eyeing the white undergarment I had tossed there. "No wonder. That's what underwear is for, Nicodimus. Well, one of the things it's for, at least."

"I might suggest you tell me things of such import a bit sooner, in the future, lady."

Again her full lips pulled into a smile she quickly hid. Still kneeling, she touched my hands. "Move them aside and let me see."

I went still, my jaw dropping.

"Oh, come on. Now don't try to tell me you're shy, Nicodimus. I know better. Let me see if you've been completely emasculated."I grunted in derision, but moved my hands aside. She examined me for a moment. She touched me, and I caught my breath at the surge of energy that sizzled from her hands when she did. But it was brief, all too brief. Then she stood and nodded. "It's just a tiny scratch. You'll be fine." Was she slightly breathless?

"Of course I will. The healing will take place in moments." I disliked that she had seen me howling in pain over such a seemingly minor injury. However, it truly *had* hurt incredibly. Already, though, the pain was easing, and my flesh tingled as the skin began to regenerate itself. Or was that simply the tingling sensation remaining from her touch?

"Take them off," she told me, "put on the underwear, and be careful when you use the zipper. Okay?"

"Zipper. So that's what that vicious contraption is called."

She nodded. "You need any help?"

"I believe I can manage to dress myself, Arianna."

"You could have fooled me," she said, eyeing the shirt. I looked down, and realized it hung crookedly. I had misaligned the little discs. I sighed, and shook my head, feeling doubts as to whether I would be able to adjust to this new world. I hadn't even left her house yet, and already I was floundering.

Her hand came to my cheek, soft, warm. "You're going to be fine," she told me as if she had sensed my misgivings. "You're smart, and you're strong, Nicodimus. More so than any of the other men I've met in this century. You'll put them all to shame, I promise."

That soft-spoken faith in me did wonders for my spirits. I had already recalled the years I had spent grieving my wife and sons. And while it made me sad, it gave me some peace, too. It took the edge of newness from my sorrow, and helped the shock to ease away as well. I had been without them for centuries. I had learned to go on. And I would have to do so again, now.

A knock sounded at the door. Then Duncan's voice followed. "Is Nic okay in there?"

"Fine," Arianna called. "Cut himself shaving."

"Shoot, I do that everyday," Duncan returned. "I say we go on strike, grow long beards and never shave again."

I felt myself smile. Arianna had chosen not to embarrass me by revealing the truth; and Duncan, it seemed, thought nothing of the explanation she had given him. So commonplace, this shaving accident, that he had made a jest of it.

"I believe I shall join you in that movement," I called to him.

Arianna's palm skimmed over my cheek, and meeting my eyes, she shook her head side to side. "That would be a shame, Nicodimus. Covering up this face . . . it would be a crime."

Instinctively, I caught her palm in my hand, and drew it around to my lips. I kissed her there. Her eyes grew dark and smoky before she lowered them and quickly drew her hand away. "I'll leave you to change," she told me, and stepped out of the room again.

I sighed after she'd gone. Truly, there were feelings surfacing within me that I did not understand. If this woman had been my enemy, if she had betrayed me, if she had caused my death—none of which she denied—then why would my body react to hers the way it did? Why would I now feel myself wanting her ever more strongly each time I looked into her eyes? Why would these tender, aching feelings keep welling up inside? It made no sense.

I shook my head. The memories would come. Soon, they would come. Perhaps I would understand my emotions better then. One thing was certain. I would not leave this place until I did.

—

Marten grew more and more frustrated as he watched the small house at the edge of Stonehaven, awaiting his opportunity.

Nicodimus was alive! There inside that small house. Marten had followed Arianna, and he'd been watching ever since. He had even crept close enough to peer through the cracks between the shuttered windows—and he'd glimpsed his enemy inside.

Alive. Fully, completely, alive.

It seemed impossible, but he could not deny what he'd seen with his own eyes. So he watched, and he waited.

So many people around! Yes, he'd like to wreak his vengeance on Arianna for trying her best to make a fool of him. But she wasn't his main quarry. Nicodimus was. The thief who'd stolen his sister so long ago, and left his father mortally wounded and dying, and he and his brother without a woman to tend to their needs. It had been Anya's place, her duty to care for them.

Nicodimus was old and his heart was powerful—or had been once. As he peered through the windows, Marten thought it was again, and growing more so all the time. Marten wanted that power, craved it for his own. But the two strangers, immortals both of them he sensed, stacked the odds strongly against his success. And then the Dark One had shown up—insane or nearly so. Nidaba. He'd heard tell of her before. Dearborne had once claimed she was the eldest immortal he'd known of. He'd wanted her for his experiments. Whether he'd ever had her, Marten did not know. But he had no wish to lock daggers with her now.

Too many. Too many for him to take on alone. He would likely be killed himself before he managed to get to Nicodimus, if he stormed the house the way his instincts told him to do. No, he needed a plan. A way to get them outside, to scatter them, leaving his quarry alone and vulnerable.

Nicodimus was still weak. Though healing, his body was still weak. And Marten wanted to spring on the ancient immortal before he grew strong again.

At first, Marten had thought to wait, that the others would leave eventually. But when days had passed and they still hadn't done so, he knew the time had come to make his move.

Every Witch had some innate skill that stood out in him, and that skill grew stronger when the Witch in question was an immortal High Witch.

Marten had such a skill. One he had honed down through the ages, until he'd achieved near perfection. It was that skill, he realized at last, that would bring this standoff to a head. He could drive them from the house most easily.

His skill was the art of telepathic combustion.

Marten could make things burn.

20

Nicodimus held the remote control in his hands, and thumbed buttons as his eyes remained riveted to the television screen. "Amazing," he kept muttering. "No matter how often you explain this, I still do not understand."

He looked, Arianna thought, like a man out of time. Big, and finely developed, but from work rather than workouts. A balanced, muscular power that emanated from him even when you couldn't see what lay beneath his clothes. But Arianna had seen. And she wished she could again.

Lying beneath him as he moved on top of her, around her, inside her, had been like riding the untamed fury of the elements. He was the physical perfection and strength of earth. He was the life and breath of air. The sizzling heat of fire, and the depth and silken caress of water. Gods, no wonder she'd loved him from the moment she'd laid eyes on him.

He stood now, wearing jeans and a black T-shirt, which had become his uniform, though he admitted to missing his kilt. She'd promised to get him one. Frankly, she couldn't wait to see Nicodimus in a kilt again.

Nidaba rested in a large beanbag chair in the rearmost

corner of the room. She had refused to don modern clothes. Arianna had tried to convince Nidaba to bathe and wash her hair, but the woman had only finally given in when Nicodimus had begun telling her about the wonders to be found in the bathroom.

If she were familiar with indoor plumbing, she didn't say so. In fact, she refused to say anything at all about where she had been, how she'd managed to get by for all the centuries since Arianna had last seen her. When asked, she retreated behind a wall of silence, and her eyes went blank.

Sensing it might be too much for her to bear talking about, Arianna stopped asking.

Arianna had found a black dress of similar cut to the one Nidaba had been wearing, and she'd replaced the tattered one with it while Nidaba had been in the bath. Nidaba wore that now. Her own had been so old it had fallen to bits when Arianna had tried to wash it. Nidaba gave no indication whether she had noticed the change or not.

She brooded, Nidaba did. Her gaze was always hostile. Her reactions were nervous and startled all the time. She simply sat, watching. Silent and watching.

Arianna went to her with a plate of food now, holding on tight to the sides of the dish in case Nidaba tried to knock it to the floor with a swipe of her hand, as she had done no less than three times in the past week. "Are you hungry, Nidaba? Would you like to eat?"

Nidaba gave the plate a thorough looking over. Fried chicken tonight, with french fries. Nicodimus had fallen in love with greasy modern cooking.

"I detest it," she said, "all of it!" but she took the plate out of Arianna's hands and ripped into a chicken leg like a lion ripping into a rabbit. "Why do you not roast your meat as is proper?" she mumbled around the food. "Why must you try to kill us with this horrible fare? It is unfit to eat!" Within seconds she'd stripped the meat to the bone, and was yanking up the second piece. She paused, and glared up at Arianna. "Do not think I am fooled by your make-believe kindness, wench. You may have taken Nicodimus in with your wiles, but not me! I'll not let you destroy him again. Not again!" Then she went stiff and her eyes widened.

"What is it, Nidaba?"

At Arianna's question, Nicodimus turned from the television set to look at Nidaba's frightened face.

"The window! Someone is watching from the window!" she shrieked. The food flew from her lap as she leapt to her feet. The plate shattered, French fries and chicken bones scattering over the floor, and Nidaba ran into the bedroom. The door slammed hard behind her.

Arianna sighed. Duncan and Raven had hurried in from the kitchen at the noise. "She throw another tantrum?" Raven asked softly.

Nodding at the mess on the floor, Arianna bent to begin picking it up.

"Let me," Duncan said. "You'll cut yourself." He moved her aside and tended to the mess himself.

Nicodimus met Arianna's gaze as she sighed and sank into a chair. "I just wish I knew how to get through to her," she whispered.

"I mentioned Dearborne's name to her," Nicodimus said softly, glancing at the door as if afraid Nidaba might overhear. "Just as you suggested I should. But she became like stone. As if she could neither hear nor see me. Just went still, barely breathing, it seemed." As he spoke, he moved to the window to stare through the glass, looking around in wonder at the town outside. "I see no one."

"I doubt anyone was there," Arianna replied, but she too, looked when Nicodimus moved away. "She's so frightened. I feel sorry for her."

"Oh, Arianna, for goodness sake, how can you?"

Raven's exclamation drew all three sets of eyes. But she only rushed on. "She's mean, and she hates you, and she threatens you at least ten times a day. It's obvious she wants Nicodimus all to herself and sees you as her only obstacle. My Goddess, Arianna, I can barely sleep nights for fear that creature is going to sneak into your room and murder you to get you out of her way."

"That is not going to happen," Nicodimus said quietly.

Arianna tore her gaze from her sister's to stare at him. But he said no more. So she turned back to Raven again. "It's not like you to be so cruel. The woman is ill, Raven."

"The woman is insane, Arianna. And if I had my way, she'd be out of this house before she starts acting on these delusions she has that you are to blame for what happened to Nic almost five hundred years ago. She wants you dead. I can see it in her eyes."

Arianna lowered her head. "Maybe she does. But they are not delusions, Raven. As much as you love me, you cannot admit that I am less than perfect. But I am, and my mistakes did cost Nicodimus his life."

"And you haven't punished yourself enough for that all these years? Is that it? Do you feel you have to let her punish you now, too, just so you can feel you've suffered thoroughly enough?"

Arianna sighed heavily, but said nothing.

Nicodimus moved closer to her, and took her arm gently in his big hand. "Is that true, Arianna? Is that why you allow Nidaba to stay? Due to some sense that you must pay for whatever you did to me in the past?"

She looked up slowly and met his gaze. "No, Nicodimus. It's nothing to do with that, I just—"

Nicodimus held up a hand for silence, and without taking his eyes from Arianna, he said, "Duncan, Raven, if you would not mind . . ."

"We'll give you some privacy," Duncan said quickly, and taking Raven's arm, he led her up the stairs to the bedroom they shared.

"Come," Nicodimus said when they had gone. "Sit with me for a time."

With a sigh, Arianna did as he asked. She sat down on the small sofa. Nicodimus took a seat beside her, his body turned toward her, and gathered her hands in both of his. "It is long past time we had this talk, do you not agree?"

Not meeting his eyes, she nodded. "I suppose so."

"I have not told you this, Arianna, but I have had . . . memories. Of you. Of us."

She looked up quickly, drew in a short breath.

"I remember only small glimpses into the past. Riding together, this one is clear. You had long, golden hair. It flew behind you in the wind and captured the sunlight. I could barely keep my attention focused on guiding my mount because it was so beautiful."

She blinked in surprise, a lump coming into her throat so suddenly she nearly choked.

"And there are other things, too. I remember how I loved listening to you talk. I remember your voice, and the song of the highlands in your speech. And your quick temper, and your impulsive nature and how often I feared it would get you into trouble."

She smiled a bit, nodding at him. "It often *did* get me into trouble. But you were usually nearby to get me out again."

"I remember holding you as you cried at your sister's grave. I remember when some lad cut you to see if you would bleed, and the fear and horror I felt as I tended the wound." He shook the remembered fear away. "You were furious at him."

"*You* punched him in the nose," she said softly.

He smiled. "I should have done more." He met her eyes, and his smile died slowly. "I remember making love to you, in a sacred place surrounded by stones, Arianna. In the midst of the falling snow. And I remember what I felt for you then—"

"Don't." She got to her feet quickly, putting her back to him. "Stop now, Nicodimus. Your thoughts are confused. You didn't feel anything for me then."

"But I did." He got up, and came behind her, his hands sliding over her shoulders as he turned her gently. "I still do."

She closed her eyes as tears threatened. "You will change your mind when you remember the rest."

"It will come soon enough," he said. "But it will not change my mind. I was suspicious of you at first—"

"With good reason! You came to hate me before you died, Nicodimus."

"But you've shown nothing but kindness to me, and to

Nidaba as well. No, Arianna, I could never have hated you. If anyone has cause to hate, it is you who have cause to hate me. For you loved me, freely and generously, you loved me. This I remember very well. Yet I, in my stubbornness, continued to deny feeling anything for you in return, even when I—''

''Please don't,'' she whispered. ''If you say it now only to take it back later . . . Nicodimus, I don't think I'll ever get past it.''

''Perhaps I don't want you to 'get past it'. But I will not say the words if they frighten you so. I will hope instead that my heart can speak for itself.''

He drew her closer then, and bent to press his lips to hers. For the life of her, Arianna could not pull away. He kissed her so tenderly, so gently. And when she parted her lips on a shuddering sigh, and wound her arms around his neck, he kissed her harder. Deeper. He pulled her hips tight to his own, and drove his tongue into her mouth, tasting all within his reach, plundering her until her head was spinning and her heart, pounding.

And then he lifted his head away, and his eyes sparkled down into hers. ''I would like very much to hold you in my arms tonight, Arianna. I want to take you to my bed. Will you let me?''

She couldn't speak. So she only nodded, then panicked and the words spilled out before she could stop them. ''I will never love you again, Nicodimus. I won't let you break me that way. Not again.''

He stared at her, and finally sighed and shook his head, ''I hurt you very badly, then, didn't I?''

She nodded in jerky motions. ''I gave you all of me, all I had to give. But it was never enough for you. And you only threw it back in my face.''

''Then I was a fool. And whatever you did to me in the end, was likely well deserved, Arianna.''

Lowering her head, she shook it slowly. ''No. You warned me after all. You told me you could never feel anything for me. I just couldn't accept it.''

''Nor should I have asked you to.'' He searched her eyes,

saw the way she trembled, she was certain of it. "I want you very badly, Arianna."

"I . . . I . . ." She stared up at him, incapable of refusing him. She was his, tonight and every night, if he wanted her. She hated feeling powerless, craving him this much when she ought to know better than to fall into the same old trap. Loving a man who could not love her back. It was self-destructive. And painful. And she deserved better, dammit.

"No, Arianna," he said softly, his eyes roaming her face. "Not tonight. Not now, with this unsettled between us. You'd give still more of yourself if I asked you now, wouldn't you? No, don't answer. I will not ask any more of you. Not now, not like this."

"Nicodimus?"

He shook his head. "Go on, little cat. Go up to your bed. And do not worry about Nidaba. I will hear her if she moves from her rooms. I will keep you safe, I vow it."

Little cat. He did remember. Arianna drew a deep breath, hating the weakness only he could bring to life in her. Damn him. She was strong. She didn't need him to love her, didn't even need him to forgive her. Much less to protect her.

She didn't!

And she didn't love him, either.

Only a fool would love a man who'd rejected her as many times as Nicodimus had rejected Arianna.

Only a totally hopeless fool. And Arianna was nobody's fool.

Marten focused his intent on the small house. His eyes bored into it as he drew the heat up from the core of him, holding it and letting it build. Hotter. Stronger. Sweat broke out on his face and arms. His breaths came short and fast, and his body shuddered with the effort of containing the energy. And yet he held it inside him as it grew. His body heated, and he knew his skin was turning bloodred. A white-hot haze filled his vision, brighter, blinding, but still he did not blink, did not close his eyes.

Finally, with a shout, he released the energy. It shot

forth, a ball of spectral flame that penetrated the house at its base, near the back. As it flooded out of him, Marten went weak. Nothing remained inside him, no strength, no energy, and his body sank limply to the ground. He lay there, still, waiting. His strength would return in a few moments. It always did.

While he waited, he watched the house as his vision slowly cleared and returned to normal. He saw the soft glow from within. Saw it build. Watched it spread.

Marten smiled.

Arianna lay awake in her bed, restless and troubled. So Nicodimus wanted her again. It was no surprise, or at least, it shouldn't be. He'd wanted her before. He just hadn't loved her. And although he might think that had changed, she knew better. She had spent too much time convincing herself he could never love her to believe so easily now. Once he remembered, it would all change.

And why would he bother with her anyway, when it was obvious his feelings for Nidaba ran far deeper, and were far older than anything he could ever feel for Arianna? He spent countless hours with Nidaba. Whenever she ventured out of the room she'd claimed as her own, he would be at her side, talking to her about the amazing things he'd seen or learned about in this new world. Or reminiscing about the past, recounting various adventures they'd shared together. Asking gently if she remembered.

She always did.

He spent time with Nidaba in her room as well. Less now that she was venturing out more often, but still, a lot of time passed with the two of them holed up back there. Arianna didn't like to think about what they were doing. She'd barely restrained the urge to walk in on them and find out. At least Nicodimus didn't sleep in there with Nidaba. He'd taken to spending his nights on the sofa. Insisted on it, in fact, though Arianna had offered her own room to him. Maybe because it was closer to Nidaba. Maybe because he could get up and slip into the bedroom with Nidaba in the night, and no one would know. Maybe . . .

Maybe it was none of her business. She had no claims on Nicodimus.

Well, one claim, but it hardly deserved consideration. Still, technically at least, she was his wife.

He didn't know that yet. Hadn't remembered that far. But he would, in time. And she wondered what he would make of it when he finally did remember.

The scream from below ripped through Arianna's psyche so deeply that she was on her feet before she was aware of moving at all. She yanked the bedroom door open, smelled the smoke, and felt her heart leap within her chest. Racing into the hall, she peered down over the railing into the living room, and saw Nidaba tugging with all her might on Nicodimus's arm.

"Fire! There's fire! Come with me!" Nidaba shrieked.

Nicodimus only pried her hands away, and pointed to the front door. "Go, get outside, now! I have to get Arianna!"

"Damn Arianna! She'll only get you killed again, Nicodimus! Come with me now!" She gripped him again, clung to him.

Again he freed himself, shoving Nidaba forcefully toward the door, and turning he started up the stairs.

"I won't leave you," Nidaba was screaming.

Nicodimus ignored her, stopping halfway up when he glanced up and into Arianna's eyes. "Go," Arianna told him. "Get Nidaba outside. I'll get Duncan and Raven and join you."

He shook his head firmly, just once, and a cloud of smoke wafted up between them. Nicodimus took the stairs rapidly, even as Arianna turned to race through the hall and pound on her sister's bedroom door.

Nicodimus came up behind her as she pounded and screamed, but there was no answer, and it was hot here. Hotter by the minute. From below she could hear the roar and crackle of flames now, accompanying Nidaba's panicked shrieks, and a glow hovered beyond the smoke like some evil eye.

Nicodimus moved her aside and swiftly kicked the bedroom door in. Smoke billowed out of the room, and he held one arm before his face as he charged inside.

Numbly, Arianna realized the fire must have started in Nidaba's room, just below this one. The crazy woman must have set her house on fire! But Raven . . . Duncan . . .

They were not in the bed, and only when Nicodimus bent to the floor did she see them lying there. They had apparently been overcome by the smoke as they made their way toward the door.

"Raven!" Arianna rushed forward, even as Nicodimus hauled Duncan up, and flung the unconscious man over his shoulder.

Arianna gripped her sister under the arms and lifted her. Thank the Gods for preternatural strength. Though slender, Raven was both taller and bigger than Arianna. Were she mortal, she'd never have been able to manage it. Even now, Arianna struggled, but she held her sister close to her, and dragged her feet over the floor, through the door into the hallway, following Nicodimus's lead.

"Stay close," he called, and she could hear the rawness of his voice. Her own eyes burned and watered, and her lungs seemed starved for air. Nicodimus reached the top of the stairs, but looking down, Arianna saw only a pool of fire.

"My Gods, Nidaba!" she cried, wondering if the woman had gone outside, or if she still cringed by the door allowing the fire to devour her.

"This way," Nicodimus said, turning around. He headed back to Arianna's bedroom, and straight through it to the window. Without hesitation, he opened the window and thrust Duncan's upper body through. "Were you not immortal, my friend, I would not attempt this. And I fear it shall be painful, all the same." Then with a shove, he launched Duncan into the night.

Arianna heard sirens wailing. The village's volunteer fire department, no doubt. Another spectacle of modern life for Nicodimus to wonder at.

Her bare feet began to blister, and as she looked beneath her she saw tongues of fire licking up through the floorboards. Her sister's weight was taken from her arms, as

Nicodimus pulled Raven into his own. Carefully, he maneuvered Raven's body through the open window, dropping her just as he had dropped Duncan.

"Come," he rasped, gripping Arianna's arm. "Hurry."

The flames licked higher, and she heard the floorboards cracking beneath her blistering feet.

"Now!" he commanded, jerking her forward. She hooked one leg over the sill, gazing back at him. She held his arm. The floor wouldn't hold long. She didn't want to leave him. He wouldn't make it in time.

"Nicodimus—"

He gave Arianna a mighty shove, and she sailed through the night, hitting the ground with a bone-shattering impact that rattled her teeth and sent pain searing through her body. But even as she managed to draw a pain-racked breath and stared back up, she realized he hadn't followed. The window was a dark hole, now, and Nicodimus no longer stood there. Beyond the darkness, she could see only the dancing flames.

"Nicodimus!" Nidaba screamed.

Arianna whirled to see the woman standing nearby, staring up with anguished eyes at the spot where Nicodimus had been. Near her feet, Duncan was slowly stirring awake, as Raven shook him and spoke to him. The both of them were all right. And Nidaba, too. But Nicodimus . . .

"You've done it again, haven't you, Arianna? You've killled my son all over again!"

Arianna blinked, stunned by the words, confused, but unable to devote even a moment's thought to the crazy ramblings of a madwoman. "The floor must have given way," she muttered, calculating in her mind, where he would have landed if it had. The kitchen, he would be near the kitchen. She raced round to that side of the house while Nidaba shouted in some unknown language after her. Curses, no doubt. Hurled in the tongue of the desert lands from whence she came. Arianna gave one brief thought to hoping the woman was too crazy to cast a decent spell, then put Nidaba from her mind and kept on running.

The town's only fire engine came to a squeaky stop, and

men piled out. But she had no time for them. Arianna found the hatch door in the ground and jerked it open, racing down into the pitch darkness of the basement, and then up its inside stairs to the door that opened into the kitchen. Smoke here, but not as much. Heat, too, but maybe . . .

She pressed her palms flat to the door. Hot, yes, but not blistering. Bracing herself for a blast, she opened the door. A wall of fire danced before her eyes. It coated the kitchen walls like living paint, and licked out across the floor in pools. She eyed the gas powered range, thought of the propane tanks just outside, and dropped to her knees to avoid the smoke. "Nicodimus!" she cried. "Nicodimus, where are you?"

She couldn't see. Perfect night vision was worthless when smoke burned her eyes like acid. So confusing was being in the heart of this fiery beast, that she no longer knew which way she was moving, just kept crawling along on all fours, choking out his name before drawing in more smoke-laden air.

Then she felt him. Warm, soft, his arm, yes it was his arm! She gripped it, and slid her knees backward over the floor, dragging his weight. Carefully, she moved, trying to retrace her path exactly. She moved a few feet, then she tugged, dragging his body over the floor, then moved a few more feet and tugged again, mightily, pouring all her strength into moving him. She shouldn't be this weak. It shouldn't be this difficult. But she knew it was the smoke, the heat. She was dizzy. She knew damn well she could die from smoke inhalation just as she could die by any other mortal cause. She'd revive again . . . unless the fire consumed her body—and her heart with it. If that happened, she'd be truly dead. Permanently dead.

And Nicodimus with her.

Blackness threatened, but she battled it. Dragging him still farther, she called on her Witchly senses to guide her to the basement door. She moved back farther, and pulled him along, and finally she ran out of floor.

It seemed to vanish from beneath her knees, and she fell,

her body banging hard all the way to the bottom, her hand wrenched free of Nicodimus's arm.

No!

She pulled herself upright when the tumbling ended, realizing she'd fallen down the very stairway she'd sought. But without Nicodimus. She gasped, inhaling in a huge amount of the relatively clean air there, and lunged back up the stairs again. Gripping both of Nicodimus's arms, she pulled him back down the stairs with her. There she collapsed, finally unable to fight the darkness any longer. It closed in and she knew nothing for a time.

"What did you mean by that?" Duncan asked Nidaba after she'd stopped screaming.

"Never mind her, Duncan, we have to find Arianna!" Raven cried, her head pressed between her palms as she searched in vain for her sister. "My Goddess, I think she's gone back inside after Nic!"

The firefighters manned hoses now, aiming them at the flames and soaking the poor little house in an effort to save it. But Raven thought it was going to be a total loss. She didn't care, she just wanted her sister.

"That way," Raven screamed. "She went that way!" She started forward, only to be pulled firmly back by Duncan's strong hands.

"Look, there," he said, pointing to the open hatchway door. "I'll go. Stay here. I mean it, Raven."

She met his eyes, nodded hard, and watched in terror as he raced away. "Be careful!" she cried.

Duncan ducked into the basement, out of sight. Trembling, Raven glanced behind her, only to see Nidaba curled into a small trembling mass on the ground. She had come to hate the woman. It was unlike her to hate anyone, but Nidaba had been heartlessly cruel to Arianna ever since she'd arrived here. And Raven didn't take kindly to *anyone* who mistreated her beloved sister.

But now, seeing Nidaba in this much pain, Raven was touched in spite of herself. She moved forward, bending close.

"My son, my Nic," Nidaba was muttering, and Raven felt her own eyes widen as understanding dawned, almost blinding in its brightness.

"By the Gods," she whispered. Was this just more insane rambling from a lunatic driven beyond reason? Or could it possibly be true?

"They'll be all right," Raven whispered. "Duncan will get them out . . ."

"Don't touch me!" Nidaba jerked violently away from Raven's hand on her shoulder. "I hate you, I hate you all!"

Raven knelt beside her, and Nidaba lifted her head, her wet, red-rimmed eyes fixing on Raven's, the ruby in her nose glinting the fire's reflection.

"No, you don't," Raven said. "You just love Nicodimus. But we all do, too, don't you see that?" Raven fought a sob. "The man I love is in there, too, and my sister . . ."

Then, without warning, Nidaba collapsed against Raven's chest, shuddering with sobs that seemed too powerful to contain. Unsure how to react, Raven put her arms around the woman's shoulders and just held her while she cried. "I cannot lose him again," Nidaba sobbed. "I lost him twice . . . and I cannot lose him again."

"You won't, I promise, you won't."

Nidaba shivered, lifting her head, looking at Raven, and for the first time since she'd met the woman, Raven saw some fleeting kind of lucidity in her eyes.

"He died for the first time when he was but nine years old," she whispered. "I didn't even know what I was then. . . . He . . . was all I had."

Raven frowned, puzzled, and gently brushed the hair away from Nidaba's eyes. "When was this?" she asked softly.

"So long ago . . . so very long . . . millennia passed before he was reborn as an immortal High Witch. But I knew he would be. . . . I knew, for he died stepping between a soldier's sword and his mother's heart. He died to save my life. So did I, but I revived, and my son . . . my precious Nic, did not."

"My God," Raven whispered. "My God, you really are . . . You're his mother?"

"Nicodimus!" Nidaba cried, rising to her feet and staring through rivulets of tears at the inferno. "Don't leave me, Nicodimus, not again!"

Raven turned to gaze back at the blazing house. And then Duncan emerged, Arianna hanging limply over his shoulder. And as he came up the last steps, Raven saw that he was dragging Nic behind him.

Nidaba collapsed on the ground then, retreating, perhaps, to insanity. And for once, Raven thought she understood why. Millenia, she'd said. Gods, could anyone live that long and remain sane? She left the woman alone with her ghosts, and ran forward to help Duncan carry Nic and Arianna to safety.

"They'll be all right," Duncan assured her as she eased her sister's body from his arms into hers. He bent to scoop Nicodimus up. But Duncan had taken in a lot of smoke. It coated his mouth and nose in black soot, and he moved slowly, awkwardly, choking often, pausing to catch his breath. Eventually, the two managed to carry Nicodimus and Arianna back to where Nidaba had been waiting.

Raven lowered Arianna to the ground, and Duncan dropped Nicodimus beside her. "The fire didn't get to them," Duncan said. "They'll revive."

"Thank the Gods," Raven muttered. She bent over her sister, stroking her soot-streaked face. "You see Nidaba? I told you they'd be okay."

As she spoke, Raven looked up. Nidaba was no longer where she had been before. Turning her head, Raven scanned the area, but still, there was no sign of the strange woman.

Instead, she spied a jeweled dagger, thrust into the earth, and a small scrap of paper pinned there by its blade. She frowned at Duncan, who quickly went to pull the dagger up. Duncan scanned the note, then met Raven's eyes. "Nidaba has been taken by someone named Marten, who says he'll release her only to Nicodimus. 'Come alone,' it says. 'You know where to find me.' "

Duncan frowned, his face tight with concern. "Do you have any clue what this is about, Raven?"

Raven shook her head slowly, but her eyes burned with tears of worry for the woman she sensed she had never really met until tonight.

21

"Nic, come on, wake up."

I heard Duncan's voice just before my body went rigid, and the life force flooded back into me. Then I went limp, lying still on the damp ground, opening my eyes slowly.

Before me were a massive machine with flashing lights, and men wielding lengths of soft tubing that spouted water at the house. The house . . . Arianna's home was a sodden, charred mass now. A ruin. Tongues of flame shot forth still, but the fire was nearly extinguished. The sight of it stirred some memory. A brief glimpse of a similar scene from the distant past. A flicker, then gone, leaving me with a sickening feeling in my stomach. I turned my head, not wishing to look on that sight any longer, only to see Arianna lying beside me on the ground. Still.

"Arianna?" I sat up immediately, moving closer, bending over her. Her face was dusted with soot, her hair dulled with it. I touched her face, lifting my gaze to her sister's. "I do not understand. I pushed her from the window."

"But you were still inside," Raven said softly. "She went back in after you. We couldn't stop her."

Something twisted in my heart. "She could have burned," I whispered. I gathered her limp body gently into my arms, pulling her upright, so she rested against my chest. One hand at the small of her back, one cupping her head and holding it to my shoulder, I rocked her back and forth. "You're such a fool, little cat. Risking death for a man you say you do not love. I think you lie."

As I held her, she went stiff, sucking in a great gasp, then relaxing in my arms once more as she came awake. "Nicodimus?" she whispered, her voice hoarse.

"Right here. It is all right. Everyone is safe." As I said it, I realized I had not seen Nidaba, and sent a questioning glance over Raven's shoulder to Duncan.

The man nodded. "Yes, everyone got out of the house."

Good. Nidaba was likely frightened by the noise and lights and people. She was probably hiding somewhere nearby.

One of the men who'd been fighting the fire came toward us with a stack of blankets. "The house is lost," he said, and his voice was thickly laced with a Scottish lilt. "But there be rooms for you at the inn. No charge. An' by the time you get there, you'll find a change o' clothes a'waitin'. Some o' the local ladies keep such things on hand for emergencies such as this."

"That's very kind. Thank you," Raven said.

In my arms, Arianna was still shaking. Still, I thought, trying to sort through the confusion in her mind. I'd been here with this woman for several days now. And with each one that had passed, my feelings for her had grown. All the suspicions, all the instinctive sense that I must not trust her, and even the knowledge that she had indeed been somehow involved with my death, did nothing to dampen the feelings growing wild within me. There was something about her. Her keen mind and quick wit. Her boldness and intelligence. Her kindness and generosity. Her temper—even that drew me to her. She was small and quick and, I sensed, passionate. I had made love to this woman once, though the memory of it was vague and sketchy now. Knowing it only served to make me want her more, a desire that burned hot within my soul, and seemed to grow daily. But it was more than lust I felt for this woman. A great deal more . . . perhaps more than she wanted me to feel.

I felt it all the same, and sensed she did as well. And I would tell her so, if only she would let me.

It was, however, something she did not wish to hear. And I would respect her wishes. For now. Only for now. She loved me, though she might deny it. I knew that. She had risked her life to save mine tonight. She loved me. She simply needed time to accept the idea.

I took one of the blankets from the stack the man had left with us, and wrapped it around her shoulders, brushing ash from her hair.

"Nic, we um . . . we need to talk. Something has happened," Duncan said.

Arianna's head came up, her eyes alert now, and searching the area around us. "Where is Nidaba?" she asked.

Raven averted her eyes. "Nidaba . . . told me some things a few moments ago. Things you both need to know . . . especially you, Nic."

I frowned, wishing Nidaba would show herself and ease this sudden kernel of worry that seemed to be gnawing at my belly. "What did she tell you?" I asked.

Licking her lips, Raven lifted her gaze to meet mine. "She . . . she's always been very close to you, hasn't she? Very protective of you."

I nodded. "Yes. Sometimes to the extreme."

"But she's never told you why, has she?"

"No."

Raven bit her lip, nodded slowly. "I didn't think so. Do you know why you were born into this lifetime as an immortal High Witch, Nic?"

I nodded. "Of course. I must have died trying to save the life of another, in the lifetime before."

"Right. Well, Nidaba . . . she was the one whose life you saved."

I blinked in surprise, glancing quickly at Arianna. She said, "It doesn't surprise me. I always knew there was an incredible bond between you two."

"More than you could even guess," Duncan said.

I glanced his way. Raven cleared her throat. "Nic... When you died to save her life, Nidaba was..."

"Was...?" I prompted, when she stopped mid-sentence.

"She was your mother."

I heard Arianna's soft gasp, even as Raven's words made their way to my ears. It felt as if my heart jumped into my throat. I parted my lips, but could not speak, could not even breathe for a moment.

"Sweet Goddess," Arianna whispered. "Your mother... Oh, it all makes so much sense now."

The large vehicles began to rumble away. My gaze seemed to search the darkness around us as if I were seeking some sense, some explanation that could be found there. There was none, of course. There was the house, reduced to smoking, sodden ash and charred beams that dripped and hissed away the last of their heat. There was Arianna's driving machine sitting out of harm's way, and apparently untouched by the flames. There were three people watching me as everything I had believed in my life simply melted away beneath a revelation too shocking to comprehend.

And there was Arianna, still in my arms. I suddenly held her more tightly. "My mother," I whispered, staring at Raven in disbelief. "She said this?"

"Yes. She was your mother, an immortal High Witch, but she didn't even know that at the time. You were nine years old, she said, when she was attacked by some soldier.... She didn't say why. Just that you leapt in front of her, and were killed by a blow from his sword. And that it was a very long time before you were finally reborn in Scotland."

My head low, I shook it slowly. Arianna sat up slightly, and ran one palm gently over my cheek. "Why?" I asked of no one in particular. "Why would she not have told me these things...?" Arianna only shook her head, her big brown eyes wide with concern for me.

"I don't know why, Nic," Raven said. "But I think it's

true. "I . . . I know Nidaba is not in the best of mental health right now, but I saw her eyes when she was speaking, and . . ." She drew a breath, then nodded hard. "She was speaking from the heart, I know that much."

"No wonder she hated me so much," Arianna said. I looked into Arianna's eyes, saw the pain there, the reflection of my pain, and perhaps Nidaba's as well. So caring, this woman. The most caring I'd ever known. "I understand everything now," she said.

"I do not," I told her. Reluctantly I released Arianna's small, warm body, and got to my feet. "I must speak to Nidaba. Where is she now?"

Raven and Duncan exchanged a worried glance. Then Duncan extracted a small scrap of paper from somewhere beneath the blanket wrapped around him, and handed it to me. I frowned down at the words . . . English, I thought but unfamiliar to me. I could not read what was written there.

"We only left her alone for a minute . . . just long enough to pull you two out of that basement," Duncan said. "I guess that's when he got to her."

My head came up fast, and just as quickly, Arianna jumped to her feet beside me, and snatched the note from my hands.

"Marten," she whispered.

"Marten?" The name brought his image clearly back to my mind. My nemesis. My onetime brother-in-law, and lifelong enemy. "That bastard is still alive? Damn him. Are you saying . . . Gods, are you saying he has taken Nidaba?"

"It looks that way," Duncan said. "Read him the note, Arianna. Maybe he can make some sense of it."

Arianna met my gaze, and I saw her reluctance. But she nodded, and read aloud. " 'Nicodimus, I have taken your precious Nidaba. I will kill her if I must, but I fear taking the heart of a lunatic might well infect me with her madness. Still, I will risk that, if you force me. I am willing, however, to make a trade. Nidaba, unharmed, for you, Nicodimus. Come alone, old friend. You know where to find me. Marten.' "

I stopped my pacing and lifted my head. "But . . . I *do not* know where to find him. What . . ." Then I let my question die on my lips and gazed at Arianna. She looked quickly away, shielding her eyes from my probing stare.

"Arianna, if you know what this means, tell me."

She only shook her head, still not meeting my eyes. "I don't know."

"You must know!" I went to her, gripped her shoulders, and stared into her eyes. "Arianna, please."

"I don't know, Nicodimus. It must be something from the past, something you still haven't remembered. But if it is, it's something I didn't know about."

I saw something in her eyes. A shadow that seemed to hide her soul from me. I did not know if she were telling me the truth, or why she would want to lie. I did not feel as if I knew anything just then. Everything I'd ever believed seemed to have been shaken to the core by Raven's revelations. "I must find her," I whispered.

"We'll find her," Duncan said, his voice firm and strong. "He can't have taken her far. Arianna, maybe you can at least give us a physical description of this Marten character to go on."

Arianna nodded, but I saw the way her jaw was set, and the determination in her eyes. I also saw the suspicion with which Raven was eyeing her. She, too, thought Arianna knew more than she was saying.

But why? Gods, could she be jealous of my affection for Nidaba still? Even knowing the woman had been my mother?

My mother. Gods, I could not get over it. Nidaba, my own mother.

"So what is it, exactly, that you're keeping from Nic?" Raven asked.

Arianna looked up fast. Nicodimus and Duncan had gone off into the woods beyond the town in a hopeless attempt to track Marten and Nidaba. "I don't know what you mean. . . ."

"You damned well do, and I won't let you deceive me,

Arianna. Not me, of all people. I know you better than anyone. I love you better than anyone, and I'm not going to let you get away with this any more than you would if our situations were reversed. Now what is it?"

Arianna dropped her gaze, unable to withstand the impact of her sister's accusing eyes. She was shaken, right to the core. All this time she'd been half convinced that Nidaba wanted Nicodimus for herself . . . when she'd been his mother all along. Protecting him just as any mother would do for her son.

"You know where Marten took her, don't you?"

Arianna shrugged. "I have an idea."

"And you don't plan to let that poor woman die in Nic's place. I know you better than to think that. You're going to go after her yourself, aren't you? Aren't you, Arianna!"

Arianna sighed deeply, knowing better than to try to fool her sister on this point. "What choice do I have? She's his mother, Raven. He loves her, and he needs her, especially now."

"He loves *you*, Arianna."

"No. He thinks he does, but that will change once he remembers. . . ."

"Oh, for the love of heaven, you're so blind! The man adores you! That's not going to change because of something that happened centuries ago."

Arianna shook her head. "If he goes after her himself, Marten will kill him. It's that simple. Hell, that snake would probably kill them both."

"And if you go after her, he'll kill you instead."

"No. I can beat him. Nidaba is unbalanced, and Nicodimus is still weak. But *I* can beat him, Raven. And I will—for Nicodimus. Just as you would do for Duncan. You know you would. Don't even try to deny it."

Raven lowered her gaze, unable to argue with that simple truth. "Yes. I would. Because I love him. And you love Nic the same way, don't you?"

A stabbing pain pierced Arianna's chest as she nodded. "Yes. I love him. But I can't have him, I can't make him love me, and I'm not going to try. I've made that mistake before, but I learned from it. Yes, I love him. . . . I love him enough to let him go, Raven."

"And enough to die for him?"

Arianna didn't answer that. Instead, she just looked away.

"Fine, go after Marten in Nic's place if you must. But not alone. I'll go with you. And Duncan will, too. With three we'd have Marten outnumbered."

Keeping her gaze carefully averted, Arianna nodded. "You must promise not to tell Nicodimus. We'll have to slip away, without his knowledge. He's still not strong enough to do battle."

Raven eyed her warily. "All right. Agreed."

"Good then."

"Why do I get the feeling that was far too easy?"

Arianna shook her head and plastered a false smile on her face, hoping against hope her sister would believe her lies. "We'll go tomorrow. We both need rest after this night's mayhem."

"Yes. All right." Raven paced away, then back again. "Let's get to the inn then. The fireman said they would have rooms for us."

"One room," Raven said. "One large room. I don't plan to let you out of my sight tonight, Arianna."

Meeting her sister's gaze, Arianna murmured, "You're going to have to, love. I plan to spend this night in the arms of my husband. Just in case my plan goes wrong. It might be the last chance I ever have."

"Your . . . ?" Raven's eyes widened as she searched her sister's face.

Arianna simply nodded. "Nicodimus and I were married once, a long time ago. He doesn't remember it yet, but I do. I'll never forget." She lowered her head, to hide the color she felt staining her cheeks. "So give me this night with him. And tomorrow, we'll do what needs doing."

"Oh, Arianna." Raven enfolded her sister in her arms, and held her tight. "Why is it you feel you have to try so hard not to love him?"

"Because he can never love me back. I thought . . . I

thought if there were no love, there could be no pain. No hurting and longing for what I could never have. But it was never a choice, really. I've always loved him."

Raven stroked her hair. "Things will work out. Have faith, sweetheart."

Arianna lowered her head to Raven's shoulder. But she was out of faith, and determined, at last, to right a very old wrong. She couldn't have Nicodimus's love, she knew that, had accepted it. But she could save his life, and she could give him back his mother. She could make up for the mistakes she'd made in the past. And she would. Even knowing full well that it might be the last thing she ever did.

Marten had left no sign. Duncan and I searched for hours, to no avail. We found no track, no path, no clue. I thought of Nidaba, of the horrors she must have suffered in the past, likely at Dearborne's hand, and of how she must be feeling right now . . . a captive once more. Anxiety for her, and a deep fury against Marten, boiled in my belly.

"We might as well go back," Duncan said, a hand on my shoulder. "Maybe Arianna has remembered something more about all this by now."

"Arianna will not tell us any more than she wants us to know," I said wearily. "She's always been the most stubborn girl I . . ." I stopped speaking for a moment, and Duncan looked at me, waiting. "I remember her stubbornness. The way she would sneak away from her mother's home by night to study the ways of magick with The Crones. Even knowing the danger such actions brought with them."

Tilting his head, Duncan studied my face. "The Crones?"

I nodded, Arianna's face clear in my mind now. The way she had looked then. I had followed her, spied on her to be sure she was safe. I'd seen her with the old women, her cheeks bathed in the glow of their balefire. "She looked the same . . . but different somehow. Physically, she hasn't changed, except that she has cut off her hair. But there was an innocence in her eyes then. She seems . . . hard now."

"Not so hard as you might think," Duncan offered. "With her sister, she's as soft as a breeze."

I nodded in agreement. "Her hardness is selective then. She dons it to protect her heart from the likes of me."

Duncan couldn't seem to think of a response to that. Instead he said, "Tell me about these old women who taught her their ways."

I nodded, searching for the memories, finding them where before there had been but shadows. "They were Witches, mortal ones. Even before she knew of her own nature, Arianna sensed her power. She was determined to learn about it, about what it meant, and why she possessed it when others did not. She sought out the knowledge in the only place she could find it. The Crones were outcasts, feared by the clan, but left alone for the most part."

"Still," Duncan mused, "it must have been risky for Arianna to spend time with them. Especially in those days."

A darkness settled in my brain, and a chill shivered up my spine. "It nearly got her killed," I said. Then I blinked and searched my mind some more.

"This is a new memory, isn't it, Nic?"

I nodded. "It was the fire, I think, that brought all of this back to me. I recall . . . I was searching for Arianna, and could not find her. And . . . there was smoke, and noise coming from the edge of the woods where The Crones lived. I went there and . . ." I pressed my fingers to my forehead, as if to force the memory clear, and then I lifted my head, felt my eyes widen. "The clan murdered them. Hanged The Crones and burned their bodies. It was like a nightmare. Charred remains dangling from the limb of a mighty oak. The house in ruins. The entire clan, milling about, some bearing torches . . ."

Duncan grimaced. "You're right. Seeing Arianna's little house burn tonight likely jarred some of this loose for you."

I didn't care what had caused the memory to return. I only needed to follow it, for I sensed its import. "Arianna was there. Gods, she was devastated, and furious. The crowd turned its attention on her as she shouted accusations at them. Someone cried out that she had been seen with The Crones, that she was likely a Witch as well, and should suffer the same fate." I lowered my head as the breath rushed out of me, and felt again the sick-to-my-stomach fear that had assailed me then. "I remember her father, standing in front of her, ready to defend her against that murderous mob with no more than a fallen limb as a weapon. He'd have had no chance against them all. But I stepped in to protect her as well."

"How?" Duncan asked. His gaze riveted to mine, he seemed fascinated by the tale. "Two men against an entire clan? How did you defend her against that?"

I closed my eyes as the past rushed over me. "I was known as close kin to their chieftain. They wouldn't have dared defy me. But I knew Arianna would be in grave danger again the moment I was gone. I had to link her to me in a way so permanent and so real that she would be safe, even without me at her side."

Opening my eyes, I stared up at the stars, and saw the past unfolding in my mind. The dress she'd worn, the flowers in her hair. The excited uncertainty in her eyes. "I married her," I whispered. "By the Gods, I married her. Arianna . . . Arianna is *my wife*."

I felt as if my legs would buckle beneath me, and suddenly Duncan was there, gripping my shoulders, and easing me downward until I sat on a partially rotted stump. The fragrance of the moist, decomposing wood and moss rose up to wrap around my senses, but my mind refused to stop whirling.

"Your wife? For the love of heaven. She never told us any of this." He shook his head in wonder. Then he eyed me again. "It's all just a bit too much to deal with in one night, isn't it, Nic? Discovering a mother and a wife, all at once? Are you okay?"

"I . . . Gods, why didn't she tell me?"

Duncan hunkered on the ground beside the stump. "I could hazard a guess. If you want me to?"

I looked at him and nodded hard.

"Arianna is . . . a proud woman. No, that's an understatement. It's more than pride. At any rate, if you only married her to keep the clan from murdering her, then she must have known it. Right? I mean, frankly, knowing her as I do, I'm surprised she even agreed to it."

I frowned fiercely, searching my mind. "She did not agree . . . not at first. But in the end she realized she had no choice. Her mother and father urged her to accept, and I pushed her as well. Her only other option would have been to run away. To leave all she knew and loved behind, and to try to exist on her own. In the world as it was then, she would have been in just as much danger that way as she had been that night at The Crones' execution."

Duncan nodded. "So she agreed . . . knowing you didn't love her."

I blinked and met Duncan's eyes. "I was a fool. So determined to protect my heart from the touch of hers and the pain I believed that touch would bring. Gods, I set terms. Can you believe that? *I* laid out terms, expecting *Arianna* to agree to them."

"Might as well set terms for the wind as to how it should blow," Duncan remarked, shaking his head and smiling slightly at the very idea. "Arianna sets her own terms."

I nodded wryly. "Yes. She did then. She agreed to wed me, but informed me she would never be content with the rules I laid out: that she would be my wife in name only, that I would never be capable of loving her, or being her husband in the truest sense of the word. She said . . . she said she would make me love her. That my defenses would crumble beneath her slightest touch. That it was I who would surrender to *her* terms, and that I should be aware of it from the start."

Duncan smiled fully now. "You should have run for the hills, Nic. You never stood a chance, did you?"

"If I ever thought I did, I was fooling no one but myself," I admitted. "My pride . . . it wasn't pride really. It was fear. My old wounds ran deep. I had lost my wife, my sons, my family. I had no wish to let her reopen those wounds, and I knew that she could. That she would if I let her. But I could never admit that I was afraid of a young girl like Arianna."

"Don't feel too bad, Nic. I was scared to death of her sister." Duncan got to his feet again. "But I have a feeling you should be telling Arianna all of this, instead of spilling your guts to me. Don't you?"

"I suppose I should." I rose slowly, brushed the dust from my jeans. But there were more images making their way back to me as we walked toward the village. No clear memories, but a sense. A sense that Arianna had indeed conquered my heart, and that once she had held it in her small hands, she'd crushed it mercilessly. The old fear of her crept over me once more. The feeling that I must protect myself from her this time, or suffer complete destruction at her hand.

And yet, I had no desire to obey my mind's warnings. No desire at all. Let her trample my heart if she would. I would not resist her. Not this time.

I was shivering when we arrived back at the site of her burned house. A chill of foreboding ran all the way to my soul.

Arianna and Raven were waiting there, but looking far better than they had when we'd left them. They were clean and dressed in fresh clothing.

"Any luck?" Raven asked.

"No, none at all." Duncan touched the blouse she wore. "Very pretty."

"Some of the locals donated some fresh clothes to us. And Arianna and I have rooms waiting at a local inn for the night. There are clean clothes waiting for you both there, as well."

"And a hot shower, I hope," Duncan said.

Arianna had a hold on my eyes that wouldn't let go. I could not look away, and found I did not want to. She took my hand, and saying nothing, led me along the streets and through the town to the inn.

22

The inn was a large building, likely once a farmhouse, with brown slabwood siding, and a railed stairway leading up to solid doors, painted red. When we went inside, Raven led Duncan directly up the stairs, leaving Arianna and I alone below.

Arianna seemed nervous. Naturally, she would be, I reminded myself. She'd just lost her house to fire, and likely the sight of the flames had elicited the same memories in her mind as they had in mine.

Licking her lips, she led me to the foot of the stairs, then paused and looked up at me. The nervousness fled however, and her full lips quirked upward into a teasing smile. "You're still covered in soot," she said. "And your hair is practically gray with ash."

I returned the smile, though still sick with worry for Nidaba, and reeling with shock from the night's revelations. "You can see then what I would look like as an old man."

"You already are an old man."

I lifted my brows. "True enough. But you are an old woman, as well. I suppose I can no longer argue that you are too young for me, can I?"

Her smile faded, and she broke her gaze. "You remember that?"

"I have remembered a great deal tonight, Arianna." I reached out to stroke her hair, then paused, noting the dark smears of soot that coated my hand. "I will bathe first, and then . . . we will talk."

"All right." She seemed to lift her chin a bit as she started up the stairs, and not meeting my eyes, she said, "Our room is this way."

Our room? My mind leapt on those words. Did she mean . . . could she want . . . but . . .

She was moving quickly away from me, and I hurried to catch up. Turning at the top of the stairs, she moved along a corridor, paused at a door, and inserted a key. Then she opened the door and stepped inside.

The room was a simple one. There was a large bed, a pair of overstuffed chairs, and a television like the wondrous one that had been in Arianna's house. She was already moving through, opening an adjoining door, calling over her shoulder, "The bathroom is right here." But I was focused again on the bed: one bed. Only one.

Shaking myself, I went to join her in the bathroom.

"No tub," she said. "Just a shower stall, but I showed you how to work that at home."

I nodded mutely.

"Your clothes are here." She patted the top of a folded stack of garments. "Towel is on the rack." With that she quickly backed out of the small bathroom, leaving me with a head full of questions, and not a single answer.

Sighing, I reached into the stall to turn on the water and adjust its temperature. I hurried through the process of bathing, though I did a thorough job of it. I was eager to speak with Arianna . . . with my wife. To find out just what she intended to do about tonight's sleeping arrangements. Perhaps there had been only the one room available, I thought as I scrubbed the soot from my body, and watched the dark water swirl down the drain. But surely if that were the case, she'd have spent the night with her sister, and sent Duncan to share this room with me. Unless Raven objected to that.

Then again, I did not think Raven the kind of woman who would deny her sister anything she asked.

I shampooed my hair, ridding it of the ashy residue, and was rinsing the lather away when there came a tap on the bathroom door.

"Are you almost done?" Arianna called.

"Yes."

"Can I come in?"

I went still, standing motionless beneath the spray. Soap bubbles trickled down my face, into my eyes, and still I could not move. "Yes," I finally managed.

The curtain of the shower was pulled closed, but I heard the bathroom door open, heard her small, soft footsteps as she came inside. And then closer. "I . . . got some more soot on me when we were back at the house," she said, her voice very soft now. Almost timid, which was so unlike her it made a shiver dance over my spine.

Bracing myself for her rejection—for it would certainly come—I spoke softly. My voice seemed incapable of anything louder just then. "I would like nothing better than to wash it away for you, Arianna."

She did not answer. Reaching up to the curtain, I curled my hand around it, and drew it slowly open.

She stood there before me, not a stitch of clothing covering her beauty. Her cheeks were pink, her eyes wide and shining. My eyes devoured her, from her blush-stained face to her slender neck, and lower. Her breasts, round and peaked, and perfect. Her waist, narrow and tempting. The shadowy hollow of her navel, and the silken curls between her legs. Beautiful legs, slender and strong, and small bare feet, toes curling and relaxing over and over.

"I see no soot," I whispered.

She licked her lips. "I lied. There isn't any."

I clasped her waist in my hands and pulled her into the shower with me, turning her so that she stood directly beneath the spray. The water coursed over her, drenching her hair and running down her face. Her arms curled around my neck, and every part of my body seemed to tingle with new life, as she stood on tiptoe, and pressed her lips to mine. Her mouth tasted sweet, her tongue, warm and moist as I stroked it with mine. Wet flesh pressed to the front of me, her breasts warm, nipples taut against my chest.

I slid my mouth from hers to drink the moisture from her jaw, and her neck. "My beautiful Arianna," I muttered. "My beautiful wife."

I heard her soft gasp, felt her body stiffen. "Then you remember that, as well."

"I remember that. How I ever forgot it, I will never know." I bent over her, capturing a breast in my mouth, tasting it, teasing its hard crest with my tongue while I held her tight to me. Her taste . . . yes, I remembered this as well. And more. I fell to my knees before her, and as the water rained down upon us, I kissed the droplets away from her skin. Licked it away from her belly, her hips, her thighs. Then I pressed my mouth to her center, darting my tongue inside to sample the salty moisture there.

Moaning softly, she clenched her hands in my hair, and parted her thighs, opening to my gentle invasion. Inviting me to take more of her. I swelled and ached for her, wanted to devour every bit of her, and I drove my tongue deeper. The taste of her was maddening to me as I stroked her, sucked at her, used my lips and even my teeth to make her tremble and shake. She whispered my name, then cried it out loud when her pleasure reached its peak, and when she would have backed away I caught her buttocks in my hands and held her still, pressing my face tight to her and licking deep. Refusing to let her go, flushing her with my tongue until she was shaking so hard her knees buckled beneath her, and she would have collapsed had I not been holding her so tightly.

Gathering my shuddering lady into my arms, I carried her from the shower, reaching back to shut off the water. I took her to the bed, and lowered her to the mattress. Then I eased myself atop her, parting her thighs with my hands, pressing them wide for me. I slid inside her. She was warm, and wet, yes, but tight. Very tight, and still convulsing with the echoes of her climax. Slowly, I began to move deeper, and when I had filled her, I pulled back again. Very slowly.

In a moment, she was moving, too, her hips arching up as I thrust into her, pulling away as I drew back. Her legs wrapped themselves around me. Her arms imprisoned me. I bent to feed again at her mouth as I moved faster, drove harder. She reached the pinnacle again even as I felt my seed spilling into her, drawn from the depths of my soul, it seemed. Draining me dry.

I lay there inside her for several long moments, during which neither of us spoke. The very blood in my veins seemed to sing with joy, and my soul itself sighed in sweet release. Sweet union.

I moved to lie down beside her, and she curled into my arms, her head nestled upon my shoulder.

"Arianna," I whispered. "Sweet little cat, does this mean that you—"

Her fingertips came then to press softly to my lips. "No talk now, Nicodimus. Not now. I want to fall asleep in your arms. Let's save the talking for tomorrow."

I frowned, but agreed. There was nothing, *nothing*, I would not do for her. So if she wished to sleep in my arms, that was what she would do. And in the morning, I would convince her somehow that my love for her was true, and abiding, and too strong for any ghosts of the past to threaten.

Arianna slipped away before dawn. Doing so was far easier than she had expected it to be. She stood for a long moment beside the bed, in the darkness, just looking at him. Nicodimus lying there with his eyes gently closed, his magnificent chest rising and falling in the rhythm of slumber. That was the way she left him, and the image she would carry with her of him, in her mind. She found she didn't want to face Nicodimus when he woke, didn't want to see what might be in his eyes when he opened them. Not the misguided notion he had that he had ever cared for her... loved her. And not the memory that might very well have returned by then, and the hatred that would come with it. To see either of those things would hurt too much to bear. Both would tear at her heart and leave it bleeding. So when she slipped away it was with a sense of relief.

And longing. Bittersweet longing for something that could never be. Something that *had* never *been*. She'd been foolish enough to hope for it once. But she was harder now, and wiser, and she knew the difference between fantasy and reality. And yes, it hurt, but the pain would be far worse if she let herself fall into that bottomless pit of hoping again. Her feet were firmly on the ground. She knew exactly where she stood with Nicodimus.

She also knew where to find Marten and Nidaba. The keep where Marten had taken her all those years ago—the place it had taken days to reach on horseback. Now it was only a couple of hours away by car. She could locate Kenwick again, she was certain of that, although she had never tried to do so in the years since.

She exited the inn by a rear door, and stepped out into the dead silent, still streets of the sleeping village. A soft purple hue colored the sky, and the only sounds were the occasional cry of a nightbird, and the fluttering wings of insects swooping by. Morning was still a couple of hours off. It would give her all the time she needed.

She walked briskly back to the remains of her house, and thanked her stars that she never worried about such things as taking the keys from her car in this peaceful little place. Within a short while, she was heading south, along a road that hadn't even existed the last time she'd traveled this way. But the direction was right. Easy enough to keep the coast in view. Easy enough to recall the odd shape of the hills that surrounded that place.

And easy enough to wile away the time the journey took, reliving every moment of the night she had spent in Nicodimus's arms. It had been so good. So beautiful. She had no regrets, not one. It had been right to make love to him. Right, and perfect, and wonderful.

By the time she reached her destination, the sun was up, brilliant and orange and fiery in the sky. It spilled like liquid fire over the rugged hilltops, and painted the lush grasses in shades of crimson and gold.

Arianna stopped the Jeep along the roadside and got out.

Shielding her eyes, she stared at the spot amid those craggy hills where centuries before, the dark, hulking form of Kenwick had risen like a brooding giant pointing at the sky. Now there was nothing.

"Gods, what if I was wrong?" she whispered, squinting, straining to see. "What if this isn't what Marten meant at all? It doesn't look as if the keep is even standing after all this time."

Doubts crept in. If she had been wrong, it could cost Nidaba's life, and as much as the woman seemed to hate her, Arianna couldn't return the feelings. She remembered too well the woman Nidaba had been. The strength of her tempered by wisdom—strength a young rebel had admired to no end. Nidaba . . . she'd been unaware of it, but Arianna had idolized her for a time. She'd tried to emulate her, wanted to be like her.

Nidaba was a broken woman now. Wounded so deeply she'd curled up inside herself and seemed unable to find her way out again. But she would. In time, and with Nicodimus's help, she would. Arianna would at least make sure she had the chance to do just that.

She couldn't turn back now. Not until she made sure nothing remained of Kenwick.

Stiffening her spine, she struck out on foot across the land, plotting her course mentally as she went and aiming for the spot dead center of the surrounding hills, where that keep had once stood.

The terrain was rough and rocky as she climbed higher and the grass thinned. The chill morning breeze battled with the fiery sun, so she was alternately hot and cold as she pushed on. It took no real effort for Arianna though. In fact, she took it with ease, enjoying the stretch and flex of her muscles, and the increased flow of her blood. She had been cooped up too long in that cottage in Stonehaven. She had been inactive, playing nursemaid and housemother to her guests, and reining in her natural tendency to run wild.

She guessed she had been reining in a bit more than that, too. Her emotions had been imprisoned inside her since Nicodimus's return from the grave. Even now, they beat at their prison bars in protest, straining to break free. But she knew better than to let them out. Not now. She needed all her focus now, all her attention for the battle ahead.

If she let her feelings reach the surface, she feared she would be useless in a fight. She would be kneeling on the stony ground, aching for a man she could never have. Moon-eyed with a love she had sentenced to death long ago. She'd been so blind. Her feelings for Nicodimus were just as alive as he was. They had been all along. Merely dormant, waiting. She had resurrected her own weakness, her only vulnerability, when she'd resurrected Nicodimus.

Arianna topped a rise, and peered downward into the basinlike clearing. Crumbling stone walls staggered below, some towering to a height of fifty feet, while others barely held themselves upright at three. Stone masonry littered the ground. What remained of the place seemed almost ready to crumble. Yet she spied the arching entryway, its wooden doors long gone. Dust by now. Beyond that opening, a yawning darkness seemed to beckon.

She crept closer, glancing at the ground, seeing a rusted iron hinge lying there. Then drawing herself up, she stepped through, and ventured into the cavelike depths of the keep's ruin.

Her eyes adjusted quickly, as always. She stepped over broken stones and a broad beam that lay across her path. Her very breaths seemed to echo here. The sound of every step she took seemed magnified a thousand times. Deeper she trod, and deeper, following the only path possible, a twisting, writhing, ever-narrowing path that seemed to have been cleared deliberately. For no structure could crumble in just this way. And as she moved forward, she realized she was also moving *downward*. The angle sharpened, leading her into the bowels of the very earth.

"The dungeons," she whispered, startled at the loudness of even that slight sound here. This silence must be like death itself. But she soon saw that her prediction was an accurate one. The tunnel opened out wider, and the dirt floor leveled off.

She paused at the edge of this wider place, sensing danger. A man stepped out of the shadows to stand in front of her.

Marten.

"Well, now," he said. "This is pleasant, but not what I expected. Where is Nicodimus?"

Arianna drew her dagger. "He is not coming. You'll have to face me, Marten."

"Will I?" He stepped away, vanishing, it seemed. But she knew he'd only ducked into the shadowy recesses of the crumbling dungeon.

Arianna followed slowly, stepping with care, scanning the darkness, then blinking in the sudden light as she rounded a corner. Torches flickered from where they'd been thrust into chinks in the stone walls. Before her, Arianna saw a nightmare.

Nidaba lay still, strapped down to an ancient table. The pendulum high above her was drawn back and seemingly suspended in the blackness. But its blade hung low. And though it was rusted and pocked with corrosion, its edge gleamed in the dancing torchlight, as if recently honed. Yes, honed by the hand of Nidaba's heartless captor, no doubt.

Nidaba's eyes met Arianna's and held them. "Kill him," she said, and her voice was level, and for once, seemed perfectly sane.

"That would be a very bad idea."

Arianna's gaze shifted to where Marten stood beside the table, his hand wrapped around a tall lever.

"One tug," he said, unnecessarily, for it was already obvious. "One tug, and the blade will swing. I've adjusted it carefully, Arianna. It will slice her tender belly on the first pass. On the second, it will sever the organs, and by the third pass it will neatly cut her in half." He shrugged, a slight smile toying with his thin lips. "Well, maybe not so neatly I suppose. In any case, it would be difficult even for an immortal to revive after being cleaved in two." He lifted an eyebrow. "Then again, it might be rather amusing if she did. I might enjoy seeing that before I finally take her heart."

Arianna's grip tightened on the dagger she held. "Are

you so afraid to face a woman that you'd resort to this? Release her, Marten, and fight me, if you dare."

He simply shook his head. "It is not you I want," he said. "It is my dear brother-in-law. Nicodimus. I've waited centuries to kill him."

"You'll have to wait longer, because he's not coming. I told you—"

"Oh, he'll come. He'll come when he realizes I now have both his women in my . . . tender care. Put the dagger down, Arianna. Now."

Nidaba shook her head. "Don't listen to him! Kill him, Arianna, or he will kill Nicodimus! Do it!"

"I'll pull the lever. Take one step toward me, and Nidaba suffers unbearable pain while you watch. Drop the weapon, Arianna." His hand twitched on the lever.

"Marten, listen to me," Arianna said, trying to keep her voice calm, but shivering at the way it echoed in this place. It was as if a dozen ghosts mocked her, repeating her every word in deathly whispers. "Nicodimus won't come. He can't. He doesn't remember this place. He doesn't even know I've come here. The centuries of death did something to his mind, and his memory is not—"

"You are an accomplished liar, Arianna. Do you really think I would believe you again? No, you fooled me once. Pretending to want me. Throwing yourself into my arms the way you did, all just so that you could win my trust and try to escape. I had truly begun to care for you, did you realize that?"

"You don't know how to care for anyone but yourself, Marten. You murdered my family! How could you think I would have ever forgiven that?"

He shrugged, averting his eyes. "No matter. Put the weapon down, Arianna."

She swallowed hard, darted a glance at Nidaba.

"Let him do as he will with me," Nidaba whispered. "I beg of you, do not trade my son's life for mine!"

Marten glared at Nidaba. "Shut up, woman!"

"I will not shut up! My son died to save my life once,

and I cannot bear to let it happen again! Kill him, Arianna! Forget about me, and kill this cur! Now!"

Arianna clutched her dagger and lunged toward Marten. He jerked the lever instantly, and the blade lurched forward with a terrible groan, only to come to a creaking, shuddering stop again, mere inches from Nidaba's belly. Nidaba's eyes were shut tight, her jaw clenched in readiness.

Arianna froze where she was.

"It's up to you," Marten said. "But I feel I must warn you, Arianna, I am running low on patience. Dangerously low. Put it down."

Nidaba's eyes opened, damp with unshed tears. She turned her head toward Arianna. "No," she whispered. "You mustn't. No, no, no . . ."

"I'm sorry. I have to. Forgive me, Nidaba. I can't watch you suffer such an agonizing death." Arianna faced Marten again. "All right. You win." She dropped her dagger to the dirt floor. Its tip sank into the rancid, packed earth.

Marten smiled, but his hand remained on the lever. "Very good. Now, come here. We have plans to make, you and I." She remained rooted to the spot, and he held up a hand. "Come here, Arianna. Or I'll kill her all the same."

Chin lifting slightly, Arianna went to him. The dank place was filled then with the soft sound of Nidaba's sobs, echoing endlessly.

I woke with a feeling of dread. Something horrible had happened in my dream, but though I tried, I could not remember what. It had to do with Arianna . . . and with death.

My death.

I strained to recall the details, but they eluded me like thieves in the night. Sighing in frustration, I opened my eyes, reaching for her, needing to hold her close to me and feel her there and know that it wasn't real. That it was only one more taunting memory of a past that was long dead.

But Arianna was not there.

"Arianna?"

No answer.

I got up slowly, looking around the room, eyeing the

door of the adjoining bathroom, which stood open. I saw no movement inside. A slow fear spread through my veins and I moved faster, hurrying to the bathroom to look for her. "Arianna?" I called again.

The bathroom was empty. Her clothes, I realized as I turned to scan the bedroom in search of them . . . gone. I snatched up the clothing I'd never donned the night before, threw them on haphazardly, and ran back into the bedroom. I yanked open the door, stepping into the hall just as Duncan and Raven came 'round a corner from their own room, smiling, hands joined.

"Where is Arianna?" I all but shouted.

Their smiles died. Duncan looked puzzled. Raven, terrified. "I assumed she was still with you," Duncan said, his frown deepening as he looked past me into the empty room my wife and I had shared the night before. "You mean she's not—"

"Gods, I was afraid she'd do something like this," Raven said, interrupting him. "I knew it! I never should have believed her!"

I rushed forward, gripping Raven's hands gently in my own and striving for patience. "Tell me."

Bowing her head, Raven closed her eyes. "She knew where Marten had taken Nidaba . . . or . . . she thought she knew. But she wouldn't tell me. Nicodimus, she felt you were still not strong enough to fight Marten and win."

"So she went to fight him in my place?" I asked, my stomach clenching. *"And you let her?"*

Raven's head came up fast. "Of course I didn't *let* her! She promised we'd go together, this morning. She said we'd stand a greater chance that way."

"And you believed her? Believed she'd allow you to risk your life in a battle with an immortal as old as I am! She's your sister, Raven, and you didn't see through so obvious a lie as that?"

"Come on, Nic, this isn't Raven's fault," Duncan said, his hand on my arm. "When Arianna sets her mind to something, she's as stubborn as they come. If you know her at all, you ought to know that."

I sighed and closed my eyes. "I know that. I am sorry, Raven. But Gods, she can't fight Marten alone. He's older than she, more experienced in battle. The last time he took her, he held her for . . ." Then I blinked, and looked up slowly. "The last time he took her . . . yes. Yes, I remember now! His men attacked our village . . . murdered her parents, and everyone else in their path. And he took Arianna. He took my wife the same way I had taken his sister so many years before. It was vengeance, in his twisted, perverse mind."

I paced the hall, pressing one hand to my forehead as I sought the memory.

"Where, Nic?" Duncan asked urgently.

"I'm trying. . . . I remember following the trail of his soldiers. But it was a trick. The soldiers headed north, leaving an obvious path for me to follow. But Marten struck out alone with Arianna. He went south. . . . Yes, two days' ride—south. There was a keep . . . on the coast. . . ."

Duncan gripped my arm. "Can you find it again?"

I looked up and met his eyes. "I *must* find it again. And I will."

We had no choice but to travel by car . . . that amazing vehicle I had only observed from the windows of Arianna's house until now. Duncan quickly procured one from a local man, explaining that it was an emergency.

Raven and Duncan eased me into the rear seat of the machine, and I held on and battled nausea as Duncan manned the controls, setting the beast into motion. Such speeds! It was dizzying, sickening, and yet I paid little heed to the protests of my head and stomach as we bounded over the rutted dirt roads of the new Scottish countryside. I was glad of the contraption that could, by some miracle, reduce a two day journey to one of mere hours. It would get me to Arianna sooner.

It would carry me to my wife . . . sooner.

As we traveled, I directed Duncan as best I could, my memory still hazy. But more and more came back to me. I recalled this same feeling of rage and dread and helplessness filling me in the past. The thought of that vermin having Arianna. The love I felt for her, burning inside me. It had been there before. I knew that now. I may have told Arianna I could not love her, but love her I had, and still did.

I'd done too thorough a job convincing her of my lie, then, hadn't I? For even now, she believed it. Even now, she thought my love an illusion. But it beat in me strong and sure, and old. Very old. She had changed me. I'd been a bitter, lonely man, living to fight, fighting to live, existing in a world that held no joy for me. She had given me joy again. Such joy. Gods, just looking at her face, seeing her smile had filled me with it. Touching her, holding her delicate form in my arms . . . I had been born again, it seemed. Brought back to life long before she resurrected my body in this strange, new century. For I had been dead then, before I'd known her.

As I would be now, did I have to live on without her.

"I am coming for you, Arianna," I whispered. "Hold on, my love. I will be with you soon."

Raven turned in her seat, and clasped my hand in hers. "She'll be all right," she said, teary eyes at odds with the confidence in her voice.

"She has to be."

"Do you understand what you are to do?" Marten asked softly, eyeing Arianna, suspicion in his gaze.

"I keep telling you, it won't matter. Nicodimus is not coming here."

"And I keep telling you, he will. It is fate, I believe. Things must come full circle. It's the way of the Universe. This will end just as it began. He *will* come for you, Arianna. And when he does, he will find you in the arms of your lover. He will be beaten, utterly, long before I take his heart. I want him to suffer the ultimate defeat at my hands, and you will perform your part *exactly* as I have told you. You will recite the lines precisely, and *convincingly*, Arianna, or Nidaba will pay the price. Now again, do you understand?"

Arianna stared at him, hatred blazing from her soul. Nidaba remained strapped to the table, gagged now so that she could not cry out. No longer in sight, though. Marten had brought Arianna back to that place where she'd first spotted him. The place where the tunnel widened, lit now, with a torch of its own, leaving Nidaba helpless and silent, in the dim, flickering light of a single, dying torch. The frayed length of rope tied to Marten's wrist led back around the corner to that deadly lever. He need only pull to cause Nidaba excrutiating pain before ultimately ending her life. And he would, unless Arianna did exactly as he said.

But it wouldn't matter. Arianna wouldn't be forced to play out this gruesome act, for there would be no audience. Nicodimus did not remember.

He must not remember!

Marten pushed her to the floor, then took a seat beside her. "Now we wait," he told her, "for your hero to arrive. And when he does, Arianna . . ." Marten smiled grimly in the dancing light, and she could see the evil emanating from his small, piglike eyes. "He will die. And this time, he won't be coming back."

23

We stopped the vehicle each time I thought I saw a familiar place and got out to explore. But I was so disoriented. Things had changed. Not just by the appearance of villages where none had been, and the utter absence of some that had existed long ago, but by the building of roads, the disappearance of forests, the leveling of hills. Meadows thrived where barren moors had rolled before. Pastures that had once been dotted with grazing flocks, now grew up to woodlands. I could only follow the coast, wondering if even its shape had changed. If the constant barrage of the sea had eroded it away to the point where I would not recognize even its familiar form.

But at last, I spied the odd-shaped hills poking into the sky like a circlet of spikes, and I knew this was familiar. Within them, a keep nestled, protected from attack by its natural fortress.

And then, Raven pointed and sat up straight in her seat. "Look! Arianna's Jeep!"

I saw it. But no sign of Arianna anywhere near it, nor from within. I got out at once, racing to the machine to check for her presence all the same. Knowing I would not find her there. My heart fell, and my hands clenched into trembling fists at my sides. Without a word, I turned and began walking toward where I thought the keep had been. In silence, Duncan and Raven followed. I knew that they, too, were wondering what we would find here. Arianna's lifeless corpse, sentenced to death without her heart?

Her heart. Gods the thought of Marten draining the life force of the most vital woman I had ever known. But I could not allow myself to think that way, for the pain of it was nearly crippling. I *would* get her back. I would find her again and restore her to life just as she had done for me. I would, no matter what.

"Nic, hold up," Duncan said, his voice a harsh whisper, his hand on my shoulder. I stopped walking, and he pointed past me. "Look."

I saw it then, the ruins of the keep. It struck me anew how very long it had been that I'd been away . . . from life. From Arianna. To my mind it had been only days ago that I had come here, stood in this very spot, quivering with rage just as I was now.

"That looks like the way in," Duncan said.

I took only a single step before he gripped my arm. "Wait, Nic. It could be a trap. God knows the bastard will be expecting us. It's why he took Nidaba in the first place. He'll be in there, waiting for you."

"Then I will not disappoint him," I said, starting off again.

"Nic, will you use your head?" Raven cried.

Again I stopped, turning this time to face the two who had become more than just my allies in the past several days. They had become my friends. I knew their concern for me was genuine and heartfelt. And likely wise. But wisdom did not concern me. Getting to Arianna was my only thought.

"Look, we'll go 'round this thing, see if there's another way inside," Duncan suggested. "That way we can approach from two directions at once, maybe catch this Marten character off guard."

I nodded. It was a good plan. One that made perfect

sense. "Go then. I'll wait here. Signal me when you are ready to go inside."

Duncan eyed me, and finally nodded once. "Be careful," he warned me.

"I intend to."

With that, Duncan and Raven raced off around the crumbling remains of broken stone. The moment they were out of sight, I started inside. I could not wait. Not while visions of what Marten might be doing to Arianna played havoc with my mind. I would kill him.

Kill him!

The tunnel I entered was long and winding, littered with debris. Silence was impossible, and I knew that if Marten were listening—as he surely must be—he would hear my approach. Dagger in hand, I moved on all the same. I peered around each corner, fully expecting ambush.

At last, I emerged into a spot where the tunnel widened, and there I saw the last thing I had expected.

Arianna, in Marten's arms. Not fighting him. Not kicking or pulling away. Her arms were twined 'round his neck, and he was kissing her. And *she* was kissing *him*. A red haze of fury colored my vision when at last he lifted his head. And he stared at her, never looking my way, though he had to know full well I was there.

But then, so must she.

"I am so glad you came away with me at last, Arianna," Marten said.

Arianna said nothing. She turned her head toward me, and I saw in her eyes a message, words she could not speak, feelings spilling with the tears. "It has always been you," she said softly, her voice breaking. "I've never loved any one else the way I love you."

The words, apparently spoken to Marten, yet her eyes were on me. That was when the final memory returned to me. I saw it all unfold in my mind in the mere space of an instant. I had crashed through the doors of Kenwick, surprised to find them unbarred, and I found my wife in Marten's arms. I had seen the same message in her eyes then—just before I was leapt upon and killed.

As I had lain dying, Marten had gloated, "Our plan worked perfectly, Arianna." And for one brief instant, I had believed it. I had *believed it.*

Just as I was no doubt meant to believe it now.

I let my body sag, let my head lower, and my hand and my weapon with it, fell to my side. "So this is the way of it," I muttered.

"Nicodimus, no—" Arianna began. I saw Marten grip her arm painfully and nod toward his hand. Glancing downward, I noticed what I hadn't before: a length of hemp tied 'round his wrist.

"Tell him, Arianna," Marten said.

She closed her eyes to prevent the tears spilling over. "I . . . I never loved you," she whispered, her words hoarse and broken.

I had to wait until Martin let her go, before doing anything at all. He was hurting her, I could see that. And the implications of that rope on his arm . . .

I dropped my dagger to the floor. "Then I have no reason to fight, Arianna. No reason . . . at all."

"That will make this much easier," Marten all but crowed, his face alight with the anticipation of his triumph.

"Come then," I said. "Take me if you will." I opened my arms out to my sides and waited. He would have to release Arianna to come to where I stood. And that rope, whatever it was, as well.

He paused, glancing down at the rope with a hint of alarm in his eyes. "No, Nicodimus. *You* come to *me*. You must at least wish to say goodbye to . . . to your faithless wife."

But I wouldn't. For it was what he wished me to do. Instead I sank to my knees, hoping my act would be a convincing one. I lowered my head and made my shoulders shake as if with the force of sobs too violent to contain.

"So be it then," Marten said. "I never intended to let the Dark Woman live anyway."

Even as I lifted my head to see what he meant, Marten removed the rope from his wrist with a flick of his hand, clenched it in his fist, and gave it a brutal tug.

Arianna screamed in utter horror, and another scream came from the depths of this place. A faint one that was terror-filled, and very brief. Arianna leapt on Marten, even as he charged at me. He carried her on his back as she pummeled and clawed at his face and eyes. My hand closed 'round the dagger I had dropped. Marten flung Arianna from his back, lifted his dagger high, and brought it down at me. I drove mine upward. It pierced him just beneath the rib cage, at a sharp upward angle, and I buried it to the hilt, and gave it a twist for good measure.

He froze where he stood, eyes bulging, blood surging over my hand. Then he staggered backward two steps. I yanked the blade free as he did. He fell to the dirt floor. Beyond him, Arianna knelt with her head bowed. Getting to my feet, I went to Marten, bent over him, and quickly cut the heart from his chest. I flung it into the dirt at my feet, and left it there, to be disposed of later.

Arianna needed me now.

I wiped my hands as best I could, and went to her where she knelt, sobbing. Gripping her shoulders I pulled her up and into my arms. "Arianna, it's over. He's dead, my love. You're safe now."

But she was limp in my arms, and trembling violently, uncontrollably.

I eased her away from me just enough to stare down into her haunted eyes. "He made me say those things, Nicodimus . . . I never meant . . ."

"I know that."

She frowned hard at me. "You . . . you know?"

"Just as I knew the last time, Arianna. Even as my life slipped away from me, I knew you could not have betrayed me with him. I believed in you. With my very last breath, I believed in you, Arianna . . ."

She shook her head, eyes wide. "You knew? Even then, you knew . . . ?"

"I knew."

But then her face crumpled, and she sank against my chest. "Oh, Nicodimus. Nidaba! Gods, what Marten has done to poor Nidaba!"

She continued sobbing, crying, but I could no longer understand her words. Something about the rope, something about a pendulum. All but carrying her, I followed the trail of that hemp, 'round the corner. And as we moved onward, she pulled away from me, turned her back, covered her eyes. "I can't look! I can't see her that way! Oh, Gods, Nidaba, I'm so sorry! I tried, truly, I tried. . . ." Again her words degenerated into unintelligible gasps and sobs. She bent nearly double, arms folded 'round her middle as if she were in pain. Choking on her tears, she seemed lost to me.

I could not comfort her, so I turned instead, to see the fate of Nidaba. The mother I must have known as such once, but could only remember as my friend. My dearest friend. My most cherished companion.

A table, straps dangling from its sides, stood empty before me. A blade, suspended from far above, swung in ever decreasing arcs, back and forth above it.

And beside it, on the floor, I saw Duncan, getting to his feet, brushing himself off, and reaching down to help Raven to her feet as well. And then the two of them bent down, and I saw a slender hand reach up, and then another, to clasp theirs. They pulled, and Nidaba rose to her feet with the regal grace of a desert queen.

"I tried, Nidaba. Oh, Gods, I'm so sorry!" Arianna was still whispering brokenly.

"You not only tried, child, you succeeded," Nidaba said softly.

Arianna went still and stiffened. Nidaba came closer, moving with the grace and dignity I remembered so well, and hadn't seen in so long. She settled a hand on Arianna's shoulder. "I'm all right. Alive . . . at least. And I owe you my thanks, Arianna," she said.

"Nidaba?" Slowly, Arianna turned around, and then she flung herself into Nidaba's arms, and held her so hard I thought both women might well break.

After a time, they stood apart again. Arianna, stroking Nidaba's hair away from her face, searched the older woman's eyes again and again as if to be sure she was truly real and not some vision. "How did you escape that horrible blade?"

"Duncan and Raven came in through some other way. They freed me just in time."

"Well, not quite in time," Duncan said, glancing down at his arm.

I saw that it was cut and bleeding. He'd risked his very life to save Nidaba. To save . . . my mother. "I am in your debt, Duncan," I told him.

He only nodded. Nidaba took Arianna's hand in hers and stared into her eyes. "My . . . my mind . . . is not as strong as it once was, Arianna. It was becoming less so even before my time as Nathanial Dearborne's captive, and I fear the things I experienced then have broken it beyond repair. But there are some . . . lucid moments. More so, since I found my Nicodimus again." Here she paused to look at me with tear-filled eyes and a trembling smile.

"You'll heal, Nidaba . . . Mother," I said gently. "I'll see to it. You'll be well again."

Her gaze lowered. "Perhaps," she whispered. "But I fear the life span of a High Witch's mind does not equal that of her body. How long can one live on and remain truly sane, do you suppose?"

I swallowed the lump in my throat. "How long have you lived?"

She sighed wearily, bowing her head. "Four thousand years, my son."

I could only stare at her, dumbfounded. By the Gods, she must be the oldest of us all. Was she? Or were there others, even more ancient than she?

Nidaba faced Arianna again while I stood there, trying to digest the magnitude of a life span so long.

"There is something I should have told you long ago, Arianna, when I met you on the road to Stonehaven, taking my son's body to the Stone Circle. But I was too distraught to think clearly, and I . . . I blamed you for his death."

Arianna lowered her head. "As you should have. I blamed myself."

"But it was not your fault. And the one thing you didn't

know, Arianna, the one thing you deserved to know, was that he loved you then."

Arianna lifted her gaze to mine, then quickly looked at Nidaba again, her eyes wide.

"He told me so many times as we searched for you. He told me that he loved you, and that he had never admitted it to you. It was driving him mad that he had never told you the truth of his feelings, and his greatest fear was that he would never have the chance."

Arianna shook her head in wonder. But Nidaba simply pulled her closer to me and placed her hand in mine. "Tell her, my son. You love her still, do you not?"

I nodded once, my eyes on Arianna's. "I do. I always have." Arianna parted her lips, but I hurried on before she could speak. "No, let me finish. I remember it all now, Arianna. Everything. Everything about you. I was like a dead man already before I returned to Stonehaven that last time. But you wouldn't allow me to remain that way. You made me feel again, for the first time since I lost my wife and my sons. You brought joy back into my life. You made me whole, Arianna. And I realized it on the night I lost you. You are my heart, little cat. You are my love, and I will spend the rest of my days making up for the pain I caused you in the past. I swear I will . . . if you will let me."

Her tears spilled over, and Arianna spoke through a watery smile. "I swore I would never love you again, Nicodimus. But the problem is, I never stopped. Not ever. I couldn't. I never will."

I smiled down at her, and then I swept her into my arms. My woman, my wife, my very soul. My Arianna. I kissed her, and I knew that at long last, I truly was alive.